ALSO BY CAROLYN HAINES

Smarty Bones

CAROLYN HAINES

St. Martin's Paperbacks

This is a work of fiction. All of the characters, organizations, and events portrayed in this novel are either products of the author's imagination or are used fictitiously.

SMARTY BONES

Copyright © 2013 by Carolyn Haines.
Excerpt from *Booty Bones* copyright © 2014 by Carolyn Haines.

All rights reserved.

For information address St. Martin's Press, 175 Fifth Avenue, New York, N.Y. 10010.

EAN: 978-1-250-04660-4

Printed in the United States of America

Minotaur hardcover edition / May 2013
St. Martin's Paperbacks edition / May 2014

St. Martin's Paperbacks are published by St. Martin's Press, 175 Fifth Avenue, New York, NY 10010.

10 9 8 7 6 5 4 3 2 1

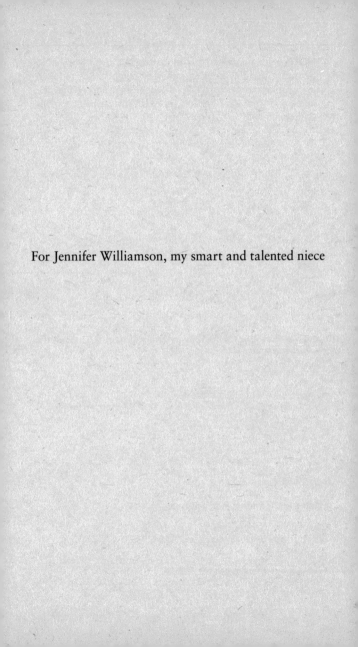

For Jennifer Williamson, my smart and talented niece

Acknowledgments

I stumbled upon the legend of the Lady in Red while I was on a book tour crisscrossing Mississippi. The grave is real and can be found in the Odd Fellows Cemetery in Lexington. And the story of how the casket was found accidentally by a backhoe and the body reinterred by the owners of Egypt Plantation is also true. The rest of this story comes from my imagination and love of legend and lore. In real life, the Lady in Red remains as big a mystery as she was the day the backhoe brought up her coffin.

I grew up on local legends such as that of the Singing River (the real name is the Pascagoula River), so named because a tribe of Indians joined hands and walked into the river to drown singing their death chant. They chose death over enslavement by another tribe.

My grandmother was George County's first and only historian and she was also the first city clerk in Lucedale, Mississippi, founded in 1910. She was a wonderful storyteller who kept us grandchildren enthralled with tales of heroes, heroines, ghosts, and fairies. My parents, too, were wonderful storytellers. My father told me stories of Leo the Friendly Lion every night of my childhood as I went to sleep.

So it's no surprise that when I stumbled on the Lady in Red, I had to tell her story—even if it isn't the truth.

I want to thank my editors, Kelley Ragland and Elizabeth Lacks, at St. Martin's Minotaur. My good friend Suzann Ledbetter, who gave me invaluable advice and the benefit of her sharp pencil. My agent, Marian Young, who indeed proves that patience is a virtue and one that works best with wisdom and knowledge. My friends who read over the manuscript to be sure the story hung together—thank you, ladies and gentlemen.

And again, thank you, Hiro Kimura, the talented artist who brings such fun to the covers of my books. Another outstanding job.

For more information about me, the books, or Daddy's Girl Weekend, our annual gathering of readers, writers, and merrymakers, you can go to www.carolynhaines .com (where you can also sign up for my newsletter). I also have Facebook pages at Carolyn Haines and Carolyn Haines Fan Page. Please join me.

And remember to please spay and neuter your companion pets. Pet overpopulation is at a crisis. Millions of animals are killed in shelters each year because there aren't enough loving homes. Support your local humane organization and urge your family and friends to spay and neuter. This is really a problem we can solve if we all work together.

1

Heat and humidity commingle to form a thick haze over the cotton fields, muting the lush green plants to monochromatic grays. The haunting vista captures my heart, and I stop my labors and lean for a moment on my broom. I've only swept half the front porch of Dahlia House—not exactly hard work—yet sticky sweat trickles down my spine. The autumnal equinox has come and gone, and in another week the calendar will flip. October will arrive and break September's stifling heat. The cotton bolls will split and mechanical harvesters will comb the fields like huge insects that produce boxcar-sized bales of long-fiber cotton. Fall has officially arrived around the nation, but it is still hot as hell in Zinnia, Mississippi.

Gazing out over the fields, I'm flooded with memories

and emotions. This is Delaney land, my land, the heritage handed down from generations of farmers and planters who grew cotton and built wealth, and then lost the money—but not the land. Never the land. When my father plied his law degree, Dahlia House shone like a crown in the sun. My mother was the prized jewel; everything around her sparkled.

The tragedy of a perfect childhood is that it ends. Adulthood brings worries and responsibilities. Perfection fades. I remember a conversation I had, not long ago, with Sunflower County sheriff Coleman Peters. He told me the best any grown-up could hope for was a sixty-forty decision, meaning that whatever choice was made, it would be, at best, sixty percent right. He's a wise man.

My childhood was a hundred percent marvelous. I had it all: parents who loved me and our community, land that produced amazing crops, an environment that encouraged me to dream big and go for it, a heritage of honor and courage. I also live with the daily knowledge that it all disappeared one night as my parents drove home from a political gathering in Jackson. On a dead-straight Delta road, Daddy flipped the car. Both of my parents died instantly.

The cause of the wreck has always been a mystery. Most folks think a deer or a dog ran out of the cotton fields and my father swerved to avoid hitting it and lost control. Some people have been insensitive enough to posit the idea that my father fell asleep at the wheel. Even though the autopsy proved otherwise, some folks insist my parents had been drinking.

The truth is, there is no truth. I've gone to that lonely stretch of road more times than I can count. It's straight and flat, bordered on both sides by cotton fields. Few roads intersect it. The night of the wreck was clear, the stars out in abundance. I remember, because I sat on the front porch with Aunt Loulane for an hour or so after dinner, talking about my studies, waiting for my folks to come home and fill me in on their adventures.

At twelve years old, I thought I should be allowed to stay home alone, but Mother insisted Aunt Loulane come and "keep me company." A good thing, too. The news that your world has exploded shouldn't be heard alone.

I inhale deeply and slowly to release the anger and frustration roiling in my chest. I cling to the memories of my parents in the good moments, the times of laughter and joy. Trips back to the night of their deaths do nothing but upset me. I've gone over it a million times. I've read the accident reports, viewed the photos of the Volvo my father preferred to drive because it was safer than a convertible. Twenty-two years have passed, and the grief is as close as my own skin. Some wounds never heal, but as Aunt Loulane would say, we learn to carry the pain and keep walking.

I pick up the broom. Work is my solace. Perhaps my abilities as a private investigator come from the puzzle of my parents' death. Why did they wreck? What happened to make my father lose control of the car? No one has ever answered those questions to my satisfaction. For more than two decades, I've chewed on what I know to be the facts. Still, to misquote Mick Jagger, I can get no satisfaction.

A noise on the side of the house makes me think Jitty is about to put in an appearance. She's a self-centered ghost, but she also has a keen ability to ferret out those times when the past looms larger than the present for me. The idea of a confrontation with my own personal Civil

War–era ghost perks up my spirits. Jitty is feisty, opinionated, and the yin to my yang. I wouldn't go so far as to call her the voice of reason, but sometimes she makes a good point.

Hurrying around the corner of the house, I stop. Jitty isn't in evidence. My horses graze peacefully in the pasture beside the barn, and my hound, Sweetie Pie, and the newest member of the Delaney household, Pluto, a fat black cat I semi-acquired from my last case, are digging for a mole. My dead relatives rest without interruption in the family cemetery behind the house. That I'm rooted to this place in a way many people don't understand slams hard into me.

Some might say my connection to Dahlia House is Southern in nature, or perhaps part of my Irish heritage. I say that folks who don't cherish the place of their birth, the residence of their family, the home and land where memories are created and linger, and the final resting place of cherished family, have never known what it means to love. While I *love* my fiancé, the most talented Graf Milieu, I *need* the expanse of land that spreads before me.

Instead of calling Jitty, I return to the porch and my chore. It's nice to have the time to do a little something for the grand old lady, Dahlia House. I've contracted a painter to fix her up with a new coat of white as soon as the weather cools and the humidity drops. Other repairs will require carpentry skills and more money. Thank goodness our last Delaney Detective Agency client—despite a bit of confusion over who hired whom—paid us. My partner, Tinkie Bellcase Richmond, doesn't need the cashola, but I sure do.

I wipe the sweat from my forehead and wonder how

Graf is handling his golf game in the torrid zone. He's spent enough time in Mississippi to understand the danger of heatstroke, but for a lot of the summer, his film work had kept him in balmy Los Angeles. Graf Milieu is a name destined to glow in neon on movie house marquees. My man is not only handsome and smart, he's talented.

Sweetie Pie's mournful howl alerts me to impending company. A car I don't recognize—a brand-new silver town car—tears down the driveway. Leaning on my broom, I wait to see who will alight. In the old days, company often showed up on the porch for an afternoon cup of coffee or a highball. Those days, when my mother, Libby Delaney, dispensed advice and help to anyone who darkened the door, hold great fondness for me. I learned much about human nature listening to people talk at our kitchen table.

Times have changed, though, and I wondered if the driver of the car was a new client for the PI agency.

To my surprise, one of my mother's friends got out from the driver's side. Frances Malone wore a smart yellow sundress with a matching jacket, a black-and-white-striped straw hat with a yellow ribbon, and yellow sling-back shoes. There wasn't a speck of dust or a single dog hair anywhere on her. She looked like she was going to a fashion luncheon.

"Mrs. Malone," I said, propping the broom against the column and walking down the steps to meet her. Over the last few years at home, I'd run into her in town and at the grocery, but she hadn't paid a visit to Dahlia House in years—at least since before I left for college, and that was better than a dozen years ago. Frances was a Delta society lady, but she had also been my mother's friend. "What brings you to Dahlia House?"

"I need your help," Frances said. "I'm desperate, Sarah Booth. You have no idea how awful this woman is, and what she intends to do. She has to be stopped. You have to stop her."

I put a steadying hand on her elbow and guided her up the steps to one of the rockers. "Take a seat, Ms. Frances. May I get you some lemonade?"

"Water would be nice, Sarah Booth." She calmed a little and assessed me. "You look so much like your mother." She blinked quickly. "There's not a day goes by that I don't miss Libby Delaney."

"Me, too." I patted her shoulder. A memory of Frances sitting at the kitchen table drinking a mimosa on a Sunday morning came back to me. Mama had been at the stove making her famous French toast, and Frances recounted some foolishness at The Club, Zinnia's bastion of culture and golf. I'd walked into the kitchen from outside, struck by the beauty of the two laughing women.

"Libby would know what to do," Frances said, her agitation returning. "She'd know how to fix this monster."

I hustled to get some water before I asked any questions. I'd never seen Frances so rattled. Whatever was happening had to be pretty awful.

When I returned, I found Pluto sitting in her lap purring. After she'd sipped the water and her respiratory rate had slowed, I pulled up another rocker. "What's going on?"

"It's just too awful." She shielded her eyes with a hand.

"You have to tell me, if you want me to help." I wasn't certain it was as serious as Frances thought, but I needed the facts.

"A woman has come to town. A scholar from New England. Dear me, I think I'm going to be sick. She's driven me to public vomiting! It's the final humiliation."

"Calm down, Ms. Frances." I put a steadying hand on her arm. "I'll help you, but I'm confused. An academic is here, and this is a bad thing?" Surely this would be right up Frances's alley. She and her friends loved learning and education. While Ole Miss was thought to be a superior school, many of the children of her set aspired to attend Yale or Harvard. The Ivy League seal of approval went a long way in business relationships.

"You have no idea. She's a historian at Camelton College. Impeccable PhD. The school is well respected—one of the new Ivy League contenders. Its campus appeals to the snow set. Skiers and hikers"—she waved a hand—"those tedious cold-weather sports New Englanders love."

Frances's reverse snobbery amused me. "What's she doing in Zinnia?" We weren't a hot spot for historical research, unless it involved some of the Native American tribes that enriched area history or the well-trod terrain of the Civil War.

"She's here to stir up trouble and besmirch the good names of your friends." Frances burst into tears. "It's just the most awful thing I've ever heard, Sarah Booth. And she's going all over town saying the worst things about the families of Cece Dee Falcon and Oscar Richmond. She *claims* the Richmond and Falcon families were involved in President Lincoln's assassination."

Smote speechless would be the correct term for me. I tried to digest what Frances had said from several directions, and none worked. "Wait a minute. She's saying Oscar's and Cece's ancestors plotted with John Wilkes Booth to kill Lincoln? How could she possibly have any evidence? I mean, this is nuts."

"Then you have to stop her." She brought a tatted-lace handkerchief from her purse and dabbed her eyes.

"Who is she?"

"Her name is Dr. Olive Twist and—"

I held up a hand. "Olive Twist? Are you kidding me? As in the female version of the Dickens character, Oliver Twist?"

"Her parents were Victorian scholars, or at least that's what she said." Frances didn't even crack a smile at the absurdity of it. She was that upset. "She's a horrid woman. Skinny as a rail and with huge feet. Poisonous. So how are you going to get her out of town?"

My breath escaped on a hiss. "Frances, this really isn't my area of expertise. I'm a private investigator. This sounds like something the mayor or supervisors need to probe. Or maybe a lawyer. If she's slandering people, she can be sued."

"You're a detective. Go detect! Find out what she's really up to, and then we'll figure a way to thwart her."

I gave her fingers a squeeze. Although thwarting sounded like fun, I wasn't sure it was appropriate. "It isn't that easy. Is she breaking any laws?"

"She stormed into the September meeting of the Daughters of the Supreme Confederacy right in the middle of Hallie Harper's speech on the mighty efforts of the women of Magnolia, Mississippi, to send buttons and thread to our soldiers in the field. At the time, many buttons were made of bone, and they wore thin and came loose. Soldiers had no means of—" She stopped herself. "Poor Hallie was so rattled by this harpy's conduct she lost her train of thought and couldn't finish her talk."

The Daughters of the Supreme Confederacy was a low-key group of ladies who enjoyed brunches of chicken salad, mimosas, and programs highlighting the efforts of Confederate womenfolk to support the men they loved. I knew many of the stories because my ancestor Alice Delaney, with the help of a smart young slave, Jitty, had worked tirelessly to support the Confederate troops and to save Dahlia House from the destruction of war, and later from the carpetbaggers.

"Okay, the woman is rude," I conceded. "But what harm can she really do? Oscar and Cece will sue her for slander if she keeps this up, but you need to chill, Frances. Remember, sticks and stones can break—"

"You sound exactly like your aunt Loulane, and I don't mean that as a compliment. Dr. Twist means to drag the Richmond and Falcon names through the mud and enjoy doing it. Cece is your friend. And Tinkie Bellcase Richmond is Oscar's wife and *your* business partner. You have a vested interest in this. Friendship demands that you take action."

"We're talking about events that happened nearly two hundred years ago, Frances." One of the worst—and the best—things about Southerners is their total devotion to the reverence of the past. "This is over and done."

Frances started to rise. "I thought you valued your friends. Yet you'll sit back and allow the character of their families to be assassinated by this . . . this . . . Yankee pseudo-intellectual."

I thought of those long-ago mornings when Frances and my mother plotted and laughed. They were women as different as night and day. My mother didn't give a fig about society or ladies' luncheons. She didn't belong to a single social organization and refused to join The Club because it was elitist. Yet she and Frances had shared a love of land and a deep appreciation for heritage and good friends. "Let me look into it. At least I can talk with her and see what she's up to."

"Oh, Sarah Booth. I knew you were the person to come to. Since you're totally outside society, you can put that woman in her place with whatever means necessary."

Now, that was a nice way for Frances to say I could put a dog-cussing on Olive Twist without behaving in an unladylike fashion, since I wasn't a lady to begin with. I had no honor to lose by getting down in the mud with the hogs.

I walked Frances to her car. "I'll pay a call on Dr. Twist."

"She's staying at The Gardens B and B." She slammed her door and drove away before I could protest.

I had a history with Gertrude Strom, the owner of the B and B in question. She hated me and had since I'd come home to Zinnia from New York. I already rued my offer to intervene. Chances were, if Dr. Twist were left alone, she'd tire of poking at the old, tired Delta society and take herself back home to her teaching duties.

The single good thing: I'd only agreed to speak with Dr. Twist. This wasn't a new case. I could still devote my time completely to my fiancé.

Graf would be with Oscar at The Club until after lunch. As much as I disliked the idea of going to The Gardens, it would be best if I got the chore behind me.

Propping the broom by the front door, I went inside with my hound at my heels and a plump black feline capering along the hardwood floors. A quick cleanup and fresh clothes and I'd be on my way to meet the caustic Dr. Twist.

I turned on the upstairs shower, disrobed, and lathered up. I was towel drying my long chestnut hair when I heard a noise in my bedroom. If Graf was already back from golf, Oscar had skunked him. Still, the prospect of seeing Graf made me rush out of the bathroom and come to a screeching halt.

A woman with a huge head of black curls and wearing a red dress, red shoes, and a garter pointed a cane at me. Perched on the side of her head was a top hat. "Boo-boop-de-doop," she said in a high-pitched baby voice.

Jitty had incarnated as Betty Boop. The resident haint at Dahlia House had gone vintage cartoon on me.

"Boo to you!" I wrapped the towel around me. "I swear, Jitty. Betty Boop? Why don't you just get a whip and flog me. It would be kinder." My decade-hopping haint had shown up in garb from the eighteenth century to *Star Trek,* but a cartoon character was taking it just a little too far.

"You ought to get you a little red dress and a garter," Jitty said, leaning on the cane and poking out her butt in a provocative calendar-girl pose. "Graf's shoes would smoke he'd be in such a hurry to jump out of them. Just think of the possibilities."

"Maybe I could suck on a helium balloon while I'm at it. If your voice gets any more babyish I'll have to drink formula to converse with you." I had no time for Jitty's antics.

"Jealous, some?" Jitty asked. "Betty Boop was the sex symbol for generations of men."

"That is too sad to even contemplate." I took a long look at her. "Your head is huge."

"And so are my boobs," she countered. "And my waist is tiny. Men love me."

"Oh, for heaven's sake. You're talking about men suffering from retarded adolescence." I went to the closet and dragged out ironed jeans and a purple shirt.

I heard the tapping of the cane and her high heels as she came closer to me.

"What do you want, Jitty? It has to be something spectacular if you're wearing that getup."

"Just giving you a preview of what's coming your way like a freight train. Better eat your spinach."

"Spinach?" I turned to confront her, but in typical Jitty fashion, she was gone. In her wake, though, a burst of tiny red hearts floated around the spot where she'd stood. In an instant, they vanished.

The long, tree-lined drive to The Gardens brought back memories. Bad ones. I didn't relish asking Gertrude Strom where to find Dr. Twist, but I had no choice. Gertrude ran the front desk like a barracuda guarding a sushi buffet. She would make life as tough as possible for me. The only person Gertrude was consistently nice to was my partner, Tinkie. Zinnia National Bank held the mortgage on The Gardens, and Tinkie's husband, Oscar, was president of the bank. Her father owned it. Money might not buy happiness, but it sure as heck could purchase obsequiousness.

Whatever my personal feelings for Gertrude, I had to hand it to her. The grounds were incredible. Mums in every shade from purple to russet to gold brightened the flowerbeds, where fuchsia-veined caladiums offered pinks and lime greens. Closer to the building, I was smitten by the riot of spider lilies, their coral petals dancing on a gentle breeze.

"What are you doing on my property?" Gertrude popped up from behind a hedge like one of those horrible jack-in-the-boxes. Even as a child I'd hated those things.

I'd hoped to at least get in the door before she launched an assault, but fate was against me. She wasn't a tall woman, but she was cantankerous as a snake with its tail in a mousetrap. "Gertrude, fancy seeing you here. Where can I find Dr. Olive Twist?"

"I don't have to tell you anything. In fact, I can call the sheriff and have you arrested for trespassing. Now that you're no longer sleeping with Sheriff Peters, maybe he'll cuff you and haul you off to jail."

Gertrude's red hair, dyed to a shade between fire engine and Bozo the clown, caught the sunlight like copper wires. Bride of Frankenstein might be a phrase used to describe her.

"Gertrude, I'm well within my rights to visit a guest."

"We'll see about that. Maybe Dr. Twist doesn't want to see you."

"If she doesn't, I'll leave. But I intend to ask her." I started past Gertrude, only to be stopped by a garden rake thrown like a spear. She missed my foot by about an inch.

"Don't take another step. You're not so special you can make yourself at home here." Gertrude came out of the flowerbed, dusted her gloves, and maneuvered her body between me and the front door. "Wait here. I'll ring Dr. Twist and see if she'll speak with you. Of course I'll warn her what a busybody little snooper you are and how ineffectual your detective agency is."

I sighed and took a seat on a bench. It was still ninety-two in the shade, but it was better than standing in the sun. Also better than arguing with Gertrude. She could waste endless amounts of my time, and I wanted to talk to the professor and then get home to stir up some fried chicken, field peas with okra, and cracklin' cornbread for Graf. Fattening up a man was one of life's little joys. Soon enough he'd be in Hollywood with his trainer, but for the moment we were tossing dietary concerns to the wind.

Speaking of trainers, I made a discreet grab at the flab accumulating around my middle. Since finishing my last case, during which a vile butler had tried to starve me, I'd shoved my face in the trough and lived life large. Graf was an excellent cook. And Dahlia House's kitchen was made for two to share. We worked well together, and we enjoyed trying new recipes, all of them saturated with calories. Soon, though, the excess would stop and the suffering would begin. Graf would be gone and I'd have to address the wages of gluttony.

"Ms. Delaney?"

Startled from my food fantasy, I swung around to face the skinniest woman I'd ever seen. She wore a long blue pencil skirt and a white blouse ruffled around the neck and sleeves. She was a vision of a 1980s secretary or bank teller. Except for her feet, which were encased in the ugliest brogans ever cobbled. They were boats. A small village could have floated on them. A size fifteen, at the very least.

"Are you Ms. Delaney?" Her voice had an irritating twang whose origins I couldn't place. She wasn't British or Canadian or even Northeastern, and she sure as heck wasn't from my neck of the woods. Jitty's warning came back to haunt me—indeed, I should have eaten some spinach because I was staring at Olive Oyl. The stick-thin, shapeless body, the blue-black hair clasped at her neck with a scrunchie, the huge feet. Popeye's girlfriend, in the flesh. Except this Olive had the visage of an angel.

"Can you hear me?" She leaned down into my face and spoke slowly. "I know you people are slow."

"You people?" I bristled. "What do you mean, *you people*?"

Her answer was a strange movement of her lips that could have been a smile, or possibly a gas bubble.

"Gertrude said you wanted to speak to me. She also told me you're a Nosy Parker." Dr. Twist sprawled beside me on the bench. "She failed to tell me you were mentally challenged."

I ignored the jab and forced my gaze away from her clodhoppers. She could water-ski with those feet. She could use her feet for Ping-Pong paddles, and something about the way she flounced on the bench told me she was probably limber enough to actually do it.

"I'd like to ask a few questions about your research." It was the least offensive opening I could come up with.

"My, how gossip flies around a small Southern town. Do you people communicate by telephone?" She looked around as if searching for physical evidence of communication devices. "Do you actually have phone service here? I was surprised to find flush toilets."

Gertrude had undoubtedly given Dr. Twist a negative impression of me, but the professor had arrived in Zinnia with a stereotype of the area already embedded in her brainpan. I was tempted to yuk it up with some hambone slang, maybe a few one-liners about how all the DNA in town was similar, but I didn't. Feeding the prejudice would only make matters worse.

"Let me treat you to a drink," I offered as I stood up. While we were the same height, I had her by forty pounds. If she took those ass-ugly shoes off, maybe fifty. I'd really never seen anything quite like them. They were stacks on a platform of glittery black plastic. Open-toed lace-ups, they appeared to be leather painted in a camouflage pattern. With a cuff of gray faux fur. Why would any sane person want to call attention to a foot that size?

"A drink would be lovely," she said.

A serving or two of free booze might oil the hinges of Olive's jaws. Patience was a virtue, and one I didn't come by naturally. Still, I played it cool and got us settled at a small table in a corner of the bar.

Even though I didn't care for Gertrude, I loved The Gardens' bar. It was all dark paneling, but there were plenty of windows. The parquet floor was polished to a shine, and plants hung in baskets and sprouted from planters. The ambience was wealth mingled with a green thumb. Gertrude knew her clientele. And one of her guests, a distinguished-looking fellow with salt-and-pepper hair and a small, Clark Gable mustache, seemed very interested in either me or Dr. Twist. He pretended to read a newspaper, but he watched us.

With a Long Island iccd tea in front of her and a Bloody Mary at my fingertips, I started out casually. "I'm fascinated by history, and I heard you were here to do local research."

She nodded. "If my theories are correct, I'll publish a monograph that'll impact American history from the Civil War period. And that's just the beginning. I have a rip-roaring tale that will translate into bestsellerdom." She stood up abruptly. "Would you mind changing places with me?"

"What?"

"The light is better where you're sitting. So my assistant can film." She pushed me out of my chair and scooched into it with a provocative wiggle. "We're documenting every step of this journey. This could be as significant as the first walk on the moon, or Admiral Peary's trip to the North Pole."

"Wasn't that claim challenged?"

Olive grinned, and I swear I saw wicked canines. "You're not as stupid as you look."

"I'm not the one who thinks every move I make is noteworthy." I glimpsed a young cameraman behind a potted plant. He held an expensive piece of equipment trained on the preening historian.

"I'll put this hick town on the map." Olive leaned back in the chair. "Whether you people like it or not."

If she said "you people" one more time I might deck her. "Most folks don't find Mississippi's history all that fascinating, unless you're writing about the Civil War or civil rights. You've come a long way to work on a tired, overdone project."

"I have," she agreed. "No one told me it was so hot here." She wiped perspiration droplets from her forehead. "I've never been anywhere so intolerably hot. Is it the heat that makes you Southerners so slow? Honestly, I think if I stayed here six months my brain would turn to goop, too."

I smiled. "Tell me a little about yourself." Some folks loved to talk about their favorite subject—themselves. I suspected Dr. Twist was one of them.

"What's the big interest in me?" she asked. "You don't strike me as the kind of person who gives a flip about academics or the pursuit of knowledge. Do you even read?"

It was hard, but I ignored the insult. "Oh, that's where you're wrong. I'm a big fan of facts. Facts are my stock-in-trade." I sipped my drink, amazed that her glass was drained. She might not weigh a hundred pounds, but she sure could Hoover down a drink. "Lay some knowledge on me." Yeah, I couldn't help myself from goading her just a little.

"Maybe you've got a personal interest in what I'm doing." She tapped her straw against her glass and assessed me. "Booth is a rather interesting name in a small Southern town. Booth. Ring any historical bells for you? A would-be actor, a theater, a gun." She chuckled. "I hadn't counted on such good luck on my first day here."

This wasn't going to be easy. Whatever else Dr. Twist might be, she was nobody's angel—and nobody's fool. "Are you referring to John Wilkes? No relation to my family, I assure you."

"DNA tells out. Have any family branches from Maryland?"

I refused to rise to the bait. "I'm trying to figure out what your interest in Zinnia is. Why don't you just spare us both a lot of hemming and hawing and tell me why you're here."

She signaled the barkeep for another drink. "Research."

"Could you be more specific? It's possible my friends could assist if your project is interesting."

"I don't think you or your friends will help me. No, not at all." She took the drink the bartender brought and sucked down half of it. "I don't think you'll approve of my . . . research."

"History's history. It's either fact or not. It's not up to me to approve or disapprove."

"Very enlightened attitude, but you're not a convincing liar. I know your type. Defend the family honor no matter the truth. It's been said that in the South, blood is always thicker than water. In some instances, I've been told, blood carries more weight than money. Is that true, Ms. Delaney?"

She didn't really know me at all, but she'd locked in on a partial truth. I was extremely defensive about my family's honor, and also my friends. Money came in a distant second to honor in my book. "So what are you researching?"

"I don't have to tell you a damn thing about my work here. Or your friends. I doubt any of you could understand what I'm doing. And if you did understand, you wouldn't approve of it. Besides, I have Boswell. He provides every service I need."

My brain flipped through a mental Rolodex and came up empty. "Boswell? From *Charlie's Angels*?"

"That's Bosley, you . . ." She stopped herself. "Boswell is my assistant. The one with the camera." She waved at him. "I've promised him a credit and a tiny percentage of the royalties on my book if he works hard. There'll be plenty of glory to share, and Boswell is all I need. He works tirelessly, and he's very good at what he does. He loves to please me."

She'd managed to dodge the question of her research as well as my insincere offers of assistance. What she needed was a good dose of Aunt Loulane's wisdom—she sure could catch a lot more flies with sugar than with vinegar. I wondered what had made her such a sour person.

"I guess polite questions won't work for you. Let's get down to the nit-picking." I was pretty certain that colorful phrase would please her, because I was sure she believed everyone in Zinnia had nits. "Are you researching the genealogy of the Richmond and Falcon families?"

"What if I am?"

Saint Peter with rigor mortis, she was an aggravating varmint. I signaled the barkeep for another round for her. She drank like she had a hollow leg. I'd run up a bar tab and gotten nothing in return. "Both the Richmond and Falcon family are personal friends. Slander or, worse, libel is not a good idea."

"Are you threatening me?"

"Pope Paul at a clambake! I don't know what you're up to and I don't care, but if you've come here to make trouble for my friends, it won't end pretty." Dang, that was a Freudian slip. Dr. Twist could have been a real beauty, if she had better taste in clothes and a foot transplant.

"Threats don't scare me. Your friends' ancestors were involved in some low-down, dirty business that resulted in the assassination of one of the greatest men to ever lead this country."

"JFK? No one in Zinnia had anything to do with that."

"Not Kennedy. Lincoln."

"That's the most ridiculous thing I've ever heard." She really was a fruitcake.

"I have evidence, and as soon as I get the order to disinter the Lady in Red, I'll have proof beyond a shadow of a doubt. Her DNA will match either Oscar Richmond or Benjamin Falcon. She is the mastermind who plotted the murder of Abraham Lincoln. Mary Surratt was falsely accused and executed. It should have been the woman in that grave, Tilda Richmond or Tilda Falcon, who swung from the gallows."

The ghoulish scene she evoked made me blink. "You don't know which family?"

"There's a connection between the families I haven't

figured out. But I will. Once I'm on a scent I'm better than a bloodhound."

Color me flabbergasted. I opened and closed my mouth like a guppy, unable to form words. Her accusations and leaps of logic were so astounding, no sane person would give them credence. She'd taken a local mystery and embroidered it into a tablecloth for a banquet of crazy lies.

The Lady in Red, an unidentified female, was accidentally disinterred on Egypt Plantation in Cruger, Mississippi, in 1969. The details of the incident were well known, at least in the Delta. Few folks outside the region knew—or cared—anything about a mysterious grave.

A backhoe operator unearthed the sealed coffin of a beautiful lady wearing a red gown and gloves. The glass-topped coffin had been filled with alcohol and sealed so that the body inside was perfectly preserved. No one identified the body. No one claimed her. She was reburied at a local cemetery, and the plantation owner erected a monument inscribed: Lady in Red, Found on Egypt Plantation, 1835–1969. Her birth date was presumed, based on her clothes and age. The year 1969 was when she was accidentally dug up and reburied. No real facts were known.

The grave was a local attraction for teens and tourists for years—for those who could find it.

"No one knows who's in that grave," I said. "If she'd been a Richmond or a Falcon, trust me, her family would have claimed her."

"Would they?" She gulped down the last of her drink. When she tried to signal for the barkeep, I grabbed her wrist. I'd had enough.

"Where did you come up with this cockamamie idea?" I asked.

"You'll have to read my book to get those answers, but I'll give you a hint. Lincoln had one cabinet member, Edwin Stanton, who loathed traitors, and he viewed all Southern sympathizers as such. He kept tabs on a woman who fits the description of your Lady in Red. I have some of his private letters, which are enlightening on the subject of Lincoln's seduction and betrayal."

"That's the most ridiculous thing I've ever heard."

"Is it?" A smile lifted her features from haughty to beautiful.

"After all this time, new evidence is suddenly discovered? Sounds to me like you're desperate for something sensational."

Olive's expression shifted to consternation, and I glanced behind me. A very handsome young man had walked up. Light brown curls topped his six-three frame, and clear gray eyes met me head-on. He held an expensive digital camera in his hand. He nodded a hello. "Jimmy, this is a private detective sent to scare us out of town. Does she frighten you?"

He laughed. "Dr. Twist, it's time for your massage."

"Thank you, Boswell. I'll be right there. Go and heat the rocks. I've had enough tension for the day."

"I'll be ready for you in fifteen minutes." He nodded good-bye before he left.

"That's your assistant?" It was my first good look at him sans the vegetation. He looked more like a boy toy.

"Boswell has a bright future, as long as he does what I tell him."

"No doubt." Anyone who bucked Dr. Twist would suffer. "But I can tell you the woman in that grave has no relationship to Sunflower County families. It would behoove you to stop that kind of gossip. Oscar won't tolerate it, and if Tinkie hears any of it, she'll take you to court."

"I'm the only one who has access to Stanton's letters, and I intend to make the most of it. Truth is the only defense against slander or libel. I'm going to prove my hypothesis is true."

"How?"

"Once the body is on an autopsy table, I'll compare DNA to the living family members."

"And how do you intend to prove that the woman in that grave had anything to do with Lincoln's assassination?"

"Oh, I have my ways, Ms. Delaney. And I'm willing to stake my professional career on it. Now I must go. I can't miss my massage. There's so much tension in this kind of research, and I can't afford to stress my back."

2

Chablis, Tinkie's lionhearted Yorkie, greeted me with a little dance and yips of pleasure when I slipped through the front door of Hilltop, Tinkie and Oscar's home. Now, while she was alone, would be the best time to tell Tinkie about Olive Twist. Oscar was still on the links with Graf, and Tinkie would have a couple of hours to calm down before he returned.

My friend was not a hothead or a brawler, but she'd married a Richmond, and woe unto anyone who messed with her family. Since I hoped Twist would be a passing nuisance—a kerfuffle among the heritage dames of the county—I'd considered keeping the situation from Tinkie. But I would hate it if someone hid things from me. Especially something involving family. Perhaps Tinkie could straighten out Dr. Twist and send her packing. Tinkie's social skills were sharper than a surgeon's blade.

"Sarah Booth!" Tinkie sang as she came out of the kitchen waving a spoon covered with something brown. And stinky. Really stinky. Even Chablis took a whiff and ran to hide under the sofa.

"I'm so glad you're here," Tinkie continued. "I'm making doggy treats for the local animal shelter fund-raiser." She grimaced at the sad apron she wore, spattered with gunk that reminded me of an explosion in a turd factory. "The first batch I baked turned into rocks. I was afraid Chablis would chip a tooth. I didn't have to worry. When I tried to give her one, she hightailed it and ducked behind a chair."

"You're making doggy treats?" This did not sound like my detective partner. Tinkie and Oscar had a cook. And a maid. And a gardener. Tinkie was more inclined to get a pedicure than to bake. Judging from her apron and the smell wafting from her and the counter area, life was better in the Richmond household when she stayed out of the kitchen.

"It's for a good cause, and Madam Tomeeka assured me it was a simple recipe." She was dangerously close to a pout. "I don't understand why it won't come out right. Tammy predicted I would be the hit of the bake sale."

Madam Tomeeka, known to her close friends as Tammy Odom, was a psychic of sorts and a loyal friend of the highest order. This time, though, she'd led my partner astray.

"Did she also tell you that you'd wreck your kitchen and create something akin to toxic waste?"

Tinkie took a halfhearted swipe at me with the spoon. I almost gagged. "What in the hell is on that spoon?"

The color, consistency, and odor ignited convulsions in my throat. "God, it's awful."

"I know." Tinkie plopped the spoon in the sink. "I did something wrong."

"Understatement of the year. Put the baking aside, I need to talk to you."

Tinkie untied her apron and threw it on a chair. Her gaze swept over the kitchen and she picked up a bowl filled with foul-smelling brown goop and dropped the whole thing in the trash. It was swiftly followed by a pan of baked brown things shaped like bones. "I'll buy some gourmet dog treats and donate them to the fund-raiser. I don't think any dog in its right mind would eat one of these things."

Silence was the wisest choice. When the kitchen was tidy again, Tinkie motioned me to follow. "I have an appointment. We can talk while I'm getting dressed."

Tinkie was a clotheshorse, and I had total appreciation for her élan and taste. She'd look good in a feed sack, but her closet was filled with the latest fashions. I settled onto an overstuffed burgundy velvet chaise and gave her a chance to ask me the news. I wanted her full attention.

She shook out her blond curls. "You never come to Hilltop if it's a case, so this has to be personal. What has you picking your cuticles? You and Graf have a lovers' spat?"

I shoved my hands into my pockets. Tinkie had the vision of an eagle. "Graf and I couldn't be better. It's something else. It's not as bad as it may sound at first, but—"

"Spill it, Sarah Booth, before you give me a coronary." Tinkie tapped her bare foot on the carpet. "It must be horrible for you to be so afraid to say it."

"A university professor is in town doing research on the Lady in Red."

"That old grave they found out in a field?" Tinkie opened the closet door. "Whatever for? And more importantly, why is this news? Folks have speculated about the woman in that grave for fifty years and nothing has ever come of it."

I wanted to broach the subject with finesse and calm. Those were not my strong suits. The end result was silence.

"Well, what is it?" Patience exhausted, Tinkie put her hands on her hips. "You look like you're constipated. Tell me or let me get dressed."

"There's a crazy bitch in town who claims the Lady in Red is a relative of Oscar's and that she intended to assassinate President Abraham Lincoln. She's a university professor and she's come here to prove her theory."

Tinkie's cheeks turned pale, then flushed. I could see her body temperature rising with every passing second. "Who is this person? Surely not someone from Ole Miss. The history professors there have far more breeding than to try to stitch together this ridiculous tale."

"No, not Ole Miss."

She caught the scent of the story. "Where the hell is she from then, and who is she?"

"Her name is Olive Twist. She's a—"

I got no further. Tinkie burst into her tinkling trademark laughter. "You are pulling my leg, aren't you? Olive Twist. What is she, a martini garnish?"

"A toothpick would be more apt. Her parents were Victorian scholars."

"Olive Twist. Like the Dickens character, only female." She caught on fast.

"Correct. Or so I've been told." One thing about the education we'd received from our literature teacher, Mrs. Nyman—we knew our classics.

"So she's from where? Duke? Emory? Vanderbilt?"

"Camelton College. In Maine. It's an up-and-coming Ivy League—"

"I know where it is. But why is someone from there interested in the Lady in Red?" She caught the fabric of the whole quilt. "Oh, I see. She believes one of Oscar's relatives was mixed up in the assassination of Lincoln. This is a big deal. She can come down here and dig up crap on prominent families and hope she gets enough notoriety out of it to publish a paper or get tenure."

"Not just Oscar's ancestors, but Cece's, too. And she said something about a bestseller. Her ambitions go beyond academia." Oscar was the most even-keeled man I knew. Olive Twist wouldn't get under his skin, because he wasn't invested in the past. Cece was another matter. Her past was a wound. She lived with it, but I knew how deeply she hurt. "If Twist gets wind of Cece's background, she is going to have a heyday."

Our friend Cece Dee Falcon had once been Cecil. Now he was a she and she was the head of the society pages and the best investigative reporter at the *Zinnia Dispatch*. When Cece had demanded the right to be her own person, her family had disowned her. This would all be grist for the mill of Dr. Twist's book. Cece had lived through this once. She shouldn't have to confront it again.

"I don't like this one little bit." Tinkie snatched clothes out of the closet without even looking. "Where is this person staying?"

"The Gardens B and B. I've already been there and

tried to talk to her. All she did was run up a bar tab and thumb her nose at me."

"One call to Gertrude and Miss Sassy Britches will be out on her ear." She slid into a cute pair of capris and sandals. "You've seen her. What's she like?"

"Really skinny. Like a number two pencil. And glamorous with a peculiar sense of fashion. And mean as a pit viper. She enjoys upsetting people. She disrupted the meeting of the Daughters of the Supreme Confederacy. That's how I got on to her. Frances Malone came by Dahlia House and asked me to speak to her, for all the good it did."

"Then I guess I'll have to take a swing at her. I'll cancel my appointment."

That was exactly what I feared Tinkie might do. "First, let's go out to the Egypt Plantation and see what we can find out. Maybe if we talk to the folks there we can find a reason to make Olive Twist go away."

The drive to Holmes County was beautiful. Fall temperatures wouldn't arrive in the Deep South for another four weeks, but I could see hints of approaching cooler weather in the quality of light. The sun was still brutal, but the pale yellow of approaching October edged the horizon and seemed to linger in the green leaves of the trees. I loved this time of year, the last, lingering days of summer's heat. When I was a child, September had meant excitement. A new school year filled with potential and fun—though everyone wore shorts to the Friday-night football games.

I wasn't a geek or a bookworm, but I liked school. I

loved the workbooks in which language and math problems could be solved with a sharpened pencil. September included the dizzying smell of a new box of crayons, opened for the first time. It was as if each color had its own special scent. Recess was kickball and jumping rope.

If I could go back in time for a week, or even a day, I would halt life and step into the past. I'd had no cares, no worries, no guilt, and no regrets. What a shame we grew out of utopia and into adulthood.

Tinkie's manicured fingers touched my shoulder. "You're far, far away, aren't you?"

"The past." I could confess such things to Tinkie. She had a kind and understanding heart.

"Not a bad place to visit, but don't put down roots. People who live in the past are doomed to unhappiness. You have me, Graf, and all your friends anchoring you right here in the present."

"Thanks." With so little effort, she'd pulled me into the moment. "I think we're almost there."

The little town of Cruger, population under five hundred, was really only a blink. Holmes County had the lowest life expectancy of any county in the United States. The soil grows excellent cotton and soybeans, but the people struggle.

I'd driven my antique roadster, and we tooled down a two-lane road bordered by fields and kudzu. The kudzu vine, originally introduced to halt erosion, had taken to the Southern states like a tick to a dog. The vines could grow twelve inches in twenty-four hours. They wrapped around fences, trees, lampposts, buildings—anything that couldn't move away. Some farmers considered it good fodder for cattle, but most did everything they could to eliminate it because of its propensity to take over.

"That looks like a dragon," Tinkie said, pointing to several trees and possibly a billboard buried under kudzu. "I wish I could breath fire. I'd toast Olive Twist's hair."

I caught the incredible scent of the purple kudzu flowers in bloom. It was so intense I could almost taste grape. "They've virtually eradicated kudzu in Sunflower County."

Oversized sunglasses shaded Tinkie's blue eyes, but consternation hardened her features. "Just like I intend to eradicate this Olive Twist person. She has no right to be here tampering in our history."

She was aggravated, and I understood. Tinkie didn't mean legal right, she meant something far more difficult to pin down. The legends, stories, and places were ours. Not personally hers or mine, but the collective "ours" of the state. We passed folklore and tall tales down from generation to generation. This community knowledge partially defined us. The Lady in Red was part of this, a story every Delta child knew, and most of us had made up our own interpretations of where she'd come from and who she was. And none of them involved Abraham Lincoln.

My mother had told me the Lady in Red legend when I was nine. She and my father had driven me to Egypt Plantation to see the manager's house where the coffin had been accidentally unearthed.

I could still hear my father's voice. "They were digging a field line for the septic tank here at the manager's house when they hit the casket. They brought her up and discovered she was a beautiful woman. Lots of red hair piled up on her head. And she wore a red velvet dress with a white collar. Whoever buried her had loved her, because the casket was cast iron and made to order. It was shaped to her body and then sealed with a glass top. The coffin was filled with alcohol, and the body was perfectly preserved, but only for a short time. The backhoe cracked the seal on the coffin, and as the alcohol leaked out, the body decayed." My father had put a hand on Mama's back. "Something sad transpired to bury her here, alone, without any of her loved ones around."

My father had been a lawyer, and he didn't spare me from the realities of life and death. He protected me, but he didn't try to paint a pretty picture when it didn't fit the scene.

"When did you first hear about the Lady in Red?" I asked Tinkie.

"I was maybe seven. I was at the bank spending the afternoon with my father. Mr. Sampson from Holmes County came in for a visit. He and Daddy were friends, and the subject of the Lady in Red came up. They both told me about it and how no one knew who she was. I remember thinking how sad it was. She was buried in the yard of a house with none of her people around her."

"That's exactly what my father said." I pondered another question. "Do you think she's one of Oscar's or Cece's relatives?"

"Anything is possible, but I doubt it. If she were a cousin, the Richmonds would have gotten her body to Sunflower County for burial. They wouldn't have left her in a backyard. It just doesn't make sense."

"Remember the stories we made up about her? She was always exotic, always a woman of wealth." The memory came from that point of innocence that made childhood so wonderful. Children seldom fantasized about starving or ugly people, at least not little girls in the Delta. It was always princesses or movie stars or women who had a grand destiny.

"It doesn't matter where she came from, she's ours now. She isn't up for inspection or dissection by outsiders." Tinkie pushed her sunglasses up her nose. "I won't have it."

"Legally, I don't know how to stop Twist. She can write what she wants." I had to be up-front. Once Tinkie dug in, she didn't give up.

"Do you think she was murdered?" Tinkie asked.

"Murdered and then preserved? The casket had to be expensive. Probably shipped up from New Orleans." In a weird way, it made sense. Sometimes people killed the very thing they loved the most. The expensive funeral preparations and the unmarked grave would follow that train of thought.

"Maybe she was running away from her wealthy New Orleans husband," Tinkie said.

"Maybe she was meeting her lover. A tryst that went wrong."

"Maybe she was foreign, like a mail-order bride." Tinkie pulled down her sunglasses so she could look at me. She really liked that theory. "And she got here and met her husband-to-be and hated him and ran away. Maybe she got to the plantation and they tried to help her, but he caught up with her and killed her."

"Surely if there had been a gunshot or knife wound the law would have investigated."

"Not if she was buried without anyone ever notifying the law. People could do a lot of things back then. Folks believe she died right after the War Between the States, from what I can remember of the story. There was a lot happening around here. Union and Confederate troops had been all over the area. Remember, Sherman burned Jackson to the ground, and Jackson isn't that far away."

Tinkie had a point. Anything could have happened. Our dead woman could have been a prostitute, or a thief, or a con artist, even a card sharp. People had been shot for a lot less. As far as that went, she could have been the wife or sister of a soldier searching for a lost relative.

"Maybe there's more solid information at Egypt Plantation," Tinkie said.

"Let's start there. They reburied the Lady in Red in a cemetery in Lexington. But maybe someone at the plantation knows the history."

The flat land of the Delta broke at Holmes County and became more rolling. We drove to the plantation—six thousand acres of cotton, corn, soybeans, and peanuts. There had been a time when the plantation was like a small town. Workers had lived on the property. Churches and stores had sprung up within walking distance. The community of Egypt Plantation, like all of the large plantations in the Delta, would have been self-sustaining.

Things had changed. Folks had cars and drove into Lexington for shopping and supplies. Huge pieces of equipment did the work of hundreds of hands. But the land was the same, and the crops growing were lush, abundant, and well tended.

The manager had no new information for us and wasn't aware of any recent interest in the woman once buried there. He sent us on to Lexington, the county seat, to the Odd Fellows Cemetery where the Lady in Red was reinterred. Tinkie and I found her without any trouble.

"I wonder who paid for the gravestone?" Tinkie asked, her finger tracing the lettering on the marker. "Nineteen sixty-nine . . . that's when she was found . . . 1969. I guess they judged her age by the clothes she wore."

My family members were all buried at Dahlia House

in the family plot. Mama, Daddy, Aunt Loulane, Great-great-great-grandma Alice, Uncle Lyle Crabtree, and Jitty rested among the markers with names I didn't know. This woman was all alone. "I don't want to be buried," I said.

"Well, it's not something we have to worry about today, Sarah Booth."

"Excuse me, ladies. Are you here about the exhumation request?"

Tinkie and I both started and whirled around. A distinguished-looking gentleman stood only ten feet away. He wore a suit and a starched shirt even though it had to be over ninety degrees. "Who are you?" Tinkie asked.

"A request to dig up the body has already been filed?" I asked.

He chuckled in a deep baritone. "So you aren't the woman who petitioned to exhume the Lady in Red?"

"No," we answered in unison.

"I don't like the idea of disturbing the dead," the gentleman said. "Excuse me, ladies. I'm Meshach McFail, the coroner of Holmes County."

"Who requested the exhumation?" I asked, though I knew the answer. Dr. Twist had been a busy, busy lady.

"She didn't sound like she was from around here," McFail said. "Had a clipped voice with a strange twang. And real bossy."

"Olive Twist."

His smile widened. "She's filed a petition with the circuit clerk to have our Lady in Red exhumed. She said it was really important." He tilted his head to indicate the grave. "Since there's no one to speak for the dead lady, I guess she'll be dug up. Seems like a shame, though. She was already brought up once before. By accident."

"How can we stop this?" I asked.

He gave me an approving nod. "I'd speak to the circuit court clerk right up there in the courthouse in Lexington. He'll know what you need to do. Like I said, it would be a shame to disturb this poor lady's rest a second time."

"Who has the authority to exhume the body?" I asked.

"Anyone can request such a thing. Usually it's in cases where homicide is suspected. But Red, that's what we call her, she's been dead over a hundred years. No one has ever mentioned murder. Even so, the person who killed her would be dead, too." He gazed down at the headstone. "To be honest, I didn't care much for Ms. Twist."

"Everyone she meets feels the same way."

"She was awful to the young man who was with her." His lips compressed. "When he asked a question about the exhumation process, she told him he was stupid. She dressed him down right in front of me and the clerk. The young man was embarrassed. Why would a mother treat her son with such disrespect?"

"He's her employee, not her son."

Meshach whistled softly. "I'd be looking for another job if I were him."

Far be it from me to figure that one out. "What reason did Dr. Twist give for wanting the exhumation?"

He hesitated. "The clerk should tell you this, not me. But I can't see where it's a secret. She said she believed the Lady in Red was poisoned, and she wants a DNA sample as well as tissue to test for poisonous substances."

"Would any poison remain in the tissue after a hundred years?" Tinkie asked.

"Arsenic, for sure. I don't know about anything else." Meshach brought his watch from a pocket in his pants.

"I'm not a medical doctor, just a coroner. Someone with medical training could answer that with more certainty than I."

In Mississippi, coroners were elected. Requirements for the office didn't include a medical degree.

"Who can stop an exhumation if there are no relatives?" Tinkie asked.

Meshach pondered the question. "Can't say for sure. The clerk will know, and if he doesn't, Odie Williams will sure find out for you. He's not too keen on digging this poor lady up, either."

"Thanks, Meshach," Tinkie and I said simultaneously.

It didn't take ten minutes to reach the Holmes County Courthouse in Lexington. The graceful redbrick building was the third to serve as the official center of the county. Two predecessors had been destroyed by fire.

Odie Williams was serving his fourth term as clerk. The first thing he did when we walked in the door was offer us coffee. Meshach had obviously been on his cell phone, because Odie knew exactly what we wanted.

"My job is to help people," he explained as he poured two mugs full of aromatic coffee. "That Twist woman, though, she just got under my skin. She was rude to Ruby, my assistant, and to Meshach, and when she unloaded on that young man she brought with her, it was hard to watch."

"Has her petition to exhume been granted?" Tinkie asked.

"Judge Colbert has it. I assume he'll rule on it sooner rather than later."

"Would it help if we protested?" I asked.

"Couldn't hurt. I don't know what business this is of

some professor from out of state. Seems to me Dr. Twist has her own interests that may not go along with what's best for the Lady in Red or Holmes County."

Or Tinkie, Oscar, Cece, and our friends, but it would profit no one to point that out. "Where can we find Judge Colbert?"

"He's gone fishing. It might be best to hire a lawyer to draw up an official document protesting the exhumation. Might give him some legs to stand on to oppose it."

"Good idea," Tinkie said. "I know just the lawyer to talk to."

3

Oscar and Graf were sitting on the front porch of Hilltop when Tinkie and I returned to Zinnia. Ice tinkled in their drinks, and though I hadn't even had lunch, I accepted Oscar's offer of a "little libation."

In old planter tradition, morning alcohols are mostly mixed with breakfast fruit juices—tomato, orange, something with nutritional value to kick the day off to a good start. Noon opened the door to wines. Afternoons called, traditionally, for sherry for ladies and whiskey or port for men. Cocktail hour started any time after work and hard liquor, martinis, and such were the rule. Occasions such as a lazy Sundays were wide open in the realm of "libations."

Oscar returned with two salty dogs, one for me and

one for Tinkie. "A little grapefruit is good for the body," he said.

"I'm sure the vodka doesn't hurt." I licked the rim of the glass and caught my fiancé watching me with wicked intent. If Graf stayed in the Delta much longer, I would be totally corrupted, and loving every minute of it. The tart drink exactly hit the spot, and would certainly make it easier to tell Oscar what was going on in the heart of his hometown.

"How was the golf game?" Tinkie asked. Her level hand indicated that I should hold steady for the moment. She would break the news.

"Graf won, but only by two strokes." Oscar was a gracious loser and an equally gracious winner. There had been a time when I'd viewed him as a totally humorless stuffed shirt—a man who'd been handed everything on a silver platter. While Tinkie had married well when she joined her future with Oscar, he had also married into one of the most prominent Delta families. Tinkie was Mr. and Mrs. Avery Bellcase's only child.

Funny, but as I got to know Oscar, I saw depths in him I'd failed to acknowledge. That was even more true for Tinkie. Her high-gloss Daddy's Girl polish had once made me underestimate her generous heart.

Sitting on the front porch with a breeze cooling the day, we chatted aimlessly for half an hour before Tinkie broached the subject of Olive Twist. Oscar was, at first, amused, which quickly built to anger when he learned Olive had filed a petition to exhume the Lady in Red.

"Exhumation would be a sacrilege," he said. "I won't stand for it."

"Is there anything we can do to stop it?" Tinkie asked.

Watching the play of emotions across Oscar's face, I could only admire Tinkie all the more. She'd put the problem squarely in his lap, yet she made it clear she supported him. She wasn't just the good wife, she was his partner. And before the conversation was over, she'd made her points about what she thought should be done. Her gentle approach encouraged Oscar to listen.

In comparison, I was ham-fisted. To quote a poet laureate of the nation, I had "miles to go before I sleep" when it came to learning how to work with men. Or work men, as I occasionally viewed it.

"Let's go talk with this woman." Graf was more West Coast in his approach to the problem. "She can't just come to town and start digging up bodies."

"Do you happen to know Circuit Court judge Colbert?" I asked Oscar.

"I do. I went to school with Delbert." Oscar leaned forward. "Is he the judge hearing the petition?"

"Yes."

"I'll put in a call. We can certainly delay the exhumation."

That was a relief. It gave us a little time to figure out how much we wanted to stop Olive. "Her research will come to nothing," I said. "Even if she gets DNA, the poor lady isn't related to anyone around Sunflower County."

For half a minute, no one spoke.

"Oscar? Is she a relative?" I frowned at Tinkie's husband.

"Whoever she is, it's ridiculous to think she was involved in a plot to assassinate Lincoln. It would take days for a woman in a buggy to travel from Mississippi to Washington, D.C. Remember, Sarah Booth, women didn't ride all over the country like you do. A *lady* only traveled in a buggy, coach, or wagon. The going was much slower."

"Maybe riding astride was the first declaration of independence by women." I couldn't help but tease Oscar. He was raised with a code of conduct as strict as the one Tinkie had been held to. In his world, the distinction of the genders was still clear and not the blurred line of more metropolitan areas.

"Let's see what this Olive Twist has to say for herself." Graf stood up and I followed.

I wasn't certain this was a great idea, but I didn't see any way to stop it.

Gertrude fawned over Oscar, Tinkie, and Graf as she led us to the suite of rooms Dr. Twist occupied. She didn't even acknowledge I was there.

"Dr. Twist may be napping," Gertrude explained. "She's been very busy working on material for her book. Isn't it exciting? She's going to write about the history of Sunflower and Holmes Counties. Let me knock."

The door opened instantly. Jimmy Boswell gave us a slight nod before he asked Gertrude what she needed.

"Mrs. Richmond and her . . . friends would like to speak with the professor."

"Dr. Twist is napping," Jimmy said in a low voice. "She'll be up around three o'clock. Could you come back?"

"No." Tinkie slipped past him. "I have a busy schedule." She walked into the room and stopped.

Since I was right behind her, I nearly collided with her. But then I saw what had halted her. A pallet of blankets and a pillow were on the floor beside the lush bed Olive Twist reclined in. She made her assistant sleep on the floor beside her bed.

Jimmy rushed to pick up the pallet, and to my surprise, Gertrude helped him.

Tinkie's red face told me all I needed to know. She was about to blow a gasket. I intervened as best I could. "Dr. Twist, this is Oscar and Tinkie Richmond, and Graf Milieu."

Olive had eyes only for Graf. "I know some of your work. I saw you once Off-Broadway in *Bedlam*. I thought you were exceptional."

"Thank you, but we aren't here to talk about my acting career." Graf was not a man won over by praise.

And Dr. Twist was not one to be deterred from her goal. "I heard you just wrapped a western. The buzz is that it will rival *Unforgiven* for Oscar nominations."

Graf didn't respond. He'd zeroed in on Olive's feet. Her lovely face and model-thin body could never offset those gunboats. She was barefoot, and her toenails were painted black with silver lightning bolts. He couldn't tear his eyes away from the enormous mud flappers. I pinched him on the back of his arm.

"Uh, yes. I mean, awards are hard to predict. No one knows what will happen. But as I said, we're here for another reason."

Oscar and Tinkie, too, focused on Olive's feet. She dug her toes into the carpet and released them. It looked like some strange machine that wanted to harvest the carpet but was unable to move forward.

"Dr. Twist has a very busy schedule." Boswell broke the strange tension. "It would be best if you left." He held a video camera and was taping everything we did.

"Please, put that away." I made a move to cover the lens, but he stepped back.

"I record all things related to Dr. Twist. It's for posterity. People will be fascinated by Dr. Twist's research techniques and her original thought processes once her book is published. She'll have her own television show before this is over." He spoke in a completely flat tone.

"Please turn the camera off," Oscar said.

"Put it down, Jimmy," Olive said. "Let's hear what the locals have to barter. Whatever it is won't make a difference, but they can try. Make notes, Jimmy. We might get some leads." Olive's infatuation with Graf was gone and now she was all business.

Gertrude, who'd stationed herself by the door, inserted herself. "I'll escort Sarah Booth and Boswell to the lobby so the four of you can have a conversation." Obviously, Boswell and I had been culled from the herd.

"Sarah Booth isn't going anywhere." Graf's arm encircled my shoulders in a gesture both protective and romantic. "She's my girl."

"There's no accounting for taste," Gertrude said. "I'll be at the desk." She wheeled around and left.

Graf closed the door. "Now let's get this sorted out."

Oscar, Olive, and Tinkie settled at a small breakfast table in the kitchenette. Graf and I stood near the door, and Jimmy Boswell began straightening the room. "Shall I make some coffee, Dr. Twist?" he asked.

"That's my personal coffee, Jimmy. Absolutely not. It's very expensive. Why don't you fetch some coffee for everyone from the dining room."

He refused to look at any of us, and I felt a rush of sympathy for him: Had he known how he would be treated when he signed up to be Olive's assistant? The better question was why he didn't leave her employ. By the time she finished with him, he wouldn't have a shred of self-respect left.

I did a visual survey of the room as the Richmonds and Olive got down to business. The accommodations at The Gardens were exceptional and filled with amenities such as plush bedding and windows that offered stunning views of the back gardens. The kitchenette glowed with polished granite counters and chrome. I noted the gourmet coffee beans, electric grinder, and French press beside a Bose stereo system with satellite radio.

A large-screen TV topped an antique desk in the parlor. There was even a bookcase with shelves of books written by Mississippi authors Miranda James, Charlaine Harris, Ace Atkins, and David Sheffield. All mysteries. So Gertrude had a thing for complicated story lines.

On the bedside table were several romance novels. Dr. Twist didn't strike me as someone who courted *amore*, so her choice of reading was illuminating. The titles intrigued me: *The Rogue with a Brogue, Paradise Peccadilloes, The Viscount's Verdant Vixen*. She had a thing for alliterative titles. I picked up the last one, intrigued by the cover.

"Put that book down," Olive ordered me. "None of you has authority to interfere with my research." She stood up so abruptly she bumped the table. Graf grabbed it before it toppled over.

In that moment, I couldn't say exactly what happened. A crash erupted, and window glass shattered as a missile flew into the room. A sliver of the window zinged across my forearm, leaving a thin line of oozing blood. A split second later, an explosion in the center of the Turkish rug sent everyone diving to the floor. Black smoke filled the room, and a fire broke out. The flames spread across the expensive carpet.

"Everyone! Outside!" Graf took charge, and Tinkie, Oscar, and I obeyed.

Not Olive. She ran around the room grasping notebooks, the video camera, computers, and files. "My research! Help me! Boswell, get back in here right now and help."

We met Boswell in the hallway holding a tray of coffee. Graf found a fire extinguisher in the hall, and in a few moments, he had the small blaze extinguished. Except for the noxious smoke, the burned carpet, and the broken window, the damage was minimal.

Oscar whipped out his cell phone and called the sheriff.

"I must be on to something good," Olive said. "Why else would these rednecks go to the trouble of trying to stop me?"

"How do you know it was a redneck?" I asked. "Did you see someone?"

Before she could answer, Gertrude stormed into the room and let out a wail of dismay. "That's an antique rug worth thousands. Who did this? Who's responsible?"

Grasping her shoulders gently in his hands, Graf led her from the room and into the hall. Whatever he said calmed her.

"Is everyone okay?" Tinkie motioned to Boswell to cease cleaning up the bits of scattered glass and debris.

"Don't touch anything," Oscar directed. "Let the sheriff handle this."

"Boswell must take care of my papers," Olive insisted. "And the camera. We can't lose this valuable footage.

He's been taping me for the past six months. These are the critical moments leading to the point where I prove my theory correct. We must have this footage to support the climax of my documentary."

I stage-whispered to Tinkie. "I think she's ready for her close-up."

Oscar barely suppressed a laugh, and Tinkie didn't bother trying. "Where is Mr. DeMille when we need him?" Her dramatic tone drew a cough from Graf.

"Take your half-wit remarks into the hallway," Olive commanded.

We were only too glad to do so, at least until the law arrived.

We didn't have long to wait. Fifteen minutes later Sheriff Coleman Peters strode toward us with DeWayne Dattilo, his deputy, in tow. I'd come to like DeWayne and respect his attention to detail, skills, and loyalty to Coleman.

As DeWayne collected the physical evidence, Coleman questioned us. I could read the curiosity on his face—who was this Olive Twist and what were we doing in her room? He'd get around to asking soon enough.

"Was Dr. Twist the target?" he asked me.

Olive jumped in with both enormous feet. "Of course it was me. Boswell, get the camera running. This will make an excellent episode—how I was nearly killed by those who don't want the secrets of the past to come out. I can see it now. Oprah may host a special just to interview me."

"Don't hold your breath," I said under mine.

Coleman stepped aside. "Sarah Booth, Oscar, Tinkie, I think you should go. I'll catch up with you later. Right now, I need to have a heart-to-heart with Dr. Twist and determine exactly what it is she thinks she's going to expose."

Olive sashayed up to him and gave him the once-over, head to toe. "Oh, I think I'd enjoy exposing myself to you."

Nebuchadnezzar eating a Kit-Kat! She was coming on to Coleman. "I beg your pardon," I said before I thought. "I don't want to see our sheriff turned to a pillar of salt."

"Are you one of those religious nutcases?" Olive asked.

"Sarah Booth is not any kind of nutcase, religious or otherwise. But she and her friends are leaving. Now." Coleman winked as he pushed me toward the door.

Jimmy joined the huddle as we all bumped together trying to get out. My left eyebrow inched up my forehead. "Good luck, Coleman." I was only too glad to leave Olive to his tender mercies. Coleman was first and foremost a lawman. But the Richmond and Falcon families included his friends. He would not take Olive's stated goal lightly.

After the excitement of the explosion in Olive's room, my sweet man, my best friend, and Oscar repaired to the bar at The Gardens. Thank goodness we managed to avoid Gertrude and settled at a table with a round of drinks. We could see the front exit from where we sat, and Coleman would not escape us. I had a lot of questions for him.

At the first sip of my drink, my shoulders relaxed. The bomb or Molotov cocktail or whatever it was had upset me more than I realized. "My goodness, we could have been injured or killed. And we aren't even on a case."

I was surprised by the coolness on Graf's face. "You were certainly protective of the local sheriff." He sipped his Jack and water. "I thought you might claw Dr. Twist's eyes out. Are you sure you aren't still carrying a torch?"

His question caught me flat-footed. I'd reacted to Olive's blunt come-on to Coleman not because I wanted him for myself, but because she was poisonous. I wondered if I could explain my reasoning to Graf.

"Shut your mouth, Sarah Booth, before you catch a fly." Tinkie put her arm through Graf's. "He's teasing you."

"I am," Graf said. "But I did notice."

"I'm glad you noticed, but you have nothing to worry about. My point was, Olive Twist could go through a man like a buzz saw through bologna. I just didn't want Coleman to get his clean shirt bloody."

"Coleman can handle himself," Oscar assured me, "though Dr. Twist probably eats raw meat, and I suspect cannibalism wouldn't be much of a stretch for her. She considers herself quite the vamp, and she certainly liked the looks of Graf and our fair sheriff."

"I'll bet she likes handcuffs," Tinkie threw in.

"Oh, stop it. I think we should investigate who threw that incendiary device through the window." I didn't want to sit around twiddling my thumbs and making up sexual scenarios for the history professor. I'd just had my fill of witnessing kinky sexual moments, thanks to the butler at a wealthy estate during my last case.

"I think we should let Coleman and DeWayne handle the attack or whatever it was. Once they finish, we'll have a look for ourselves." Tinkie turned to me. "Do you think that bomb-thing was meant to scare Olive off?"

"Maybe. Or it could be she set the whole thing up

to—" I stopped mid-sentence when the handsome man I'd noticed at the bar earlier that morning came up to our table. This time I paid a lot more attention.

He wore an expensive tweed sports jacket with leather patches, brown slacks, casual and expensive leather shoes. His salt-and-pepper hair was carefully cut, and the dark mustache highlighting his sensual mouth was trimmed to perfection. This was a man who cared greatly about his appearance.

"Excuse me, I'm Dr. Richard Webber," he said. "I couldn't help overhearing your conversation. Did someone try to blow up Dr. Olive Twist?"

"We're not certain what happened," I said smoothly. "Are you a friend of Dr. Twist's?"

"Some would say colleague, others might say competitor. I believe the good doctor's premise is flawed and I intend to prove it." His charming grin revealed twin dimples and eyes that crinkled at the corners. "I see a giant flapdoodle brewing. I predict excellent fun."

A man who enjoyed a "flapdoodle." Now, that was a development I hadn't expected. "Are you psychic or do you intend to start this . . . flapdoodle?"

"I like to think I'll be instrumental in putting the wheels in motion. You see, Dr. Twist has behaved in a most unethical fashion."

"How?" Tinkie was on it like a chicken on a bug.

"It's not a simple story. May I join you?"

Oscar got a chair from a nearby table and we made room for Dr. Webber to sit with us. When Oscar offered a drink, Dr. Webber opted for iced tea. "Dr. Twist has stolen my concept and research. Worse than that, though, she's intent on perverting the true facts and she'll stop at nothing. I have the real documentation for the Lady in

Red. Olive Twist is a dangerous woman who won't let anything get in the way of her ambitions."

"Then you know her intentions about the Lady in Red?" Tinkie was grim.

"I know them and I abhor them." He swallowed and glanced out the window for a long moment as an angry flush rose up his neck.

"Can you stop Dr. Twist from using the Lady in Red for her own personal gain?" I needed to know what silver bullets he might possess.

He inhaled slowly, controlling his temper. "There's a ninety percent probability I can halt that mule in her tracks."

I loved his colorful language, and I could see my friends approved, too. He actually made a set-to with Olive sound like fun, but big talk did not necessarily mean effective action. "How will you accomplish this?"

"I can't give away all of my trade secrets," he said. "Just believe me, I have ammunition that will stop her."

His secretiveness led me to question his credentials in the "torpedo Twist" realm. "Do you know each other?"

"That's a complicated question, my dear. I slipped in under the radar and I've been watching her for the past two days. All I can say is, thank god I'm not her assistant. Why that boy doesn't slit her throat while she sleeps, I'll never know."

He'd pretty well captured my feelings about Jimmy Boswell. The only thing worse than being Twist's paid employee would involve marriage or blood kinship. "He sleeps on the floor beside her bed."

"So I've been told." Webber drank his tea. "There's a long tradition of strange relationships in the world of letters. The young and eager subjugate themselves to the older and experienced."

"Oh, bull hockey!" I'd had enough. "No one should treat another living creature the way she treats Boswell."

"It's a peculiar arrangement, even by the standards of eccentric academics." He shrugged. "But the young man accepts it. He isn't an indentured servant or a slave. He can leave any time he chooses."

"He could pack his gear and make a run for it while she sleeps," I said.

"Do you think she sleeps?" A mischievous grin lit Tinkie's face. "Vampires don't require rest, do they?"

"Good one, Tink," Oscar said as everyone chuckled. My partner had a quick and ready wit.

Yes, we were a jolly bunch as we waited for Coleman to free himself from Olive's machinations. To pass the time, Richard Webber entertained us with tales of historic battles where competing academics vied to outdo each other and win acclaim. One thing about Richard Webber—he loved an audience. "Academia is a war zone fraught with the blood of the innocent and the naïve."

"He's a bit over the top," Graf whispered in my ear.

"No kidding. I'll bet the students love him."

Oblivious to the murmuring in the audience, Webber continued, "The stakes are important to only a handful of people, but to those people this is life or death. If Olive is able to prove her cockamamie theory that Tilda is a Richmond or Falcon ancestor and the Lady in Red, and that she was involved in Lincoln's assassination, we'll be watching Olive on national television. She would love that, wouldn't she? She'd throw over her academic career for a host position on an entertainment network in a heartbeat." His lips pursed. "If she's right, though, this would impact the entire Mary Surratt execution."

"Was Mary Surratt guilty?" I'd heard two different sides of the story about the Southern woman who owned a boardinghouse in Washington, D.C., where John Wilkes Booth was often seen.

Webber held up both hands. "She was the first woman executed in the United States. Charged with conspiracy to assassinate a president, she was rushed to a trial, never allowed to defend herself properly, and summarily hanged as a conspirator. The trial was a sham, engineered by Secretary of War Stanton as a military trial rather than a civil one. Most historical experts agree the evidence against Mary Surratt was not enough for a conviction. She ran a boardinghouse where Booth and his co-conspirators gathered at times. Being a Confederate sympathizer is a far cry from participating in an assassination."

"I never learned any of this in a history class," I said.

"History is written by the victors. Surely you know that, Ms. Delaney. The Surratt hanging brought shame on a government viewed as occupiers by half the country. You understand how some actions require deep burial in the shifting sands of time."

"Indeed, I do. I—"

My comment was short-circuited when Coleman strolled up to the table. An impression of lips in bright red graced his right cheek. Olive had kissed him! I couldn't believe it. "You'd better go disinfect yourself." I hadn't meant to speak those words aloud, but the whole table laughed. Even Graf.

"If you're thinking of bedding that woman, I'd be careful," Oscar said with mock concern. "She's lovely and could make a burlap sack look elegant, but if you rolled on top of her, one of her ribs might poke you and puncture a lung."

Everyone laughed, except me. I didn't find it funny that a woman who plotted the destruction of Coleman's friends would have the audacity to kiss him—and that he would let her.

"Who's responsible for the bomb?" I asked, getting down to business. I didn't want to know the details of Olive's play for Coleman. Or that she got close enough to leave evidence of a smooch on his cheek.

"Molotov cocktail," Coleman corrected. "Whoever made it was an amateur. They didn't put enough gasoline in the bottle to spread the flames."

"Maybe the bomber didn't intend to do real damage. Maybe it was someone Olive paid to have her little moment of drama. She's a diva if ever I saw one." I sounded stiff and hateful, and I didn't care.

"Your ability to judge character is excellent," Webber threw in. "Dr. Twist is a barracuda. Her exploits are legendary. She craves the limelight and would do anything—or anyone—to be the center of attention."

"The same thought occurred to me, " Coleman said. "My first assumption was the event was staged. Now, after examining the scene, I'm not so certain."

"You found evidence of an intruder?" Tinkie asked. "Tell us."

"There were footprints made by a large shoe in the dirt outside the window," Coleman said. "Very large."

"Have you checked Olive's clodhoppers?" I asked maliciously.

Coleman arched an eyebrow at me and kept talking. "We tracked the prints from the porch to Olive's window, and then back. Someone ran to the window, threw the bottle, and then rushed back to the porch and disappeared into the main building. DeWayne tracked the person through The Gardens and then out to the front parking lot, where the trail ended. We're acting on the belief the bomber was male."

His gaze drifted pointedly to Richard Webber. "Where were you?" Coleman asked him.

"Right here at the bar. The barkeep will verify I didn't leave my stool to even go to the john."

"I will check," Coleman said pointedly.

"So whoever it was likely drove off in a car." I didn't believe Webber was guilty. He was too collected and urbane to be a mad bomber.

"Exactly." Coleman eased into a chair Graf provided for him. "As far as I can tell, the only person Dr. Twist knows in Zinnia is her assistant. Both of them are accounted for at the time of the explosion. As were you, Sarah Booth. Otherwise, based on your obvious dislike of the professor, I might have you on the prime suspect list."

Graf laughed out loud, which only made me more annoyed with Coleman. "You tried that once before with a murdered actress. How did that work out for you?"

"*Touché*." Coleman's grin didn't slip an iota.

"So who did throw the cocktail?" Oscar asked.

Gertrude Strom appeared out of nowhere. Leaves from a ficus tree and other flora were trapped in her red hair. She'd been hiding behind the potted plants eavesdropping on us.

"Sheriff Peters, you find the person who did it and make him pay for all the damages. Whoever did this is gone, but I fear he'll be back. Once word gets around about Olive's project, every yahoo and half-wit in the area will be after her, and I don't intend for my bed-and-breakfast to become a war zone. But I believe this book needs to be written. A lot of hoity-toity people will get their comeuppance."

"You like what she's proposing to write about?" I asked.

"I like the truth," Gertrude said. "Sometimes it takes centuries for it to finally roll around. If the Lady in Red was involved in killing President Lincoln, the whole world needs to know about it."

Dr. Webber drew himself up to his full six-foot-two height. "I can assure you, madam, that such is not the case. I've done extensive research in this area, and the woman in that grave was Abraham Lincoln's lover, not his assassin."

"Oh, King Solomon with a meat cleaver! Where did that come from? Lincoln's lover? And just how do you intend to prove that?"

"I've been working on this premise for the past two years. Dr. Twist became aware of my research and has stolen my concept and tagged a ridiculous assassination charge onto the end of it. Tilda Richmond, and I'm reasonably certain she was a Richmond and not a Falcon, though there is some blurring to be cleared, was in love with Lincoln. She would never have conspired to harm him. I personally believe she returned to Mississippi to try to mend the wounds of the war. She loved her homeland and she loved Abe Lincoln. She was a woman caught between two gigantic forces. But I scoff at the notion she wanted Lincoln dead. Olive Twist is the worst kind of intellectual thief—one who takes a solid theory and bastardizes it into soap opera drama. Next thing you know, she'll be a cable TV pundit."

"Why haven't you sued her?" I asked.

"You can't copyright an idea." Tinkie knew a lot about business law. "She took your findings and built on them. It's how academia perpetuates itself."

"I realize that." Webber's chin lifted. "But there is a code of ethics involved here. Twist has violated them. Professors don't steal each other's research."

"Like drug companies don't steal research, or movie studios pilfer writer's ideas," Oscar said. "I think research is fair game, Dr. Webber."

"Legally, you are correct. There is no recourse in a court of law. But that doesn't excuse what she's done."

"This is hogwash," Gertrude said. "She beat you out fair and square. She got busy and came down here. You should have pushed aside your cabal of devoted graduate students and gotten busy." Her smile was smug. "You might better plan on being at the press conference Olive has called for eleven o'clock tomorrow morning at the Lexington Odd Fellows Cemetery. She plans to announce approval for the exhumation."

"Over my dead body," Oscar said, rising from his chair.

"I'm sure that wouldn't bother Dr. Twist a lick," Gertrude replied before she pivoted and walked away.

4

The ceiling fan in my bedroom swirled round and round, casting a lazy breeze over our sheet-clad bodies. It was late afternoon, and while I knew I should feel guilty for wallowing around in bed when there were grave robbers to snare, I couldn't deny the time with Graf had been well spent. We'd come home from The Gardens and raced up to the bedroom like teenagers.

I stretched and fought the temptation to curl up beside him and sleep. I'd never been one to take naps, but then I'd never had such a pleasurable bedmate. Snuggling against Graf made a nap sound as tempting as a slice of Chocolate Decadence cake.

A delicate black paw patted my chin, and I looked into the green gaze of Pluto the cat. "Hey, big boy." I pulled him against my side for a few strokes. His owner was recuperating from a near-death experience. It was still up in the air if she'd leave Pluto with me permanently, but I was already attached to the handsome and smart feline.

Pressed between Graf and Pluto, I wanted to drift back to sleep. Unfortunately, I owed Frances a call to report how our meeting with Olive had gone. And I wanted to check in with Coleman to see if his crime analysis had revealed any clues about the bomb thrower.

Sliding from beneath the sheet, I stood up and stared at my handsome lover. Graf had it all—movie-star good looks, talent, personality, charm, and me. He was one lucky devil. And just to prove it, I decided to slip downstairs and stir up dinner. I could multitask with the best of them.

The thought generated a growl from my stomach. We'd had drinks at The Gardens but no food. It was time to find something to eat. I pulled on a pair of shorts and a T-shirt advertising an Irish liqueur and padded barefoot to the kitchen.

My mother's favorite cookbook was open on the countertop, and I put on a pot of coffee while I leafed through the entrée selections. I decided on couscous with fresh cucumbers, tomatoes, bell peppers, and mango chutney, corn on the cob, and sweet potato salad. Even with the air-conditioning and fans churning, it was too hot to eat a heavy meal. To that end, I began peeling and cubing the sweet potatoes while rehearsing in my head what I'd say to calm Frances and yet keep her from having any false hope I could send Olive packing.

The next thing I knew, a slender hand sporting a honking diamond ring was shoved under my nose. No surprise, Jitty had joined me. What was unexpected was the black pageboy hairdo, the cute little skimmer dress with a black patent belt emphasizing her tiny waist, and matching pumps. "Who this time?" I asked wearily.

"Archie proposed to me. Not Betty. Me. After more than sixty years, he finally popped the question."

"Archie Bunker?" I knew she meant Archie Andrews, but I couldn't help tormenting her. If she could appear as vintage comic characters, I could pretend not to recognize her.

"You are a meathead," she said in disgust.

"You spend way too much time watching television. Too bad I can't book you on a trivia show. You might win us money." I returned to my pursuit of creating the perfect sweet potato salad. From the cabinet I pulled out local honey and then chopped celery while the potatoes cooked.

"You know who I am, Sarah Booth. The classic triangle. Betty, Veronica, and Archie."

"I do." I refused to look at her. I'd deduced Jitty hated it when I ignored her special outfits. "Veronica Lodge. I get it. So Archie asked you to marry him. After sixty-something years. Your eggs are probably all dead and shriveled and I doubt Archie is going to be worth the wait, sexually. I mean, he's been a virgin forever. Low libido. Stifled sperm. Bad choice, Jitty. I figured you'd be more the Wolverine type. Howling at the moon and all."

"Well, I never—"

"Can the outrage. If the shoe were on the other foot, you'd dog me to my grave about my aging eggs."

"That's true, but it's also beside the point. Comic-book characters and ghosts don't procreate. Humans do. Or at least those who aren't too hardheaded to manage wrangling a man into bed for a little contribution to the cause of motherhood."

There were some days when Jitty made me so mad I thought my hair would catch on fire. This was turning into one of those days. "I don't have to trick Graf into making love to me."

"Where's the proof?"

"Where's Betty? You know, the girl Archie *should* have proposed to." I hoped to distract her.

"Check the Kleenex factory. She's still boo-hooing. Wholesome just doesn't cut it when it comes to a man." She grinned, and I swear she looked exactly like Veronica Lodge. Why would Archie choose her over Betty? Could it be Veronica was an heiress? What in thunderation was I doing trying to figure out the motives of cartoon characters?

I gathered my focus. "I don't care for this incarnation, Jitty." I had to be honest. "I never liked Veronica back in the day when I read comic books. I don't really care for Betty, either. Or Archie for that matter. And Jughead was too weird, though I liked his crown." I flicked wet fingers at her, showering her with water. "Go away and come back as someone interesting."

"Stop that! Ghosts don't like water."

"What? Will you melt?" I tried to look eager at the prospect.

"I'm a ghost, not a witch," she grumbled. "Instead of flapping your hands like a hysterical female, you should do something useful."

"I have a better idea. Why don't you make contact with the Lady in Red and find some answers for me? Was she associated with Lincoln? Did she conspire to kill the president? If you could get a few basic answers it would make my life a lot more wholesome."

"You think I got nothing better to do than your leg-work?"

I put down my knife. "Yes. That's exactly what I think. If you can come here as a comic character, I think you have time to burn. If you aren't going to help me, then don't devil me with my lack of a child. Graf and I aren't even married yet. All things in time."

"Graf's asked for your hand, and I think you should speed up those wedding plans. Time's a'wastin'."

"Go talk to Graf. He wants to marry in Ireland in April."

"As long as it's just the wedding in Ireland." She preened a little. "I could be right popular with some of the departed Irish if we went over for a celebration. But you are both coming back to Dahlia House to live, right? You're not thinking of moving to Ireland, are you? Why, that would be as bad as living in Hollywood."

I had no idea what had her in such an insecure mood. "Of course we won't live in Ireland." Like it or not, Dahlia House was my anchor and my millstone. I could never leave the land I loved.

Jitty walked across the room, her hips swaying. "Sarah Booth, you don't have the stretch of time a cartoon char-acter has. There's only dust and mold for most people. Have that baby, a Delaney to carry on the name and the lineage. Think of the joy of watching your daughter grow up here. And a son. You want at least two children."

Jitty always pushed me to follow the regime she'd out-lined. I seldom obliged, but this time she snared me with her fantasy. I could envision a little chestnut-haired girl running through the rooms searching for her handsome father.

"Don't you want a family?" she asked.

"I do. And it will happen. Soon enough. The clock is ticking, but I have time left."

Jitty perched one hip on the edge of the kitchen table. Her beautiful face took on a pensiveness Veronica Lodge could never have managed. "Time goes so fast, Sarah Booth. That's one of the shocking things you learn when you've been around for a few centuries."

I'd also felt the speeding up of the clock's hands. "Everything will work out."

Jitty was staring out the kitchen window at the cemetery where she and her husband were both buried. "After the men left for the war and it was just me and Miss Alice to work this land and tend the young-uns and try to keep body and soul together, it seemed like each day was a century.

"We'd go out to those fields in the hot sun and work until we staggered back to the house to eat. And then the long afternoon called us back out there. There was never enough time to get everything done, yet it seemed each day would never end."

I slipped beside her, looking out at the gravestones. "I never had to work that hard, but I understand. After my parents died, it felt like I was trapped underwater and time had stopped. I'd fall asleep and it would seem years passed, but I would wake up and only ten minutes would be gone. I thought I would die before I found a way to stand against the grief."

"In the good moments, time speeds up and goes much too fast." She gave me a hint of a smile. "These are the fast days for you, Sarah Booth. In the blink of an eye, you'll look in the mirror and see an old woman. It goes way too quick. Don't let it slip away without havin' those children."

"I won't." I wished to comfort her, but I didn't know how. "I promise."

"Promise what?" Graf sauntered into the kitchen in jeans and nothing else. "And who were you making a promise to?"

"Myself."

"You're talking to yourself and you're very pleased about it." He caught me in his arms and pressed me against him. "What did you promise yourself?"

I kissed his chin and then his jaw. "That I'll love you with every bit of my heart every day. I won't waste a moment of this precious time together."

He eased me back so he could look into my eyes. "I love you, Sarah Booth. You constantly surprise and amaze me. I'm the luckiest man alive." He brushed his lips against my ear in a way he knew drove me crazy. "Let's not waste any more time."

Reaching behind me, I turned off the sweet potatoes. Food could wait a little longer.

The sun had set when I got Frances on the phone. I invited her to Dahlia House so I could update her on Olive Twist. I hoped Graf's presence would help her maintain her calm. Ladies like Frances never created a spectacle in front of a handsome man.

When she arrived, Graf walked her into the parlor and poured her a glass of sherry. She was old-school. I abstained, until I got past the bad news.

"I'm so sorry, Frances, but Dr. Twist isn't planning to leave town. In fact, she's holding a press conference tomorrow to announce the exhumation of the Lady in Red." I blurted the facts before she interrupted.

"This can't be true." Frances looked at Graf, hoping I was playing an awful practical joke. "Surely she won't be allowed to desecrate a grave?"

Graf sat down on the horsehair sofa beside her and patted her free hand. "She's petitioned for the right to exhume the body. I don't know if she'll be granted legal permission. It's up to Judge Colbert. Do you happen to know him?"

"Delbert Colbert? Of course I know him. And his daddy, and his granddaddy."

"Then I suggest you make a few phone calls. If there's a protest against the exhumation, it will at least delay it. But you have to have grounds to stop it."

Frances drew herself up and belted the entire glass of sherry. "That grave is a historic site. It should not be tampered with so an interloper can test out a ridiculous theory she's concocted."

"Exactly what you need to tell the judge." I felt relief. If nothing else, we could create a delay.

"This is already causing trouble in our community. Serious consequences will occur if this desperate woman isn't stopped," Frances continued.

I didn't think heart palpitations in the Daughters of the Supreme Confederacy would really be viewed as a dangerous situation, but who was I to discount the weight of a clique of heritage ladies? "The judge needs to hear this."

"And so does Oscar Richmond," she said.

"I'm not sure I follow." Graf rose from the sofa and refilled her glass.

"Then you haven't heard?" Frances sipped the sherry.

"No, ma'am. What have we missed? Sarah Booth and I were . . . rehearsing some movie parts this afternoon."

I'd thought I heard the phone ring, but to be honest, I hadn't paid a lot of attention. I'd been very, very busy with other things. "What happened?"

"Tinkie was supposed to call and tell you that Buford Richmond, Oscar's ne'er-do-well cousin, showed up at The Gardens this afternoon and got into it with Dr. Twist. Some harsh things were said, mostly about her feet." Her eyes widened. "Have you noticed how huge her feet are?"

Olive's tootsies didn't interest me. "What did Buford say?" Oscar's cousin was a loose cannon. He was a survivalist nut who'd once bought every roll of toilet tissue in the Piggly Wiggly and refused to share. Several folks in town who'd run out of Charmin had wanted to string him up. He said he was storing the tissue and soap for "the coming apocalypse."

"Well, he heard Dr. Twist intends to connect the Richmond and Falcon families with a conspiracy, and that's all it took. He had a gun, actually an old derringer—and he threatened to blow Olive's 'mud flappers from here to eternity.' "

"Oh, for heaven's sake." Buford acting like an idiot would be fuel to the flame of Olive's prejudice against Southerners. "I wish the townspeople had whipped some sense into him when he hoarded the toilet paper."

"It gets worse. I can't believe you haven't heard anything about all of this. It was a real scene." Frances gave me the stink eye. "What were you doing all afternoon?" She watched the blush rise up my cheeks and then she looked at Graf, who to my amusement also blushed. "I see," Frances said.

"What else happened?" I tried to put the conversation back on track.

"Jeremiah Falcon showed up looking every inch the buffoon. He had on the blue seersucker suit with the white panama hat, acting all lord of the manor."

Cece's brother, Jeremiah, was a good ten or fifteen years older than she was. He fancied himself a planter, except he'd never done an honest day's work in his life. Well, at least in the last twenty years. He lived in the Falcon family home, Magnolia Grove, and survived off the fortune his parents had amassed and he'd cheated Cece out of.

"Jeremiah never comes to town. He's virtually a recluse. How did he hear about Olive?"

Frances considered. "I guess Buford called him. Those two have been thick as thieves since grade school. They had the potential to do amazing things, and both have squandered their lives."

That they were in cahoots didn't surprise me, but it did concern me. Every kook in town had come out of the woodwork. "Does Cece know?" Jeremiah had been a total jackass about her sexual reassignment and was instrumental in getting Cece disinherited. He'd done everything in his power to make sure his sister, who was smart and talented and kind, had been left out in the cold.

"She knows by now. Everyone in town knows, except you."

"I'll call her right away."

"People will be hurt by Olive Twist. She's doing a lot more than digging up graves. She's resurrecting a lot of pain and hurt. And your friends are the ones who will suffer, Sarah Booth."

I could clearly see that. "Gather the Daughters of the

Supreme Confederacy and get them all to call Judge Colbert down in Holmes County to stop the exhumation.
We each have as much standing to stop it as Olive has to
request it."

Graf interrupted. "If Olive presents a case the Lady in
Red was murdered, that could weigh in her favor."

He was right. But my immediate worry was Cece. She'd
been wounded by her family's reaction to her sexual reassignment. They'd told her they would rather see her
dead than a "thing." Sometimes words hurt more than a
bullet. "I need to talk to Cece."

"I'll discuss this further with Frances," Graf said.
"You check on Cece."

My love for Graf was a constant, but his offer to chat
with Frances, a woman he'd just met, so I could attend to
Cece sent my love spiking off the charts. "Thank you."

He kissed me lightly on the lips. "Sarah Booth and
I will be married in the spring," he told Frances. "I'm the
luckiest man alive."

She beamed at both of us. "I think Libby would
approve of your choice, Sarah Booth. He puts me in
mind of James Franklin, your daddy."

"Me, too." I could barely get the words out past the
lump in my throat. I grabbed my car keys from the table
and whistled up my hound. Sweetie loved to ride in my
convertible, and I had reason to believe she could comfort Cece in a way I could not.

"Take your time, Sarah Booth. Pluto and I will feed
the horses."

"You are a saint." I blew a kiss and ran out the front
door.

I tried calling Cece on my cell phone as I drove toward her house. When she didn't answer I tried Harold,

Oscar's right-hand man at the bank and a member of Delta high society. He might be a good ally in figuring out how to handle Jeremiah and minimizing the damage to Cece.

Harold answered instantly. "What can I do for my favorite girl detective?"

I gave him a rundown on what was happening.

"I'll meet you at Cece's house."

"Thanks." I hung up and called the newspaper just to be sure she wasn't working late. No dice. The receptionist told me Cece had left around noon and hadn't been back.

I wasn't worried. Not really. Concerned. A little. When the phone rang, I was relieved the ID showed Tinkie. But the relief was short-lived.

"Oscar's disappeared." Tinkie was close to tears, judging by her voice. "He isn't at Hill Top, or the bank, or The Club. It's just not like him to disappear. This whole thing with the Lady in Red and Buford acting a fool has upset him more than he lets on. Cece, too."

"You don't think Cece has gone hunting Jeremiah, do you?"

"I hope not."

I didn't have to be a mind reader to know Tinkie and I envisioned the same bloodbath. Cece had fought Jeremiah in the courts over the Falcon estate, and she'd failed. The last words she'd spoken to her brother included the phrases "rot in hell" and "too dead for backtalk." If they clashed, I didn't trust Jeremiah not to hurt her.

"Do you know where Jeremiah might be?"

"Jeremiah doesn't socialize much, but I heard Buford was holding court in the bar at The Gardens. If Jeremiah is with Buford Richmond, they'll be knocking back the whiskey. The two egg each other on. Normally, Jeremiah is standoffish and aloof, but he's changed lately. Buford, too. I can't put my finger on it, but I don't like it. I hope Oscar hasn't gone there to try and talk sense into Buford. That's a waste of breath."

Testosterone and liquor were never a good combination. Especially not when mixed with rampant ignorance, a sense of superiority and entitlement, and guns. Buford had an arsenal, including illegal automatic weapons. Everyone in town knew Jeremiah carried a derringer in his boot. A boot he didn't have enough sense to pour piss out of when he was in his cups.

"I'll go to Cece's and then work my way to The Gardens." I would rather take a beating than return to Gertrude's den, but Cece was my friend. Jeremiah and Buford were both crazy enough to shoot her if she got in their faces.

"I'm sorry, Sarah Booth, I can't go with you. I have to find Oscar."

"No apologies, Tinkie. If I run across him, I'll call."

Harold was waiting at Cece's when I pulled into the drive. "She's not here," he said. "I peeped in every window. She isn't home."

"The Gardens."

"Okay." He knew my history with Gertrude. A wicked smile lit his face as he petted Sweetie in the backseat of my car. "Can I bring Roscoe? He's here with me."

Roscoe was a demon with four legs. That his vet file labeled him "canine" didn't mean a thing. A DNA test would prove he was a descendant of Beelzebub. "Sure."

If I could give Gertrude Strom a stroke by taking Sweetie, it wouldn't hurt to have Roscoe along, too. "Maybe Roscoe will pee on Gertrude's foot. I don't know why she hates me so much. It's almost as if she thinks I've plotted against her."

"I wouldn't lose any sleep over it, Sarah Booth." Harold held the car door open for Roscoe, who flew across the porch making a noise somewhere between grumbling and snorting. He was a vile little customer.

The dogs loved my old roadster convertible, and we set out for The Gardens just as the sun slipped behind the tree line. When I turned into the lane, shaded by beautiful oaks and brilliant with blossoming shrubs and beds of flowers, I had to stop the car and take it in. The peachy light of sunset saturated the golds, russets, and purples of the mums. As we idled in the drive, shadows overtook the day.

"I love dusk," Harold said. "The soil seems to absorb the sun's light. The day is over; the night begins."

"I love it, too, but it's a sad time for me." I couldn't say exactly why, but the day's ending brought the past closer. As light slipped from the sky, memories took on the texture of reality. Many of my remembrances were sad, moments lost in time. "I prefer sunrise. New potential."

"When the night is burned away by the golden orb. You've had enough shadows in your life, Sarah Booth. You deserve to bask in the sun." Harold patted my shoulder. "You're a good friend. We don't tell you often enough."

"As are you. I'm blessed with good friends." I pressed gently on the gas and put the car in motion. "Gertrude will be angry about the dogs."

"Gertrude is angry at you no matter what you do. Want me to ask her why she has such a burn-on for you?"

I laughed as we found a parking spot. "Nope." I turned to the backseat. "Sweetie, Roscoe, stay in the car." Sweetie sometimes obeyed, but I had no expectations for Roscoe except trouble.

"There's Cece's car," Harold said. "And the ancient Jaguar Jeremiah inherited from the Falcon estate. He probably drives it twelve miles a week. What a sad and lonely creature he is. I've often wondered why he never married. He's not bad-looking. When he was younger, he was quite the local heartthrob."

"It's hard for me to remember anything except how awful he was to Cece. Speaking of which, let's find them before Cece gets arrested."

We hurried down the flower-lined pathway just as the solar lights came on. I thought of Peter Pan and Wendy when Harold grabbed my hand. We ran like children rushing to recess.

Gertrude was not at her normal sentinel post at the front desk. Harold and I giggled as we slipped down the hallway to the bar. When we were fifty yards away, I heard the harbinger of war to come.

"You're a stupid bastard without an ethical bone in your body," Cece yelled.

I could make a good guess whom she was talking to.

"And you're a freak of nature," Jeremiah tossed back.

"Oh, shit," I whispered. No time for fancy curse phrases now.

Harold doubled down on speed, and I was hot on his heels. He hurled himself through the bar's doorway and threw a punch so perfectly devastating, Jeremiah was lifted off his feet. He fell back on a table and crashed it.

I patted his back. "Mike Tyson in disguise." Cece stood beside me as stunned as I.

"I can brawl when it's necessary." Harold straightened his jacket. "A gentleman seldom finds himself in circumstances requiring fisticuffs. This time it couldn't be avoided."

"I'll sue you for everything you're worth." Jeremiah sprawled on the debris of the table. "You rush to the defense of that he-she. You have a taste for trash."

Harold drew back his foot, and Cece and I both rushed forward to step between him and Jeremiah.

I hadn't seen Jeremiah in years, and his appearance was shocking. The classic Falcon good looks had eroded from anger and drink. Sure enough, he wore the same tired trademark seersucker suit. Stains littered the front of his jacket. His panama hat lay on the floor beside him. Even in the wreckage of what was left of him, I saw something that reminded me of Cecil's older and very sophisticated brother. He let bigotry and ugliness eat him from the inside out.

"Get out of here," Cece said.

"I have as much right to be here as you do. Maybe more, since I'm a genuine person."

Harold cocked a fist, but I stepped up to Jeremiah's ear and whispered, "If you say another hurtful word to my friend, I will figure out the thing that makes your life a living misery and then I'll make certain it happens."

"You can't threaten me." He straightened his spine. "No one threatens Jeremiah Falcon." A trace of lord of the manor still clung to him.

"Yeah, leave him alone." Buford Richmond, Tinkie's cousin by marriage, pushed between us. When the fighting started, he'd ducked behind the bar. Buford, shorter and rounder, was a physical contrast to Jeremiah. The things they shared in common included lack of ambition, lack of love, and a lack of joy.

"Buford, if you say another stupid word, Oscar will shut down your allowance. You dishonor the Richmond name with this behavior." Harold didn't raise his voice. "Now, the two of you pack up and head for home. If either of you needs a driver, I'll have someone take you home safely."

I saw the movement of Buford's hand as he brought a gun from his waistband just as Cece stepped in front of Harold. She meant to block the bullet with her own body.

Before anyone could do anything, Sweetie Pie came flying through the air in what would pass for a doggy-Olympic event. Her teeth clamped on Buford's gun hand just as Roscoe sank his fangs into Buford's calf. Buford hit the floor screaming. For good measure, Roscoe whipped around and bit Jeremiah on the inner thigh, dangerously close to his family jewels. His scream rivaled a banshee's.

To my mortification, Cece and I burst into laughter. Harold picked up the gun Buford had dropped. Jeremiah tried to gain his feet, but Harold put a foot on his blood-soaked leg. The slightest pressure brought another howl. "Stay down. I think we need to call the sheriff."

"Well, well, if it isn't what Faulkner might describe as a good down-home family reunion." Olive Twist stood in the doorway. She wore a dress Little Miss Muffet might wear for tuffet sitting. For a woman whose body would love the slinky look of couture fashion, Dr. Twist was hopeless in her choice of dowdy.

"The redoubtable Dr. Twist," Harold swung the gun

in her direction. That took the smug off her puss. She jumped behind Jimmy Boswell, using him as a human shield.

"Oh, forgive me." Harold opened the clip to show it was unloaded and then put the gun away. "Harold Erkwell." He extended his hand. "And this is Cece Dee Falcon, and I believe you've met Sarah Booth."

"I know all of you." She swept us with a scathing glance. "And the people on the floor? Relatives, I suspect. I've heard about the family shindigs you people find so endearing. They usually involve guns and incest."

Sweetie's hair bristled, and a low growl slipped from deep in her throat. "My dog doesn't care for your ignorance," I said.

Twist had sense enough to edge away from Sweetie. She was unprepared for Roscoe, though, who slipped behind her. She stumbled into him, and in a moment she was sitting on her butt in the middle of the floor.

"Dah-link, camo-platform shoes are so . . . tacky," Cece said. "Those with such an obvious lack of grace might want to wear Crocs. Are your toes webbed by any chance? I see Olympic swimming in your future."

Boswell helped Olive to her feet, and his thanks was a dirty scowl. "Have any of you seen Dr. Webber?" Olive asked. "He sent me a bouquet of lobelia. I wanted to let him know I'm not in the least intimidated."

"Why would flowers intimidate you?" Flowers were normally signs of affection.

"If you had any education whatsoever, you'd know that flowers convey a message. Lobelia, also known as pukeweed or vomitwort, signifies malevolence. There are deeper meanings in everything, Ms. Delaney, but you have to educate and train your mind to think."

"No one ever sent me a bouquet of pukeweed, Dr. Twist. I guess that's part of an education I missed. My beaus send me roses, orchids, and sometimes birds-of-paradise. Those flowers *mean* they view me as exotic and like me."

"You are such a simpleton," Olive said. "No quality of mind whatsoever."

"There's an old saying down here in Mississippi," Cece said. "Book smarts never made a woman attractive."

I started to say that I'd never heard the expression before, but I asked something else instead. "Did anyone call Coleman?" I was ready to go. "He should come and pick up Jeremiah and Buford and lock them up until they sleep it off."

"Don't arrest them," Cece said.

"I've got a good mind to press charges against you, Harold," Jeremiah said, but he was already easing toward the door, with a wonderful limp. "I'll consider my options and talk with my lawyer. Your assault was unprovoked."

"The fact you breathe is a provocation," I told him. "Be careful what hornets' nest you stir, Jeremiah."

"You can't scare us." Buford swaggered to his friend's side. He sneered at Olive. "We have resources you can't conceive of. And you can't use us for your research. The Lady in Red is a revered historic site. We've already started a petition to stop the exhumation."

"What's the Lady in Red to you?" Olive waited like a cat stalking a bird.

"She's a Southern lady who met an unfortunate end. That's all we need to know. We won't have our womenfolk violated." Buford's chest swelled with pride. "We men defend our women. I don't know how you do things where you're from, but down here, womenfolk are treasured."

"Buford, you are a moron." I wanted to beat him with a stick. Talk about a stereotype. He should have just brought a Jeff Foxworthy joke book and started reading: You might be a redneck if . . . you think a woman is a delicate flower.

Harold glared at him. "Beat it, Buford. Oscar is going to stop your monthly check if you speak another word."

Buford grabbed Jeremiah's sleeve. "Let's go. You can drop me by my house."

"Understand, Dr. Twist, we won't lie still for this. You will not besmirch the noble blood of our forefathers." Jeremiah tried to wrap himself in the glory of the battered South. "We are a proud people. We won't tolerate having our dead tampered with. You'll pay a heavy price if you don't heed our words. We are not people to be trifled with."

He swept past Buford and marched out the door. Buford scooted after him.

"Charming relatives," Olive said. "*Enchantée!*"

"Gag me with a spoon," I responded. "Come on, Cece. Let's head to Dahlia House for a drink."

"I'll be right along," she said. She'd locked on Jimmy Boswell. Cece loved young, pretty men, and Boswell certainly qualified. "I need a word with Mr. Boswell."

To my amusement, Boswell edged toward the door. "I have a prior engagement," he said.

"That's news to me." Twist turned on him. "You're on the clock for me. You have no other engagements. Only those I set up or approve. Is that clear?"

"Yes, Dr. Twist." He cowered, but there had been a hint of anger before he tilted his head down. Twist might bully the young man, but he wasn't the doormat he pretended to be. There was fire beneath the cool exterior.

"Harold?" I had Sweetie Pie by the collar, and Roscoe was sniffing at a potted plant with the clear intention of watering it. Any minute now Gertrude was going to show up at the bar. Of course everything would be my fault.

"Let me pay for the table." Harold peeled money from his wallet. "It was worth every cent to knock Jeremiah on his ass. He's needed it for the past twenty years. You know, a lot of us younger men once looked up to him."

I linked my arm through Harold's. Boswell had left the room and Cece was, discreetly, right behind him. Olive Twist might well lose her assistant if Cece had her way.

5

The morning sun slanted in through the kitchen window and mingled with the mouthwatering smell of fried bacon and coffee to create the perfect morning. Graf, wearing gym shorts and a wifebeater that showed off his muscled shoulders, stood at the stove flipping French toast while Tinkie and I sat at the table, fresh coffee steaming before us. She was unusually quiet, so much so that I nudged her.

"What's going on?"

"It's Oscar. When he came home yesterday evening, he was in a terrible mood." She spoke softly. "I asked him where he'd been, and he said something about an appointment but wouldn't give any details."

That didn't sound like the Oscar I knew. He didn't

keep secrets from Tinkie. They'd had a rough patch in their marriage a few years back, and they'd laid ground rules. One was total honesty. As far as I knew, they'd both abided by the rule. Until now.

"Where do you think he went?"

"I don't have a clue." She was puzzled more than hurt. "It had to be important, but why not tell me?"

"Maybe it's a surprise. Like a fall trip to Europe." Oscar planned surprise vacations sometimes.

Tinkie's smile returned. "Thank you, Sarah Booth. I'll bet you're right."

"Are you girls done with your whispering session and are you ready for breakfast?" Graf asked.

"Yes to both questions." Tinkie's tone was impertinent. "Serve us, master chef."

Sweetie curled at my feet, one eye on Pluto, who wove figure eights around Graf's legs. Pluto was not above sucking up for bacon. He was a conniving cat, and I'd fallen hard for him. If Marjorie Littlefield demanded I return him, I'd be in a world of hurt.

"Did you know Pluto's last name was MacTavish?" I asked Tinkie. She'd talked to Marjorie as much as, if not more than, I had.

"Pluto MacTavish?" Tinkie slipped off her sandals.

"Marjorie insisted the cat is of Scottish descent. He even has a coat of arms."

She rubbed Pluto's head with her manicured toes. "How does one go about proving a cat's geographic ancestry?"

"She sent a copy of the coat of arms to my cell phone. His family motto is 'We Stalk and Thrive.' Or that's what Marjorie told me. The verse was in Latin, so I had no idea what it really said."

"You two aren't so gullible you believe the cat has a coat of arms?" Graf crumbled bacon on a paper towel for Pluto. "I wonder if they make kilts for cats?"

The most amusing image popped into my brain, and I sat back with a goofy smile.

"Where in the world has your mind gone?" Tinkie jabbed me with her elbow. "You're a million miles away."

"Scotland with a black cat wearing a kilt."

"I worry about you, Sarah Booth." Tinkie was serious.

"Do you know what's under a kitty kilt?" Graf asked. "Fur balls!"

Tink and I both groaned and threw napkins at Graf.

"Don't even try to explain." Tinkie rolled her eyes. "Your mental function is a mystery they couldn't map with a CAT scan."

"My humor is unappreciated, but Pluto approves of my cooking." The cat had eaten the bacon and was licking the paper towel. "How many pieces of French toast, Tinkie?"

"Two. And they do smell good, Graf. I think you've improved on Sarah Booth's recipe, and I didn't think that could be done. Is that nutmeg I detect?" Her complimentary tone shifted to a pout. "Oscar won't even try to cook."

"You don't cook, either," I pointed out. "And that's a good thing."

"Oscar makes wonderful pasta dishes; he simply won't do it. I *can't* cook. I've tried. Remember the dog treats?"

Even the mention of that fiasco made my stomach quiver. "Enough said."

"You know, Graf looks like he should be in a black-and-white movie with Marilyn Monroe or Claudette Colbert. With that dark, tousled hair, the shadow of a beard, hummm. Romantic comedy might be a good move after this noir film the two of you are doing."

Tinkie referred to *Delta Blues,* a tale about two private investigators. I'd agreed to play one of the PIs, and Graf the other. Filming was set to start in the Delta in November. "You're right, Tink. He does."

His dark hair hung over one eye and gave him a "devil may care" look as he spun the spatula in the air and caught it. His grin oozed charm. "Thank you, Tinkie. How many slices, Sarah Booth?"

"Two for her, too." Tinkie winked at him. "No, better give Sarah Booth three, but only if she agrees to work them off doing the horizontal boogie."

"Oh, for heaven's sake. Does Graf look deprived?"

"Graf looks rather fetching." Tinkie couldn't suppress her grin. "And I have to say, he appears well bedded. There's a certain . . . looseness in his posture."

I had to change the subject. Tinkie was determined to tease me, and I was terribly vulnerable in front of my man. "Graf, are you coming to Lexington with us for Dr. Twist's press conference?"

"I should look over the contracts my agent emailed, but I think I'll ride along." Graf served us each a heaping breakfast plate. "Will I be in the way?"

"Of course not." I was thrilled he wanted to join us. We weren't really on a case, more of a mission for Frances Malone. "It shouldn't take long."

The phone rang and I picked it up, wondering what Coleman was calling about.

"Sarah Booth, I think you should hurry over to The Gardens."

"What on earth for?" That was the last place I wanted to go.

"Jimmy Boswell is dead, likely murdered."

My fingers tightened on the phone. "What happened?" I asked.

"My best guess is poison. Doc will know more after the autopsy."

"Do you have a suspect?"

"I have half a dozen. That's the problem."

"Why would anyone want to poison Jimmy Boswell? He was harmless."

"Maybe not. It's complicated, but Oscar's cousin and Cece's brother are both suspects, as well as Dr. Twist. And Dr. Webber. By the way, Olive Twist is asking for you."

"You have got to be kidding."

"Afraid not. She wants to hire you. I told her I would pass the message along."

I looked down at my mountain of French toast. The morning had been going so pleasantly. "I'm not sure I want to be hired." Both Tinkie and Graf gave me their full attention. "Any leads on the bombing yesterday?"

"DeWayne made a cast of the prints outside the gallery. We found a pair of shoes that fit."

"Where were the shoes?"

"In the ditch in front of Jeremiah Falcon's driveway."

"Not good." But another thought occurred to me. "If he was the bomber, he wouldn't be stupid enough to throw the shoes at his own driveway."

Coleman took a deep breath that showed his frustration. "I know. Jeremiah and Buford are plenty smart, in their own twisted way. But I don't see them as killers. Buford is an old blowhard who lives in a fantasy world of a past that never existed. Jeremiah is more difficult to figure out. Acting like he's planter class and everyone else is inferior—it's an act. Deep down, Jeremiah knows better."

"I wish that were true, Coleman. For Cece's sake if nothing else."

"They're cowards pretending to honor and nobility they've done nothing to earn. I just can't see them as killers."

I could read between the lines. "So you're seriously considering Dr. Twist as the killer." Delight colored my voice.

"Keeping an open mind, Sarah Booth. All of the evidence isn't in. But Twist is asking to hire you, and that tells me she knows she appears guilty. There's some circumstantial evidence that points to her. What do you want me to tell her?"

I started to say he could tell her to kiss my patooty, but I didn't. "Tinkie is here with me. We'll discuss it." My partner was about to pop at the seams with curiosity. And Graf was almost as eager. Besides, business was business. I needed steady income, and Frances Malone hadn't really hired me. She'd asked me for a favor, which I was glad to do. She'd be upset if I signed on with the enemy, but I had bills to pay. Ultimate justice was my goal, so if Twist was innocent, I could help her prove it. But that was a mighty big if.

"Don't take too long," Coleman said. "I could use your judgment."

"Okay. Tink and I will be there as soon as we can." I hung up and faced Tinkie and Graf. "Jimmy Boswell has been murdered, and Dr. Twist wants to hire us to prove she didn't do it."

"Boswell?" they said in unison.

"Why Boswell?" Tinkie mused. "He was harmless."

"Coleman thinks he was poisoned. Maybe it was meant for Dr. Twist." I cleared my throat. "Although Olive is, apparently, the number one suspect."

Graf put his spatula down. "Does this mean I'll get to spend more time with Dr. Twist? She's such a compelling woman. Brilliant. Perhaps she can improve my mind."

His behavior was so off-the-wall I was stumped for a response. Tinkie, though, caught on fast.

"You cannot devil Sarah Booth that way," she said. She picked up a dish towel and snapped it at Graf's bare thighs. "I'm the only one who can tease her!"

"Ouch!" He jumped away. "Okay, I won't torment her."

"Don't mess with my partner," Tinkie said. "Especially about someone like Twist."

"I guess our trip to Lexington has been canceled," Graf said with mock innocence.

"Let's head over to The Gardens," Tinkie said. "If we take the case, we need to examine the murder scene."

I was less than enthusiastic. "Are you coming, Graf?"

"No. I've had my fill of Dr. Twist. The morning will be more profitably spent making business calls. I'll hold down the fort here, but if you need me, I'm only a phone call away."

"But you were going to Lexington with us," Tinkie protested.

"Lexington sounded like fun. Talking with Twist at The Gardens sounds like work. If I have to labor, I'd rather hammer down business details."

"Coward," I whispered as I kissed his neck. "You're afraid of Olive Twist."

"She is rather . . . scary." He put his arm around me and dipped me backwards as he planted a big one on my lips. Tinkie applauded.

"We'll be back," Tinkie said as she gathered up her keys.

There was no sense of urgency at The Gardens. The sheriff's car was there, along with a hearse, but the grounds were quiet. Too quiet. Tinkie and I walked along the beautiful paths, and even though the sun was shining brightly, solemnity was in the air. A young man was dead. Murdered. I'd hardly spoken a full sentence to Jimmy Boswell, but he'd seemed nice enough.

We skirted the B and B's front door and headed around back—the way the bomber had gone, according to Coleman's calculations based on footprints left in the soft earth. As I retraced the path, I realized how easy it was for someone to sneak in this back way, toss the bomb, and haul ass to the parking lot and a getaway vehicle.

As we edged around behind the main building, there was no sign of Gertrude, for which I was thankful. She was likely fit to be tied. A murder on her premises would not sit well. Bad for business. And I'd seen Gertrude eyeing Jimmy Boswell. She might act like she was the most uptight prude on the planet, but her eye had wandered over the contours of Boswell's lean body with more than a passing interest.

When we'd gained the back gallery, I paused. DeWayne and Doc Sawyer stood just within the doorway of Olive's suite. Coleman would be inside with Olive and the coroner.

Doc would escort the body to the local hospital for the autopsy. Doc Sawyer had been our family physician for as long as I could remember. He'd closed down his office and retired—until he was rehired as the emergency room doctor. Now he worked eighty hours a week instead of the hundred he'd worked in private practice.

"Let's bag him up and move him out." The voice of the county coroner, ripe with a country twang, floated on the morning breeze. "He sure was a purdy boy. He didn't die easy, though."

In the last election, Ely Wattles, an itinerant preacher, had won the post of county coroner. As far as I knew, his qualifications involved his talents for hellfire oration in a pulpit and the fact his daddy had been one of the biggest bootleggers in the adjoining county.

Juby Wattles had cooked high-grade corn mash for LeFlore County and most of Sunflower County, until his still blew up and killed him. A piece of copper, powered by 190 proof whiskey, launched through the air and pierced his throat. Juby had bled out while his friends watched.

Ely hadn't taken up bootlegging—the cost of sugar and transportation made it a small-profit business, especially since liquor was available for purchase in most Mississippi counties. The big money was in meth and other drugs. Ely, in my opinion, was too lazy to run a still and not smart enough to do so without endangering his clientele and himself. Lead poisoning was a risk of careless bootleg whiskey, and Ely was a careless man.

In other words, I had zero respect for Wattles. The idea of holding the office of coroner of Sunflower County seemed to draw the woodchucks out of the woodpile. They went in for a four-year term and were regularly voted out in the next election.

"Who is that yokel?" Richard Webber asked from behind me. I almost jumped. He'd sneaked up without a sound.

"You gave me a start." Tinkie recovered with far more grace than I could muster. She leaned toward him and batted her thick lashes. "You could be a spy, Dr. Webber."

I inched back in awe and wonder. When Tinkie was at work, the male of the species didn't stand a chance. A man with an ego the size of Webber's would be easy plucking for her.

"When I was a Boy Scout, I practiced these skills." He crooked up one side of his lips, Errol Flynn–style. "I used to daydream about being a spy. I'd never repeat this to my peers, but I was hooked on Robert Ludlum's books. And Ian Fleming. James Bond, what a character." His demeanor took on gravitas. "Webber. Richard Webber."

"I'll bet you have a way with the ladies just like 007. Your classes are probably the most popular on the campus." Tinkie served up that line with enough sincerity to keep me straight-faced.

"I've had a few colleagues and even some of the older graduate students imply they might be interested in more intimate studies, but such things are a violation of ethics. While I find them flattering, I would never act upon them."

"I could tell you were a man of character." Tinkie slipped her hand through his arm and took possession. "Are you here to commiserate with Dr. Twist or just nosy like me and Sarah Booth?"

"Actually, I'm here to speak with Ms. Delaney." He

finally realized I was still there. "Could we have a moment alone?"

"Tinkie is my partner," I said. "She's the brains behind the operation. And the fashion sense."

"She is certainly the most stylish person in the room." His baritone chuckle was rather sexy. "On a more serious note, I have evidence in Boswell's murder."

Tinkie shifted away from him. She was all business. "What kind of evidence?"

"I'm afraid it implicates Dr. Twist." His glee was impossible to hide.

"You think she murdered her assistant? Why?" Olive was hard to swallow, but everyone was jumping to the conclusion that she'd killed Boswell. It made me wonder if she was too easy a target.

"I know she killed him. Boswell tried to blackmail her, and she took the expedient route. She poisoned him." Webber spoke with great authority. "I watched the complex interaction between Twist and Boswell. She was the authority figure, and she belittled Boswell and then praised him to keep him in line. Classic manipulation by an abuser. I have to say, I'm not shocked to discover Boswell wanted to bring her down or that Twist is capable of murder."

And I wasn't shocked to hear Webber point the finger at his competition. "This doesn't make a lot of sense. What was Boswell attempting to blackmail her about?"

"He'd been videotaping every moment of Twist's life."

"I know it and so did Twist. She ordered him to do it," I pointed out.

"But he taped her when she wasn't aware. From what he told me, he had some outrageous footage. Temper tantrums, sloth, greed, lust, gluttony, cruelty—pretty much a rundown of the seven deadly sins. She's a binge eater and bulimic. He captured her in all her mental disorder. She wanted to star in her own documentary, but Boswell said the things he'd recorded would paint her as a sociopath."

"Are you certain this is true?" Tinkie threw in. "Boswell seemed . . . devoted. Or at least totally cowed by Twist."

"Even the most humble man can take only so much," Webber said.

"Where's the film?" I asked.

Webber frowned. "I don't actually have it."

"Have you seen it?" I asked.

"Not exactly. Boswell told me about it, though. He confided in me because he felt Olive had wronged me. He all but said Olive heard about my research and climbed on top of it to make her own name. According to him, she hacked into my computer and stole my research."

"Can you prove it?" The accusation Webber leveled was serious, and also unsubstantiated. "If you have evidence, you should turn it in to the sheriff. But tread carefully, Dr. Webber. Slander applies."

Coleman came out of Olive's room as if on cue. He saw me and walked toward us. "Tinkie, Sarah Booth, Dr. Webber," he said. His gaze pinned Webber. "Do you have something to add to the investigation?"

"Not really. I believe Olive killed him, but I can't prove it."

"Thanks for the unsubstantiated opinion," Coleman said. He clasped my wrist and led me to the side. "What have you found out?"

So far, Twist hadn't hired me, so I relayed Webber's

accusation, and had a few questions of my own. "Was Boswell really poisoned?"

"It would seem so. I'll know more after Doc finishes the autopsy."

"Could it have been accidental?"

Coleman lifted one shoulder. "Twist insists Boswell was fine, up until this morning. He was drinking coffee and slumped over. By the time the paramedics arrived, he was dead. But it seems Olive has plenty of reason to want Boswell dead. And I did find a printout of poisons and their symptoms in her suitcase. She claims someone planted it on her, but who knows. If Boswell was actually trying to blackmail her with extra footage, that would certainly be a motive for murder."

"Boswell was drinking coffee. Was it made from Twist's special beans?" I remembered the coffee, the dark-roasted beans, and the grinder. "Did Olive drink coffee this morning?"

"So you suspect it was in the coffee beans instead of just his cup?"

I nodded. "If that should prove to be the case, I can't help but wonder if the poison was meant for Dr. Twist rather than Boswell."

"And that's exactly why I want to hire you and your partner," Twist said as she came up behind us. "The sheriff is paid to find the guilty party. I want you and Mrs. Richmond to pursue proving my innocence. I didn't harm Boswell. Why would I? He was an invaluable part of my team."

To my amazement, Twist wore baby doll pajamas. I hadn't seen a pair since college, and these showed off her slender, mile-long legs and narrow hips and waist. I had to admit, she was very sexy in them.

"Hiring private investigators isn't necessary, Olive. You haven't been charged with anything," Coleman pointed out.

"But I will be. Someone is setting me up. I want Ms. Delaney and Ms. Richmond to find out who."

"Why don't you leave it to Coleman?" I didn't relish the idea of working for Twist. She treated her employees like crap. Besides, it would be better for everyone in Sunflower and Holmes Counties if Twist was arrested and put in jail. The whole Lady in Red controversy would dissipate. History wouldn't be perverted by the likes of Twist.

"Someone is framing me for a heinous crime. I don't want to stand around and wait to see what happens next." Twist glared at all of us. "I want you to be proactive. Find out who's trying to destroy me."

"What about Boswell?" Tinkie asked gently.

"He's dead. What about him?" Twist lifted her chin. "I mean, it's terrible that he's dead, but I didn't kill him. I'll never be able to properly train a replacement. This has thrown a monkey wrench in my work schedule."

"Poor you," I said.

"Will you take the job?" Olive asked.

"Of course she will." Coleman pressed my elbow. "Won't you, Sarah Booth?"

I looked at Tinkie, and she nodded, blue eyes sparkling with amusement.

"We'll take the case. It's five grand, payable now." Sometimes we didn't charge a retainer, but with Twist, I figured we should get the money up-front.

"I'll have a check for you. Shall I drop it by, or will you be at Holmes County today?" Twist sidled away as if she had something more important on her mind.

"You're going forward with the exhumation hearing today?" I couldn't believe it. Boswell was dead.

"Of course. Jimmy would want me to continue with the project. I'll give him a credit on the academic book I intend to write. But not the bestseller. That's all mine. And naturally, the film documentary will bear his name." She beamed at all of us. "He'll be more famous dead than he ever was alive. And all thanks to me. By the way, can you run a camera? I might ask you to videotape some of the events. For my documentary. It's easy as pie. Now I must get collected for today's battle."

She strode back into the room, and I could hear her ordering the coroner and paramedics around—or at least giving it her best effort.

"She is a piece of work," Coleman said. "She doesn't intend to let anything slow her down. Not even death."

By eleven o'clock, I was hoping the poisoner would return and take Twist out. Boswell was barely cold and she was as good as her word. She intended to push forward with her exhumation. She'd rescheduled the press conference at the Lexington Odd Fellows Cemetery for one in the afternoon.

Frances Malone and the Daughters of the Supreme Confederacy were organizing a picket line. Members of the Heritage Pride Heroes, a national organization that claimed to have roots in honoring acts of home-front bravery, would likely put in an appearance. In my opinion, they were nothing more than a bastard offshoot of survivalist mentality organizations. This kind of shindig was right up their alley. It was all adding up to be a nasty confrontation.

Tinkie and I had no choice but to be there. Lexington was out of Coleman's jurisdiction, so we couldn't expect any help from him, though he was on standby in case the Holmes County sheriff needed him. I could only hope that Frances, Oscar, Cece, and others of influence had been able to convince Judge Colbert to block the petition to exhume. We'd find out when we reached Holmes County.

Tinkie drove this time, and I rode shotgun. Graf's original plan to chauffeur us to the cemetery was crushed when his business calls yielded an interview for a voice-over job on an animated film—the role of a sexy wolfhound in a Disney production of *Castle Dark,* an intriguing tale of werewolves and vampires in Ireland. It was work Graf couldn't turn down, and I was happy for him.

"Oscar is really mad at Buford," Tinkie said, her focus on the highway but her thoughts clearly on her husband and family. "He is such a disappointment."

"I don't blame Oscar. Buford is a fool."

"Oscar said, 'Maybe they'll shoot Buford, the silly bastard. Buford is a moron. He's got a thousand rolls of toilet tissue and the IQ of a dead snail. I hope Coleman puts him under the jail.'"

Tinkie was damned good at impersonating her husband. And I thought I had acting chops. Something wasn't right, though. "So why are you upset? Everything Oscar said is true."

"There're rumors that Buford also has weapons."

I wanted to come up with a witty reply that would explain everything, only I couldn't. "All those good ole boys have guns. It's compensation for . . . well, men who are inadequate need to feel powerful in some fashion. Guns and killing helpless animals make them feel strong."

"Oscar said if Buford gets arrested, I'm not to bail him out. He also said he'd cut off his allowance if he made a public jackass of himself."

"A few weeks in jail might smarten him up." Doubtful, but why dash her hopes.

Tinkie motioned she wanted to pull over. I needed a cup of coffee so I pointed out a fast-food drive-through. Tinkie eased off the highway and joined the line. An emotional storm moved across her face.

"What's wrong?" Worry ate at her with sharp little teeth.

She ordered two coffees, and I didn't press. The sun was hotter than six degrees of hell even with the air conditioner blowing hard. She found a shady spot and parked.

"Exactly what is wrong with Oscar?" I asked.

She checked the rearview mirror as if we were being followed. "I found this in his jacket pocket." She pulled a folded piece of paper from her purse and handed it to me.

Meet me tonight. Dr. Twist has fabricated material about your family. I have evidence, but it will cost you.

There was no signature. I considered the many implications of Tinkie's revelation. "Who gave this to Oscar?"

Her lips quivered, as if she might cry. "I can't be certain, but from the paper and handwriting, I think it was Jimmy Boswell. After the firebomb incident. I think he slipped the note in Oscar's pocket."

"Did Oscar meet with him?"

"I don't know." She cleared her throat. "Last night, Oscar disappeared for a couple of hours. He could have met Boswell then."

"So what? Surely you don't suspect Oscar of trying to poison Boswell or Twist."

"Of course not." Righteous indignation pushed her tears away. "I'm worried Twist caught on to what Boswell was doing and killed him herself. But if that's the case, she's smart enough to implicate Oscar. She'd do it for meanness."

Traffic whizzed by as we sat beneath a pecan tree beside a strip mall and a fast-food joint. The thermometer in the car showed ninety-four degrees.

"How do you want to handle this?"

"Find out if Oscar met with Boswell, and if he did, what happened between them." She shifted into drive and edged to the highway. "Why didn't Oscar just tell me? We promised not to keep secrets from each other."

"I don't know." But I had a guess. "The Richmond family honor is at stake. Maybe Oscar doesn't want to taint that for you, especially if all of this is made-up bullcrap Olive is trying to sell as fact."

"I married Oscar, not his name. Who cares what happened two hundred years ago?"

I laughed, but I wasn't mocking her, because her heart was true. Yet family name and reputation carried a lot of weight in the South. In the current climate, the charge of being Lincoln's lover might shock a few people, but to be labeled an accomplice in his assassination was completely different. Time wouldn't fade that stain. "A logical attitude, but if the Bellcase name were linked with political assassination, you might see things differently. And don't forget, we're looking at current illegal acts. Someone tried to blow up Olive Twist and killed Boswell."

"If Buford and Jeremiah killed that young man, they have to be punished. It's just that . . . Buford used to be somebody. And Jeremiah, too. People looked up to them. We were little kids, so we don't remember. Buford served on the bank's board of directors. He went into financial advising and made money for a lot of people. He only started drinking when the economy tanked. Now he's like a joke. It just hurts me."

Her conversation triggered an old memory. Buford coming out of the courthouse with my father. They both wore suits and laughed as they walked in dappled sunshine to Millie's for coffee. Buford was handsome, well groomed, and well liked by my father and the people they passed. I'd been a kid, as Tinkie said. And I'd forgotten the admirable Buford.

"All I'm saying is Oscar and Cece may act like this doesn't bother them, but it does. There's history here. Everything isn't black-and-white."

"I'll keep it in mind."

"It doesn't change what we have to do. I just wish Buford would consider the impact of his actions on others."

Drunks had no conscience, as far as I could tell. Their needs were all they thought of. No sense saying it, though. Tinkie knew it as well as I did.

Easing into the traffic, Tinkie aimed for the southbound lane of the highway that would take us to Holmes County.

"Who do you think killed Boswell?" I asked as the sun-soaked fields of green slipped past us.

She didn't hesitate. "I think Olive did it. He betrayed her on two fronts. With Webber and Oscar. She found out and acted out of rage."

"But you agreed to work for her to prove her innocence." Her lack of even a shade of gray surprised me. Tinkie wasn't duplicitous.

"And I'll do my best. But I'm convinced what we'll

prove is her guilt. And I won't be unhappy by those results." She cut a sly look at me. "Dr. Webber makes a lot of sense. And he's very persuasive."

"You think he's handsome, don't you?" I slapped the dashboard. "You've got a crush on the professor."

"I've always had a weakness for academics, or anyone with doctor in front of his name. Why, when I was a junior at Ole Miss, Dr. Mitchell was the Canterbury scholar. He whispered old English in my ear when we were making out. Honestly, it just weakened my knees."

"Tinkie Richmond!" I couldn't believe it. "You dated your professor? And Old English turned you on?" I wasn't certain which part of her revelation was more provocative.

"Of course we didn't date. That would've been against the rules. We just kissed in his office. It was really innocent, but very exciting. You know, forbidden passion. And I swear, 'The Wife of Bath' is exquisite. So bawdy!"

"You are a scandal."

Tinkie laughed. "Oh, don't play innocent with me. I'm sure you had your flirtations in college. The theater department was a hotbed of steamy sex. Do you remember Carlos Rodriguez? Oh, he was the heartthrob for many girls. Of course I couldn't date him because he didn't belong to a fraternity, but he was so sexy."

"My lips are sealed." I'd had a crush on the handsome Carlos, but I'd never acted on it. He was the Latin lover who made the rounds—and won the male lead in every production for the four years he was in school. Had he not been so busy putting notches on his belt, I might have fallen for him.

"You'll end up telling me everything," Tinkie said with confidence. "You always do."

She slowed for a roadblock as she approached the Odd Fellows Cemetery. "Uh-oh. Things are heating up." She parked on the roadside. "Grab my camera, Sarah Booth. We may get a photo of Boswell's killer. And of course I want to document this for our client. God knows she loves being filmed."

I took in the chaotic scene. "Half of Zinnia is here."

Several hundred people milled in and around the cemetery. Many were society ladies, wilting in business suits and pumps. They'd come to protest the exhumation.

Tinkie couldn't mask her disapproval. "You know, a Daddy's Girl would never cause a spectacle like this. It's unseemly to dig up a dead woman and hold a press conference about it."

"Bad taste is the least of our troubles," I said, pointing to four men armed with hunting rifles. Second Amendment nutcases took the Bill of Rights to the extreme. I was always leery of an emotionally unbalanced person carrying a loaded weapon. With their sweat-stained camo T-shirts, beer guts, swagger, and guns, they seemed more than half a bubble off plumb.

"Sarah Booth, this could get out of hand." Tinkie had the same thought.

"An understatement, Tink." We stopped halfway to the cemetery. "If Twist persists in this, someone *will* be hurt."

"There's the coroner." Tinkie pointed through the crowd to Meshach in his hot suit. The man believed in personal presentation. He held an envelope in his hand and approached Olive Twist with it extended. He spoke a few words and left the way he'd come. Olive opened the envelope and read for a moment.

"Uh-oh, her desires have been thwarted and she's

mad." Tinkie's eyes twinkled. "Look how her face went pale and then red. Sure sign her temper is up."

"Ladies and gentlemen," Olive called out. "My request for exhumation has been denied. I will pursue this matter legally. I promise the mystery of the Lady in Red will be solved. I will prove she's a relative of prominent Delta families and that she was involved in a nefarious crime."

When the first tomato flew through the air, I thought Olive had been shot. The red splotch on her white blouse looked, for a second, at least, like blood. By the time three or four rotten tomatoes had splattered her, I realized a troublemaker was pelting her with spoiled fruit.

An enraged shriek let me know Dr. Twist failed to find a scintilla of humor in the situation. "Who's responsible for this?" she demanded. "Sheriff, arrest whoever did this. I want them charged with deadly assault."

"Ma'am, it's a tomato, not a hand grenade." Holmes County sheriff Adams Peeples was a tall, slender black man with studied calm.

"It's that idiot Buford," Tinkie whispered in my ear, and pointed to a tall holly hedge where the fruit pelter had hunkered down. "At least he isn't shooting hollow points. Let's take him out."

"Are you serious?" I checked out her expensive sundress and bejeweled sandals. "You want to tackle him in a dress?"

"I don't intend to get dirty. You tackle him. Once he's on the ground, I'll stand on him. I can put a hurting on him."

It was pointless to argue with Tinkie. I was the one wearing jeans and boots. I was the taller and heavier partner. I was the muscle. "Okay." I broke away from the crowd and circled behind the hedge. It wasn't just Buford involved. Jeremiah was handing him the overripe tomatoes and he was tossing them with deadly accuracy.

Twist had taken refuge behind the sheriff's car, and a swarm of tomatoes burst against the white and green cruiser. So far, the local constabulary showed no interest in stopping the fruit attack.

"Buford, dammit!" I slapped a tomato out of his hand just as he was about to hurl it. "Stop this shit or you'll go to jail."

"I doubt it," Jeremiah said. "We don't listen to the likes of you anyway."

Jeremiah had made it abundantly clear that anyone who supported Cece was his enemy. I'd given him a piece of my mind several years back and it had rolled off him like water off a duck's back. The only thing he'd accomplished in his miserable life was to shut out his last remaining family member and doom himself to loneliness and hate.

"You think it's fun throwing tomatoes?" I asked.

"Yeah. It's fun," Buford said. "Big fun."

"Yeah," Jeremiah brilliantly added.

I picked up a crate of tomatoes and started throwing at both of them. I scored a few direct hits before they reorganized. By then, Tinkie had arrived with the sheriff.

"Arrest them," she said. "They're a danger to the community. Vandalism. Flat-out stupidity—I don't care what the charge is, just lock them up."

A cluster of armed men stood beneath an old cedar tree in a corner of the cemetery. They talked and nodded toward Twist. The sheriff was well aware of the potential for violence.

"This is a volatile situation. Dr. Twist will keep stirring

the pot until she gets media attention. She's willing to risk her life for a spot on the six o'clock news. Those two buffoons"—I indicated Buford and Jeremiah—"will be goaded into acting so stupendously stupid the national media will be down here. Lock them up for their own protection."

"Not a bad idea." Sheriff Peeples snapped cuffs on Buford and Jeremiah before they knew what happened. "Let's head to the jail so you can tell me all about your rights as citizens of the great state of Mississippi."

Like it or not, I needed to talk to Olive. I herded Tinkie in that direction. "Should we drop her case?"

"Nope. This way we're on the inside. We'll know what she's up to."

I considered it as we crossed the cemetery, moving from one shady patch to the next to avoid the sun. "Do you believe what Dr. Webber said about Boswell's secret stash of videotapes?"

Tinkie stared at Olive as she berated a group of Heritage Pride Heroes. The professor obviously had a serious death wish. "Maybe. Olive is certainly self-destructive. Look at her." She used her palm to remove a sheen of perspiration from her brow. "On the other hand, I don't trust Webber as far as I can throw him."

"I thought you liked him." I was surprised.

"Oh, he's sexy and smart. But he's a snake. He certainly thinks well of himself, as does Olive."

"I don't understand the standards academics judge themselves by." Things were very different in the theater department at Ole Miss. The measuring stick of success was a role on Broadway or in a film in Los Angeles. "Is Webber successful?"

"He's a prince among paupers in his own reviews. And Olive is a princess. We walk amongst royalty."

We were still chuckling when we approached Olive's side. "Thank you for saving me from those nabobs," she said. "Lord, the ignorance here is abysmal."

"Our pleasure," Tinkie interjected before I could point out we weren't really concerned for her safety when tomatoes were the weapon of choice.

"It seems a petition to stop the exhumation was presented to the judge. He halted the process to consider the petitioner's views. I'm positive I'll prevail, but it'll delay things." She tried brushing tomato pulp from her clothes to no avail. The stain only spread over the left side of her blouse. "I should sue those cretins for ruining my clothes."

"I'm sure you can replace the whole outfit for little or nothing. There's a Nickle-Mart not far from here." Tinkie let that bomb roll toward Olive with a smile.

"I hate shopping," Olive confessed. "It's such a waste of my valuable time and intellect."

"Not to mention your fashion sense." A smile plastered Tinkie's face.

"Yes, you're exactly right." Olive bestowed the warmest smile on my partner. "You understand how valuable my time is. I have moments of sheer brilliance, but those breakthroughs require hours of thinking. To be totally original, one must struggle to find the enlightened path. Mental labor is intensive. I don't like to waste my energy shopping."

"Oh, I understand." Tinkie played right along.

Since I was behind both of them, I took the opportunity to pinch the snot out of Tinkie's waist. She bolted forward but suppressed a squeal, bumping into Olive, who cast a furious look at my partner.

"Sometimes Tinkie has a flash of brilliance, like just now, and she almost has an out-of-body experience," I chattered away. "The surge of intellect is so powerful, it's almost as if she were possessed. I wish I could feel something like that."

Tinkie's expression promised retaliation. "Oh, trust me. You will. At the most unexpected time."

Olive pulled her shoulders back. "You're so generous, Mrs. Richmond, but you really can't expect someone with an ordinary mind to feel what you feel. There are those of us who have quality of mind, but the majority of the population simply doesn't."

"Yes, we elite few can only pity the fools who suffer in mental darkness." Tinkie heaved a big sigh.

I'd had enough. "Since you can't dig up any dead people today, what's on our agenda? Maybe Tink and I could deposit our retainer?"

"Oh, dear, I forgot the check." Olive almost fanned herself. "Let's head back to The Gardens for it and to prepare my legal plea on the exhumation. This pleading is vitally important. I'm sure I'll get my way. These dolts have simply set me back a few days, but they haven't foiled me."

I didn't like her persistence or optimism. "Surely there are other projects. Why not research Leland Stanford's or J. P. Morgan's railroad schemes. There's bound to be plenty to write about there."

"Of course there are numerous historical events to excavate. Unfortunately, Sheriff Peters informed me I can't leave the area. Even if I wanted to abandon this project and move on to something that doesn't remind me so much of the loss of my research assistant, I can't. I'm stuck here. So I might as well work."

"I could put in a word with the sheriff for you," I offered.

"No thanks. I'll put a few words on Coleman Peters all by myself." She simpered, and her chest emitted the strangest little trill. "He's one burning hunk of man."

Tinkie grinned over her shoulder. "He is a fine example of man flesh, and he's single."

I'd kill her as soon as I got her alone. "But he supports his ex-wife, a nutcase who tries to kill all of his girlfriends."

"Another chapter for my book," Olive said. "That's why I love the South. Such eccentrics. It's like Faulkner's characters are hiding under every rock around here."

"You cannot put anything about Mrs. Peters in a book," I blurted.

"Of course not." She gave me a withering look. "I'll use it in the romance novel I'm writing. With my active brain and linguistic abilities, I should be able to pen a bestseller in a matter of weeks."

"Yeah," Tinkie agreed. "Simple as pie."

"But don't you have to be able to convey human emotions to write a successful romance?" I asked.

She missed the point completely. "Emotion schmotion," she said. "I want to convey far more than just the ordinary 'he loves her, she loves him.' I want to write about destiny. In my novel, Ian and Enya are fated to share the most intense love imaginable. At first she hates him, and he must teach her obedience. Then, of course, there's a war. She thinks she's in love with this simpering Englishman who only wants to destroy her clan. In the end, Ian spanks some sense into her and they live happily ever after. A good spanking really spices up the love scenes, don't you think?"

Tinkie rolled her eyes. "Fascinating. What do you call it?"

"*Gone with the Heather*. It all takes place on the western moors. The story starts at the beginning of the heather blooming season, which is August, and ends when a big storm sweeps through and fog blocks out the view of the heather. Enya realizes Ian is the man for her, but she can't find her way to him in the fog."

"This sounds vaguely familiar," I said.

"If I find out someone has plagiarized my story, I'll sue." Twist squared her shoulders. "Brilliance is often stolen."

"No doubt," Tinkie said. "No doubt."

6

When I returned to Dahlia House, Graf was out jogging. I knew his route so I saddled up Reveler and Lucifer. Miss Scrapiron, the lady of my herd, could have the day off. With Sweetie at my side, I took off along the trail Graf had taken. I rode Reveler and ponied Lucifer. Lucky for me the two geldings had bonded.

The heat was almost intolerable, so I walked the horses. My favorite ride took me around the edges of the cotton fields and along the banks of a small creek, shaded by scrub oaks, cypress, and willows. Coker Creek, named for Jitty's husband, wound through the property of Dahlia House and then back into acres and acres of cotton and corn.

Delta farmers long ago learned the value of windbreaks,

and so the trees along creeks and waterways were spared from the ax. A good thing for me and the horses on a scorching day.

As we ambled along, I noted evidence of Graf's passing. His footprints were sporadically embedded in the creek bank or in a damp spot beneath the overhanging tree limbs.

My heart was troubled by the web that Twist had thrown over my friends. While I didn't believe Oscar had done anything wrong, I was worried that he'd shut Tinkie out. I knew from experience such behavior could destroy even the best relationship.

I arrived at a straight stretch and put Reveler into a gentle, ground-covering canter. Ten minutes later, I spotted the familiar figure of my man jogging. He must have heard the pounding of horse hooves and stopped, hands on his thighs, to catch his breath.

"Why, Sarah Booth Delaney, you are a sight sent by the angels," he said when I drew abreast. He took Lucifer's reins. "Thank goodness you brought me someone to ride home. This heat is a killer. The climate in California is far more hospitable."

"Live long enough and we'll have California's climate right here in Sunflower County, thanks to global warming. If we aren't underwater." I tossed him a pair of sweatpants. Riding in gym shorts was not a great idea for man or woman.

"Thanks!" He slipped into them and mounted Lucifer and I passed him the bottled water I'd packed. "You are a goddess. Anything new to report on the case?"

"Nothing solid."

We eased the horses into a walk and made for the nearest shade. "Why would anyone kill Boswell?" Graf asked. "Did he even have a life? I mean, he slept on the floor beside Twist's bed."

"I'm beginning to suspect there was more to Boswell than the shadow servant he presented to everyone." Webber had painted a different picture of the assistant. There was also the note to Oscar indicating Boswell would sell out Olive to the highest bidder.

"What happened in Lexington?"

"The exhumation was stalled, but there was an angry crowd. Buford and Jeremiah were arrested for hitting Olive with rotten tomatoes. I'd expect that conduct from Buford, but Jeremiah was also so . . . classy. I mean, he's an ass because of the way he treated Cece, but he was dignified. I guess Aunt Loulane would say, 'If you lay down with dogs, you get up with fleas.'"

His laughter rang over the fields. I realized with a catch in my heart how much I loved him. He was born to be a movie star, and it scared me. At one time I'd wished nothing more than to be successful as an actor. Life had changed me and my ambitions. Coming home in desperation after my failed Broadway career, I'd learned Dorothy's lesson. There's no place like home. Could I reasonably expect Graf to be happy with a woman who lived in Mississippi while he traveled the world making films? I knew only too well how many women would devote themselves totally to fulfilling his every whim or desire.

"You're too serious for your own good," Graf said.

"Just thinking about the case." I would not burden him with my own insecurities. "How did your business talks go?"

"They've offered me the voice-over job. I need to leave soon for Hollywood. I'll be there a week and can come back after I finish. I can stay in Mississippi a while before the next shoot starts."

I forced a wide smile. "I'm thrilled for you. And you are the perfect person. Kudos to the studio for seeing your talent."

"I wish you could come with me." He wasn't pressuring me, just expressing his wishes.

"Let's see what tomorrow brings. This whole case may have blown over by then."

"Wishful thinking, Sarah Booth. But I thank you for the thought. And I accept your work is as important to you as my acting is to me. We'll navigate around our schedules. Plenty of people do it, and they don't love each other half as much as we do." A devilish glint gave me warning. "How about a trot?"

"I think the horses would love a trot."

Neck and neck, we made our way back around the cotton fields to the cool shade of the barn. We hosed the horses and put them in a pasture. They both rolled, aligning their backs in what passed for horsey chiropractic maneuvers. "I'll make us a drink," I said.

"Let me run a little oil over the tack and I'll be right in," Graf said.

I'd turned the corner to the house when Coleman pulled up to the front. His expression boded trouble. "Coleman's here," I called to Graf.

By the time Coleman got out of the patrol car and stood beside me at the steps, Graf had joined us.

"Sarah Booth, Graf," the sheriff greeted us. "I just got Doc's autopsy report. Boswell was definitely poisoned. We found the source—Olive's gourmet coffee beans. The poison was mixed into the whole beans. When they were ground and used to brew the coffee—it was more than a lethal dose. We have a homicide on our hands and a dangerous killer on the loose."

"Have you arrested anyone?" I asked.

"The evidence against Twist is circumstantial at best, but she did have motive. I understand Boswell was working behind her back, trying to sell her out to Webber and Oscar."

I couldn't deny that. Nor did I want to. "Olive's mean as a snake. Why would she expect loyalty—the way she treated Boswell."

"Speaking of Twist, she's looking for you and Tinkie. I thought I'd give you a heads-up. I'm not certain I believe she did it, Sarah Booth. It's possible she's being set up, but she has it in her head that she needs her own investigators. Forces paid to serve her self-interest, as she put it."

"If Twist isn't the murderer, then she's likely the intended victim," I noted. "I find it a lot easier to believe she was the target, not Boswell."

"I agree," Graf said. "She's the instigator. Boswell was just a bit player."

"We found fingerprints on the coffee bag. Twist, Boswell, Gertrude, the cleaning staff, and unidentified prints that may belong to the stock boys at the specialty coffeehouse. We're checking on it. We're also comparing the prints with Buford's and Jeremiah's, once Sheriff Peeples uploads and sends them over."

"Are those two smart enough to use a poison?" I asked. "The way they've been behaving lately, I think they're back to about second-grade intelligence."

Coleman frowned. "Don't underestimate them, Sarah Booth. Both men were brilliant in their day. And Buford has several degrees in finance. He knows how to make money if he wants to. I'm checking Boswell's background. The tip you gave me has merit. Boswell had archived extensive footage of Twist that he'd surreptitiously taped. She comes across as a tyrant, bully, and complete ass. I don't envy DeWayne the job of going through it, but that's what he's doing."

Better Deputy Dattilo than me, I thought. "What about the Heritage Heroes or whoever they are?"

Coleman's frown deepened. "A bunch of peckerhead haters is one thing. A bunch of haters with plush bank accounts is something else. From what I'm hearing, Buford and Jeremiah are revered by the group. I've gotten reports those guys are dedicated survivalists. They've kept a low profile in Sunflower County, but I've got my ear to the ground. There's something here that disturbs me. I don't like covert organizations, and especially those that cloak themselves in patriotism and the glory of the past. Sometimes that's just a cover for racism or misogyny or greed. They can be very dangerous, and my sources tell me these guys are armed."

"I had the impression they were just a bunch of bigots strutting around, talking foolishness," Graf said. "It's frightening to think they actually have weapons and ammunition."

"Most of these good ole boys want to blame someone for a bad economy or a wife who took a runner. They like to drink and shoot off their mouths. They kill animals that can't shoot back, and they re-tell stories of the past when things were 'good.' Twist is messing with what they view as their sacred heritage. Some of them have serious brain deficits, and I worry they'll do something rash. Now it looks like they've found leaders willing to show them the way. Jeremiah and Buford can create real problems. Particularly Jeremiah. He's painted himself as a symbol of the fallen South. A man betrayed by his brother. Sort of the worst of the dead South. The Falcon inheritance was substantial. Big enough to cause serious problems."

I saw his point. Money could buy a lot of trouble in the wrong hands. "This seems a little sophisticated for a bunch of yahoos."

"Jeremiah went to Harvard. Buford has a doctorate. They aren't stupid, but they've chosen a life of stupidity."

"What about Richard Webber?" I was curious how Coleman read the Ole Miss professor.

"I don't normally view academics as killers." Coleman wiped sweat from his forehead. The heat was leeching the life out of us. "But the jealousy and ill-will between Webber and Twist is pretty epic. If he was sure he wouldn't get caught killing her, he might be tempted to try."

"Anyone else on your list of suspects?"

"Frances Malone was certainly upset. She made public threats."

"She's harmless and you know it. She wouldn't hurt a fly."

"I still have to speak with her and check her alibi."

I didn't envy Coleman. For all her bluster, Frances was delicate. The idea she might be *considered* a murderer would send her into a hissy fit. "Be gentle. You know she isn't capable of harming Boswell, or Twist."

Coleman's crooked smile told me he didn't view Frances as a real suspect. But a good investigator followed every lead.

"Any news on the exhumation?"

Coleman's amusement vanished. "Twist will eventually get the order. The identity of the woman in the grave is a mystery. If Twist is willing to pay for the exhumation and the necessary DNA tests to identify the dead woman, I'm willing to bet the judge will rule in Twist's favor."

"And no one can stop this?"

Coleman shook his head. "A family member, but there isn't a proven one."

"Digging up a body seems wrong," Graf said. "I mean, rest in peace should mean something."

I completely agreed, but I understood the law wasn't our friend in this instance. "I'll call Tinkie and we'll talk with Twist. I honestly don't want to work for her, Coleman."

"Then don't." Coleman didn't pull any punches. "This will divide Sunflower County and the Delta all the way down to Lexington. If I could steer clear of this rolling stink bomb, I would."

"Sarah Booth's curiosity has been stirred." Graf rumpled my hair. "Might as well let her feed it. I suspect Dr. Twist will be headed north by the end of the week. Might be delicious for our little Southern flowers to fleece the carpetbagger."

"From your lips to God's ears." Coleman touched the brim of his hat. "Let me know if Twist confesses. And a word to the wise: get your retainer up-front, Sarah Booth. Olive likes to live large."

Graf and I watched him walk away. "Let's get that Bloody Mary," I said. "I need to be fortified to deal with Twist, and I have to talk with her."

"I'll expect a full report when you get back."

"Come with me," I suggested.

"Not just no, hell no."

I didn't blame him. Not even love could drag him down that long, rocky road.

Tinkie climbed into the front seat of the roadster. "I thought about this all afternoon. I don't want to work for her."

"Neither do I."

"Then why are we going to The Gardens to talk with her? Send her an email or a text message. Tell her we don't have time."

I had to laugh. Not so long ago, Tinkie had read me the riot act about the horrors of breaking up with a man by text. I would have thought the same applied to a business deal. When I asked her, she gave me an exasperated expression signifying I was gaucher than a grub.

"Twist is not a lady, nor is she a friend. We've never been involved with her in any way. She's a *potential* client, who has yet to pay our retainer. We can decline the job by text." She swatted my shoulder. "Stop laughing at me. It's rude."

"If we're not going to continue with her as our client, we owe it to her to tell her face-to-face."

"Since when did you become a maven of good manners? Last I heard, you were threatening to send Graf's ring back to him by FedEx."

She had me there, but I still had a little mischief in me. "We'll find her and you tell her we quit."

"Did she really hire us? No money crossed my hand."

I turned down the beautiful drive to The Gardens. "She agreed to our price. When we went to Lexington, it might be construed as working for her."

"I was working for Frances Malone. She's a lady with some class. And Twist is a . . . I don't know what she is, but it isn't a lady."

"Point taken."

Tinkie lowered her sunglasses and pierced me with a blue gaze. "Go dancing with Satan for the price of a song, Sarah Booth, and just see what happens."

"Hang on!" I swerved the car as someone jumped out of the shrubs in front of us.

"Holy shit!" Tinkie slammed forward, but the seat belt caught her before her face hit the dash. "Who the hell was that?"

Behind us Gertrude Strom stood in the middle of the drive shaking a fist at me. Tinkie's jaw jutted forward.

"Let me handle the old bat." Tinkie unbuckled her seat belt and opened the car door. "I've about had it with her low-class conduct. I'll set her straight."

Because I really wanted to hear it, I turned off the car and followed Tinkie.

"Do you realize you almost made us wreck?" Tinkie hurled the words at Gertrude as she stormed toward her. "Even a cow has more sense than to walk in front of a moving car."

"Not really," I whispered to Tinkie. "Cows don't comprehend vehicular right of way."

"Shut it!" Tinkie whispered back. She zeroed in on Gertrude. "What is wrong with you?"

Gertrude put the back of her hand to her forehead. "Thank goodness you're here. I need help."

"What help? Maybe shoving little children into ovens?" Gertrude was not my favorite person and I saw no reason not to devil her.

"Twist and Webber are at each other's throats. They've hurled insults to the point they've declared a duel! I overheard them in the hydrangea garden. They're set to fight it out at high noon."

"There's still time to find a good seat," I said, consulting my watch. "Is it to be swords or pistols?" I had no real concern that the two academics would physically harm each other.

"I won't have blood shed on my hydrangeas! High iron content in the soil will change the color, and I've worked so hard to achieve this dusty shade of pink."

The woman was madder than a hatter. I couldn't even compose a witty comeback.

"What are they quarreling about?" Tinkie, always the practical partner, asked.

"I don't know. I have to stop it, though. Think what it will do to my B and B's reputation if two guests try to kill each other."

"It might increase business," I said.

All expression dropped from Gertrude's face, followed by sudden hope. "Do you really think so? The economy has been awful. Business is down forty percent, and I could use a boost."

"Where are they?" Tinkie pushed me toward the car.

"The hydrangea garden," Gertrude said with some irritation. She didn't like repeating herself.

"Where are the hydrangeas?" I asked.

"Behind the summerhouse."

I had a general idea. The grounds of the B and B sprawled for hundreds of acres. Gertrude had developed gardens on thirty acres centered around the physical building, but there were nature trails and wooded acreage behind us. I jumped behind the wheel of the car and Tinkie and I took off. We went straight through the parking lot and behind the tennis courts. I halted beneath the branches of an incredible old oak. In the distance I heard, "I'm gonna gitchew, you sonofabitch-chew."

I was stunned Dr. Olive Twist knew the lyrics to a Kinky Friedman tune—much less could imitate a Texas-Jewish accent. Perhaps there was hope for her.

Instead of musing on musical heroes, Tinkie sprang from the car and ran into the clearing. "What the hell?" was her bemused comment.

I followed and found Webber and Twist standing inches apart, facing each other. Neither held a weapon, and both were red-faced from fury.

"You aren't a historian, you're a terrorist!" Olive shouted at Webber.

"And you, madam, are no lady!" Webber responded, making me ponder where I'd heard that line.

Twist beat me to it. "So you fancy yourself a modern-day Rhett Butler! Dream on, you bloodless ponce." Twist's smirk was a victory lap.

Webber drew himself up to his full height. "And you fancy yourself a human being. Better get your DNA checked."

"My DNA is registered, which can't be said for your intellect. Can you even hit double digits on the IQ scale?"

Oh, ouch! Tinkie and I took seats on the roots of an old oak tree. It was like a tennis match, only much slower and there were no racquets or balls.

"Published much?" Webber sneered. "Let's see, your last publication was in *Weekly Reader*. But oh, yes, it was peer-reviewed, I believe. A panel of second graders."

"And your last book sold what, six copies? Didn't your mother buy all of them?"

"At least my mother can read."

"Thanks to a prison literacy program!"

Bada bing! Score one for Twist.

"You listen to me, you bone with a hank of hair. You leave my mother out of this."

Too bad for Webber. He showed the first weakness.

"Got a few mommy issues, do we, Dr. Webber? You probably started your history career doing genealogy for dear old Mum. Plundering the musty bones of your dead relatives give you a boner for history?"

"What type of mother could produce the academic version of a cross between Marilyn Manson and Charles Manson?" Webber asked.

Twist muttered what sounded vaguely like "helter-skelter" and lowered her head and charged. She butted Webber's midriff with enough force to send him staggering backwards.

Tinkie and I rushed into the fray. Enough was enough. The war of words had turned physical. I caught Webber before he fell. Tinkie dragged Olive back.

"Get a grip!" Tinkie ordered. "What is wrong with you two? This isn't elementary school. You can't punch each other like six-year-olds."

"As usual, words fail her!" Webber pivoted and strode toward the B and B, leaving me to wonder if plagiarism applied to stealing great lines.

"What in the world is wrong with you?" Tinkie asked Olive. "Your assistant has been murdered, and you're out in a garden head-butting a grown man."

"He deserved everything he got." Twist was breathing hard, but she was calming. "He's just . . . mean!" She burst into tears.

Tinkie rolled her eyes at me. "Will you drive the car back to the parking lot? I'll walk with Olive."

I knew then she wouldn't quit the case. Olive's show

of helplessness was all it took to bring out the defender in Tinkie. Great. I wouldn't be flying to Hollywood with Graf, and Olive Twist and Richard Webber wouldn't be leaving Zinnia, either. We would all stew in our juices until poor Jimmy Boswell's murder was resolved.

I found Tinkie and Olive in the bar. Olive was sucking down Bloody Marys, on Tinkie's tab, of course, and was feeling much better. "Webber stole that last line from Gore Vidal," she said. "He's so unoriginal he rips off barbs."

"Let it go," Tinkie said. She inhaled her drink, working on the premise, I presumed, that if she couldn't beat them she'd join them. She signaled the waitress for a round for all three of us.

"I'll sue Webber." Twist dared us to disagree.

"That should be fun." The waitress set a glass in front of me. The Gardens' bartender made an awfully good Bloody Mary. Lots of big fat olives. I chomped one in half.

"What big teeth you have," Olive said.

"The better to eat you with, my dear." I wasn't in a mood for her foolishness. If she messed with me I might bake her in a pie.

"Listen, it's imperative I exhume the body, get the DNA samples, and get out of this place. The heat, the crazies, it's just too much for me." Olive fished around in her empty glass for the pickled green bean. "I have to return to a cultured environ. This is a desert of ignorance."

Tinkie grabbed her wrist. "You're not endearing yourself to us, Olive. If you want our help, stop acting like an arrogant jackass. Boswell is dead. From what I gather, you're the prime suspect."

"I speak the truth, no matter whom it offends."

"Then let me give you an etiquette lesson." Tinkie slid from her chair and stood up. "You don't insult the people who work for you or try to help you. I realize you were likely raised by bloodthirsty barbarians, but it's time for an education. You will treat Sarah Booth and me with respect, or you'll be on your own."

Olive simply couldn't help herself. She bared her teeth. "That sheriff won't arrest me. He questioned me and knows I wouldn't hurt Boswell. Besides, there's a spark between us."

Now I stood. "Coleman is a good man. He's off-limits."

She smiled. "Got a crush on the sheriff? Does your fiancé know?"

"Off-limits," Tinkie said. "That's all you need to know."

A hard pause settled between us. At last Olive broke the silence. "How can I prove I didn't kill Boswell?"

"Convince us." I propped on my elbows.

Twist pushed her hair from her face, and sadness settled around her mouth and eyes. "I treated Boswell poorly, I know. But he knew I cared for him. He paid attention to all the little details. His research was thorough, and he was smart. He pursued a lead until he exhausted it. He cared about this work as much as I did. Sometimes, late at night, he'd get up and work more. Why would I harm someone so valuable to me?"

In Twist's logic, she had no reason to want the young man dead. It was a start, though I wondered if she was aware he had been working behind the scenes to betray her.

"Have you noticed anyone strange following you?" Tinkie asked.

"Half the people in this town are strange." Twist held

up a hand. "Sorry. No one has followed me." She frowned. "So you think the poison was meant for me?"

Tinkie nodded. "I believe Boswell was collateral damage. You have a knack for pissing people off."

"Where did you buy the coffee beans?" I asked. "We'll start by tracing the beans and everyone who touched them."

"They were special ordered from a little market in Costa Rica. The beans are organically grown on a private plantation. One pound runs thirty dollars, but the coffee is worth every cent. Of course, there's nothing to compare here in Mississippi. Do you even have imported beans?"

Tinkie sighed. "Your arrogance is exceeded only by your ignorance. We have specialty coffees, gourmet cheeses, chocolates—anything you can find in the big cities you love so much. And we also have clean air, and land that grows things other than gangs and litter."

I gave Tinkie a high five. When she put it on someone, she lowered the boom.

"Look. I don't mean to sound so—"

"Officious. Repugnant. Bigoted. Ill-mannered." Countless options were available to me.

"Rude," she said. "Small towns are not sophisticated, no matter where they are. I require cultural stimulation. I'm a creature of refinement."

"Creature, yes. As to the rest, I'll withhold judgment." I couldn't help myself any more than she could. My reward was a hard stomp on my toes from Tinkie.

"We have to stop this one-upsmanship if we're to accomplish anything." Tinkie spoke with fervor. "Can you two stop needling each other?"

I looked at the ceiling.

"I'll do my best," Twist said.

"Me, too." My fingers crossed behind my back.

"Good. Let's track down those coffee beans."

7

Three hours later I knew more about La Hacienda coffee than I ever wanted to know. The upshot was the coffee had been shipped to a gourmet shop in New York City. Olive ordered it from there, and it was mailed to her home. She'd opened and used the beans—without ill consequences—before she'd brought them down to Zinnia.

Logic led me to believe the poison had been introduced into the coffee *after* Twist and Boswell checked in at The Gardens.

I gave Doc Sawyer a call. Normally I'd stop at the hospital for a face-to-face, but my focus was on getting the info and getting rid of Twist. I'd visit with Doc another day when we had more pleasant topics to pursue.

"Coleman tells me you're working for the professor," Doc said, amusement in his tone. "I hear she's something else."

"Nobody ever said private eyeing would be easy work."

Doc's chuckle took me back to the past. He'd always been able to finagle a smile, even when I was in panic mode about shots. "You could retire and let your movie star take care of all your needs."

"Not likely. I love Graf, but nobody takes care of a Delaney."

"Or a Booth. You get a lot of your independence from Libby Booth, and don't ever forget it."

"Not possible." Forgetting my parents was akin to forgetting to breathe.

"Some days, Sarah Booth, I see you and think for just a split second that Libby's back."

I had the same fantasy, but I wondered what had Doc waxing nostalgic. "If I had time for therapy, I'd ask if I'll ever recover from missing my parents. But there's a murder to solve, so what's the story on the poison?"

"It was the coffee, as everyone thought. Someone mixed a form of rat poison in the coffee beans. It was the only thing in poor Jimmy Boswell's stomach."

The ingeniousness of the murder method stopped me in my tracks. "So when Boswell ground up the beans and made coffee, that was it."

"Doesn't take much." Thanks to Tinkie and me, Doc had become expert in murder methods. Especially poisons.

So the issue I had to resolve was how did the d-CON, or whatever brand it was, get into the coffee beans in Olive's room. And were they intended for Boswell or Olive? The latter seemed the logical answer. She was abrasive, superior, and determined to piss off the old-school grumblers who wanted to pretend the Civil War had been about nobility. War was always about money, and nothing else. Pretending otherwise didn't change the facts.

I told Doc what I'd found out about the coffee beans. "So why didn't Olive drink coffee? Her beans. Her fetish for this boutique coffeehouse bean. She's not generous enough to stock such things for Boswell. It was her coffee. So why did she not die, too?"

"Questions you and Coleman will have to answer. By the by, best keep an eye out for our sheriff."

"What do you mean?" I asked.

"Twist showed up at the hospital for the autopsy results and she was all over Coleman. He wasn't exactly fighting her off."

My aggravation factor climbed to red-hot. "Coleman isn't a fool. She's a suspect in the murder of her assistant. Surely he has more sense than to involve himself with her."

"He's a lonely guy."

I couldn't tell if Doc was teasing me, baiting me, or warning me. "I'll have Tinkie speak with him."

"Music to my ears. Now I have a motorcycle accident victim to tend. At least he was wearing a helmet, but it probably won't make his leg heal straight."

I hung up and considered calling Coleman. Best to leave it to Tinkie, though. She could be no-nonsense with Coleman in a way I couldn't. Poking my nose in Coleman's romantic affairs, even for his own good, was forbidden to me.

I left a callback message on Tinkie's phone and returned to my computer. While I couldn't do anything to save the sheriff from a romantic debacle, I could research Dr. Olive Twist. If the Molotov cocktail and the poison were meant for her, she might have brought her enemies to town with her.

I had Dahlia House to myself. Graf had gone to town to buy new shirts. While shopping opportunities abounded in Los Angeles, Graf preferred the boutique men's shop, Butterfield 8, where Oscar and Harold bought their clothes.

Sweetie Pie's snores resounded in the house. Even Pluto was asleep on a pillow on my desk. He lolled, half off the brocade, and opened slanted green eyes. He watched my fingers move across the keyboard with sudden interest. Pluto wasn't above attacking my digits. He made his demands known.

I'd been working on the computer too long, and I stood to stretch.

"Care for a bite of apple?"

It was no big shock when I turned to find Snow White standing behind me, a Red Delicious in her outstretched hand.

"Let's see. Snow White succumbed to a poisoned apple. And Boswell died from poisoned coffee beans. Maybe it's time to diet."

"A pure heart is the only protection from evil," Jitty said. Her voice was high and singsongy and I wondered if her black hair and pale, pale white skin were compliments of Disney.

"Where are those pesky dwarves when you need them?" I wasn't really annoyed with Jitty—more amused than annoyed—but I certainly didn't intend to let her know it.

"Why are you such a crank?" Jitty asked. "I'm here to help you out."

"I don't think so." I stretched side to side and leaned forward to rest my hands on the floor. My hamstrings screamed. I needed to reclaim my stretching and exercise regime. Since Graf was home, I'd focused on horizontal action. My aerobic routine had fallen by the wayside.

"Lord, Sarah Booth, whatever you do, don't bend over in front of Graf." The cartoon voice was gone and Jitty's familiar voice came through loud and clear.

"Why not?"

"He's gone see that wide ass of yours and run for the hills."

I slowly stood and glared at Jitty. "You are infuriating. My butt is not that big."

"If you were goin' down the street, you'd have to wear a sign that says 'Wide Load.' Girl, throw them 'taters out the back door and make you a green salad."

I checked my backside in the front parlor mirror. I'd put on a few pounds since Graf had been cooking, but it wasn't that bad. Jitty was going to give me a complex. "My butt looks fine." I tightened and released the muscles, making it jump. "See. Nice and firm."

"Mirror, mirror on the wall, who's the jigglyist of them all?" Jitty smirked.

I wanted to throttle her, but she was already dead. "No point in you gazing in the mirror. You don't have a reflection. Are you sure you're a ghost and not a vampire?"

"Very funny." Jitty put her hands on her hips. In the fitted blue bodice and long yellow skirt, she came across sweet as pie. I knew better. This was my heritage haint, and she meant to hold my feet to the fire. About love, life, honor, even weight. It was time to turn the tables on her.

"Okay, what gives? Betty Boop, Veronica, Snow White? I realize Twist bears an uncanny resemblance to Olive

Oyl, but I don't get the connection with these cartoon characters."

Jitty shook a finger at me. "Your fantasy life is sadly lacking." She was starting to fade. "What happened to your imagination, Sarah Booth? What happened to giving yourself to a fancy? You used to daydream and create scenarios. You were softer, more feminine then. What happened to the girl who sang 'Moon River' with her daddy and danced across the parlor?"

Her questions were wicked and sharp. It had been a long time since I'd allowed a daydream to fully capture me. I'd been living with both feet planted firmly in chores and necessities. I'd lost the magic of make-believe. But I was also in the middle of a case where my client seemed to live in a world of pretend. Her whole scenario of the Lady in Red was like a bad melodrama. I had to focus on the truth.

"I wish I could give myself to a dream." I wasn't just saying it to placate Jitty. A longing for the softer, gentler Sarah Booth took hold. It was hard to always be practical and on-target.

"Remember when you used to go down to the oak trees with your mama? You played with elves and fairies."

The memory Jitty called forth made me long for those days. "I remember."

"Your mama knew how important it was to imagine things. She knew, and she would be sad to think you'd lost that. She never did."

"What do you suggest?"

"Don't ever forget how to play, Sarah Booth. You and Graf got some good times ahead. And some hard times. But if you remember to play, you can get through anythin' the world throws at you."

"Did you and Alice play?" Alice was my Civil War–era ancestor who'd survived the brutal hardships of a defeated nation—with Jitty's help. She'd kept Dahlia House and the land, even though she and Jitty lost their husbands in the war. They suffered poverty and near starvation by holding on to each other.

"We did." Jitty picked up a basket filled with apples. The sunlight from the window shafted through her. She was almost ready to leave. "We played cards and we talked about the past and the future. Folks might say we built sandcastles, and that the war and the poverty and the sickness came in wave after wave and knocked our fancies down. Bending over, backs breaking in the fields as we struggled to grow potatoes and turnips, we made up our future. And we clung to those fancies even when we had nothin' to eat. We lived on pretend."

I walked toward Jitty as she faded in and out. "Thank you for reminding me."

"You're mighty welcome, Sarah Booth. Now find you some fancy lingerie to slip into and play a game with your man. I believe that's him pulling up right now."

The game I chose was Afternoon Delight. When Graf walked in the door, packages in his arms, I let him know I'd been fantasizing about him. I left him a happy man. Exhausted but happy.

I didn't always give Jitty credit, but this once I had to hand it to her. Thanks to her nagging, I'd recaptured a bit of the girl in me, and Graf enjoyed the rewards of my femininity. He was smart enough not to ask what had inspired me.

He was sound asleep when I returned to the computer

and finished my research on Twist. What I found wasn't completely surprising, but it was interesting enough that I copied most of it and emailed it to Tinkie. And to Coleman. I was pretty sure he'd done his own research, but just in case.

The thought of Twist laying her snares for Coleman was like salt under my skin. I couldn't stop him from making romantic mistakes—I had no right to interfere at all—but I wanted to be sure he knew the score. Knowledge was power, so I sent him her entire bio.

Twist's parents were British. No big bombshell based on her name and the references to Charles Dickens's fictional character. Olive grew up in London until school age, when the family moved to the United States. Her parents took jobs at the University of Montevallo in Alabama. Twist was sent to boarding school in Connecticut. About as far away as they could send her.

It got worse. When she was twelve, her parents returned to England *and left her in the States*.

I pondered that for a moment. The tiniest grain of sympathy for Twist began to grow inside me. What would I have become had my parents abandoned me and moved halfway around the world? And why would they have done so? Olive was an unpleasant, pretentious person, but was that a result of abandonment issues or the reason she was abandoned?

"Saint Peter jumping hurdles. I sound like some softsop talk show." And on top of that, I was talking to myself. Sweetie looked up with red eyes and flopped back down with a sigh.

Time for action—I'd had enough sitting. I checked my backside in the glass doors of the bookshelves. My butt wasn't that big. Maybe it was an inch or two wider than in

college, but I was older. I couldn't expect to keep a fresh-
man figure forever.

Beneath the bookshelf, I rummaged around in the
cabinets until I found my leg weights and a DVD of exercise routines. Time to wage war against the inches.

Wearing gym shorts and sneakers, I launched into
step aerobics with weights. Thirty heart-pounding minutes later, I collapsed on the floor for sit-ups. My thighs
screamed against the abuse I'd heaped on them.

"A hundred sit-ups." I spoke aloud to seal the commitment.

I crunched up and down. Pluto sauntered over and
pawed at my hair as it splayed on the floor. Bored with
hair, he climbed on my stomach. His little kitty pile-driver
paws went straight through the layer of fat into my internal organs. It was unbelievable a cat so fat could have
such dainty paws.

"Get off, Pluto." I continued to lever myself up and
down. "Fifty-two!" I huffed. "Get off me!"

Pluto was unimpressed with my self-improvement routine or my sweaty midriff. I figured fifty-two sit-ups with
the cat's weight added to my own would count for a hundred normal crunches. I rolled onto my hands and knees
and paused to catch my breath—and convince my trembling legs they could, indeed, support me.

I'd begun to think I would spend eternity on all fours
when the phone rang. That propelled me upward into a
chair, where I snatched the device out of the cradle and
answered.

"Dah-link, were you in the middle of hot, sweaty sex?"
Cece asked. "If so, I want details."

"Dream on," I managed. "I was exercising."

"Trying to trim your caboose down to a manageable size?"

"You are a bitch." And she was. Cece was a woman, but she'd retained rights to the slender hips and tight butt of her years spent as Cecil. It was graphically unfair, and she loved to rub my nose in it.

"Calm down, dah-link! I'm only teasing you."

"What's the haps?" I asked, stealing a line from one of my fictional heroes, Dave Robicheaux.

"It's Jeremiah."

She didn't have to go into detail. Her brother was in jail in Holmes County because he was a mental midget and a nutcase. "I'm sorry, Cece."

"I'm not. Please, don't think I'm calling because he finally ended up behind bars. I hope they keep him until he's too old to harm anyone else."

"What can I do for you?"

"I've been digging into the Heritage Pride Heroes. They inhabit a crazy damn world, Sarah Booth."

Up until recent events, I'd honestly viewed them as a dozen old farts who met up in the woods, got drunk, and shot off their guns to prove their manhood. I'd never given them serious consideration. Cece was on the right track, one I should have already gone down. "What have you found?"

"They're redneck morons, but some of them have guns."

"Everybody in the South has a gun."

"Maybe so, but not all gun owners are emotionally unstable. While Jeremiah was in jail, I made a trip home. Magnolia Grove is in ruins."

"You should have called me to go with you." I didn't

like the idea of Cece tripping down a razor blade–filled memory lane. The Falcon estate, the home she'd grown up in and been kicked out of, held only pain. She needed a good friend for such a journey into the past.

"It's done now. It's distressing stuff."

Cece never used the word "stuff." She was a reporter. Details colored every sentence.

"What?"

"I don't want to say on the phone."

"Paranoid, some?" I tried to make light of it.

"Maybe." She wasn't laughing.

"Come over. Graf's asleep." I didn't want to mention I couldn't walk after my exercise-a-thon.

"Meet me at Millie's Café."

Then again, I could force myself to move if it meant Millie Roberts's homemade apple pie. Screw exercise! Screw my caboose! "I'll meet you there in ten minutes."

When it came to hot apple pie, I could drive like the wind.

Millie's was hopping with the late-afternoon crowd of coffee drinkers, the teenagers who gathered after school, and the farmworkers who'd been hitting it hard for the past ten hours and wanted rib-sticking food. Millie's was the common ground for all segments of Delta society.

I'd hobbled to a table by the time Cece arrived, exquisite in a pale amber sundress, black heels, and an amber sunhat with black polka dots. Along with slender hips, she had shoulder blades to die for, and the halter-style sundress showed them off to good effect.

"Sarah Booth, why are you trembling?"

"Anticipation of pie. I must have burned off two

hundred calories all at once doing aerobics. My body is about to go into shock."

She laughed as she sat down, and every man in the place gave her an appreciative look. "If you're not careful, you'll get fat."

"Graf likes a woman who doesn't stab him with bones."

Cece caught Millie's eye and waved her over for a hug. "It's been ages, it seems," she said to the café owner and head cook.

"I stay in the kitchen," Millie said. "We're busy from the time we open at five a.m. until we close at nine p.m. And I'm not complaining."

Millie worked hard, but she loved her work. She frowned at me. "What happened to you, Sarah Booth? Have you been afflicted with palsy?"

"She worked out and her muscles are spasming." Cece grinned wickedly. "Chunky-girl syndrome."

"Enough." They tickled me, but I didn't want a dang complex about my weight. "Apple pie. Hot black coffee."

"I'll have the same," Cece said.

"You're in luck. Deep-dish apple pies are just out of the oven." Millie touched my cheek with a fond gesture. "I read in the *National Enquirer* Elvis and Elizabeth Taylor were caught dancing at the Beau Rivage Casino in Biloxi, Mississippi. Wouldn't it be something to see those two together? I think we need to make a road trip."

Millie loved the outrageous tabloids that reported fake movie star news and other questionable tidbits of science and society. "A road trip sounds like a great idea. The four of us haven't been on a junket in a long time." Tinkie, Cece, Millie, and I were the four musketeers. Tammy Odom, aka Madame Tomeeka, was the fifth.

"There was a photo," Millie said. "A clear one. I don't think it was faked. They were dancing. Cheek to cheek. They were young and gorgeous. It just did my heart good. They both suffered a lot in this lifetime. I believe they're happy now."

"Me, too," I said.

"Gives me hope for the future," Cece threw in. "I would like to see a little unrestrained joy and dancing before I die."

"Now that Sarah Booth has her a man, we need to focus on finding one for you, Cece. A great man. Someone who will love you for the remarkable person you are." She bent down and kissed Cece's forehead. In a lot of ways, Millie played a maternal role for all of us even though she wasn't much older.

When she was gone, Cece looked at me. "Why couldn't she have been my mother?"

I didn't have the wisdom to answer that question. "So what did you find out about your brother?"

"I found incriminating things at the house. Jeremiah is into crazy shit up to his eyeballs."

This was not what I wanted to hear. Jeremiah had once had a future. Now he was like a scorpion in a hole. He only came out to bite. If anyone dared poke a stick at him, he plotted revenge. "How bad is it?"

"Homeland Security, twenty-five to life. Maybe execution, depending on how you define treason." She sighed. "I'm exaggerating, but it's pretty damn depressing. My brother has lost his mind."

"What's he into?"

"That stupid group, the Heritage Pride Heroes, they're plotting all kinds of ridiculous events. They want to surround Twist and march her out of town." Her lips twisted into disgust. "They think they're the freaking Minutemen, that they're protecting the honor of the South. My parents would be so ashamed of Jeremiah. He was educated. He should know better."

Jeremiah had a degree in chemistry and a doctoral degree in biochemistry. I could only imagine if he put his mind to mayhem. "It's not bombs?" I whispered.

She stiffened. "No, thank goodness, not bombs. At least I didn't find any indication of firepower to that degree. The idiot has been teaching an online class in surviving the coming class war. Like how to hide wealth and necessities from the hoards soon to be roaming the landscape." She gripped the table. "He's become one of those nabobs who feel entitled to a certain life. One only the elite deserve. My family home is the location for a cell of the Evergreen Tree Identity group."

"Saint Joseph on a trapeze."

"Stop that silly saint cursing, Sarah Booth. Just say it. The stupid bastard is in a world of shit. He's sitting in the Holmes County jail, but if anyone really looks into him and Buford, they'll both end up at the state mental institution."

I wanted to ask if that would be a bad thing, but I didn't. "What, exactly, is the Evergreen Tree Identity?" I'd never heard of it.

She rolled her eyes in vexation. "Don't you keep up with the news?"

I considered a moment. "No, but I'll hazard a guess and say it isn't a horticulture group."

"Absolutely not. They're religious kooks. They claim they're God's chosen people. You know, like the Aryans are the master race. Mostly, they're white, male pinheads who have bought into a conspiracy theory similar to Bilderberg."

I knew a little about Bilderberg. It claimed to be a group of the world's wealthiest and most powerful men. They were rumored to control the president—any president from Nixon to the present—and plotted to create a world order that would ultimately be administered by them.

"This is dangerous, Cece."

"You've only heard the tip of the iceberg. From what I ascertained, they honestly think a class war is not only imminent but necessary. They want this. It's the final step before they all go up in the Rapture."

A lot of things tumbled through my mind, and none were good. FBI shoot-outs, crazy cult people, racists, Nazis, people driven by ignorance and a desire to be better than someone else. "Tell me about the Evergreen Identity."

"They believe only males of pure Aryan extraction should have a vote. They think the government is controlled by a tiny group of wealthy people. And Jeremiah, bless his poor demented brain, wants to be one of them. He's lost it, and I feel partly to blame." Her brow was a thunderstorm. "He wants to take the vote—and driver's licenses—away from women. Keep them home where they belong."

"Cromwell in a top hat, this is crazy."

"I need help getting his computer." She blinked back tears. "He's turned my mother's art studio into this vile place where he holds classes in survival technique. There are cots all over the house where these idiots have been sleeping. A bunch of grown men acting like kids in a fort. The place stinks to high heaven, and it's filled with tracts and pamphlets dripping venom."

"I'm here to help. Whatever you need."

"He is such a spoiled, entitled bastard he thinks he won't be punished for this insanity." One lone tear rolled down her cheek and she dashed it angrily away. "I should let them take him. If they can prove he's crazy, they'll take Magnolia Grove for back taxes. Of course he hasn't paid in the last three years. If the county confiscated the property it would serve him right. I don't know why I even care."

"It's your home, and he's your brother." That said it all to me.

"He's renamed the place. There's a big sign: 'Falcon Crest.' Like the old TV soap opera. I'm sure he doesn't even see the irony of it."

I rubbed her arm lightly. "I'm sorry."

She bowed her head and put a hand to her brow. "I thought I was done with that place. After I left with such bitterness, I really thought I'd grieved and gotten over losing my home. My parents didn't want me there. My brother hated me, fine. But, Sarah Booth, when I saw the way the house and grounds have deteriorated . . ." She turned away to gather her emotions. "No repairs have been made in years. The house hasn't been painted in over a decade. Shingles are off the roof. And did I say it stinks?"

"I'll go with you to clear out what we can. You need to get someone to take Jeremiah's website down." I wondered about the implications of even taking the damn thing down. "Hopefully, no one but his crazy buddies know about it."

"Should I tell Coleman?" Cece asked.

Millie brought the pie and coffee, and I had a minute to think through my answer. "I think you have to. Jeremiah hasn't broken any laws, as far as I can tell. He's mean-spirited and nuts, but if that were illegal, half the county would be locked up."

Forkful of pie halfway to her mouth, Cece halted. Her eyebrows rose. "I'm so humiliated."

"You aren't responsible for his craziness." Cece had successfully killed my appetite and I signaled Millie for a go-box.

Cece took another bite of pie. "Maybe I should just kill him and be done with it."

"That would be the simplest solution." I hesitated to bring this up, but I had to. "Did you find anything relating to poisons?"

Cece bit her bottom lip. Her gaze dropped to the table and even though I waited a full sixty seconds, she didn't answer or look up.

"You did, didn't you?"

"The place is overrun with rats. There was some rat poison in the kitchen cabinet. I'm surprised one of those morons hasn't accidentally knocked it into a pot of gumbo or something. But he wouldn't poison a woman." Cece's eyes pleaded with me to convince her that her brother wasn't living on the lunatic fringe. "Would he?"

"Let's just hope this is a fantasy world and not something they intend to actually bring about."

8

The old Falcon estate looked sad and forlorn as Cece drove us down the long, winding driveway to the house. Since Magnolia Grove wasn't visible from the road, the decay hit me hard. Once upon a time it had been a beautiful plantation with fields of cotton, corn, soybeans, and peanuts. Once upon a time it had been a place where high school kids gathered for barbecues, dances, and fun. Back when Cece was still Cecil and the apple of his mother's eye.

Now most of the large tract of land was under lease with a farming concern, but the property around the house was sadly neglected. Weeds and scrub trees clumped in small islands in what had historically been fertile fields and a lawn that had hosted tennis, croquet, and touch football matches.

Jeremiah's stewardship of the property was remiss.

I hadn't set foot on the property since Cece was in high school, but my heart ached for her. She had grit, though. Tears glittered in her eyes, but she held them at bay.

She drove over the stone bridge across Black Water Creek built by Lucien Falcon during the Civil War. The Falcon land dated back to prestatehood. Lucien moved to Mississippi from Georgia in the early 1800s. He'd purchased the land on both sides of Black Water Creek and constructed a traditional two-story antebellum house with four rooms on each floor and galleries running the length of the front and back.

Over the years, wings had been added. And outbuildings. A pool in the shape of a four-leaf clover featured tiles fired by "old country" Irish master masons. Everything was done with taste and a sense of permanence.

Twenty years ago, it was a showplace, and Jeremiah and Cecil were heirs apparent to a productive farm and a fine tradition.

Cece slowed. "Depressing, isn't it? In my heart, I knew Jeremiah was running the place into the ground. My solution was to avoid coming here."

"Yes, it's depressing." There was no point lying. "I want to beat Jeremiah with a stick."

We passed the ornate sign announcing Falcon Crest, and I said nothing. Jeremiah's fanciful creation was complete with some made-up family crest showing a pheasant, cotton, and a Latin phrase. "The man has lost his mind," I said. "What is this family crest bullshit?"

"He wants to be somebody. The curse of inherited wealth. When a person is handed everything, he's never tested to learn who he is. In a way, I was lucky because I was forced to stand on my own two feet." Cece saw it clearly. "I haven't come here because I didn't want to cling to the past. But honestly, Jeremiah has turned this place into a ghetto."

"He should have married. Maybe a wife could have kept him straight."

"Maybe he could marry Snooki." Cece aimed for comedy and hit her mark.

I grinned. "I think even she has more taste than to settle for Jeremiah. How has this happened to a man who had everything—brains, looks, and money?"

The curving driveway passed the gazebo where I'd first kissed Coleman on a dare. It had taken all of my middle-school courage to boldly kiss an older boy, but it was a bang-up memory. And now the scene of my daring foray into adulthood was in ruins. Half of the gazebo's roof had collapsed. The foundation, built with bricks hand-fired by slaves, was still in good shape, but the wooden structure was a lost cause.

"What the hell has he been doing here? Everything has gone to hell." I was angry. Jeremiah had destroyed Cece's family home, *and* he'd tromped all over a bunch of my memories. "I think you should have him committed and take the property over."

"My parents didn't want me to have it," Cece reminded me.

That would always be salt in her wound. "They wouldn't want to see how Jeremiah has treated the place."

She nodded. "Legally, it's his to do with as he chooses."

"*Legal* and *just* can be two different things. And if he ends up a ward of the men in white coats, maybe the place will revert to you."

Cece parked in front of the house. "Let's see if we can figure out the extent of his survival activities and beat it back to town. There's nothing on this property for me except pain."

I hurried after her. She wore five-inch heels and I had on flats, yet I still had trouble keeping up.

She opened the front door with a key. When I stepped inside, the smell hit me. It was like the dankest, moldiest men's high school locker room ever invented. The stench was like a physical slap.

"It'll knock you down and make you cry 'Mama,'" Cece said. "Disgusting!"

"That is some funk!" I tried hard not to breathe. "Let's grab his computer and hit the road." I didn't have enough oxygen to come up with creative curses.

Cece led the way to what had been the front parlor. In sixth grade, we'd gathered in a circle on the floor and played spin the bottle. Now the room was a barracks/classroom. The once-vivid antique Persian rug was clotted with mud and gunk.

Diagrams of weaponry adorned the walls, covering valuable artwork. Semi-automatics, powerful assault rifles—someone had diagrammed the parts and uses of the guns in great detail. Pamphlets filled with kooky theories of the poor waging war against the rich were scattered over the floor. The brochures included Jeremiah's prediction of the coming battles and his theories of how the "righteous and ordained *men*" would prevail.

"This is some sick shit," she said, her face pale and sweat forming on her forehead.

"Should we box this crap up?" If Jeremiah kept acting like a total idiot, this might be evidence for Cece to use in a sanity hearing.

"A pox on Jeremiah and his stupidity. If he goes to the mental institution, then he goes. The house and property aren't mine. They'll never be mine. I can't believe I let sentimentality get the better of me. I don't even know what I'm doing here, to be honest with you."

I put my arms around Cece and gave her a hug. At first she stiffened, but then she hugged me back. "I'll do whatever I can to help." I was there for the long haul, like a friend should be.

"Let's open some windows and air this place out. Once the man musk is gone, maybe we can think more clearly."

We set to work and an hour later, a hot wind blew through. In the Old South, homes were designed to allow cross-ventilation. We hadn't explored the wings of the house, but the main rooms smelled much better.

Judging by their ankle-deep garbage, Jeremiah's merry band of recruits had none of the military's discipline or neatness. These were the dregs of a dying world. Folks who couldn't fit into society and had become survivalists, gun lovers, men who were impotent in their regular lives and therefore had to hide out in a fantasy where weapons gave them power over people.

They were also nuts. And dangerous. Jeremiah, who hadn't worked a day in the past two decades, was a member of the class he feared. He could no longer consider himself part of elite Delta society. He lived off a trust fund, which in my opinion was little better than the dole. All he had to do was look around at the decay and filth to get a picture of who he really was. Of course, self-blindness was part of his narcissism.

My emotions twisting, I stopped to open the draperies in the dining room. Mrs. Falcon's once beautiful mahogany dining table was covered by a flip chart, papers, tracts printed by radical organizations, and notebooks filled with Jeremiah's scrawling handwriting. I thumbed through the pages of a notebook.

Instructions and diagrams on making Molotov cocktails stopped me. Had one of Jeremiah's minions tried to harm Olive Twist? Had Jeremiah done it himself?

"Saint Thomas doing handsprings," I said as I took it to Cece. With the air clear, my creativity in cursing had returned.

Her hands clenched as she read the damning evidence. "You don't really think this bunch of yahoos would put something like that into action, do you? I mean, talking about it and doing it are two different things."

Reality loomed large between us. Someone had attempted to bomb Olive or Boswell or both. Fact. And the notebook held a recipe for just such a firebomb.

I wanted to cheer her up, even if I offered false hope. "Most guys like this are blowhards. They talk the talk but then go home and drink a six-pack, kick their dogs, smack their wives, and fall asleep on the sofa."

"Are you just saying that to make me feel better?"

I punched her arm lightly. "Sort of." But I had to be honest. "Jeremiah isn't rational, Cece. The man you loved as an older brother—he's not in residence these days."

"It could've been one of Jeremiah's disciples."

I couldn't argue with her logic. "We'll take this to Coleman. It isn't evidence Jeremiah did anything, but it's evidence. In fact, all of this," I waved my arm to indicate the state of the house, "is evidence Jeremiah isn't thinking with all parts of his brain."

"First the Molotov cocktail, then poison. Twist was the target, wasn't she?" Cece asked.

"Probably. But there's another possibility. Did Twist poison Boswell because he meant to blackmail her?"

"What do you think?"

"Twist is twisted." I'd been wanting to say that since I met her.

Cece groaned. "You need better material, dah-link! Your punning sucks."

"But you did smile," I pointed out. "Mission accomplished."

"I have to tell Coleman about this," Cece said. "The class warfare bullshit, the Molotov cocktail diagrams—Jeremiah needs to be institutionalized. I can't risk he'll declare war on the whole town of Zinnia just to protect his cherished—and *fabricated*—heritage."

"They'll likely send him to Whitfield." Mississippi State Hospital in Whitfield was a public mental health institution. For those without insurance or families unwilling to spring for pricey private institutions, the state facility was a viable option. Jeremiah had inherited wealth, but I was willing to bet he'd run through all the cash. If the Falcon lands were in an unbreakable trust, which I hoped they were, Jeremiah would be destitute.

"He doesn't have medical insurance. He hasn't for years. He doesn't believe in it." Cece was growing angrier by the second. "I mean, the man inherited a fortune and he's squandered all the savings. He leases the land for a tidy amount. And he has *no* insurance!"

"Take it easy. He can get care at MSH." I understood her frustration.

"I think I have a great case for involuntary commitment, don't you?" Cece asked.

"I wouldn't count on that, Mr. Cecil," a deep male voice said.

We whirled around to find a man standing in the doorway. He was enormous. At least seven feet tall and three hundred muscular pounds. He blocked the doorframe in all direction.

Cece squared her shoulders. "I don't know who you are, but get out of my house."

"It isn't your house. It's Jeremiah's, and he sent me to collect his things. When he hears you've been trespassing, he's not gonna like it." His grin was like a jack-o'-lantern's. Crooked teeth, big head.

"If I report to the sheriff what Jeremiah's up to, he'll never see the light of day. I'll have power of attorney to sell everything here, including the land. The proceeds will be used to defray his medical bills."

"You can't do that."

"What's your name?" I stepped forward.

"You're that nosy private investigator. You're so smart, find out yourself. I'm going to talk to Jeremiah, and he'll put a stop to your plans. Now, you two get out before I toss you out. And you can put the notebook back where you found it. In fact, you'll walk out of here empty-handed, just like you came in."

"My brother is in serious trouble. I'm trying to help him."

"He don't want help from the likes of you. He's told us all about you. Every disgusting detail."

I moved in front of Cece. "I suggest you shut your piehole."

"I'd love it if you tried to make me. Uppity bitches need to learn how to act in front of a man. You'll learn your place quick enough, which is flat on the floor, crawling.

He was big, and he had plenty of sense. If I went for him, he could slap me silly and call it self-defense. I wished for a loaded gun. A .22 would be fine. I'd pop him in the foot and listen to him holler.

"Let's get out of here." Cece latched on to my arm. She knew how my mind worked. "It isn't worth it, Sarah Booth. Let's go. Coleman will obtain a search warrant and take care of my brother."

"Call the law on your kin. That's what creatures like you do." His disdain for Cece was palpable.

"Listen, meathead, give me a reason—"

Cece snatched me backward. "Outside," she whispered. "Now!"

Tension radiated from her and I didn't argue. When we were at the car she almost pushed me into the passenger seat. "What's wrong with you? He had a gun tucked in his waistband."

"I have a gun, too." I did, but it was in the trunk of my car.

"Maybe you're comfortable restaging the shoot-out at the O.K. Corral, but I don't want to be shot. I think that guy would have killed us without blinking an eye. We're less than roaches in his opinion."

She was right, and when my nose was rubbed in the reality, I realized how dangerous he could have been. "Let's hit it. I'll call Coleman while you drive."

Cece tore down the drive while I punched my phone. Before I could connect with the sheriff's office, I received an incoming call from Harold.

"Where in tarnation are you, Sarah Booth? I'm driving all over Sunflower County hot on your trail."

"Cece and I are leaving Magnolia Grove. It's a long story."

"Meet me—"

"At the courthouse." I wanted to speak with Coleman in person.

"I'm on my way."

Folks in Sunflower County were laying low from the heat, so we wheeled into town in record time. Cece and I were standing on the courthouse lawn when Harold Erkwell pulled up.

"Tinkie said to call her," Harold slammed the car door. "She's determined to go to Lexington, even though Oscar told her she couldn't. She was having a confab with Oscar, and I'm a little worried."

"What were they talking about?"

"I don't eavesdrop on my boss and his wife, but I'd be willing to bet Buford and Jeremiah were a main topic. Whatever it was, Oscar is mighty upset and Tinkie was about to cry. No matter you how cut it, Buford is a Richmond, and Oscar feels an obligation toward him."

"What are you doing out of the bank?" I asked. It wasn't part of Harold's normal routine to drive around the countryside during work hours.

"Looking for you. Olive Twist got the okay for the exhumation of the Lady in Red. Judge Colbert abruptly reversed himself. Frances Malone asked me to track you down. She left several messages, but you were out of pocket."

"I can't believe Twist. This is a hornets' nest. Someone threw an incendiary device in her room, and her assistant was poisoned. Yet she won't back off even long enough to let things cool down."

"She's going gangbusters," Harold agreed. "She keeps it up, she'll get herself killed."

"I have to do what I can to protect her." It was certainly

a thankless task, but I couldn't walk away from my duties. The last thing Sunflower County needed was for something bad to happen to Olive. "Where's Dr. Webber?"

Harold shook his head. "Don't know. I heard he checked out of The Gardens. You be careful, Sarah Booth. And you, too, Cece. To someone with good sense, this sounds like a tempest in a teapot, but I gather this whole Lady in Red situation could be a career-maker for Twist and her ilk. Or at least a lot of money. Folks have killed over a lot less. I wouldn't want my favorite journalist and unmarried private eye to get caught between the ambitions of two academics eyeing fat book contracts."

"We'll take care," I promised.

Harold gave a little salute and drove away.

"He still carries a torch for you, Sarah Booth," Cece said.

"Harold will find the love of his life. And so will you."

"I'll talk to Coleman about my brother's activities. Too bad we couldn't grab any of his papers to show the sheriff. I didn't even see a computer."

"I didn't, either. But he has to have one. Anyway, I'd better check in with Tinkie. We need to be in Lexington if they're going forward with the Lady in Red and I'm a little worried about her."

"I can walk to my car at Millie's. Might have to get another piece of that pie to take home for a late-night snack." She pecked my cheek with a kiss. "Call me and let me know that everything is fine and I'll give you a report on what happens with Jeremiah."

"It's a deal."

———

By the time Tinkie and I got to Lexington, the Lady in Red was exhumed and on her way to the state lab for tests. Dead bodies littered my history, but viewing a hundred-year-old corpse didn't headline my idea of fun events. Olive had gotten her way with the body, and she would be intolerable.

Sheriff Peeples had supervised the exhumation and now prowled the Odd Fellows Cemetery's perimeter for wayward spectators or troublemakers, his scowl an opera of disapproval for Olive and us.

Tinkie pinched my arm. "Here she comes, strutting like Tom Turkey in a yard full of hens."

We stood in the center of the Odd Fellows Cemetery in Lexington. The open grave where the Lady in Red had rested was only ten yards away. The earth reminded me of a raw wound.

"Aren't you going to congratulate me?" Olive asked. She wore a white lace blouse with a high neck, long sleeves, and a million tiny buttons. Her black skirt's hem dropped below her calves. Her huge feet were encased in black patent boots that caught the sun and winked as she walked. She had the worst taste in clothing I'd ever seen. Prim and tasteless seemed to be her fashion choices.

"Aren't you about to die of heatstroke?" I asked. "It's got to be ninety-five degrees and you're wearing boots?"

"In the Northeast, we understand fashion. We can't all run around barefoot and pregnant."

One day I would lose my control and smack Olive right in the nose. Tinkie's fists were balled. She, too, felt the need to knock some sense into Olive.

"Neither Tinkie nor I is pregnant," I assured her. "Nor are we barefoot. But when you develop a raging case of athlete's foot from those hot boots and your toes rot off, don't come crying to me."

A slice of doubt moved across her features. "Enough about fashion. Who poisoned Boswell?"

"I'm shocked you noticed he was dead," Tinkie said.

"Don't be silly. I had to make my own coffee this morning and use inferior beans I bought at the Piggly Wiggly. Of course he's dead or he would have served me in bed."

I restrained Tinkie with a touch on her shoulder. Nothing would shake Olive out of her self-involvement. Best not to allow her egotism and prejudice to get under our skins. "You do realize you're still a suspect in his murder?"

"Totally ridiculous. Coleman will never believe I did such a thing. He sees into my heart."

So now he was Coleman to her and he had X-ray vision that penetrated the black nut of her heart. Tinkie's hold on my arm restrained me. "Why didn't you drink coffee yesterday morning? It was *your* special beans, *your* grinder. You don't strike me as the generous type. Why did you forgo coffee?"

"My stomach was upset. I'm very delicate. I was afraid the acid from the coffee would engage my gag reflex. That would have been unpleasant for me, and for Jimmy."

"But you allowed Boswell to drink your coffee?" Tinkie asked. She got right to the heart of Olive's selfishness.

"He'd already brewed it when I woke up. Of course I told him I would deduct the cost of the beans from his pay." Olive sighed. "Just think. I could be dead."

"Don't tempt me," I said under my breath. "So what's on your agenda now?"

"Research. There are church records of the Richmonds, Falcons, and Erkwells. I may find something interesting."

"Search all you want. You won't find a thing." Tinkie was confident. "That woman, whoever she was, is not an ancestor of Oscar or Cece."

"Then your husband wouldn't mind giving me a DNA sample, would he?" Olive was cunning. I had to hand it to her.

"You'll have to ask Oscar yourself."

"I'll do just that. I can be very persuasive with an intelligent man. I wonder if Ms. Falcon would consent. Buford agreed, but now he's reneged. " Perplexion dropped over her features. "If they had nothing to hide, why wouldn't they give a sample?"

Tinkie's jaw clenched so tightly I heard her teeth grind. "Maybe because they view you as an elitist, bigoted bitch?"

"Oh, fiddle-dee-dee. Isn't that what your Southern heroine always said? Look, I've won this round, and I'll win the war. Just like last time."

"Olive, I think you'd best walk away." I had Tinkie by the back of her shirt. If I let loose, she'd fly all over the professor and it wouldn't be pretty.

"You two are so entertaining. It's like watching tadpoles in a mud hole." Olive pivoted and headed out of the cemetery. "Find out who killed Boswell. And figure out what Dr. Webber is up to. He's probably the killer. I suspect he meant to do me in. Now get busy. Chopchop!" She tossed her commands over her shoulder as if Tink and I weren't worth her full attention.

"I am going to kill her," Tinkie vowed. "Before the day is out, most likely."

"She's not worth the lead it would take to plug her."

Tinkie laughed. "The sooner she leaves town, the sooner our collective blood pressure will go down."

I returned to Dahlia House to confront one hungry kitty and one lethargic hound dog. Pluto sat on the front steps, his tail flicking his displeasure at being left without numerous menu choices.

I sat down beside him for a moment to try to make amends. As I stroked his sleek black fur and baby-talked him, he started to purr. I was home—order was restored in his world. He was not a happy puss when both Graf and I were out of the house.

Sweetie came over and I rubbed her long, silky ears. Hounds have the most expressive faces, and Sweetie's showed bliss. The sun was hot on my legs and face, but there was contentment in sitting on the steps, just as I had as a child during the long, late-summer days.

A sudden fantasy of walking into Dahlia House and hearing my mother, busy in the kitchen, took hold of me. She didn't cook all the time, but when she did, it was such a treat. My father and I would eat in the kitchen, sometimes with a couple of their friends. It would be festive and casual and fun.

I was startled out of my fantasy by a golden rope that fell over me and was pulled taut, penning my arms to my sides. "What the—"

"Don't you dare curse." My captor wore a red, blue, and gold formfitting costume. And brother, did she have the form to fit. Enormous, perky ta-tas rose above a nineteen-inch waist and swelling, voluptuous hips. A golden crown rested in dark black hair.

"Diana Prince!" I knew who she was. Wonder Woman! One of my favorite cartoon characters, though she was a sexist creation. Still, she had super strength, super speed, and the ability to make people tell the truth. Now, that would be useful in my current line of work.

The lasso shook free and fell. "I don't need no lasso to see you're pinin' for your mama." Jitty took the form of the Amazon goddess of the comics, but she hadn't bothered to upgrade her accent. She sounded just like Jitty.

"Okay, so you're roaming the halls of the great comic-book heroines. What message are you trying to convey?"

"Sarah Booth, you are one lazy chile. Sittin' here on the porch, moonin' about with a hound and a black cat. Put your thinkin' cap on. What's the story on Diana Prince?" Jitty was all about the lecture and never about giving a simple answer. She struck a pose and light reflected off the silver bands that encased her forearms.

"Let's see." I hadn't thought of Wonder Woman in years, though Jitty's portrayal reminded me that I'd once fantasized about her magnificent superpowers. "She's a princess, the ruler of a tribe of Amazon women. She fights to bring peace to the planet, and she can make people tell the truth with her golden lasso."

"Your brain ain't all turned to mush."

Jitty was never free with a compliment either.

"So, what's shaking in the world of superheroines? And aside from the ass-kicking costume, why Wonder Woman?"

Jitty's response came in the form of another question. "Where is that Olive Oyl person?"

"Dr. Twist is at The Gardens, I presume. Or she might be in Jackson making the state investigator's office a hellhole. She has a knack for bringing stress and discord wherever she appears."

"Forget Twist the twit. You need to find the truth about the Lady in Red, Sarah Booth."

"No kidding." She was pissing me off. "Do you have any suggestions how I might go about that? I don't have a lasso of truth."

"Have you bothered speaking with Oscar?"

"Tinkie's Oscar?" I didn't see the point.

"Maybe he'll tell you what he won't tell Tinkie."

I sat up. I hadn't considered such a thing. "Is Oscar related to the Lady in Red?" I'd never entertained the idea Olive's accusation could be true.

Jitty twirled her lasso.

"Was the Lady in Red involved with Abraham Lincoln?" Jitty could answer if only she would. Almost everyone involved in the wacky case hung out beside Jitty in the Great Beyond. All she had to do was track Honest Abe down and interrogate him.

"You know I can't tell you secrets from the Great Beyond. Why do you keep askin' such things?"

"Because you *could* tell me if you wanted." I didn't care that I sounded spoiled and bratty.

"Rely on yourself, Sarah Booth. That's what your mama would say."

She was right about that. And Wonder Woman would say the same. "I do rely on myself."

"Better get in the kitchen and cook up some vittles for your man."

I stood slowly. Pluto reached up and dug his claws into my kneecaps. I thought I'd dance off the steps backward but managed not to break my neck. "Pluto! What's with you?" When I looked up, Jitty was gone.

I disengaged Pluto's claws and walked toward the kitchen. She was right. I should prepare something fantastic for Graf. Lately, he'd done most of the cooking. I would surprise him with my culinary skills.

"Right!" Jitty's voice echoed around the kitchen.

I whirled around, but there was no evidence of Jitty at all. She just had to have the last word.

Pluto and Sweetie followed me to the cabinets. When I reached for one of my favorite recipe books, a note fell from the pages. I picked it up and discovered my mother's lovely handwriting, a recipe for curried shrimp salad. Perfect for a hot September evening. I had just enough Gulf shrimp in the freezer. And I had a plan!

"Why, Sarah Booth, I had no idea you were an aficionado of the curry." Oscar reached for a third serving of the shrimp salad.

"My mother's recipe." I opened another bottle of the crisp California pinot Graf had brought from the land of oranges, grapes, and movie stars. My intention was to help Oscar to a drunken state. Then, if my questions offended him, he wouldn't remember tomorrow.

Tinkie put down her fork and watched me. Behind her baby blues, her brain was churning. I hadn't told her of my goal—I would never solicit her help in getting her husband drunk—but she was on to me nonetheless. She wasn't my partner because she was slow.

"Have more wine," she urged Oscar.

When I began to clear the table, Graf snatched my hand and pulled me into the dining room. The swinging door closed. "What the hell are you and Tinkie up to?"

I wanted nothing more than to kiss him. I'd had a bit

of wine myself, and my libido was thrumming. I put my hand in his thick hair and twisted my fingers. "We're getting him drunk so I can question him."

"You're not far behind him." Graf's good humor was restored. "Oscar will be hurting tomorrow."

"I know." I was suddenly remorseful. Oscar was a good guy, and I'd plied him with liquor.

"Cheer up. He'll live." Graf took my elbow and led me back into the kitchen. Tinkie arched her eyebrows and I nodded.

"Graf, will you help me find a file in the office?" She kissed Oscar's cheek. "We'll be right back, sweetheart."

I was left alone with Oscar.

"Tinkie is something special," Oscar slurred.

"She is, indeed." I captured his hand on the table and held it firmly, forcing his attention to me. "Oscar, are you related to the Lady in Red?" I asked him outright.

It took a moment for his gaze to latch on to me, but then he looked down at the table. He couldn't hold my gaze and fib. "Don't lie to me, please."

"Maybe." He tried to focus but couldn't. "There are family stories about a young girl with beautiful red hair. She was a Richmond. Tilda Richmond. She was an accomplished woman, especially for those times. Though she couldn't get a degree, she studied law and was more knowledgeable about agriculture than any of her brothers or cousins." His grin was lopsided. "Family legend has it that she was wild as a March hare. Had her own mind about things, and how her future would be. She was like you, Sarah Booth, kicking against conventions."

"What happened to her?"

Oscar reached for his wineglass but then pushed it away. He was toasted, but he wasn't wallowing drunk.

"She ran away when she was sixteen. She never came back to Zinnia, at least not that anyone knew."

"Do you think she's the Lady in Red?" I asked.

He tried to stand but sank back in the chair. "In 1969, when that backhoe dug her up, the question was raised. Judging by the perfectly preserved corpse, she would have been about Tilda's age, according to family records. The whole thing was so peculiar. If you remember, the late sixties were a time of great stress in Mississippi. My family chose not to pursue the question of the Lady in Red. But she's haunted the Richmond family. If she was a Richmond, and my family knew of her and didn't bring her home because they disapproved of her lifestyle or her political beliefs, then I'm deeply ashamed."

The poignancy of that touched me. If the Lady in Red was indeed Tilda Richmond, she'd been so close to home, yet she couldn't make it. She'd died a few counties away from her family and those who had once loved her.

"Do you know any more of her story?"

Oscar was closer to sober than I'd assumed, and still willing to answer the question. "The family story goes like this. Her father had arranged a betrothal for her to a planter's son. It was a very wealthy family from Virginia that had established a huge plantation here in Mississippi. Tilda would have been well taken care of and held a position in society."

"But she didn't love him." This story was old and familiar. Why did parents never learn? Security and position meant nothing to a young girl who'd always had everything she ever wanted. She'd never experienced life's harshness. She'd been loved—and she wanted the same devotion from her husband. Not a business contract.

"She couldn't know if she loved him or not. She never

met him," Oscar continued. "She never gave him a chance. When she heard he was coming to visit and meet her, she ran. Sixteen years old and alone. She took a few of her clothes and her horse and rode out during a March storm. She was never seen again. There was talk she made it to Washington, D.C., but there were also stories she opened a saloon in Tombstone. Any or none of it could be true."

"Could Olive Twist's hypothesis that she was Lincoln's lover be true?"

Oscar blew out his breath. "She was wild. And she believed she should be free to make her own choices. She felt the same way about the slaves. She was an outspoken abolitionist at a time when such talk often resulted in death."

I let these new facts sink in. "Was she murdered?"

"I don't know. And I'm not certain the woman in the grave is Tilda Richmond, my great-great-great-grandfather's sister. All I know is that Tilda left Mississippi when she was sixteen. She never came home."

"She never sent a letter or anything?" That would have been hard on her parents, even if she'd disappointed them. They would have craved to know she was safe.

Oscar contemplated his answer. "Gossip got back to the family. There was talk she had gained President Lincoln's favor. She would have been in her late twenties, and from the only photograph I saw of her, she was a true beauty. Part of the family legend is that she became a madam in the capital. But that's as substantial as the Old West stories."

"Holy shit." Olive Twist had been striking at the right nail. If she published these revelations, she'd cause a scandal for Oscar and the Richmond family. But only a minor scandal. So, a Richmond had been an abolitionist and slept with Lincoln. Not such a big deal. But if she'd conspired to assassinate Lincoln, that was something else.

"I've thought repeatedly of digging up the grave and having a DNA test." Oscar waited for me to react.

My shock gratified his expectation. "Really? Will you submit a DNA sample to Olive?"

"Absolutely not. It's one thing to deal with family issues privately. I won't pander to her need for material for a book. And neither will that moron Buford. I've heard she's offered money if he will and I put a stop to that."

I didn't really blame Oscar. Knowing was one thing. Having the world know was something else. "Would Tilda have come back home and gone to Egypt Plantation instead of Zinnia?"

"I can't say. What was there at Egypt Plantation? Maybe someone who believed in what she was doing. Another abolitionist, or perhaps a lover. I've thought perhaps she came on a riverboat from New Orleans, based on the fancy dress she wore."

"You think it's Tilda, don't you?"

"I think there's a good probability. She was a true beauty, Sarah Booth. There's a photo of that corpse in the family Bible. Why else would it be there? But I don't want to give her over to Twist. That woman has no soul. I don't want Tilda painted as a whore or an abolitionist or a murderess. I want her to rest in peace."

"What can you do about Buford?"

"I intend to have him committed to a private mental institution. Cece spoke with me about what he and Jeremiah have been up to. I've made arrangements at Cold Springs Mental Hospital. I'm paying for both of them, if

Cece can get Jeremiah in there to dry out. They need to be locked up before they hurt themselves or someone else. I'm afraid they'll either sell out to Twist or kill her. They're both so volatile it could go either way."

That was a pretty drastic step, but I understood Oscar's impulses. If they were under medical care, Olive couldn't work on them and they couldn't hurt her or anyone else. It wasn't a bad plan—on the face of it. I didn't know the legal machinations for getting a relative committed, but I was fairly certain neither Buford nor Jeremiah would go voluntarily. Besides, while Buford tipped the sauce too frequently and too much, I wasn't certain alcohol was Jeremiah's issue. I got the sense he had bought into the baseline meanness of the Evergreen Tree group. He did feel superior to women, especially Cece, and so many other elements of society.

My immediate problem was Tinkie and her husband. "You need to tell all of this to Tinkie. She knows something is wrong and she's worried about you."

"I will," he said. "Tonight. When we get home. It's funny, but I think about this and it happened such a long time ago, none of it should matter now. It's gone and done. But I can't let it go. Tinkie deserves to know why I've been so preoccupied."

"One more thing, Oscar. Did you meet with Jimmy Boswell the night before he died?"

He paled but recovered quickly. "Who told you that?"

"Tinkie. She found a note in your pocket. She assumed it was from Boswell. Asking to meet."

"He slipped the note in my pocket the night of the Molotov cocktail in Twist's room. I agreed to meet him at a little park on the other side of town. He didn't have a vehicle, so we picked a place he could walk to. He never showed up. I figured Twist caught on to his scheme and chained him in the room."

"Or possibly poisoned him." I really hadn't taken Olive seriously as a potential killer. Maybe I needed to change my attitude.

I had other questions, and a warning for him to be honest with his wife, but I had no chance to twist his arm, because Tinkie and Graf returned.

Oscar planted a sloppy grin on his face and the evening continued.

9

The morning sun slanted through the bedroom window, chasing the predawn gray into the corners. Consciousness brought a mile-long list of things I needed to do, but Graf was too much temptation to leave all alone in bed. For a few minutes, I watched him sleep. Pluto curled into his chest, his little black kitty paws making biscuits against the dark hair. Sweetie's soft snores waffled from the floor beside the bed. There was not another thing in the world I needed. I whispered a thank-you for the wonderful life I'd somehow managed to acquire.

I'd lost so many people I loved. Jitty wasn't the only spirit moving through the hallways of Dahlia House. My parents, Aunt Loulane, a host of Delaney relatives who'd loved this land. While I couldn't see them and talk to them like I could Jitty, I knew they were never far. But Graf was flesh and bone, a man who stirred my blood just looking at him. How had I ever gotten so lucky?

My finger traced his jaw. The dark shadow of beard gave him a roguish look. He was perfect for the role of a private dick in the movie *Delta Blues*. I wanted the chance to act opposite him, to complete that part of our life.

And I wanted a lot more.

I put my left hand on his shoulder and the morning sun sparked off my beautiful engagement ring. Graf had pushed me to set a wedding date, but I was reluctant to marry at Dahlia House. I didn't consider myself a morbid person, but holding the ceremony here would only accentuate all the people who weren't around to bless the union.

Ireland. That's where I wanted to get hitched. Maybe a nice horseback ride up the western coast and a ceremony in an old church. Something casual with a small group of those close to me. The drawback involved my friends. Not everyone could just drop everything and haul butt to Ireland. So it would have to be a planned trip arranged around schedules and responsibilities.

Sweetie's cold nose poked my back as if she'd read my thoughts and wanted to say, "Hey, you can't leave me behind." I gave her the petting she craved and when I glanced back at Graf, he was also looking at me.

"What's on your mind?" he asked.

"Wedding plans."

His grin melted my heart.

"We don't have to wait for a ceremony to celebrate." I leaned into him with a kiss, and he pulled me against him.

Pluto gave a growl of protest and a big hiss before he vacated the bed.

When I finally stretched and decided I had to feed the horses, Graf had fallen back to sleep. I left him snoozing and slipped into shorts and tennis shoes to do my barn chores.

A breeze lifted my brown curls off my shoulders. Before anyone could say "Jack Spratt" it would be Christmas. Time rushed by. It was a quantum physics question—why did time flee when one was happy and drag when one was sad? The answer had something to do with perception, but I didn't want to try and figure it out.

The horses cantered to the barn the minute they saw me. Reveler gave a corkscrew buck just to let me know I was late with his chow. While they ate, I groomed them. Lucifer had settled into my herd without a problem. When the Natchez sisters who'd owned him were sent to prison, his care had fallen to me. It became less and less likely I'd try to re-home him. He was here at Dahlia House to stay. Graf adored riding him, and so did I. And Miss Scrapiron had two boyfriends to tease and torment. Life was good for her, too.

The horses finished eating, and I turned them out, then went in and made Aunt Loulane's cathead biscuit recipe. While they baked, I took a shower and got ready for the day. I wasn't exactly eager to start, but it had to be done. The fact that it was nine o'clock and Tinkie wasn't beating the door down told me Oscar had filled her in about Tilda Richmond and the possible link to the Lady in Red.

Tinkie wasn't the kind of person who let the past define her, but Tilda's story was a sad one. It would hurt her heart, and she would also feel Oscar's pain. That his ancestral aunt might have been a madam in a brothel, whether in D.C. or the Wild West, was no big deal. That she'd been Lincoln's lover—in the Old South view that would be sleeping with the enemy, literally—also had no sting in this day and time.

If Tilda had been involved in assassinating a president—that was a mark of shame, especially if she used sex as a tool to get close to Lincoln, only to betray him. Those tactics were dishonorable. Somehow, though, none of this possible historical scandal coalesced into a motive for murder. Olive might kill if she felt betrayed. And the Heritage Heroes would stoop to throwing tomatoes and trying to run Olive out of town. But murder? Now, money—that was a good motive for murder. And if Olive's boasts of financial gain to be made from her "research and book" could be believed, I had a lead worth pursuing.

I took a tray of biscuits, sausage, sawmill gravy, and fresh, hot coffee upstairs to my fiancé. To earn his rakish grin, I would have hoed a row of cotton.

"Where are you off to?" he asked, savoring the aroma of the coffee.

"To find Dr. Webber. I think it's time I had a sit-down with him alone. If he knows something definitive about the Lady in Red, I need to know what it is."

"He's a handsome man." Graf pretended to pout.

"And he can't hold a candle to you." I leaned down and kissed him long and deep. "Wait here for me. I'll be back."

The day promised plenty of sun, and I let the top down on my mother's old Chinese red Mercedes roadster and took off for Ole Miss.

To the north and east of Zinnia, the Mississippi terrain changes radically. The flat stretches of the alluvial delta buck up in small hills. The change is sudden and dramatic, and the hills rise up on the horizon like a wall of green. While I loved the delta, I also appreciated the different topography of the state.

Zinnia is a small farming town, and Oxford is an upscale college town. They might have developed on separate planets. Oxford is the home of the University of Mississippi, or Ole Miss as it is fondly called. It is also the home of William Faulkner, a man whose employment in the postal service sometimes led him to burn the mail rather than deliver it. Faulkner's stated attitude—just because a man had the money to mail a letter didn't mean he had anything worthwhile to say—appealed to me.

Whether the story was true or not, I enjoyed it. And I applauded his ingenuity.

I drove to the Ole Miss campus and parked in the shadiest place I could find. The campus was beautiful, but the asphalt lot was at least ninety-eight degrees. The walk to the history department left me sweaty and breathless. I could only hope that, after all this effort, Richard Webber would be in his office. I hadn't tried to make an appointment—I was afraid he'd dodge me if he knew I was coming.

The secretary gave me a knowing look when I asked where to find the professor. I wondered how many women had tried to track down the wily historian. I probably couldn't count that high. As far as I knew, he'd never been married.

After following a rat's maze of narrow corridors, at last I knocked on his closed door.

"Who is it?" an annoyed voice asked.

"Sarah Booth Delaney."

Rustling and the sound of furniture moving put me to wondering if he was barricading the door. It swung open as he shrugged into his jacket. Seersucker and very Southern male. He cultivated a distinct image—distinguished, bookish, a bit disheveled, and manly.

"Ms. Delaney," he said, inviting me in with a crook of his finger. "Come in. And close the door."

His office reflected his persona. Dark bookcases were filled with leather-bound volumes. A beautiful old globe gleamed in sunlight flooding in from two windows with plantation blinds half closed. There was an air of studiousness and intelligence in the room.

He pointed to a sofa, motioning for me to sit. A big leather sofa. I looked at it, and I looked at him. He clearly read my thoughts, and his grin widened.

"What can I do for you?" he asked.

"Tell me about the Lady in Red and your research."

"I like a direct woman." He rolled his office chair close. I caught a whiff of cologne. Something Calvin. He crossed his legs, ankle on knee, the picture of casual ease. "I hear Dr. Twist got her exhumation."

"She did."

"Folks are mighty pissed, I'm sure." And he was mighty pleased.

"That's old news. You accused Olive of stealing your research. How did she do it?"

He went to a filing cabinet, dug through some files, and brought out *The Aggregate of Past Events* magazine. He found the article he wanted and handed it to me.

The headline read: "Mississippi Grave Holds Secrets to Civil War."

I scanned the article, which pretty much put forth the same hypothesis Olive espoused—that the Lady in Red was Lincoln's mistress during the thick of the Civil War. I wanted a copy of the article for Tinkie to read. "But you published it, Dr. Webber. It's public knowledge. Olive didn't steal it if you put it out there."

His face held pity and contempt. "There's a code of honor among academics. Hell, among journalists and scientists and even novelists. When a colleague is working on a premise, others stay away. It's an unwritten rule. Once a claim is staked, it's forbidden for a peer to jump the claim. Everyone abides by this. Except Olive. She's a vulture picking the bones of any scholar with an original thought because she has none of her own."

"I didn't see a connection between the Lady in Red and local Sunflower County families in your article."

He harrumphed. "I didn't include them because I intended to work with the Richmond and Falcon families. Their cooperation would have streamlined my research. That was to be phase two of my work."

So, he meant to deceive Oscar and Cece into helping him and then lower the boom on them in print. Nice.

"So how did Olive find out about local connections? I mean, the Lady in Red could have been anybody. And still could. There was a Tilda Richmond, but there's no proof she's the woman Olive exhumed."

"I made the connection. I heard the story of this red-haired firebrand who swept into Washington and was accepted into the inner circle of political figures. A woman. At a time when women weren't given credit for thinking. Olive called to congratulate me on the article in the *Aggregate*. We chatted for a long time, and I was lulled into complacency. I mentioned the local connection."

The fuzzy picture sharpened. Webber was blowing hard about his project and had let too much slip. Olive jumped on it. "When you were talking with her, were you aware of her interest in the Lady in Red?"

"Academia is a small world. I've been familiar with Dr. Twist for a time. She told me she was researching slavery in the Northeast. Something about the power of the female slave in nonagricultural households. Turns out that was just a smoke screen. Twist knows damn good and well her entire premise is built on my research. She's poached my work and now she's stolen the body right out of the cemetery."

I wasn't familiar enough with academic standards to know if Webber had a legitimate legal claim or was just whining. But I would be pissed if I was working on a case and another private dick jumped into the middle of it.

"What do you know about Twist?" I'd read her CV and several articles she'd written. None of it had impressed me, but she worked in a different world.

"She's a carnivore. She eats historians for breakfast and picks her teeth with their bones. She's hated at her hoity-toity university. When she showed up down here, I made a few calls. Let's just say none of her colleagues would cry if she disappeared."

I was enjoying this academic boil-busting. It almost made me like Olive. Almost, but not quite.

"Is she a respected academic?"

"A long time ago she wrote a paper focusing on the journals of New England women during the Civil War. It was very well received, uncovering new material about the way small communities worked together while the men were at war. The details were remarkable." He frowned. "I wonder whom she stole that from?" His eyes widened. "She could have made it all up!"

"Is there a formal method to complain about what she's done?"

"None that would make a difference, I'm afraid."

"You have a motive for murder, Dr. Webber." Certainly he knew this already.

"You're right. I might have gleefully offed Twist, but I had nothing against Boswell." He draped an arm over his chair back. "I told you Boswell came to me, begging for a job. Olive treated him like an indentured servant, which is pretty ironic since she's trying to paint the Richmond and Falcon families as slaveholders who killed a relative because she supported freedom for the slaves."

"Olive thinks the Lady in Red was murdered by her own family because she was an abolitionist? But I thought she was an assassin of the South's number one enemy."

"The problem of working with legends and folklore, Ms. Delaney, is that truth is distorted by family interest. The woman—Tilda Richmond, if Olive's estimations are correct—was viewed as a traitor and a whore. Olive intends to prove the Richmond and Falcon families conspired to poison her and bury her in a grave where she'd never be found."

"But that doesn't make any sense. She was lovingly interred. The coffin was handmade to fit her. If her relatives had murdered her, wouldn't they have just dragged her into a cotton field and buried her?"

Webber leaned back and resumed in his most professorial tone. "Olive's theory is that the families were forced into the murder. Remember, my dear, the war had destroyed the South. Brother fought against brother. Families were betrayed by loved ones. If Tilda Richmond was Lincoln's lover, she would have been viewed as the ultimate whore and turncoat. If she came back to

Mississippi, then she would have been considered a spy. The Richmonds and Falcons likely *had* to kill her, or else they would be suspect, too. And I hate to say it, but if Olive can verify this, she's going to have a runaway bestseller on her hands. I don't know where she found Secretary of War Stanton's private letters, but if they can be authenticated, this will propel Twist into national prominence."

I didn't care about Twist's future. "So you're pretty much saying the entire county was in on the murder of a young woman—because she didn't agree with their politics."

"Well, if you put it that way, yes. Community pressure. Think of it, Ms. Delaney. The South had lost everything. Every family contributed a father, husband, or brother. Some lost multiple family members. The women and children were starving, their homes and crops burned to the ground. People have this idea that war is honorable, but don't believe it for a minute. Women with infants were left to starve. It would have been kinder to put a bullet in their brains." Webber waxed eloquent.

"Everyone suffered. No one disputes that. But to think people would be bullied into killing a family member because her politics were embarrassing, that's just plain nuts." Jeremiah popped into my mind and with him came a dawning awareness. It wasn't such a stretch to consider Cece putting him in an unmarked grave. Luckily Webber couldn't read my mind.

"By our standards today, perhaps. But put yourself in a country torn apart by a bloody war that was fought to preserve a way of life in the South. Whether the cause was right or wrong, the men who fought gave everything. To find a viper at their own breast . . . it would have been unthinkable. It's possible everyone in the Richmond and Falcon families would have been hanged as traitors. I presume the families did the only thing they could do for survival."

"How are both families involved? I mean, she was either a Richmond or a Falcon. Why does Olive want to involve both Sunflower County families?"

His smile was smug. "I've done a little research myself in the last few days. There's a common factor between them. Tilda Richmond—and I am certain the Lady in Red was a Richmond—was betrothed to a Falcon. She ran away from home rather than marry him. He was humiliated, especially in light of the fact that she took Abe Lincoln as her lover. And just think how delicious—if she was an assassin, she couldn't confess that and save herself. Either way, she was doomed."

My head was already swimming in boys in gray and blue uniforms doing their best to kill each other. "This is too much."

"In a very roundabout way, it makes perfect sense. Olive believes a member of both families was involved in Tilda Richmond's murder and secret burial. A Falcon, because of the rejection of marriage, and a Richmond, to save the family's honor, and possibly lives."

"This gets worse and worse."

"From your perspective, but not from that of a historian."

"The past aside, my concern is the murder of a young man. One who had no dog in this fight. Boswell had nothing to gain, yet he's dead."

"Boswell wasn't an innocent. I told you about the tapes he made of Olive." Webber rolled his eyes. "He's got her dead to rights, and those tapes, released at the right time, could have torpedoed a book deal. They cast doubt on her credibility and her sanity."

"Did Boswell show you the tapes he mentioned? Do you have any evidence they existed?"

"Unfortunately, he was murdered before he could show them to me."

I stood up. "Where were you the night before Boswell died?"

"You know very well I was at The Gardens B and B. Just as you were. And your partner, and Twist, and about twenty other people. I heard Olive's room was fire-bombed. Find any fingerprints?"

"The investigation moves forward. That's all I can say." I didn't want to admit that every lead had been a dead end so far.

"Which means you've got zilch. If I were truly a suspect, Sheriff Peters would have me behind bars." His teeth sparkled white. "You're here on a fishing expedition." He leaned closer. "And you haven't gotten so much as a bite."

He might get a punch in the nose. He grated on my last nerve.

"Oh, this trip hasn't been a total waste of my time." I gave him my sly and superior expression. "You reveal a lot more than you realize, Dr. Webber." I decided to give him the pretend-psychic treatment. "You're attracted to Olive, yet she doesn't reciprocate. That's why you excoriate her conduct. You accuse her of stealing what you've put out for public consumption, which tells me you're jealous of the fact she took this thread farther than you thought to do. You're used to opening doors with your charm, and right now it isn't working for you. You've been left without another play."

Heat jumped into his cheeks, but he held on to his smile. I had to give him credit for that. "Always an interesting tactic, Ms. Delaney. Attack on a personal level when you have nothing else."

"One you're all too familiar with, I see." I walked to the door. "My visit was unofficial. I wonder how the board of trustees of the university will react when Coleman comes a'calling."

Before he could answer, I walked out the door and closed it behind me. I felt the secretary's gaze drilling into my spine.

She looked down at her desk, pretending she hadn't been staring. I knew better. "Mrs. Blackmon," I said, reading the nameplate on her desk, "do you file travel vouchers for the professors?"

"I do." Her fingers flew over the keyboard to show she was too busy to chat.

"May I see those for Dr. Webber?"

"I can't release that data." She stopped typing. "Even if I'd like to."

"Thanks." I hadn't seen his expense sheets, but I'd discovered something else. The history department secretary was not a fan of the professor.

Tinkie was waiting for me on the porch at Dahlia House when I got home. She was sipping a bourbon, neat, when I climbed the steps. This was not the proper drink for a Daddy's Girl on a hot September afternoon. It was a declaration of intent to tie one on.

"You're violating Rule 3,394 of the Daddy's Girl Handbook." I hoped to squeeze a laugh out of her.

"I'm sure I'll break a lot more rules before Olive Twist leaves town. Dead or alive." She tossed back the bourbon and clapped the highball glass to the wood floor.

"What's going on?" I asked as I settled down beside her. I gazed out over the fields we both loved. Tinkie was on the edge of either a temper tantrum or a crying jag. I hoped for the former because the latter made me feel helpless.

"Oscar is in a snit," she said. "Coleman came and talked to him about the note Jimmy Boswell slipped in his pocket."

"And?"

"They went in the library and closed the door so I couldn't hear. After the sheriff left, Oscar wouldn't talk about it."

"Coleman doesn't seriously think Oscar had anything to do with Boswell's poisoning?"

Tinkie's lower lip protruded slightly. It wasn't a pout, which indicated the dreaded tears were a distinct possibility. "Oscar refuses to say anything. It must be bad."

I'd warned the big nudnik about holding out on Tinkie. His wife wouldn't judge him on events from two centuries ago. He was a fool not to confide his worries to her. "I talked with Webber. He believes members of the Richmond and Falcon families murdered the Lady in Red. Family honor and survival."

"You paint them like the mafia."

She wasn't far off the mark. "According to Webber, Tilda Richmond, whether she is the Lady in Red or not, was betrothed to a Falcon."

Tinkie's eyes widened. "And she dumped him?"

"Yep. I guess she didn't read the Daddy's Girl Handbook."

Tinkie swatted my arm, but her enthusiasm was restored. I bumped her shoulder with mine. "And what about you? How are you?"

"I can understand why Oscar would want to leave this bit of family history behind. Those awful men who kill their daughters if they defy tradition . . . it's a form of the basest ignorance. No one wants that personal history, but blood isn't destiny or identity. Speaking of which, the DNA results on the Lady in Red should be back soon."

"Olive must have paid a pretty penny for such a fast track."

"Obviously she thinks it'll pay out big. It was bad enough listening to her bestseller brags. Now she's moved on to movie options. She thinks Keira Knightley should play her." Tinkie swung her legs like a kid. I realized she was wearing cutoff jeans, tennis shoes, and a tank top—far more my wardrobe choices than her normal polished style.

"Frances Malone called me, too." Tinkie sat up straighter. "She's bonding Jeremiah and Buford out of jail."

"Oh for heaven's sake. They'll go after Olive."

"That's exactly what she's hoping." She bit her bottom lip. "There's a bloodthirsty streak in Frances I never suspected. She really wants Olive gone—or dead. She said if she'd never come here, none of this would be happening. I'm tired of this stupidity. I want Olive to leave town and everyone to stop hurting each other. Jeremiah and Buford are capable of tragic stupidity."

"Can Oscar stop Buford's release?"

"He tried. Too late. They were only charged with creating a public disturbance. Oscar didn't have time to get a judge to rule on sending them to an institution. Now they've gone underground. Cece talked to Coleman about arresting them on spewing hate, but he can't. Not until they do something in Sunflower County, and it has to be something more than flinging a few tomatoes."

I stood and gave her my hand to pull up. She rose to her feet, glass in hand. We walked into the cool foyer of Dahlia House, our footsteps echoing. The house was empty.

"Where's Graf?" I asked.

"I haven't seen him. I went in and mixed a drink, but I figured he was with you."

"Let's head to the office and see what we can determine about who Jimmy Boswell really was. If he offered compromising video to Webber and then tried to sell information to Oscar, he might be more than just a mistreated research assistant."

Tinkie linked her arm through mine. "There are days, Sarah Booth, you surprise me with your intelligence." The ghost of a grin touched her lips. "Then other days I realize your brain is sound asleep."

10

We hit a hot trail on Jimmy Boswell. Internet research led us to an unexpected revelation. And Tinkie's phone work yielded even more strange fruit. The shadowy Boswell we uncovered was as different from Olive's subservient research assistant as Jekyll was from Hyde.

And it all went back to the War Between the States.

The Boswell family history held every dark secret. "Some of his Boswell ancestors died during the siege of Vicksburg," I told Tinkie, scanning a document I'd stumbled on. "Adrian Boswell was a prominent merchant in Vicksburg, Mississippi, who imported antiques and fine china from Europe through the port of New Orleans and up the Mississippi River." I read aloud.

"Union gunboats closed off the river, stopping all

supplies, and Union forces surrounded the city, closing overland supply routes, so the residents of Vicksburg dug caves in the bluffs and moved furniture there to escape the constant shelling. Horses, dogs, and cats disappeared, and finally residents were forced to eat rats and boiled shoe leather."

Tinkie sat on the edge of my desk. "I hope we never have to endure anything like that, Sarah Booth. I don't think I'm tough enough to last."

"I know." Talk of war always depressed me. Jitty didn't often tell about the difficult times she'd been through— she was much more focused on the here and now and how she could torment me. The stories she'd recounted, though, were a testament to the strength of spirit of the survivors, on both sides.

Of all the Civil War battles, Vicksburg headed the list of horrific. A city under siege creates a lot of suffering. Vicksburg's citizens held out under extreme conditions, and all told, some twenty thousand people from both sides died.

"Can the history lesson," Tinkie said. "What happened to Adrian Boswell?"

"This is unauthenticated information." I wanted to be clear the tidbits I'd uncovered could have been posted by anyone, including Jimmy Boswell.

"Stop acting like you're on a witness stand. All I'm asking is what you found." Tinkie was easily exasperated today, a sure sign of stress in her marriage.

"Adrian Boswell was allegedly hanged by Union soldiers *after* the city surrendered. The Union soldiers were court-martialed, but it didn't undo the lynching."

A furrow appeared between her eyebrows. "That's disgusting. Does it say why he was hanged?"

"He called the Union soldiers cowards, and he slapped one. Adrian was weakened from hunger and crazy with grief. His wife and daughter died of dysentery during the siege. He couldn't find adequate food for them and they died in his arms." It was a bleak bit of history. "The soldiers he accosted found a rope and hanged him from an oak tree near the riverfront."

"So why would Boswell work for Twist, especially on this project where he would be confronted with the war and all the sadness involved?"

I put my hands on my hips and waited for her to arrive at the same place I stood.

She jumped to her feet and mimicked my pose. "Because he intended all along to thwart her research?"

"It's possible. I mean, he was setting up meetings with Oscar and trying to sell embarrassing videos of Olive to Webber. It would appear he was intent on ruining her."

"If she found out, she'd have ample cause to kill him."

"Exactly." We'd officially landed on the same page.

My view of Boswell had changed, which forced me to reevaluate Olive's possible motives. He wasn't the innocent victim of his employer, at least not completely. He'd joined Twist willingly and tolerated her abusive superiority, and now I believed he had an ulterior motive.

And we had evidence, or at least gossip. If Webber could be believed, Boswell was the asp clutched to Olive's bosom. Had she discovered his intention to ruin her, she really might have murdered him.

"So, we may have given some credibility to the theory that our client is a murderer. That wasn't what we were paid to do." Tinkie shifted her head left to right to loosen her neck. "In fact, we haven't been paid anything to clear Olive."

"Which is why we're behind the curve here. She keeps *forgetting* our check."

Tinkie's biggest interest wasn't money. "Do you think Dr. Webber was involved in Olive finding out Boswell was against her?" Tinkie had taken the supposition to the next level.

"I wouldn't put it past him. Will we ever be able to prove it?" I shrugged. "Probably not. What did you find out?" She'd been yakking like a magpie on the phone.

"Boswell was an exemplary graduate student at Camelton College and earned his master's in English last year. He went directly into Olive's employ. I spoke with some of his former classmates, and they said he was a loner. Most thought he was simply introspective, but his former roommate said Boswell was 'the type to climb a bell tower and take out students and faculty.' "

I'd seen nothing of that nature in the young man. But someone who could plot to destroy Twist's credibility and take the abuse she heaped on him without complaint and with seeming subservience was a master actor. "Did anyone corroborate that view of Boswell?"

"Not so strongly. He was engaged to a young woman when he started graduate school, but he broke it off. She was bitter about it, but she said Jimmy was struggling with his own demons."

I cringed inwardly at the thought of what my past lovers might say about me. Perhaps an ex-fiancée wasn't the most reliable character reference. "Anyone else?"

She withered me with a glare. "I spoke with three of his teachers. He was highly regarded intellectually, though each one said he was reserved and quiet. None characterized him as aggressive or vindictive or especially motivated. High marks came easily to him, and he didn't take on extra work for the pleasure of learning."

"So what's your conclusion?"

Tinkie hesitated. "This is gut, Sarah Booth. I think Boswell went to that particular school to meet Dr. Twist. I think he intended to ruin her, if he could."

"But Boswell had no idea Twist would write about Mississippi history. She could have gone in the direction of Native American burial grounds or seafaring tales from the Northeast. We need to look up Olive's prior publications and see where her former interests lay." I wanted to be logical, not emotional.

"You're the one at the computer and you're wasting time."

Leave it to Tinkie to batter me with the bludgeon of reality. I started tracking Olive's academic career. Top of the list was her journal article on the impact of the Civil War on the women of the Northeast. Many lost their men as more and more soldiers were poured into the war machine, and then their slaves were freed by the Emancipation Proclamation.

Farmers in the Northeast faced the same problems as those in the South. Without slave labor, there was no one to harvest the crops. While the farms weren't as vast as the thousands of acres in the Deep South, the work was still labor-intensive and required hard, long hours when crops were ready.

"I wasn't aware there were so many slave owners north of the Mason-Dixon Line," Tinkie said, reading over my shoulder.

"History is written by the victors." I clapped my hand over my mouth in horror. I truly was beginning to sound like my aunt Loulane. Not that she wasn't a wonderful woman, but she was old and given to spouting platitudes around the clock.

"This article was written five years ago. Doesn't she have anything fresh or new?" Tinkie was a bulldog when she got her teeth into something.

I typed in more search terms. Pretty soon I had a comprehensive list of Dr. Olive Twist's publishing history. Her latest articles focused on issues regarding the South. I read over the titles, which was hard to do with Tinkie standing behind me giving a running commentary.

"Why, that witch! Would you look at that! 'The Southern Male and the Umbilical Cord: How Peter Pan Lives in the Modern South.'" She spun me around to face her. "Is that history or psychology or hoo-ha?"

"Hoo-ha?" I guessed.

"Really, Sarah Booth, there's a note of contempt for the South in everything she says and does. Our men are no more tied to the umbilical cord than other men."

I looked everywhere except at her. Our view differed.

"I really can't work for her, even if she comes up with the money. Which I doubt she will," Tinkie continued. "You'll have to handle this yourself."

I considered it. "Nope. We're a team. If you can't do it, I'll resign. I don't like her, either."

"Coleman's job is to find Boswell's killer. So far, we haven't come close to proving Twist is innocent. I don't want to work for a person who so obviously dislikes my home."

We'd worked for former ballerinas, faith healers, murdering twins, and actresses gone bad, but Tinkie drew the line at geographical bigots. I couldn't help but smile.

"It isn't funny, Sarah Booth. Her arrogance and

condescension make me want to pop her upside the head."

This time I laughed. Tinkie didn't "pop" people "upside the head." I wondered how the phrase had even infiltrated her vocabulary. "I'm not arguing. But it's interesting Boswell may have selected Olive as his boss so he could keep an eye on her research."

"This is really far-fetched. You saw the way she treated him. He would seek that out?"

"This whole thing is bizarre." I had to agree. "If we aren't in Olive's employ, should we alert Coleman to this information?"

"I'd hold off, at least for right now. Oh, there was something else."

She always saved the best for last, dang her. "Well?"

"Boswell's old roommate said that Boswell had a connection in Mississippi. As in a family connection."

"Right. Adrian Boswell, the Vicksburg merchant who was hanged."

"No, someone else. He said it was a beautiful woman who'd been murdered and buried on a plantation."

The skin on my arms stood at attention and marched. "The Lady in Red? Boswell meant he was related to her?"

"The roommate didn't know who or what. He said Boswell made several references to his personal Annabelle Lee. Like from the Poe poem, a woman shut away from love who died and was put in a sepulcher."

"This is getting creepy." The web cast by the Lady in Red was drawing tighter and more complex. For an anonymous woman buried in an anonymous grave for over one hundred fifty years, she was certainly having an impact on my world.

High heels tapped their way toward us. Someone had

come in the front door. Unless it was Jitty, ready to reveal herself to Tinkie, which I didn't think was the case, we had a visitor.

Peeking around the corner of the music room, I saw a vision in a teal and yellow sundress and high-heeled sandals. Cece Dee Falcon had arrived.

"What's the word on the DNA from the corpse?" she asked, running her perfectly manicured fingers through her hair. The gesture told me that though she looked cool and unworried, her gut was in a knot.

"We haven't heard anything," I said. "And likely we won't. We're quitting. Well, we can't quit because we've never been officially hired. No contract signed, no cash changing hands."

Cece dropped her purse on my desk. "You can't quit. You can't. How else will we know what the enemy is up to?"

Good point, but I wasn't a spy. "Sorry. Tinkie thinks Olive's a bigot and I think she's a bitch. We can't work for her."

"You *have* to work for her." Cece blinked rapidly, and I realized she was about to cry.

"What's wrong?" I seated her at my desk. "What in the world is going on?"

"Jeremiah and Buford are out of prison. Jeremiah called me, furious. That oaf of a man who saw us in the house told him I was in there, poking through his business. He's going to press trespassing charges. Against both of us."

I wanted to use a very emphatic Anglo-Saxon curse word, but I restrained myself. Jeremiah was an idiot. He could charge me with ten million counts of trespassing, but he could not hurt my friend again.

"I'll take care of Jeremiah," I seethed.

"If Jeremiah presses charges, Sarah Booth, *you* might be in the calaboose." Tinkie's little foot tapped like a dancer on speed. "Have you asked him to drop this matter, Cece?"

"That's another job perfect for you." Cece had reclaimed her élan. "I don't have time for the rabble." She fought hard for that arch tone. "And you'll get a lot more out of him than I ever will. Remind him that once upon a time he was sweet on Sarah Booth."

Her words stopped me dead in my tracks. "Jeremiah?" He was working for Chemron Fertilizers when I was still in high school. He was brilliant, and handsome. Cecil was his pesky kid brother and we were Cecil's pesky teenage friends. Yet I remember him standing in the doorway, watching us as we played cards, or danced to the popular songs of high school. He'd been entertained by our antics, for sure. But was there something more in his presence?

"It's true," Tinkie said, awareness dawning. "He had a crush on you, but because he was so much older, it was inappropriate."

"I was sixteen and he was, what, thirty?" A flash of Jeremiah hit me hard. Once I'd gone upstairs to get something from Cecil's room. Jeremiah was in the hallway. He was visiting his parents over Christmas, on leave from his job at Chemron's French headquarters. Mrs. Falcon had a photo gallery of her accomplished son working at sites around the globe.

"Why, if it isn't Miss Sarah Booth Delaney." Jeremiah wore a black turtleneck and black pants, and his long, dark blond hair fell across one eye. I'd been terribly intimidated by him, but boldly tried to speak my smattering of high school French.

And he was kind. He bowed over my hand and kissed it and told me I was beautiful in perfect French.

The memory must have shown clearly on my face.

"Oh, you little Lolita," Tinkie teased.

"Sarah Booth, did you break my brother's heart?" Cece asked.

"Not fair. I wasn't even aware. He was kind to me. For one split moment, he allowed me to feel sophisticated. It was my Audrey Hepburn moment." Despair was a step off a high bluff. How had that man become the hate-filled bigot that was Jeremiah Falcon now? "I truly didn't know."

"I sometimes wonder if Jeremiah was aware of his feelings. I mean, I don't think he's ever spent ten minutes exploring what he honestly feels. He *thinks* everything. Like his brain can rationalize his way through every situation." Cece slumped. "I wonder if he understands how much he and my parents hurt me? I was his kid brother. I worshipped him. It would have meant the world to me if he'd given me his support, or even a shred of compassion."

"Most people have no clue how much they hurt each other." Tinkie hugged her. "Jeremiah fought an idea that happened to be you, Cece. It was never you he went against. It was the idea of it. People are terrified of anything sexual, and face it, to change genders is an act that forces people to define themselves in a sexual way."

"I didn't choose this." Cece's lower lip trembled. "I wanted to be Cecil. I wanted to be the son my parents were proud of. I was never the rebellious child, the one to start trouble. All I ever wanted was to please them. But in doing so, I couldn't betray who I am. But it still hurts."

The unnecessary pain people caused each other astounded me. Tinkie was right. Jeremiah stopped seeing

Cece as a person and had viewed her only as an idea—as something he didn't understand and therefore didn't like. Once he lost his compassion for his sibling, he lost his ability to empathize and love. Not only Cece, but himself and everyone around him. Hate grew in the barren fields of his life.

"Oh, Cece. We love every inch of you just the way you are! No one could ask for a smarter, more courageous, and more loyal friend. We'll continue to work for Olive." Tinkie made the proclamation with an eye toward me to make sure I agreed.

I nodded. Aside from the fact that Cece needed us to continue, I didn't like the idea of dropping a case in midstream. It smacked of unprofessionalism. Besides, I was hooked. Who *had* killed Boswell? And why? Better yet, who was Boswell—I was clearly beginning to discover that no one in this case was who he appeared to be. And what was Boswell's agenda? Was Twist the intended target?

So many questions to answer. It was better than a feast.

When we left the office, there was still no sign of Graf, and I decided to tackle Jeremiah head-on, though I didn't tell Tinkie or Cece. I didn't want either of them following me and mucking up a difficult job. My frontal assault would infuriate Jeremiah, but I had to reason with him, or at least try.

Cece had reminded me of the man Jeremiah had once been. For such a long time I'd viewed him as a heartless, money-grubbing man who disdained love and family for profit and gain—his gain and Cece's loss as he manipulated their parents against her. And then he'd let everything he'd won go straight to hell.

Almost as if he knew the cost had been his soul.

I left a note for Graf and jumped into the roadster with Sweetie Pie riding shotgun.

Graf had installed a satellite radio because I loved the old classics of forties and fifties rock. To set the mood, I pulled scarves and sunglasses from the glove box for Sweetie and me and turned the calendar back to the era of ducktails and bobby sox. The Skyliners belted out "Since I Don't Have You," but it was the Platters signature song that applied to Jeremiah, "The Great Pretender." I had to make him see that.

When we turned into the drive to Magnolia Grove, Sweetie sat up in the seat and warbled a low, mournful howl. She'd never known the Falcon estate in all its glory, but somehow she sensed the decline.

"I know, girl." I scratched her speckled back. "It's sad to see something that was once so beautiful fall into ruin."

Jeremiah's old Jaguar was parked in front of the house, and I stopped behind it, honked the horn, and got out. Sweetie waited obediently in the front seat for an invitation to disembark. She had better manners than any of my friends or family, and she was self-taught.

The front door burst open and Jeremiah stormed onto the veranda. Because I was seeking it, I caught a glimpse of a man from long ago. He was still there, hidden in the slender frame that moved with grace. Silver threaded his blond hair, and he wore shabby, dingy clothes instead of European chic. Like the house and grounds, he was in decay. And like the condition of the house, it was a voluntary choice. Whatever his reasons, Jeremiah had decided not to take care of himself.

Instead of a gun or a weapon, he held a phone. "You have sixty seconds to clear off this property or I'll call the sheriff to have you arrested for trespassing. A second offense."

"I need to speak with you." I signaled Sweetie out of the car. She bounded over the door and halted at my thigh. She didn't growl or act aggressive, but she was tense. Jeremiah recognized her posturing and knew if he so much as stumbled in my direction, she'd protect me.

"If that dog comes at me, I'll have it destroyed."

"Dream on, Jeremiah. I only want a few minutes of your time. Call Coleman if you want, but until he gets here, I intend to try reasoning with you."

"I have nothing to say to you or any of your deviant friends or associates."

I thought about the tire iron in the trunk and what satisfaction it would be to bring it down on his pumpkin-filled head. Instead, I reached for patience and understanding. What was it about Cece that sent Jeremiah off the deep end? And then I knew. "What did you really want to be, Jeremiah? It wasn't a chemist. Sure, you have a natural talent for science. But it wasn't your love. What was taken from you that makes you hate Cece so much? She didn't let your parents subvert her identity, and you did."

"You pompous bitch." He came down the steps, but he stopped short. Sweetie watched every motion he made.

His reaction told me I'd hit the nail on the head—and I knew the answer. In Jeremiah's old room were dozens of drawings—landscapes, still lifes, pen-and-ink creations of beauty. "Why didn't you pursue a career as an artist? You could have done both."

He paled, and the hand holding the phone shook. "Get off my land. No matter what you think, it's my land, and I can do what I want with it."

"Another lie. You were never allowed to do what you wanted. As the elder son, you did what was expected." And here was the seed of his cruelty toward Cece. He didn't hate her so much as he hated himself. She demanded to be taken on her own terms, and he'd folded to pressure.

"I don't know who you think you are—"

"I'm Cece's friend. Someone who cares about her, the way you should. She never harmed you. She never wanted anything from you except love."

"I'm still pressing trespassing charges against both of you."

His arrogance was nearly my undoing. "Go ahead. Show the entire county how petty you are. I'll happily pay a fine. And at the end of it, you'll still be all alone, with no real friends except the buffoons who hang out here because you've squandered your family fortune buying beer and pandering to their pathetic need for power against someone."

He crossed the yard. Sweetie's hackles raised, and she gave a warning growl. "You don't know a damn thing, Sarah Booth Delaney. Nothing. Not about your friends or the history of this place."

"Maybe I don't. But you've done more harm to yourself than anyone else ever could. I know it could stop now, if you let it."

A wild laugh escaped him. "If you knew me so well, you wouldn't be here. You'd be too afraid of what I might do to you."

Now it was my turn to laugh. "You wouldn't hurt me. Not deliberately. In some ways you're like me, Jeremiah. You've turned the past into an idealistic romance. I'm part of that past for you." I tried my rusty French, the same awkward phrase I'd spoken so many years ago. If I'd slapped him, I couldn't have stunned him more.

"Go home," he said softly.

If he would ever tell me the truth, it was now. "Did you poison Jimmy Boswell? You're an expert in chemicals. Poisons would be right up your alley."

Confusion clouded his features. "Are you joking?"

"You didn't." I'd discovered what I needed.

"Of course not. Why would I poison one of us?"

I froze, my satisfaction sliding into the dust at my feet. "What do you mean, 'one of us'?"

He laughed, and the mask of ugliness was firmly back in place. His vulnerability, if I'd ever truly seen it, was gone. "Boswell was a member of the Heritage Pride Heroes." He let it sink in, his sneer widening. "You didn't know."

"Unbelievable." No, I hadn't known. Nor had I suspected. Were I a conspiracy nut, I'd be babbling "grassy knoll" all over the place. "I knew about Boswell's connection to Vicksburg. His family, like so many others, suffered during the war and Reconstruction. A hundred fifty years ago, Jeremiah! Boswell was educated. Smart enough to see the economic factors and realize the conquered always suffer. Why would he belong to a group that celebrates ignorance and criminal behavior?"

"Maybe because we're sick of the way this country is going. Maybe because the South will never be under the federal boot heel again. Maybe because he intended to write his own book and make his own film, documenting that awful woman for what she is—an abusive overlord and the worst kind of pretender."

"What you say may all be true, but here's more truth for you. The Heritage Pride Heroes is an organization of frightened men. You want to control women and bully others with fear into following your agenda."

"We're a well-organized paramilitary organization. We don't recognize the federal authority. You'd be surprised at the people who share our philosophy."

"No, I wouldn't. There are nutcases all over the place." I opened my door and called Sweetie into the front seat. One foot on the running board, I changed my mind and went to him. "I remember you, Jeremiah. When you lived in France. You went there because you thought you could pursue your drawing as well as work in the chemical business. I realize now you intended to please your father but hold on to your dream. I don't know what happened, but you can still go after the things that are important to you. Cece would support you. She's that kind of friend, and she would be that kind of sister to you. Don't squander any more time."

"You think you know Cecil. You don't. And you certainly don't know me."

"I think I know you both. Better than even I knew. I'm happy for Cece. She's her own person. But I'm very sad for you. This whole Heritage Pride thing is just one more punishment, but this time you're heaping it on yourself."

"You'll see us in a different light soon enough. When we're ready to go public."

"Who killed Boswell? Was it one of your buddies intending to get Twist?"

"That's what I'm hoping you and Sheriff Peters can answer."

11

I took my time driving home. Jeremiah had given me a lot to think about. Because I'd never bought into the glory of war—not any war—I couldn't follow the thought processes of those who clung to "tattered glory."

How could an educated, well-traveled man like Jeremiah worship at the altar of such stupidity? It was as if he'd decided if he couldn't pursue art, he would kill everything of beauty or sense in his life.

Some would say that made him a very dangerous man.

Because my thoughts were so depressing, I telephoned Graf. He didn't answer, and I left a message asking him to call me on my cell phone. I wasn't ready to head home to an empty house, so I called Harold and swung by to collect him and Roscoe for an ice cream treat. We rolled along the drive-thru at the Sweetheart and picked up our cones at the window.

"Lick fast," I ordered the dogs. "It's hot as Satan's toenails."

Harold studied me as I held Sweetie's cone and enjoyed my own. When we were done, I pulled onto the highway.

"Let's ride to Morgan Creek," Harold suggested. "We can let the dogs swim and hang our feet in the water."

The idea charmed me instantly. Morgan Creek held many good memories of picnics, water games, hunting for arrowheads along the sandy banks, and swimming with my mother and childhood friends.

I turned down a dusty lane and aimed for a distant clump of trees marking the creek's passage. Pulling into the shade, I said, "I haven't been here in years."

"Me, either." Harold hopped out and whistled up the dogs. They abandoned the car like it was on fire. Roscoe's gravelly bark spurred Sweetie on as they ran for the water. "Come on, Sarah Booth. We have to at least wade."

Pulling me by the hand, Harold led us to the spring-fed, amber creek. It was only fifteen yards wide, and no more than four feet deep in places, but the dogs flew into it with woofing joy. Sweetie tackled Roscoe in the shallows, and the evil little beggar was caught completely off-guard. He recovered and jumped on her, knocking her into the water.

"The smile makes it all better," Harold said. "For a moment I thought you might sink through the asphalt, you were so low. Why are you so down?"

One thing I loved about Harold was how well he read me. "I went to see Jeremiah. He's filled with bitterness and anger, and he wants to hurt everyone around him. Especially Cece."

I picked up a piece of compressed earth and threw it into the creek. "I went to Magnolia Grove all determined that all I had to do was remind Jeremiah about the good old days and he'd see how he was hurting his only close relative. Like I could ride onto the scene and change the way he views life with a few pithy sentences about the importance of family. I'm as deluded as the rest of them."

"I take it Jeremiah didn't react as you expected. How dare he!" He folded onto the ground and patted a spot beside him for me to sit.

Harold had long ago accepted me as the occasionally snarky little troll I could be. I amused him. "Understatement of the week."

"Tell your uncle Harold how he can help."

He wasn't patronizing me; he was teasing me. But I took him at his word. "I can see how Jeremiah clings to the myth of the Old South where all the residents were genteel and educated and cloaked in nobility. Those nasty Yankees came along and disrupted Utopia. The fantasy appeals to a lot of people who never studied history or who deliberately choose ignorance. What I don't get is how he can so totally reject Cece. He doesn't even know who she is." I caught myself before I crashed into tears.

"Oh, he knows enough about Cece to know he hates her." Harold sat taller, monitoring the dogs playing downstream in the shallows. They chased and barked and ran up and down the banks.

"Why would he hate her?"

Harold loosened his tie, rolled up his shirtsleeves, and put his arm around my shoulders. It was a gesture of friendship, not intimacy. "Jeremiah let his parents break him. They held money over his head and he kept jumping for it. Cece gave up the family inheritance and all the power it had over her."

I put a stick in the path of a soldier ant and watched the creature's amazing dexterity. "That's exactly what I felt. I told Jeremiah he could still pursue art or whatever his dream was, but I infuriated him."

"Many people who are victimized struggle hard to reclaim their lives, but a certain type of victim never wants to be told they have the power to change their status. Fear or self-doubt prevents them from changing. So they have to believe it isn't their fault. The shame of it is that they become victims of their own belief systems."

It always amazed me when Harold and I found ourselves not only on the same page but reading the same line. "Now I'm depressed all over again."

"We live in a world of free choice, Sarah Booth. People want to be victims. Ignorance and bigotry are comfortable places, especially for victims. It's easier to hate than to be curious. Sad truth of human nature."

Harold pulled a backward Cinderella moment and removed my shoes. When he was barefoot, too, he escorted me into the water. The gently flowing creek was deliciously cool under the shady trees. As the dogs sprayed us with water and sand, I closed my eyes and soaked in the bliss of creek water and good friendship.

"As much as I dislike him, I don't think Jeremiah killed Boswell." I took the opportunity to hash out the case with Harold. He had a good head for logic, and he was excellent at playing devil's advocate.

"Jeremiah can be dangerous, and don't ever forget that. But I don't think he killed Boswell, either. Poison is a coward's weapon. Jeremiah is deluded, but he isn't cowardly."

He made a good point. Jeremiah and Buford viewed themselves as men left behind by history. They were the knights of the Round Table in a world that didn't appreciate their nobility or willingness to sacrifice. Men of honor. Throwing rotten tomatoes had a rakish humor to it. "Oscar, with Cece's help, says he'll push to institutionalize both of them."

"He can try." Harold stepped in a depression and water covered his trousers to his knees. Instead of being upset, he laughed.

"You don't think he can?"

"I don't. Oscar has influence with a few judges, and he might manage to have Buford evaluated by a psychiatric team, but not Jeremiah. He has no standing to initiate action based on questionable mental health. Cece won't pursue this. Don't ask it of her."

The cool waters sloshed our legs as we walked to a fallen tree growing sideways from the bank. It made a perfect seat, and he lifted me onto it before he jumped up himself. The limb was low enough that our feet dangled in the creek. Out of the corner of my eye, I saw Roscoe swimming toward us like a big gator.

Harold hiked his feet before Roscoe could nip them. "If you want my opinion on who killed poor Boswell, I'd vote for Webber."

"What do you know about Dr. Webber?" I moved my feet to safety, too. Roscoe circled like a shark.

The sunlight filtering through trees' canopy showered us with dappled shadows. Harold hesitated. At last he answered. "Do you remember Linley Hanks?"

The image of a slender blonde with dark brown eyes

came to mind. She'd been Miss Sunflower County my high school junior year. The little movie projector in my brain spun a reel. Linley Hanks wore a red glitter outfit and white boots with pom-poms. She twirled a baton at the head of the band as they marched around the courthouse square. Santa Claus threw candy from a float that followed behind Linley and the marching band.

"I do," I said.

"Christmas Parade." Harold sighed. "Red costume, white boots, and her baton had green tinsel."

I'd forgotten the metallic green streamers on the end of her twirling baton. "Nice stroll down memory lane, but what does Linley have to do with this discussion."

"She got pregnant and had a baby girl. The father wouldn't marry her or support the child. She never told who it was."

Working in the bank, Harold was privy to private info involving most of the region. "I hope she left town. Folks can be mighty hard on a girl who makes a mistake, especially one as beautiful as Linley."

"She moved to Oxford and took a job on campus as a secretary. In the history department."

"Oh, no." I saw where this was headed. "He seduced her, didn't he?"

"Right. They were something of a fairy-tale story— the secretary who nabs the professor. Linley was plenty smart. She could've been anything, but she fell hard for Webber. She spread the word around the university they were a couple. She said he'd offered marriage and support for her baby."

"But he didn't keep his promises."

"Not a single one. Gossip had it that she caught him

in his office with another woman. A younger woman. Linley transferred to a different department and eventually completed a nursing degree. She married a doctor and has a nice life. Her daughter is attending Ole Miss now. Things work out like they're supposed to, but Webber is a skunk."

"A lot of men wouldn't take on the responsibility of another man's child."

"Rumor said it was Webber's kid, too. Supposedly he met Linley during a senior trip for the majorettes and cheerleaders at Ole Miss. He was a research assistant for one of the other professors that summer. Later, when he had his PhD, he used the contacts he'd made to snare a job teaching."

"Linley and her daughter were just too much baggage to carry," I surmised. He was the lowest kind of bastard, not to mention the balance of power in the relationship had been weighted in his favor all along.

Harold's tone was easy, but the tension in his jaw revealed how much this still upset him. "Professor Webber is capable of anything in my opinion. Any man who would deny his own child and the woman he seduced and impregnated—he's not much of a man."

I didn't consider Harold's judgment too harsh. I certainly needed to reexamine Webber's alibi. If he would turn his back on his daughter, he might kill without a qualm. He had plenty of reason to hate Olive and to want her dead. Poor Boswell mistakenly drank the coffee.

Sweetie's soft yodeling bay called my attention back to the moment. It was time to load up and head home. "Thanks for the break." I splashed down from the tree seat and when Harold joined me, I put my arm around his waist. We headed out of the creek with the dogs bounding after us.

Before I dropped Harold at his place, he gave me the current skinny on Linley Hanks, now Mrs. Dr. Libeaux. Linley Libeaux—it had a nice ring. She lived on Highway 49 near Greenwood, not so far from the scene of her old high school reign of glory.

When I got her on the phone, she was agreeable to a meeting, especially after I mentioned the Christmas Parade and the glamorous figure she cut. Those carefree days must have been a respite for her.

I dropped Sweetie at Dahlia House and did a quick search for my missing fiancé. My friends and Graf had vanished. I was puzzled but not concerned. No telling what they were up to. I'd find out soon enough, and I didn't have time to chase them down. I was on official PI business.

Following Linley's directions, I cruised down a tree-lined driveway and pulled up in front of a home that smacked of the antebellum era.

Linley Hanks Libeaux opened the door with a warm greeting. Her well-appointed home showed quiet good taste and an emphasis on family. Linley looked older, but not by much. The last two decades had been kind to her. She offered Louisiana coffee with chicory and an apple strudel that belied her trim figure. She really did have it all, including a metabolism to die for.

"I haven't stayed in touch with Richard," she said in answer to my question. "There's no reason to." But her glance toward the back door made me wonder if she felt a need to escape the conversation.

I didn't really want to go into great detail, so I skimmed the surface of Olive Twist's research, including Webber's role in it.

Linley showed no reaction. When I finished, she asked, "So what do you want from me? I don't know about any of this. My . . . relationship with Richard is history." Her half-smile straddled amused and sad. "I was a kid easily awed by Richard. He believed he was superior, so I did, too. Like I said, I was a gullible kid."

"How ambitious is Richard?"

The sadness remained, but my question also evoked anger. "He denied his daughter and me, because he feared we'd hold him back. A man of his academic status couldn't marry a mere secretary. Besides, a wife and baby would have cramped his style as the freewheeling, seductive professor. He's ambitious enough to doom his own blood to bare survival."

"Would you say he's capable of murder?"

"Richard likes to play the game, but he never wants to pay the price. He'd kill if his comfort were threatened. He tried to talk me into aborting Kelly, but I wouldn't. I thought I could make him love our baby. I was such a fool. Worse than a fool." The skin beneath her eyes tightened. "One night, he threatened to choke me to death. He was that desperate to eject me from his life. See, I refused to be shamed into disappearing. When he wouldn't marry me, I forced him to pay for my education."

"So he has a bad temper?"

"Yeah. And no conscience. A classic sociopath. He takes what he wants and screw the consequences it causes for others." She put her hands, palm down, on the table beside her coffee cup. "Once I accepted his utter lack of conscience, it was easy to walk away. I left behind the girl in the red-sequined dance costume. I stepped into the shoes of a pregnant, unwed teenager. But I wouldn't be the person I am today, and I wouldn't have Kelly and Charles, were it not for how awful Richard was."

She spread her fingers on the table. "Charles was Kelly's pediatrician. He's a good man and he loves Kelly like his own child. I might have settled for an egotistical sociopath who cheated on me when I was pregnant. Instead I have a man who loves me, Kelly, and every child he meets."

"Does the name Olive Twist mean anything to you?"

She laughed. "Bad pennies really do turn up again, don't they? She was a graduate student he met at a history conference in San Diego."

My jaw fell. "Were you at the conference?"

"No, I wasn't there, but I pieced it together later. Twist isn't the type of person you forget." She gathered herself to recount the tale, anger sparking in her eyes. "I was almost due when Richard booked the conference. I begged him not to leave town. I was scared and on my own. But he went anyway. Weeks later, I found photos in his briefcase. Explicit photos of Richard and a lanky graduate student, Olive Twist. They had a torrid affair while I sat at home in Oxford and waited for him to call." She pressed her hands against the solid table. "Thank God the pathetic, scared young woman I used to be is long dead."

"Are you positive he was involved with Olive Twist?"

"Fake British accent and all. She called the history department repeatedly after he was home. She wanted me to know who she was and that she was educated and I wasn't. She was everything he needed, she told me."

It had to be Olive. And she and Webber had known

each other for years. He'd certainly lied to me and Tinkie, which carried only the penalty of our wrath. They both had. Had they also lied to Coleman? Now, that was a different kettle of fish. Lying to a law officer could bring harsh consequences, and Richard Webber was a man who needed to feel the brunt of the law falling on his shoulders.

I swung by Cece's, but she wasn't home. Nor was she at the newspaper office—where she should have been. I called Graf to ask if he'd heard from her or Tinkie. No answer on his cell phone or at home. I left another message to let him know I was running by the courthouse to speak with Coleman. I needed to update the sheriff on the latest Richard Webber info.

Coleman had his own set of woes when I arrived at the sheriff's office. DeWayne Dattilo, his deputy, gave me a comical moue of wild panic before Coleman caught him. "What's going on?" I asked.

DeWayne pushed himself out of his desk chair. "I'm going to Millie's. I'm having hunger pangs."

"If you don't convince Darcy Miller to say yes quick, you'll be too big to fit behind the wheel of the patrol car," Coleman snapped. "It's three squares a day, not six troughs-full. How many pieces of pie have you eaten today?"

DeWayne had stacked on twenty pounds or so during his courtship of waitress Darcy Miller, but he was a long way from being obese.

"I'll bring you a bowl of Millie's peach cobbler. Might sweeten up that foul temper of yours." DeWayne jammed on his hat and strode out the door.

I was left alone to face Coleman and his flushed cheeks. Embarrassment or anger, I couldn't tell.

"I hope you have good news," he said. "This is a frustrating case. And Gertrude Strom is driving me nuts. She could worry the fur off a bear."

"What does she want?"

"The killer arrested and the reputation of her B and B restored. She says no one will drink her coffee since word is out that Boswell died of poisoned java. Folks are canceling reservations. She wants a front-page story in the *Zinnia Dispatch* saying her facilities are top-notch and perfectly safe.

"If she wasn't always such a bitch to me, I'd ask Cece to write a story for the society page."

"Yeah, like movie star Graf Milieu dines in the shady luxury of Zinnia's premier B and B. I can see the photo spread. Graf, pensively leaning against a vine-covered post looking into the hazy, heat-soaked distance."

"If you tire of pushing a badge, you can write ad copy. You have a knack for it."

He rounded the counter, hat in hand. "Let's take a walk."

What was with the men today? A wade, a walk, next it would be a waltz. It was hot as hell outside but had begun to cool—a tad. It was still eighty-five degrees, and humid. But if Coleman needed to walk, I would stroll beside him. As a child, I'd spend endless hours bicycling around town, or walking and window-shopping. Now I seldom toured Zinnia, which was a shame.

The courthouse square and many of the downtown streets were shaded by large oaks. When the Delta land had originally been cleared, a few trees were left in areas where residential centers were planned. In other instances, trees had been planted after the town was formed. Good planning. The lacy oaks dropped the temperature at least ten degrees.

A soft breeze lifted my hair off my neck as we sallied forth. Coleman had something to say, but grilling him wouldn't make him give it up any faster, so we walked.

When he did speak, it wasn't what I expected. "This morning I caught the first whiff of fall in the air."

"You must have been up at five a.m., before the sun heated everything up." I couldn't read his profile. What the hell? I didn't need a weather report.

"I was up early. I met Olive for a jog."

"Daniel leapfrogging lions! Where?"

"At The Gardens. I wanted to tell you myself. Before Olive did."

"Oh, no. This is not happening." I grabbed his elbow and jerked him around to face me. "Look me in the eye and tell me you're dating that bitch."

"I'm not. We jogged. She likes to stay fit."

"She's so thin if she turns sideways she won't cast a shadow." My overwrought brain refused to process the information in any useful way.

"Don't be cruel, Sarah Booth. She has a high metabolism."

"I don't know what to say. She's a suspect in a murder case. Have you lost what little gumption you had?" I realized we were standing on a corner on Main Street in Zinnia. Vehicles whizzed by, and several pedestrians eased around us, looking back with concern.

I tried to compose myself. It wouldn't do a lick of good to have a come-apart on Main Street.

"We went for a jog, but I know how gossip flies around Sunflower County and I knew it would get back to you."

"I'm not your mother." Fury washed over me in waves. "I should think you'd be more concerned about what DeWayne and the voters think about the fact you're dating your own murder suspect."

"We were—"

"Jogging, I know. A euphemism for dating for the S and M set."

"Ouch!" Coleman's grin said it all. "Are you mad because we're dating or because we're exercising together?"

"Mother Teresa eating a Fudgsicle! I don't care what you do, it's doing it with Olive Twist. She's a suspect. You've made a few boneheaded mistakes in your life, but this is too much. You're displaying terrible judgment, Coleman. There'll be a backlash. People in Sunflower County will despise Olive for what she's trying to do. That contempt will rub off on you."

To my surprise, he didn't defend his choice. He didn't say a damn word. Which wasn't like Coleman.

"What are you up to?" I tried to pin him down.

"I won't discuss this, Sarah Booth, but I didn't want to sandbag you. Now you know." He pivoted and started back to the courthouse. Our little walk was nothing but a chance for him to confess his insanity. He didn't want to do it in the courthouse in case I broke bad.

I trotted to catch up to him. "I can't tell you who or what to date." I spoke with a calm I didn't feel. "Olive isn't a very nice person."

"She says the same about you."

I wanted to beat his chest with my fists. "Make fun of me if you want to, but I'm not trying to date a possible killer. The voters might not understand."

"I'm not dating her. I went for a jog."

"It doesn't matter what you call it or how you rationalize it. It looks bad. What if you have to arrest her for murder?"

"Then I will." He reached for my hand, but I pulled back. "You have to trust me on this, Sarah Booth."

"No, I don't." I did an about-face and left him standing on the Main Street sidewalk as I hurried back to my car and the fifteen-minute drive to the safety of Dahlia House.

12

Dahlia House was silent as the grave. For about sixty seconds. I'd just made it in the door when I heard frantic scratching coming from the dining room. Sweetie's excited bark followed, then the sound of a solid hound body pummeling the door. The *locked* dining room door.

I never locked interior rooms, and neither did Graf. Like in many old houses, each door was fitted with a lock. The brass keys were left in the locks. Could the door have locked accidentally?

If so, why didn't Sweetie and Pluto use the swinging door into the kitchen and then the doggy exit to the outside? It didn't make sense. I hurried to unlock the door before my critters clawed and buffeted it down.

Pluto flew at me from the darkened dining room and nearly scared ten years off my life. If Ole Miss needed a flying tackle, I had just the cat for them.

Sweetie Pie followed right behind. She rushed to my feet and sat, tail thumping a calypso rhythm on the hardwood floor, demanding my attention. The critters were teaming up on me, but I still didn't understand the locked door in the dining room.

"Where's Graf?" I asked.

Sweetie's reply was a long, sad howl. Pluto galloped to the front door and clawed at it. He really wanted out, but Sweetie lingered at my side.

"Sweetie, you've had an ice cream *and* a swim today. Why are you acting so needy?"

She circled frantically, clawed the door, and barked. Pluto, too, gave a great impression of a cat crazed to get outside. Watching their frenzied antics, I wondered if Graf had locked them in the dining room and then blocked the doggy door. But why? I'd check it in a moment, but first I released hound and kitty into the front yard. They hurtled down the steps in tandem and tore around the house toward the barn.

"Man, those two are wound up." As I closed the door, I sensed someone was behind me. Thoughts flapped through my head as I eased around. Neither Sweetie nor Pluto would abandon me to danger. And surely they'd know if a stranger was in the house. It had to be—

"Your man is on the loose and you're worried about that sheriff. You'd better keep tabs on the handsome Graf Milieu, or you're gonna lose him."

I stared into the chocolate orbs of a mocha and beautiful Jessica Rabbit. Her arched eyebrows were fascinating, and her red hair, à la Veronica Lake, spectacular. But who cared about such things when confronted with an hourglass figure. "Jitty?" I could barely get her name out. "Where did you get that body?"

"As usual, your focus is on the wrong thing. It's not my body you should be thinkin' about. It's innocence. And how the wrong people can be accused of a crime. Maybe even a crime that was never committed. You should give Eddie Valiant a call. Take a page from him on runnin' an investigation. Toontown hides no secrets from Eddie. If the same could be said of you and Zinnia, you'd crack this case."

I had no clue what she was rambling about. Now I fully understood why Jessica Rabbit had been voted the sexiest cartoon character of all time, and Jitty knew how to play her. She took long, hip-swinging steps in my direction. For a ghost who disdained her body, she worked every inch of it to get the maximum attention. The only thing I could think to say was, "Who framed Roger Rabbit?"

"Framed is the operative word, Sarah Booth." She flicked her cigarette and the ashes speckled the top of my shoe. "Watch out."

The action set off an instant craving for a smoke. I forced my attention back on Jitty. "Who's being framed?"

"That's your job—figure it out. And you'd better be quick. Missing husbands are serious business."

Her words made not a lick of sense, or maybe I was dazzled by that incredible body, wrapped in an impossible dress. How did it stay on her? There was no back to it.

"Shall I sing you a tune?" Her wicked smile teased me. "That's a t-u-n-e, not a t-o-o-n. If I could sing a stool-pigeon t-o-o-n, I'd find out who framed my husband."

She slinked across the room. "Dig into it, Sarah Booth. If it's the last thing you do."

She sashayed toward the staircase and disappeared.

Between Jitty, Sweetie, and Pluto, I was living in a madhouse. With a missing fiancé. And missing friends. And a sheriff bent on self-destruction.

I checked in the kitchen. My note to Graf was still stuck to the refrigerator door with a magnet. My messages were still on the answering machine. And the doggy door was blocked.

How long had Sweetie and Pluto been cooped up in the house? Color me annoyed. I tried Graf's cell. No answer. Same for Tinkie and Cece. At last I called Oscar.

"Harold said you pushed him into a creek, Sarah Booth." Oscar sounded peeved. "He came back to work looking like he'd been in a tornado."

I couldn't believe Harold would go to the bank and fib about how he'd gotten his pants wet. "That's a lie. He dragged me to the water and then he jumped in. Along with that rotten dog of his."

Oscar chuckled. "So, what have you done with my wife? I've been calling her all afternoon."

The old expression "my heart stopped" conveyed the sensation in my chest perfectly. Tinkie taking a powder did not bode well. "*I'm* looking for Tinkie. I haven't seen her since this morning."

The pause on Oscar's end scared me even worse. "She said she was meeting you to work on the murder of that young man, Jimmy Boswell. She said you had plans to interview people and needed her help."

"I've been on the case, but Tinkie was supposed to talk to you. She's worried about you, Oscar. Or I should say concerned. She said you've been withdrawn and won't talk to her. She thinks it's because of Buford's in-volvement in this Lady in Red mess." I had to tell him the rest. "Cece is missing, too. And Graf."

"What the hell?"

My sentiments exactly. What were they up to? They owed me and Oscar a call. "Do you have any idea where Tinkie might be?"

"I do, and I hope I'm wrong."

"What?" My anxiety level notched higher.

"I'll bet they went after Buford and Jeremiah, think-ing they'd convince them to voluntarily go to a mental facility." Oscar's finger anxiously tapped the phone. "This sounds exactly like a windmill Tinkie would take on. I just expected Cece and Graf to have more sense than to go along with her."

"Oh, no." Oscar was right. Tinkie would go way out on a limb to help Oscar.

Convincing those two idiots to check into a mental health center was wasted breath. My dealings with Jere-miah told me he didn't want help. He was mad at the world, and he wanted to inflict pain and suffering on everyone around him. Buford wouldn't give up his bottle or his sense of power. My friends had set out on a lost cause. And a dangerous one.

"Will you find them, Sarah Booth?" Oscar sounded frantic.

"Any ideas where Buford might be?" They weren't at Magnolia Grove.

"I have a hunting camp on the river. I've always let Buford use the property. You know Tinkie would chop off my fingers if I wanted to hurt an animal. Buford doesn't hunt, either, but it's a place he can target shoot, which is what I thought he was up to. Now I'm second-guessing my assumptions."

Had Oscar seen the state of Magnolia Grove—a beautiful home destroyed by gunk and funk—he'd be concerned about his property. Like the rest of us, Oscar had assumed Buford and Jeremiah drank hard, talked too much drivel, and sometimes got drunk and shot off a few rounds. No one really suspected Buford and Jeremiah were up to anything serious.

I took down the directions, hung up, and pulled on my tallest leather boots. Snakes would be crawling all over the riverbanks. Before I left Dahlia House, I tried all three cell phones—no answer. There were dead spots along the river where electronics didn't work. I sincerely hoped that accounted for the lack of returned calls from all three.

Sweetie, always ready for a ride, was panting on the front porch when I stepped out. Pluto, also exhausted, lay curled against my hound. When I made for the car, Sweetie leaped into the roadster's front seat and we set off for the river.

My cell phone rang, but sweet relief was cut short when caller ID showed it was Olive Twist. I answered with reluctance.

"Where are you?" she demanded.

"Working on the case." I wasn't about to give her specifics. To be honest, I wasn't absolutely certain I was a actually working on *her* case. Without a contract and a retainer, Delaney Detective Agency had never been officially hired, and I was more concerned with finding my fiancé and friends than with resolving her problems. On the other hand, her case and my friends all snarled together.

"I mean *where* are you? I didn't ask what you were doing." She sounded annoyed.

"What do you want, Olive?" I could sound just as petulant and even notch it up a measure to peeved.

"Someone sneaked into my room. I've been violated."

I slowed down and pulled off on a side road so I could hear better. "You've been raped?"

"No, but someone came into my room and messed through my things. It's a violation. It might as well be a rape. My intimate inner sanctum has been sullied by prying, dirty fingers."

"Have you been working on your romance novel?"

"How did you know?"

"Word choice. Sullied. It's sort of a romancey word. Never mind." I pushed forward. "Tell me what happened."

"It's high-level espionage. The intruder read my latest brilliant passage. What if he steals it? How will I prove it was mine?"

I sighed. She was more upset that someone had read her purple prose than she'd been about her assistant's murder. "I don't think you have any real worries."

"They could have photographed it. My genius shines through in each sentence, but how will I prove it's mine?"

"I'm sure any judge worth his salt will link the written brilliance to your keen ability to communicate."

"I'm not paying you to condescend to me."

Oh, snap. "As I recall, you haven't paid me anything."

"Only because you've failed to come by and pick up your check. That's what you should do right now. Hurry here to this wretched B and B and sniff out the person who intruded into my room. I'll give you a check then."

My aunt Loulane told me more than once that patience was a virtue I needed to learn. Judas on a Quidditch court, I was learning. I counted to ten before I answered her. "Was anything actually stolen?"

"I don't think so."

"How do you know someone was in your room?"

"Things are moved. My makeup and personal items. And I can sense it. Boswell used to put everything exactly as I liked it. He appreciated how fractious I can be when anything is touched. I'm positive an intruder pawed through my things."

"It doesn't appear to be an emergency."

"Fine. Don't come. I'll call Coleman. He'll take me seriously. He understands I'm delicate. I have to be tough in my work, but I'm really a very sensitive person, and he appreciates those things about me."

I wanted to throw the phone out of the car and then run over it, but I didn't. Coleman was a grown man. Olive was . . . something else. I had no place anywhere in their relationship, certainly not trying to stand between them.

"I'm working on an aspect of the case, Olive. I don't have time to stop by The Gardens. Why don't you set up your expensive video equipment and monitor your room? Kill two birds with one stone—you can continue to document every breath you take on your quest to fame and fortune."

"Good idea!"

The woman was impossible. She couldn't even tell I was goading her.

"Report the incident to Gertrude. She takes her B and B's reputation seriously. The idea that a miscreant is slipping around the rooms will motivate her to change your locks."

"Another good idea. I had my doubts about you, Sarah Booth, but maybe you are a decent PI."

"Thanks." Her insults failed to rouse me. "What did the DNA indicate?"

The long pause got my attention. "It was inconclusive."

"Meaning what?"

"They had trouble running the samples. The body was preserved in alcohol. Essentially pickled. When it was originally unearthed, the seal was broken and decay was almost instantaneous."

"The alcohol destroyed the DNA?" This would certainly crimp her entire premise. Maybe she'd leave town and take her problems and all the turmoil she'd brought to Sunflower County with her.

"Not completely, but it will require a more sophisticated lab to process the DNA. I've sent samples off. But I also need comparison DNA. I've spoken with Jeremiah Falcon. He's consented to giving me a swab, for a handsome price. He claims he needs money, but I think he's hoping to discover a connection to the Lady in Red. Especially if I can prove she was involved in an attempt on Lincoln's life."

"When did you talk to Jeremiah?"

"About ten minutes ago. He's supposed to be on his way to the hospital. They'll conduct the test there and send it in—you know, so folks can't claim later that I tampered with the results."

I really wanted to wring Jeremiah's neck. "I'll be in touch." I pressed the accelerator hard. Cece needed to know what her brother was up to.

"Don't call me tonight. I have plans. The kind that won't welcome a phone call or interruption, if you get my drift. Coleman is dropping by. And Sarah Booth, don't tell anyone about the DNA test results. You're my employee, and you have to honor my wishes."

"I didn't read that passage in the Olive Twist employment handbook." I knew the minute I said it I was picking a fight.

"There are expectations in a relationship where one person pays the other for services. Discretion is one. It goes without saying for people with ethics."

"Ethics?" I wanted off the phone, but I also had a few questions for her. "Why didn't you tell me you knew Richard Webber back when you were a graduate student? You two have a history—a sordid one, I believe."

"Did he tell you this?"

"The source is confidential. Is it true?" I didn't doubt it was, but I wanted to make her corroborate.

"You're a better detective than I suspected. So you found out Richard and I had a torrid affair. He was smitten with me, completely and hopelessly in love. He wanted me to move to Oxford and finish my degree there, as his wife. I couldn't do it, though. I'd invested everything in my studies at Tufts. That's where I was awarded my PhD, and I was deep into the degree. Tufts is an excellent school, and credentials are everything in my line of work."

My goodness, Twist could prattle on about her many wonders. "Did you know Richard had gotten a young woman pregnant?"

"Ummm, he said something about a baton twirler who was lying and attempting to trap him into marriage. He feared she'd go to the history department and report him. He languished in the final weeks of obtaining his PhD. Such a scandal would have been a righteous mess. Imagine a tramp accusing him of sexual assault. Thank goodness the little twit backed off her threats and realized she couldn't trap a man as smart as Richard."

I didn't know if Richard was a terrible bastard or if

Twist had reimagined history to suit her purposes. As far as I could tell, they both should be tied in a sack with heavy stones and thrown in a deep river. "I have to go, Olive."

"You're in my employ. We'll talk until I say we're finished."

I made a crackling noise into the cell phone. "I'm losing reception. I'll call when I hit a clear signal." I punched off the phone and tossed it into the seat with Sweetie. "Silly woman," I said aloud as I turned down a rutted dirt road that would, hopefully, take me to my man and my wayward friends.

Oscar's camp was on the wrong side of the levee, meaning it was between the levee and the water. Crossing the levee was like entering a completely different world. On the dry side was an endless vista of cotton almost ready for harvest. West of the levee was a magical land of trees, sloughs, small ponds, and abundant wildlife.

The marginal land between the river and the levee can be a quarter mile in places, and much wider in others. Oscar's property was in the latter. I drove into the brake and was instantly swallowed by a wilderness. The lushness of the green—trees, shrubs, vines—depicted my version of paradise.

Wild birds twittered and missiled in front of the car with such fearless abandon even Sweetie was in awe. There was no evidence of a camp or a cabin, but I kept driving. If this was Oscar's property, no wonder he kept it in the family. This was a rare place in a world gone crazy with development.

Of course, when the river rose, most of this land

would be underwater. Or all of it, depending on the severity of the flood.

To my left, a small herd of white-tailed deer broke cover and bounded away. They'd probably been sleeping in the summer heat, and the car had disturbed them. Though Sweetie was bred to hunt, she had no interest in chasing deer. Like me, she knew the beautiful creatures harmed no one and deserved to live in peace. Her choice of prey was evildoers who threatened those she loved.

The narrow path took a sharp turn, and the cabin came into view. It soared high into the treetops, like a boys' clubhouse dream on stilts. It had been built to withstand all but the worst floods. The weathered, dark-gray cypress blended into the natural scene. But Graf's green Range Rover told the story—my beau and two best friends were on the premises.

Curious, I pulled out my cell phone. We all used the same carrier and I had four bars. Plenty of juice to make and receive calls. So why weren't they answering? The little voice in the back of my reptilian brain screamed, "Danger! Danger! Danger!" I had learned to heed that remnant of my tree-swinging DNA alerting me to possible death or maiming.

Before I got any closer, I stopped. Sweetie, too, was on high alert. She stood in the seat and sniffed the air, letting out a low whine.

"What's wrong, Sweetie?" I laid a hand on her back and felt the way her hair stood on end. "Timmy in the well?"

Her look of disdain would have quelled a gentler spirit. But I was used to contempt, from Olive and my dog.

I eased my car into a leafy turnaround and prepared for a hasty retreat should it become necessary. I called the Sunflower County Sheriff's Office. I was outside Coleman's jurisdiction, but if I needed the cavalry, he'd figure out a way to help. DeWayne answered, and I told him where I was and my concerns.

"Why don't you wait? I'll call for assistance from the Washington County SO."

A reasonable request, except Sweetie leaped from the car and took off at a dead gallop toward the cabin. "Gotta go, DeWayne. I'll call back when I can."

"Sarah Booth, Coleman is going to skin you alive. You can't run around courting danger. It puts him in a black mood."

"Maybe he can just take a jog with Miss Skinny Britches and improve his frame of mind." I snapped off the phone.

Sweetie disappeared into the woods to the right of the cabin. I grabbed my gun from the trunk and lit out after her. Her determination roused my anxiety. Sweetie never got in a rush unless bad things were on the horizon.

I caught up with her on the cabin's south side. A soft wind tumbled the green leaves fluttering around us in all directions. On the western side of the cabin, a gallery stretched the whole length and wind chimes tinkled. The scene was peaceful, yet my nerves pulled taut.

Sweetie stood beside me, her nose delicately sniffing. She didn't make a sound, which was not like my hound. She was vocally expressive, with little snuffles, grunts, howls, barks, and full-on bays.

At last she started forward and I was right beside her. At times like this, I had to trust her nose. She could smell far better than I could see. If she was willing to move toward the cabin, I was her point man.

She halted at the steps below the gallery. The space

was used for a barbecue grill. Several lawn chairs surrounded a mountain of empty beer cans and liquor bot-
tles. And lots of spent shells. Someone had been shooting
like a Wild West show. No doubt that Buford and his
buddies had been hanging out here. Nothing more reas-
suring than drunks with loaded weapons.

Above me I heard scuffling. Sweetie's deep-throated
whine galvanized me up the steps, right on her heels.

Tinkie was the better shot, but I could hold my own
with the Glock. I didn't like to carry it, but after numerous injuries and watching my friends damaged by mean
and greedy criminals, I resolved to shoot if necessary
and ask questions later.

I crept up to eye level with the porch floor and aimed.
A shot in the leg or foot was almost as good as a kill shot
to stop a criminal. Pain worked wonders in bringing a
bad guy into line—and minimized the guilt I'd feel at
taking a life. I might fantasize about plugging Buford in
the noggin, but he was Oscar's cousin, and I really didn't
want to kill him.

Sweetie pawed frantically at the cabin door.

"Sweetie!" I took my time, checking left, right, above,
and below before I duckwalked to her. Rising slowly, I
looked through the glass into a homey one-room cabin
with bunk beds lining the walls and a cheerful kitchen
area. Graf, Cece, and Tinkie lay hog-tied on the floor facing the opposite direction.

My first reaction was gut-wrenching fear, but I saw
the steady rise and fall of their ribs, and they were sweat-
ing profusely. But then so was I. To make matters worse,
mosquitoes snacked on every inch of exposed skin. An
armed and insane Buford might be a great alternative to
the bloodsuckers biting me.

"Clear?" I asked Sweetie.

She snuffled a bark. I twisted the knob and rolled into the room behind her.

The place was like a freaking oven. "Mother Mary selling snow cones." I gained my feet and discovered duct tape covered my fiancé's and friends' mouths. Their faces were beet red. The one-room cabin was empty of Buford or strangers—I savored a moment of blissful silence and, yes, smugness. I was not tied up on the floor of a cabin, I was Wonder Woman, the rescue posse.

My self-satisfaction was short-lived. Tinkie thumped her dainty little flats on the floor. Who goes into a swamp in bejeweled velvet shoes?

"Patience is a virtue," I said, quoting Aunt Loulane, but I untied Tinkie's hands. I wasn't about to snatch the tape off her mouth. She could do that herself. I did the same for Cece and Graf.

"Sarah Booth, we thought you'd never get here," Graf said without a hint of complaint. He was simply glad to see me.

I offered a hand to pull him to his feet and into my arms. "Thank goodness you aren't hurt."

"What the hell took you so long?" Tinkie demanded. "Another half hour and I would have died of heat and dehydration. You wait until I get my hands on Buford. He will rue the day he ever thought of tying me up."

"Buford did this? Why?" I could see Jeremiah, but not Buford. "And how?"

"The door was open and Graf went inside. There were diagrams and things on the floor, like we interrupted some kind of planning session. I heard a motorcycle or four-wheeler, and Cece and I were scouting the exterior." Tinkie pulled herself together as she talked.

"When I bent down to examine the diagrams, someone whacked me on the back of the head." Graf rubbed his scalp. "While I was out, he tied me up. Then, when Cece looked in and saw me, she rushed in and she was clobbered, too."

"Same for me. I tried to call for help, but there was no reception. I couldn't tell if Graf and Cece were injured or dead. I had to check."

The important thing was they were all three okay. "Where are the diagrams?"

"Gone. Along with a laptop computer and some other equipment. Did you see the weapons down below?" Graf asked. "These people have an agenda. They aren't just kooks. They're kooks with some kind of plan."

"The guns are gone, too." My heart was pounding. Graf and my friends had come very close to being killed. "It might have been nice if one of you had left a note, or a text, or a message in a bottle naming your destination. It was only by chance Oscar mentioned this hunting camp."

"I did leave a note," Graf said. "Right beside yours on the refrigerator."

A series of flash images yielded the answer. The locked door, the animals confined—an intruder had been in Dahlia House. Sweetie and Pluto had dashed out the front door, angling toward the barn, but I hadn't bothered to follow.

"We have to go." There wasn't time to dally. "Dahlia House was burgled. The intruder stole your note, and he might have been hiding in the barn while I was in the house."

Graf rubbed his wrists where the rope had cut into his flesh. "Let's load up." Long strides took him to the door.

"What about Buford?" Cece's blood was still up and

she wanted revenge. "And the big guy we saw at Magnolia Grove. Buford called him Arnold. He was here, too, helping Buford load up the computer and stuff. I pretended to be out, but I saw them."

"I gather Buford wasn't interested in a paid vacation in a mental institution."

"After what he did, I think we have cause for involuntary commitment." Tinkie brushed at the dust on her black slacks. "He's going to pay. Oscar will see to that."

I went to my fiancé and put my arms around him. "What matters is that none of you were hurt." Even at the thought of harm coming to Graf, my heart ached. "Where did Buford go?" I asked.

"We don't know," Cece said. She'd been too quiet for too long—a sure sign the wheels were turning in her mind. "Those diagrams were important. Buford was frantic to make sure we didn't see them. And he snatched up that laptop like it was the Holy Grail. I have a really bad feeling my brother and his associates are into something seriously bad. They act like buffoons, but Jeremiah is smart. Buford, too."

I looked out the door—the sun hung above the treetops. If we hustled, we could get back to Zinnia before full dark.

13

"You don't really expect me to shake in my shoes at the idea Buford Richmond is plotting against me, do you? He's a pathetic waste of skin."

Olive's voice grated like the whine of a bone saw. "I don't care if you shake, fart, or fizzle. But you should take this threat seriously. Buford is unbalanced. He drinks too much, and he has muscle by his side. Buford's buddy looks mean, and he has the physique to back it up."

"Are you referring to that big handsome man with shoulders as wide as a doorframe?"

"How do you know what Arnold looks like?" Alarm spiked through me, because I knew the answer.

"He's in the bar, with Buford. I believe they're having

their third round of Scarlet O'Haras. Buford runs his mouth, but the big man sits back and watches. He doesn't miss much. I like a man who knows how to be attentive. Buford is a swaggering fool, but Arnold . . . has potential. I could have some fun with him. But I need the DNA sample from Buford, so I guess I'll have to stroke that pig."

"Clear out of there, Olive. Seriously. Both of those men are unstable, and your presence could provoke a saint into carnal sins."

"Very funny, Sarah Booth. I'm sure you're an authority on sin, carnal and just plain nasty." The pause lasted long enough to set the teeth of her trap. "Someone sure taught the sheriff how to do devilish things."

Even when I tried to save her life, she was the supreme bitch-a-rama. It would be a relief if Buford bashed her brains out. In fact, it might be a public service. I might even contribute to his defense fund if he did.

"What's the matter? Cat got your tongue?" she taunted.

"Olive, you make it very hard for me to care if you get killed or not."

"You're just jealous. Everyone in town says you're still half in love with Sheriff Peters."

Damn Gertrude Strom's wagging tongue. No one else in Zinnia would talk to Olive because she was a social pariah. Yet Gertrude flapped her gums about me every chance she got.

I couldn't even defend myself. Graf sat beside me in the roadster as we flew toward Zinnia and The Gardens B and B. Luckily he couldn't hear Olive's end of the conversation, but he cast a curious glance at me. When I didn't respond, his attention returned to the cotton fields speeding by. Behind us, Cece drove the Range Rover with Tinkie riding shotgun.

"The truth hurts, doesn't it, Sarah Booth." Olive couldn't resist digging a little harder.

"You're way off, Twist. And if you want me to drop you as a client, keep it up."

"You must be with Graf. That's why you won't talk. Now, Mr. Hollywood is a good-looking man. Charismatic. Sexy. Women probably throw themselves at him." She chuckled. "I'll bet he's cool about you and the lawman. Or at least he pretends to be. Old flames and all. A secure man wouldn't let it bother him. Sometimes, though, I'll bet he sees the way Coleman looks at you. I've sure seen it."

Starlings swooped above the expanse of cotton plants, elegant black shadows flitting with the grace of angels against the pink sky. Soon it would be dark, and we were racing the clock to save Olive Twist. It was an exercise in masochism.

"Olive, go back to your room and wait for us there."

"Can't argue, can you? You've got your claws in ol' Coleman Peters good and deep. Me-ow!"

I couldn't answer her charges or take up for Coleman. Not with Graf sitting beside me. "We're on the way and will be at The Gardens in a matter of minutes. Go to your room and wait there."

"I'm so sorry. I didn't realize God died and put you in charge."

"You are a stupid woman. When you're dead, Coleman will arrest Buford and his crew, the Lady in Red will be returned to her grave, and everything will return to normal."

She laughed, but it wasn't a happy sound. "You sure know how to kill a buzz, Sarah Booth."

Was it possible she was going to do what I urged? "Quit complaining and move out of that bar."

"Keep your shirt on, I'm going."

I heard the *flap, flap, flap* of her big shoes on the hard-wood floor as she left the bar area and walked along the porch to her room. She wouldn't talk and she wouldn't hang up. Nothing like being held hostage on the phone. Next thing she'd take me into the bathroom with her. This woman didn't have a shred of grace.

I tried several times to get her attention, but she mo-seyed along. I pictured those skinny hips swishing left and right. Any minute now she'd deliver the famous Prissy line, "I don't know nothin' 'bout birthin' babies."

"Olive!" I screamed into the phone.

Graf took it from my hand. "You drive, I'll yell."

My hero—he'd saved me from blowing a gasket. I snatched a quick glance at his profile, phone pressed to his ear. My love for him had grown deeper than I'd ever anticipated.

"Olive?" he said. He signaled me that she was on the line.

We flew into the darkening eastern sky, only a few minutes from Zinnia now. The Range Rover's headlights followed steadily behind me.

Graf nodded as he spoke into the phone. "Yes, Olive, what were you saying about your documentary? You believe HBO will air it? That would be incredible." He winked at me. He could do more with Olive in ten sec-onds than I could in a lifetime.

"Olive! Olive!" Graf's tone bordered on panic.

"What is it?" I asked.

"The phone went dead. She was talking about the wonders of her film and how *I* could use *my* contacts to get better distribution for her. I heard what sounded like a thud and then nothing."

I took the phone and listened to footsteps departing. Not the mud-flappers of Olive's wide shoes but quick, hard footsteps. And then moaning.

"Call Coleman. Tell him Olive's been attacked." I tossed Graf the phone and pressed the pedal to the metal.

I wheeled into The Gardens with Cece right behind me. Graf had called Coleman and then Tinkie to let them both know what was happening. We abandoned the cars and rushed inside. Gertrude Strom blocked the hallway a few doors up from Olive's room, but she stepped aside as if she were actually happy we were there.

"An ambulance is on the way," Gertrude told us. "She's still not conscious, but her vital signs are good."

I wasn't aware Gertrude had medical training, but it was good to know.

"Did you see anyone?" I asked.

"I don't have to talk to you. This is all your fault. Wherever you go, trouble follows."

So much for détente. "Did you see anyone, Gertrude? You don't want the B and B to get a reputation for endangering guests. It would be best to help us find the attacker."

She signaled us to follow her down the hall. "No, I didn't notice anyone. Buford and the giant created a disturbance in the bar. When I went there to sort it out, I sent the two of them hightailing it off the premises. That's when I realized Dr. Twist had also left the bar. I meant to stop by her room, but I was distracted by another guest. When I finally got to Olive's room, I found her unconscious on the floor. Her room is trashed. I'll bet Buford doubled back and did this."

It didn't make a lot of sense. The timing was off. I was talking to Olive when she left the bar. Graf had her on the phone when she was attacked. All within minutes. So was an intruder hiding in her room? Had the interloper remained hidden while she chatted with Graf? Or had she opened her door to the attacker?

What was he doing in Twist's room? Stealing? Not likely. Her research simply wasn't that valuable. But someone had been to Dahlia House and taken Graf's note—and nothing else. Olive's research wasn't a cure for cancer or a new app—goods people would pay money for—but that didn't mean it wasn't valuable to the right person.

"You didn't see anyone leaving?" I repeated the question to Gertrude.

"I've already said no. I'm not in the habit of changing the facts to suit myself."

Holy Swiss cheese, Olive and Gertrude shared many of the same personality traits. They were both insulting, insufferable, ornery, and prickly.

We found the door to Olive's room open. The professor sat groggily on the floor holding one side of her head. "Somebody knocked me out. Sneaky bastards. They came at me from behind."

I knelt beside her, aware that a tornado had swept through the room. When she saw the mess, she was going to be hotter than a hellcat. "EMTs are on the way. Try to stay still. Maybe you should lie back."

"Maybe you should find five aspirin and a glass of water." She pushed me away. "I need to find the a-hole who whacked me upside the head. I hate a damn ambush."

I should have known she was too freaking mean to die. "Did you see your attacker?"

"The bastard came at me when my back was turned." Olive pushed to her feet and surveyed the destroyed room. "My work! My work!" She flapped her arms as if she might burst into flight.

"Calm down, Dr. Twist." Gertrude tried to capture her.

"You stupid old bat, my work has been purloined. Can't you see, everything is gone?"

"Dr. Twist, you should remain calm until a doctor has checked you over." Graf spoke with gentleness and reason.

"Shut up! Any man stupid enough to marry Sarah Booth shouldn't be giving advice to others."

"Hey, that's enough." Cece pinned Olive's arms to her side. "Calm down or I'll sit on you. And stop being so rude to people who are only trying to help you."

For whatever reason, Cece achieved the desired result. Olive settled down and I was able to assess the damage in the room. Someone had wrecked it, and it would take time to ascertain what was missing. If anything. It might simply be an act of vandalism.

Before I could ask, Coleman entered the room. Olive pulled free of Cece and hurled herself against him. Her long arms circled his chest and she pressed her face into his starched shirt and sobbed. Every one of us, even Gertrude, looked away, mortified for Coleman.

"Let's track down Buford," Cece said with a deadly undertone. "He's stupid enough to stumble back to the bar. I have a score to settle with Mr. Richmond . . . and my miscreant brother."

"I'll call Oscar," Tinkie offered. "Buford will cooperate with us—or else."

By unspoken consensus, we agreed not to involve Coleman in the incident at the river camp. It was out of his jurisdiction, and my personal ambition was to figure out what the Heritage Heroes were up to.

"Keep an eye on Olive," I said to Coleman. "I think there's a plot afoot. She'll be safe with you."

Graf draped an arm around my shoulders as we left Olive to the tender mercies of the law.

The bar at the B and B was empty of everyone—except Richard Webber. He perched on a stool, elbows on the old teak, sipping a bourbon and reading the late Shelby Foote's last book. He never looked up when we entered.

"Engrossed in Foote's work?" I asked.

"He was a gentleman and a scholar, as the saying goes." Webber still didn't look at me. When Tinkie pushed up to his other side, I backed away. He was a man who'd respond to Tinkie's charms much quicker than to my questions. A good investigator uses the right tool for each occasion.

Graf, Cece, and I took a table in a far corner. When the bartender—Misty, by her nametag—took our order, I asked her about Buford and Arnold.

"They left a while ago. After that skinny, mean woman left. They were right on her heels." She shrugged. "Glad to have all of them out of here. Every time that woman steps foot in the door she starts a fight. She's going to get the piss slapped out of her. Or worse. And I would laugh. Lord, she rubs me the wrong way."

Color me guilty. The shame was I felt no remorse.

In a matter of moments Misty had our drinks made and delivered.

"To a long day." Cece rubbed the chafed places on her

wrist. "It's a good thing Buford isn't here. I'd have stomped a mud hole in his ass and walked it dry."

Cece seldom got colloquial, but I always enjoyed it when she did. "I could sell tickets to spectators."

She grinned at last, acknowledging the humor of such a vision. "What is wrong with the people around here?" she asked. "Why are Buford and Jeremiah still breathing? And people on the streets treat them with respect, as if they were more than a grease-based life form."

"There was a time a person's good name meant something. The Falcon and Richmond families stood for integrity and honor. Jeremiah and Buford are trading on the past."

"Not anymore," Cece said. "My parents are spinning in their graves."

I wondered if that were true. Were my parents watching what I did? Would they find Graf to be a suitable son-in-law? Were they proud of me? I'd never know for certain.

"Watch Tinkie," Graf directed us with more than a hint of admiration. "She is something else."

I had to agree. Tinkie had Webber smiling at her and bending down to listen to her every word. He whispered in her ear, and she looked up at him and giggled. He laughed heartily and his hand strayed to her back.

Soon she'd have the pass codes to his Swiss bank accounts, if he had any. It was almost unfair to unleash Tinkie on the unsuspecting. Webber might be the master of easily impressed graduate students, but he was not on a level playing field with the Tinkmeister. He would end up bruised and bloodied.

Oh, I looked forward to it. Nothing like watching a

self-proclaimed lady's man get worked over by a Daddy's Girl.

"I have to go." Cece put her empty glass on the table.

I realized then she'd been too quiet. "Either I'll go with you, or Graf will. One of us needs to stay here and make sure Tinkie doesn't tie Webber in a knot."

She stepped back from the table. "No. Please. I need a walk. And I need to decide what to do. You've held back, Sarah Booth, because one of the prime suspects is my brother. We can't do that anymore. Things will only worsen."

"Cece—"

"I think of everything I gave up just to be me." Her voice broke, but she didn't cry. "I only wanted my family to love me for who I was. I asked too much of them. And now this is visited on me by Jeremiah, who got everything. Every scrap of love they had, they lavished on him. And this is how it turns out?"

She was out the door before I could turn around. Graf caught my wrist, just a gentle tug.

"Let her go. She has a lot to think about."

"She shouldn't walk home." Cece was in terrific shape, and a walk down the deserted streets of Zinnia was about as safe as a nocturnal jaunt could be. It was loneliness that I wanted to protect my friend from, not danger. Her only living relative had hurt her, yet again.

Graf read my concern. "Wait for Tinkie. I'll go after Cece," he said.

When a man truly loves a woman, he loves her friends. "Thank you." I kissed his cheek and held him close for a moment. "I don't deserve you."

"Keep thinking that way." His grin was crooked and

naughty. "I'll tell you what I want from you later to-night."

"Whatever it is, it's yours."

He walked out the door and I had an incredible impulse to follow and stop him. I couldn't bear to let him out of my sight. What if something happened to him? I'd never recover. Love was such a handicap in the PI business.

The bartender drifted over to pick up our check and the money Graf left on the table. Misty was a respect-able distance from Webber, so I asked her if he'd been in the bar all evening.

"Most of it." She put the dirty glasses on a tray. "He left for about half an hour. He was talking to that old codger, Buford, and his friend. Then he disappeared, and I thought he'd stiffed me for the tab. He came back and paid, though, and he's been right there ever since."

"Thanks." Thirty minutes would be enough time to sneak into Olive's room, tear it up, and conk her on the head. Webber was the only person who might find value in her research—if anything was taken. It could as easily have been a Heritage Hero who just wanted to destroy her research and belongings.

Tinkie and Webber had their heads together like two old lovers. When he woke up from her spell, he was go-ing to be pissed, but it would be too late. My partner would know everything, all of his sordid little secrets.

She signaled she was ready to go. Keys in hand, I si-dled out of the bar and waited for her in the hallway. I nearly jumped out of my skin when I saw movement in the gardens. Night had fallen, and the multitude of fairy lights Gertrude normally kept on to illuminate her ex-quisite plants were oddly dark.

I almost called out, but then I caught the glint of moonlight on Gertrude's red hair. She carried a stack of linens and hurried across the yard. Probably a minor emergency like a guest needing clean sheets. The life of a B and B owner was not for me, of that I was certain.

Tinkie breezed up beside me. "Let's go." She didn't wait for me to agree. She grabbed my arm and kept walking.

"Did you learn anything?"

"Buford and Jeremiah plan to kidnap Olive. Tonight."

We rushed along the porch to Olive's room. Tinkie's tiny little fists beat hard against the solid wood door. No answer.

Very slowly she turned to me. "Maybe Olive and Coleman don't want to be disturbed?" She made it a question in an effort to spare my feelings.

I slammed my hand on the door much harder. With the same result. No one came to let us in. If they were in there, they weren't answering. And if they weren't in there, where were they?

Tink scuffed her toe on the floor. "Maybe they went to the courthouse to take a statement or something."

"Let's get out of here."

"I'll try calling him." She suited action to her words. After several rings, it was apparent he wouldn't answer. "That's not like Coleman. He always answers his phone."

"While Webber was eavesdropping on Buford and Jeremiah, did he say how they intended to abduct Olive?" Perhaps they'd already nabbed her, and Coleman, too.

"No details were forthcoming." Tinkie came to the

same conclusion. "Gertrude can open the room. Coleman could be in there injured."

We hustled to the front desk, which was empty. The key to Olive's room dangled from a pigeonhole, and I snared it. Two minutes later, Tinkie and I barreled into the room.

Papers still littered the floor. Shelves were overturned. The computer was smashed—all as it had been earlier. No Coleman or Olive.

"Maybe they went to dinner." Tinkie backed out of the room. "I'm about to starve myself."

"Coleman would answer the phone." I was worried and annoyed. "He knows the Heritage Heroes are up to something. We should have told him about the attacks at the hunting camp."

"If Olive is with him, she's safe. Drive me home and Oscar and I will search for Buford. Maybe we can talk sense into him. I'm sure Graf is back at Dahlia House now, waiting for you."

"We can stop at the courthouse and talk to DeWayne."

"Oscar and I will stop by to talk to Coleman. Buford is really our problem, and Oscar needs to handle it. Wrangle a bit of together time with Graf before he takes off for the West Coast."

We left The Gardens and walked to the parking lot—in the dark. All of the artistically placed outside lights remained unlit.

It didn't take ten minutes to reach Hill Top. I stopped at the cobblestone walk, and Tinkie put a hand on my shoulder. "Are you okay?"

"I am."

"I don't understand what Coleman sees in Olive.

Maybe he's just lonely. But keeping her safe tonight is his problem, not ours. Be thankful."

I had to draw a line in my mind and my emotions. I wasn't confused. I loved Graf deeply. I also cared for Coleman. He was my youth, my childhood. He'd known me before I was an orphan or a PI. We had a history.

She leaned over and kissed my cheek. "Tomorrow, we need to fill Coleman in on everything. We can file charges in Washington County. Which may be an asset. I'd prefer to have them in the Sunflower County jail where I can watch them, but a little distance from their cohorts might be a good thing."

"Call me when you find Buford, okay?"

"Will do. You aren't really worried they'll pull off a kidnapping, are you?"

I wasn't worried about Olive. Not really. They could cook her but they couldn't eat her—she was that unpalatable. But something niggled at me, made me uneasy. "I'd just like this to be over. The whole thing's a tempest in a teapot. Who cares what Olive writes? But a young man is dead. That's bothersome to me. The stakes aren't high enough to warrant murder, yet Jimmy Boswell is dead."

Tinkie tapped her toe. "You're right. This doesn't add up. This should be a piece of cake, but nothing plugs in quite right. Not Webber, not Olive, not Boswell. Not even those kooks Buford and Jeremiah. I see why you're edgy."

"And I'm tired." I hated to admit it, but exhaustion was making me dull.

"Get Graf to rub your shoulders." She blew a kiss and ran up the sidewalk to her house. The front door opened, framing Oscar. Chablis shot out of the house like a rocket.

I doubted the little dust mop weighed two pounds, but she was all heart. She barked and sprang into Tinkie's arms.

Oscar came down the walk and swept them both into a huge hug. Tinkie was welcomed back into the bosom of her family.

14

I fought the temptation to go by the courthouse to see if Coleman was there with Olive. The truth was, she annoyed the snot out of me. I despised her. I fought an unrelenting urge to stuff her on a jet plane headed for Maine, where she belonged. I'd never wanted this case—and in fact wasn't contractually on it—yet I felt like a wolf in a leg trap.

My headlights illuminated the cotton growing close to the road. The pulsing thrum of insects was better than any radio. I drove and pondered the chambers of my heart.

I'd never loved anyone the way I loved Graf. I had no doubt that my impending marriage was the answer to my prayers for a partner. He'd been my first adult love, and he'd broken my heart. But that heartbreak had also sent me home to Zinnia to save Dahlia House. Struggling to keep my home from foreclosure had focused me and given me a purpose I'd never experienced.

Coleman had been such a part of that journey. He was more like me than any other man I'd known. The land had a grip on him the same way it did on me. We forged a bond that only his commitment to another woman could shatter. And Connie had done that. She'd refused to release Coleman from his marriage, even when she didn't want him.

He wasn't a man who could sneak around his vows, and I'd been smart enough to know it. Had he thrown Connie over, no good would have come of it. If Life, the capital "L" kind, is all about timing, I had a lot to learn. When Coleman and I collided, our timing sucked. By the time he and Connie divorced, it was too late for us.

And then Graf came back into my life. He'd come looking for me, aware of what he'd lost. He'd been willing to give up everything to get me back.

The twists and turns of true love were hairpin at times. One degree different, and I might be living an alternate reality. I could have been the sheriff's wife. Maybe even a deputy. The bottom line: I would always love Coleman. No woman would ever be good enough for him. Certainly not Olive Twist. It was unimaginable. She would wreck Coleman's life, ostracizing him from his friends. Yet it was his choice. One I had to respect no matter how much I disagreed with it.

My thoughts had accompanied me home, and I turned down the drive to Dahlia House determined to push the case from my mind. To my surprise, Dahlia House was dark. When I exited the car, Sweetie came tearing across the porch, barking like crazy. "Where's Graf?" I asked.

He'd had plenty of time to drop Cece at home, then drive to Dahlia House. Unless he was consoling Cece. I tried to calm Sweetie as I accepted, yet again, the solid truth about my fiancé. He was a good man. In the world of Zinnia and my friends, this was far more important than being a movie star, though I had no doubt he would attain that, too.

With Sweetie at my side and Pluto, almost invisible in the night, following behind, I went to the barn. While the horses ate, I groomed them. The heat was getting to all three of them, but soon October would blow in on cool, dry air and my early-morning rides around the cotton fields would be the perfect start to my day.

I finished barn chores and put the horses out. It was nearly nine o'clock. No word from Graf. I went inside and checked the answering machine. Not a single call. I didn't want to interrupt a heart-to-heart with Cece, but worry nibbled at the edges of my brain.

I called his cell phone. On the fifth ring, he answered.

"Where the heck are you?" I kept it light.

Heavy breathing.

"Cece?" She was a prankster, but not ridiculous panting like a bad horror movie.

"Okay, guys, cut it out." I grew testy. "This isn't funny."

A long, slow inhale and exhale of breath.

"Whoever this is, I'm not finding the routine amusing." My temper kicked in, right on top of a gut-wrenching fear.

My answer was a click and a disconnect. I called back and the phone went to voice mail. "This is Graf, leave a message." I hung up and called Cece's cell phone.

"So at last you call, dah-link. I'm perfectly fine," she said, "though had I been suicidally depressed. I could already have done the deed by now."

"Where's Graf?" I wasn't intentionally brusque, but my throat constricted.

"Why would I know the whereabouts of your handsome fiancé?"

"Stop it, Cece. Is he with you?"

She heard my fear. "He isn't, Sarah Booth. I haven't seen him since I left The Gardens. I walked home and I've been here ever since."

I sat down heavily on a kitchen chair. "He left right behind you to pick you up and drive you home." The words fell out of my mouth but I wasn't certain they made any sense.

"He never showed up. I walked home and I've been here, drinking a bottle of wine. Don't panic, Sarah Booth. I'll bet he's trying to help you with the case."

"I called his phone and someone answered but they wouldn't talk." I couldn't help it. Tears leaked from my eyes. I felt them crawl over my cheeks. "He's in trouble, Cece. Bad trouble." The worry that had followed me all day jumped hard.

"Sarah Booth, don't do this to yourself. I'm sure he's fine. Where's Tinkie?"

"Searching for Coleman and Olive."

"Maybe Graf is with them."

I grasped at hope and clutched it to me. "We have to find them."

"Meet me at the courthouse." Cece took charge, and a good thing. I was in a state.

———

Sweetie was in the front seat waiting when I went back outside. The dog was psychic. And walking over the hood was Pluto. I picked him up and put him on the ground, but he jumped back on the car.

"Not now." I was gentle but firm as I removed him again.

Pluto leaped on the fender and hissed at me. I'd seen the damage he could do when perturbed. Once more, I shooed him to the lawn. His green eyes pierced me as he sat down.

"I'll be back," I promised him. "Graf may need me."

I jumped behind the wheel and eased away from the house. Pluto was lost in the inky blackness of the night. The doggy door was available to him in the kitchen, and I hoped to be back shortly with Graf.

It wasn't terribly late, but Sunflower County is still basically a farming community. Even though cotton harvesting is mechanized, farmers still rise with the sun and work all day, then hit the sack early.

I didn't think it unusual that I passed no cars on the county road into town. When I came to a sharp ninety-degree turn we called Donnie's Dogleg because of the horrific wreck Donnie Longmire walked away from his senior year in high school, I applied the brakes and slowed.

Before I knew what had happened, there was a loud noise and the car jolted. The steering wheel felt like it was stuck in drying cement. The car was completely unresponsive as I left the asphalt road and launched into the cotton fields going at least forty-five miles an hour. I was flying, flying through the night.

The impact threw me against the steering column and I had enough presence of mind to realize I could have cracked my sternum and damaged my heart. My last thought was about Sweetie Pie. Had she been thrown clear of the car? Was she alive? Before I could seek answers, a swirling blackness sucked me down to the center and held me there.

I came to my senses, aware that Sweetie's low growls came from my right side. I couldn't have been out long, because I knew exactly what had happened, and I was leaning against the steering wheel with my chest. The older car was equipped only with lap seat belts, not the shoulder harness, and no airbags, but at least I hadn't gone flying through the windshield.

"She ain't dead."

The man's voice was so unexpected, I almost screamed. Almost. But I got a grip on myself. Sweetie, though, was much less contained. Her growl warned of serious intent.

"Shoot the damn dog and let's get her." This was an older man, a voice I knew but couldn't pinpoint.

"If she dies here, it'd be the best thing."

"She's a long ways from dead, you idiot. She's just a little stunned. Now shoot the dog, pick her up, and let's move. The boss is gonna be pissed as it is."

The one thing I could not allow was for Sweetie to be shot. My hand slid toward the key in the ignition. When I'd blasted into the cotton field, I'd hit a berm at the edge of the crops and slammed into the ground on the other side. The impact killed the engine, but Mama's roadster was a tough old machine. It had cranked like a charm— after sitting unused in the barn for five years—when I came back from New York.

I was tough, too. The jolt had bruised my ribs and chest, but I wasn't mortally wounded. And I had one chance to escape. Still draped on the steering wheel, I eased the car into park, turned the key, and jammed it into drive. Thank goodness we hadn't had rain in several weeks or I'd have been up to the running board in gumbo, the thick soil of the Delta. The car started, the wheels gained traction, and I spun out.

Only to go nowhere. I didn't have any tires. The bastards had laid spikes across the road, waiting for me to drive by. They'd blown my tires, which is what sent me into the cotton field in the first place.

"Get her, Arnold!" The older man was obviously in charge.

They were behind the car, and clouds covered the moon and stars.

"Just shoot the silly bitch." I recognized Arnold's voice. Holy crap, I'd fallen into the hands of the crazy survivalists. But the older man talking was neither Jeremiah nor Buford. He was confident, though. In charge.

Sweetie's growl warned me they were approaching. One of the men chambered a round. I groped on the seat for my cell phone, but I had no idea where the impact had flung it.

"If you won't shoot my dog, I won't fight." My pistol was in the trunk. If only I'd thought to put it in the front seat with me. That was the problem with carrying a gun. I didn't have a holster like the boys in the Wild West. What good was it in the trunk?

"Get out of the car."

I tried to open the door, but it was stuck. I'd landed pretty hard. "I can't."

Footsteps brushed through the cotton, and a large man loomed at my door. "If that dog tries to bite me, shoot it."

"Sweetie, stay." We weren't far from home. Sweetie would find her way back to Dahlia House. And I would figure a way out of the mess I'd gotten myself into. I was far more worried about Graf and the Richmonds than I was about myself. But I had a hunch I was about to find my missing fiancé and friends.

Arnold wrenched the door open and his fingers dug into my arm.

"Hey, I said I'd go with you." I tried to twist free but his grip was iron. That on top of my bruised chest was agonizing.

"Shut up!" He leaned down to unfasten my seat belt and I couldn't say for certain what happened. A piercing scream burst from his throat, and he backpedaled from the car, thrashing and cursing. He fell into the cotton, writhing. Sweetie remained motionless in the front seat beside me.

"Arnold, what's wrong?" The other man sounded nervous.

Arnold bellowed a steady stream of curses and threats. "Get it off me! Get it off me!" He rolled around in the cotton, crushing plants.

"What is it?" The other man ran to his friend, but he couldn't see and hung back helplessly.

"It's clawed my eyes! I'm blind!" Arnold bucked like a rodeo bull.

I didn't have to see to know that Pluto had hitched a ride in the backseat and waylaid Arnold with his signature move.

Sweetie and I slipped out the other side of the car and took off through the cotton field. With the overcast sky, they'd never be able to track us.

I worried for Pluto, but he was a cat with more than nine lives and plenty of brainpower. Cats had superb directional abilities, and he'd return to Dahlia House.

Sweetie and I couldn't go there—once Arnold and his friend recovered from the cat attack, that would be the first place they searched.

They couldn't afford for me to contact the sheriff. Which meant they'd do everything they could to stop me.

Everything.

I knew the land. I'd ridden Reveler, Miss Scrapiron, and Lucifer through the fields and brakes, along the straight and narrow country lanes. If I headed due north, I could make it to a neighboring plantation. They'd let me use their phone and give me a ride into town.

I'd covered a hundred yards when Arnold and his friend realized I was gone.

"What had hold of you, man?" the other guy asked.

"Some kind of hell cat. It musta been in the backseat or something. We got to find that Delaney bitch," Arnold said. "If we don't get her back, the boss is gonna make us suffer."

I forced my legs to move faster. The farther away I got, the less caution I had to take about making noise, and I could run. Sweetie felt the same way. We tore through the field, panting but never slowing down.

"Go home, Pluto. Go home and be safe." I spoke aloud though Pluto couldn't hear me. Still, I used my words as a prayer to send him safely back to Dahlia House.

I tried to ignore my panic and the natural questions that arose and spurred me on. What did those men want with me? More important, what had they done with Graf?

I came to a small irrigation ditch that marked the south boundary of the McCauley land. I wasn't far from help now. I didn't know the new owners. The plantation had changed hands two years ago in a foreclosure, but the name would take decades to change. The McCauley family, who had farmed the land for several generations, had lost hard in the stock market crash. When they couldn't pay their mortgage, a national bank had foreclosed on them. I'd watched them pack and leave with sadness. Somehow, I'd never connected with my new neighbors. Now I'd meet them under pressing circumstances.

The cry of night birds and the constant chorus of insects told me no one followed me. Once I gained McCauley's, I'd call for help. I put on a final burst of speed and crossed the last wide fields to the front porch.

The house was old, like Dahlia House, built before the Civil War. A light glowed in an upstairs room, and when I peeped in the window of the front door, I saw the glow of a television in a back room. They were home and they were up. My hopes soared as I lifted my hand to knock.

Headlights jouncing down the long driveway made me pause. Sweetie's growl was all the warning I needed. We sprinted across the porch and dove into shrubs as a new-model pickup slewed to a stop in front of the house.

"Get out," a familiar voice commanded. "I can't tell how bad you're hurt. I need some light."

"Don't tell 'em it was just a cat." Arnold sounded mortified.

"The boss won't care what sliced up your head. Our problem is the private detective got away. This ain't gonna be pretty."

The truck doors slammed and both men stomped up the steps and onto the porch. They knocked three times, then twice. The porch light snapped on and the door opened.

"What the hell happened to you, Arnold?" Jeremiah Falcon asked in his arch, educated tone. "You look like you stuck your head in a meat grinder." There was a pause. "Where's Sarah Booth?"

The two men stumbled and fumbled over their explanation of how they lost me. I peeked over the edge of the porch. Arnold's face and head were shredded. One ear was barely hanging on. Pluto had surely done a number on him. The other man I didn't recognize but wouldn't forget.

"She's in the cotton fields?" Jeremiah was livid. "We have to contain her. If our plan is to work— She has the potential to ruin everything." He walked out on the porch. "Did you hear something?"

Sweetie and I huddled around the base of a big azalea.

"No, sir," Arnold said. "I didn't hear anything. I need to see how bad my face is damaged."

"Screw a few scratches. If you can't handle one little girl, you're worthless to me."

"Mr. Falcon, she had a critter in the car with her. It nearly clawed my eyes out." There was a tad of heat in Arnold's voice. He might be a Heritage Hero foot soldier, but he didn't cotton to condescension.

"You're a bagful of excuses, Arnold. You let my crazy bro-ster snoop through our plans. We moved our planning session to the river and they found us there. Now you let a half-starved girl best you."

Half-starved? Jeremiah thought I was thin? He did have at least one good quality.

"Look at my head!" Arnold had been pushed too far. "It was dark. I was attacked by something with claws. Might have been a wolverine."

"Cat," the other man said, barely able to hide his mirth. "It was a fat cat, to be sure, but just a cat. It ran in front of the headlights."

"Shut up!" Arnold said. "The damn thing was vicious and it meant to put my eyes out."

"Shut up, *both* of you!" Jeremiah thundered. "You're incompetent. I have half a mind to court-martial each of you. Organize a search party for Ms. Delaney. We have to find and contain her. Arnold, get inside and have Rob stitch your ear back on. Make it fast. We have work to do."

15

Jeremiah cracked orders left and right. "Get back in the field and search for her. She can't be far. She'll likely head toward Dahlia House. Get between her and her plantation and stop her."

"I think we should call the other members. We may need help subduing the detective." For such a big, strong man, Arnold had the whine down pat.

"You *need* to find Ms. Delaney. Now. This disaster is your fault."

The silence told me Arnold was balking. But at last he said, "Yes, sir."

"Good. I'll round up the other men on the premises. We'll load up in your truck and head out to the place where she wrecked. She has to be around there. Was she injured?"

"She hit the steering wheel pretty solid." This was the older man I couldn't identify. "She was pretendin' to be unconscious, which is how she got away."

"You *assumed* she was unconscious. Only idiots assume. Now you'd better find her and make this right."

The door slammed and in a few minutes boots tromped out of the house and onto the porch. Harsh laughter and a few ribald comments accompanied the men clambering into the pickup.

"Are you coming, Jeremiah?" Arnold asked.

"I am indeed. I'll follow in my car."

The pickup cut a sharp U-turn and sped out the drive. Another vehicle followed. The heat-soaked night settled over the fields.

I needed a telephone, and the closest one was likely in the house. I waited as long as I could, listening for anyone left behind. Worry for Graf and Pluto was eating me alive. Even if entering the house unleashed danger, I had to risk it.

"Ready, girl?" I asked Sweetie.

Her reply was a sprint around the porch and up the stairs. When I caught up with her, she was standing on her hind legs peering in a window. A television's glow illuminated the back room in a wavering blue light. It put me in mind of ghosts and creepies. My fear, though, centered on flesh and blood—men armed with guns. Ghosts I could handle.

The only sign of life came from the television, so I tried the doorknob. It turned without complaint. Sweetie was Velcroed to my leg as we entered. The house was mostly unfurnished. When the McCauleys lost their land, they took the family antiques and gracious décor that made the house such a warm memory. I'd come here with my mother on several occasions to share the garden's bounty or to have a cup of coffee. Libby Delaney looked out for neighbors, no matter how busy she was. She made it a point to stop and talk with the older folk who lived around the county, and I had often accompanied her. I'd learned a deep appreciation for the ties binding us to place and home.

Those times had passed. Now the beautiful old hardwood floor was scarred by careless misuse. Dust clouded the once burnished wainscoting that had given the foyer such a mellow glow. The beautiful ceiling medallions that centered light fixtures and crown molding handmade from plaster and horsehair had begun to crack and fall due to humidity and lack of care. In a matter of months, Jeremiah and his crowd had corrupted an antebellum beauty. He was truly a man determined to destroy anything of merit that crossed his path.

Especially his sister. And anyone who defended her right to be herself.

Sweetie and I didn't linger. We moved through the rooms as silently as ethereal spirits. My quest was simple—a phone to contact Cece and Coleman. They'd come and get me, and we'd hunt for Graf. Something had detained him. Something bad.

The empty rooms depressed me. They even worked on Sweetie. She moaned softly in her throat, letting me know she shared my emotion. When we entered the TV room, a blond bimbo on an entertainment network read the news with the startled expression of a possum in the headlights. But she was giving it all she had, trying to whip her audience into a frenzy.

This was the only room with furniture and the best bet of locating a phone, if one existed. The odds were fifty-fifty. Many people had forgone landlines. I searched every flat surface without result. Strangely, there were no computers or electronics.

"Let's head out the back and start toward town," I told Sweetie. We couldn't walk along the road for fear of being discovered by Jeremiah's militia. It would be a long, hard hike through the fields, but there were other plantations along the way where I would be received with friendship. While I might not be well known, folks remembered my parents with great fondness. Libby and James Franklin Delaney, though long dead, were still respected.

A strong impulse to check upstairs came over me. What if Graf was there, held hostage or injured? But the upstairs could also be a trap. If I went up there and the men returned, I would be caught. One foot on the first step and my hand on the rail, every impulse in my body urged me up the stairs.

"Graf?" I called softly.

Only silence.

"Graf!" I notched up the volume. If he could hear me, he'd respond.

But there was nothing, just the pounding of blood in my ears and Sweetie's soft panting. She snagged my shirt in her teeth and tugged me toward the door.

"I can't leave without making sure Graf isn't here." I wasn't being stubborn; I was terrified what they might do to him.

Sweetie gripped tighter and growled, shaking her head so hard her ears flapped. Then I heard what her keen hound ears had already picked up—a vehicle approaching.

No choice. I had to leave. Immediately.

As soon as I found Coleman, he could get a search warrant and determine if Graf was a prisoner. All I had to do was escape and get to town. I would be no good to either of us if I was captured.

I was moving to the back to vacate the premises when a small chirping noise drew my attention. On the floor beside a ratty old recliner was a small electronic tablet. Technology! Thank goodness Tinkie had insisted I learn to operate electronic devices. I could email Cece! She would alert the cavalry and come to the rescue.

I grabbed the tablet and slipped out the back door, ducking into a huge wisteria. The tangle of leaves and vines offered the perfect cover as I wasted precious time figuring out how to get into the tablet. At last I accessed the Web and sent Cece, Tinkie, Oscar, Coleman, and De-Wayne SOS messages.

"Have been waylaid by right-wing militia. At old Mc-Cauley plantation—one of their headquarters. Walking toward town. Find me! Graf is missing. Urgent."

I hit the Send button and started to drop the tablet in the dirt when I realized I held solid gold—at least potentially. I shoved it in my shirt and crawled out of my hiding place like my pants were afire. If I had to hoof it, I might as well haul boogie.

The night was like walking into lukewarm soup—hot, clammy, and unpleasant. Insects hummed so loudly I could have sung the Hallelujah Chorus and been drowned out by the busy little crickets. That was good, though. Using my best internal compass, I found a row of cotton and walked straight down it.

With her keener sense of direction, Sweetie took the lead. My dog would lead me to town. She had an insatiable love for ice cream cones from the Sweetheart Café, and I had more faith in her than I did in most people. It was going to be a long, sweaty night.

Forty minutes later, I drew close to the main road to town. Danger lurked here. But also possible rescue. The trick would be telling them apart. Approaching headlights could be Coleman or Cece, or it could be Arnold or Jeremiah. I wouldn't really know until the vehicle was too close to escape if I picked wrong.

Almost as if I'd conjured them, a pair of headlights blinked in the distance. Sweetie and I dove into the cotton. I got down on my stomach and elbows and watched the approaching lights. The vehicle crept forward at a pace that told me a search was in progress.

The pickup loaded with men cruised by so slowly I could make out Arnold illuminated by the dash lights. Several men with rifles were in the truck bed. They'd given up searching for me in the cotton fields and figured I was walking to town. They were smarter than they looked.

The red taillights disappeared just as another set of headlights came up on the horizon. This vehicle, too, cruised at a leisurely rate. It could be one of my friends, or it could be Jeremiah.

I couldn't risk it.

As much as I wanted to jump into the middle of the road and wave my hands and hope I would be rescued, I couldn't.

When the car was a good fifty yards away, I heard

music. A song with personal history for me. The Dixie Chicks belted out "Goodbye, Earl."

I jumped up and ran screaming into the road. "Stop! Stop! Here I am!"

Cece's Prius halted right beside me. "Get in quick, Sarah Booth. Coleman said people are all over the place. He thinks they're looking for you."

Sweetie and I needed no second invitation. My hound jumped in the backseat and I climbed in the passenger side. Cece was already rolling before I shut the door. And a good thing. Approaching headlights blazed in front of us.

"Get down," Cece said. She rolled up the windows and pressed the accelerator harder.

I ducked onto the floorboard and held my breath as we passed the other vehicle. Cece stared straight ahead, never acknowledging the other car.

"I should just kill that bastard," Cece said vehemently. "I should."

"Was it Jeremiah?"

"It was. Dirty lowlife."

She might call her brother names—and mean them— but he was still blood. I understood this. When the time came, she would stand for him even as he spit vitriol at her. His actions hurt her—had hurt her for many years— but he was her brother.

"Any word from Graf?"

Cece sighed softly. "No, Sarah Booth. Coleman and DeWayne are on it."

"And Olive?"

"It's a long story. I'm taking you to the courthouse. Olive is in jail."

It was the first bit of good news in a long time, but I

had better things to do then probe Olive's legal issues. "I need to go home. Pluto is somewhere in the fields between the place where I wrecked and Dahlia House."

"I can't take you there. Jeremiah has men on the lookout for you. We'd be sitting ducks."

As much as it dismayed me, I couldn't argue. Her logic was . . . logical. "What if Graf is at the old McCauley house? I should have checked upstairs. I didn't have time. Someone came back." I was working myself toward a righteous case of hysteria and guilt.

"Snap out of it!" Cece didn't backhand me, but she brought me around to my senses.

"Where could Graf be? I just have this horrible image of him bleeding out and thinking I'll be there to save him—and I don't find him."

"You're letting your imagination render you useless. Stop it this instant. I think you're right. He's been taken hostage by the Heritage organization. He's useful as a pawn to control you. So calm down. The best thing you did was to escape. Had they gotten their hands on you, they'd have no need to keep Graf."

Put that way, I felt better. "I still should have searched."

"And if you'd been trapped? At least now Coleman, DeWayne, Tinkie, Oscar, Madame Tomeeka, and Millie are all looking for him. And for you."

All of my wonderful friends were beating the bushes hunting for me and my man. If something bad had happened to him because of my work . . . I couldn't even finish the thought. Of all the times he'd been mad at me because I put myself in danger, I finally understood the emotional load he carried. An intellectual understanding of fear and worry couldn't compare to the visceral emotion I now felt. Emptiness and dread shadowed my every move, and the sensation was debilitating.

"Where have they hunted?"

"Graf isn't at Magnolia Grove. That's the first place Coleman tried." She cleared her throat several times. "They found his Range Rover hidden on the grounds of The Gardens."

Graf had been abducted before he even left The Gardens. He was taken only moments after he left me. His vehicle was moved so no one would notice. He'd been captive for hours, and I'd never suspected a thing. I'd gone about my business feeding and grooming the horses, futzing around with my leads, oblivious to the danger hanging over the man I loved.

"Do you have your phone?" Cece asked. "We haven't called it for fear they had it. We didn't want them to know we were on your trail."

"It's either on the floorboard of the car or in the cotton field. Unless they have it." I wouldn't be guilty of underestimating Jeremiah and crew ever again. What I'd learned about their willingness to harm people had given me a whole new respect for their lawlessness.

I shifted in the car seat and a sharp jab in my gut reminded me of the tablet I'd picked up in the house. "And I have this!" I pulled it from between my torso and shirt.

"That's what you sent the email on." Cece eyed it. "Anything good on it?"

"We're about to find out." Except we had no Internet connection in the middle of cotton fields.

Cece drove straight for the courthouse, where there was a strong high-speed, public Wi-Fi. I booted up the device. This was obviously Jeremiah's personal tablet— who would guess the old coot had the latest technology.

Then again, he had a highly trained brain—he just didn't bother to use it.

It might be fascinating to track Jeremiah's Internet travels, but a cache of files looked more interesting. I'd just opened up one titled Tilda Richmond—History, when we wheeled into the courthouse lot.

Coleman and DeWayne chatted beside a cruiser, a sign that didn't bode well. A security light filtered through the branches of an oak, checkerboarding the two men in shadows and light. The image struck at my soul. It spoke of so many things, of the past, the duality of life and nature, that clarity of sight or mind exists only if both light and dark are accepted. Life and death. A foreboding omen.

"Did you find Graf?" I asked, climbing out before Cece came to a full halt.

"There's not a trace of him." Coleman delivered the bad news with a clenched jaw. "He can't be far. But it's like he disappeared into thin air."

Coleman's words evoked scenes from *Ghost Whisperer* where the reconciled spirit sees the portal to the next dimension and then walks into nothingness. I choked back a sob. Coleman's arms came around me, supporting me against his chest.

"Call Tinkie here right now," he said to DeWayne or Cece, I couldn't be sure. With the lightest pressure, he guided me toward the trunk of the oak. How many hours had I played around the root system of that old tree when I was a child? I'd strung fantasies and built caves and created waterfalls with an old mop bucket and water from the fountain.

In those glorious days of remembered childhood, the light softened the edges of the hard things, the painful things. I was a child in braids, singing "Tom Dooley," a song my mother taught me, and playing in the oak's shade, until my father finished work so I could ride home with him. At nine, I'd been oblivious to the pain life meant to deliver. I'd been cocooned in my parents' love.

I would have given a lot to look up and see my father walking down the courthouse steps.

"Sarah Booth, we'll find him." Coleman held me tight against him, otherwise I might have melted to the ground. "Buck up, girl. This is no time to lose your grit."

The strongest impulse to run came over me. I pushed hard against Coleman's chest, intending to break free and sprint away. I had to move. If I didn't run as hard as I could, I might burst into flames. Or tears.

But Coleman anticipated my reaction. His arm clamped down around my waist and he used his chest as a bulwark. I fought with everything I had in me. And he held me with as much tenderness as he could afford.

We struggled in silence, neither saying a word. The only sound was my harsh panting as I fought him.

Behind me, I heard Cece's sharp sob, and DeWayne's murmured words of comfort. The shrill cry of a hawk came from high in the oak tree, another omen of doom.

I had to break free. I was suffocating in Coleman's hold, but I couldn't budge him. At last, I collapsed against him and grew still. He magically released me, knowing there wasn't an ounce of fight left in me.

"We'll find him, Sarah Booth." He said it twice.

"Those people are dangerous. I thought they were a bunch of ridiculous kooks. They're a lot more than that. They could have killed me when they spiked my car tires. I think they *meant* to kill me."

His hand cupped my elbow. "Let's go inside and review what we each know. I think Cece gave me the time frame for Graf's disappearance. His car hidden on the grounds of The Gardens tells me he was abducted there, probably on his way to the parking lot."

I felt as if a muddling fog had begun to clear from my mind. The things Coleman said sharpened the time line. Graf had been gone for nearly seven hours. They'd taken him without so much as a scuffle that anyone witnessed.

I forced calm into my voice. "I want to go to The Gardens. Maybe Sweetie can pick up his trail."

"Good thought. But let's go to my office first. I want you to speak with Olive."

"To hell with Olive." I'd had enough.

"She might be able to help."

"Seriously?" I couldn't believe it. "I should never have gotten involved with her. She came here to start trouble, and she sure has. For me, for Cece, for Tinkie and Oscar. For everyone I care about, even you."

Coleman had the grace to look away, which sent a flood of fury through me. "I'll find Graf, and anyone who tries to stop me will be sorry."

"And the quickest way to get there is to talk to Olive." Coleman's patience was running thin. He, too, felt the pressure of time. Each hour without a ransom call whittled away the possibility of a happy ending.

"Loan me a patrol car. I want to go to The Gardens."

Coleman slowly shook his head. "Tinkie's on the way, Sarah Booth. She and Oscar went out to the place where you wrecked and found your cell phone. Oscar's arranged to have the car towed to the garage. They went by Dahlia House. Pluto's safe and sound. Tinkie fed him."

Pluto's safe return to Dahlia House was one worry off my plate. "Thank them when you see them, but please give me the keys to a vehicle."

Coleman sighed. Before he could respond to my request, Cece pushed forward. Her slender arm circled my shoulders and she marched me toward the courthouse. "Twist may have information. Before you go running off and get yourself abducted, at least talk to her. If you want to help Graf, use your head, not your heart."

Every impulse told me to do something—anything. Not talk, but action. Yet Cece and Coleman both counseled me to question Twist. What could she possibly know about Graf's abduction? It was time to find out.

"Okay. Five minutes. Max."

We marched up the courthouse steps like the Fantastic Four—DeWayne brought up the rear. When we were in the sheriff's office, Coleman motioned me to the cells. "Find out what she knows. DeWayne and I will round up Jeremiah and Buford."

"Watch yourselves." Cece gave them each a quick hug.

"Will do." Coleman's gaze flicked to me. For a moment I saw his worry and determination, and then he walked out with DeWayne at his side.

"Should we call in reinforcements?" I asked.

"I don't think cavalry is stationed in Mississippi." Cece kept glancing at the door. I didn't have to read her mind to know she was hoping Tinkie would arrive.

A sudden question made me grasp Cece's elbow and pull her around. "If Olive has information about Graf, why isn't Coleman here to dig it out of her?"

A vein in Cece's temple pulsed with every beat of her heart. "She won't talk to Coleman."

"Why not?"

"We're wasting time." She pulled free. Her long stride carried her to the jail. I had no choice but to follow.

16

Olive prowled the cell like a caged lioness. If she had a tail, it would be lashing back and forth. Pluto came to mind and I wished he were with me. His interrogation techniques were simple and to the point. Claw first, and bring the suspect to her knees. Completely efficient. Too bad I couldn't wring her scrawny neck until she squawked. I was in no mood to play patty-cake with the historian.

"Good of you to drop by," Olive said.

I wanted nothing more than to wipe the smirk off her face, preferably with a Brillo pad and Red Devil lye. "Where's Graf?"

"I should think you'd ask how you can get me released. You are my employee, after all."

"In case you've forgotten, you haven't paid me a

penny. There isn't enough money in Fort Knox to get me to work for you. The fact that Tinkie and I even considered taking your case makes me question our sanity."

"Good to know, but I don't believe a word." A grin stretched her lips. "You might not like it, but I suspect you'll work for information. Especially information about a certain actor."

The jail cell was locked, which was the only thing that protected her. "If you know something, you'd better tell me now."

Perhaps it was because I gripped the bars so tightly my knuckles were white as bleached bones. Maybe it was Sweetie's bared fangs. Or it could have been Cece's flip remark, "Tell her or I'll open the cell. She's going to snap you like a twig."

Whatever—something loosened the hinges of Olive's jaw.

"You and Tinkie were buttering up Webber in the bar. Cece left to walk home, and you sent Graf to give her a ride."

But Olive hadn't been in the bar; how did she know? "You're not psychic, so that means you—"

"I set up a camera in the bar." She shrugged. "So sue me for invasion of privacy. Which you can't do. The bar is a public place. There's no expectation of privacy."

I wanted to pull her vocal cords out through a hole in her neck. "What else did you record?"

"I also installed cameras around the grounds. I wanted to catch the person who firebombed my room, and it didn't seem the good sheriff was equipped to suss out the perp."

"They don't call them perps, and Coleman doesn't suss," Cece said. "Suspect would be the word you're seeking. For an educated person, you sure don't know much—"

"Did you see who abducted Graf?" I reached through the bars and caught Olive by the bib of her butt-ugly pink and gray blouse depicting what had to be a Martian sunset. Polyester. Like bad seventies fabric. "Tell me now." Her face squashed against the bars. Her wide feet flailed for purchase on the floor.

Cece jumped into the fray and was trying to break my grip. "Sarah Booth, let her go! She's Coleman's prisoner. You can't hurt her."

"Oh, I can. And I am. And I'll enjoy doing it. Where's Graf?" I locked onto Olive and pressed my face to hers. Only the bars separated us. My intentions were easy to read.

"I don't know. But I saw what happened to him." She struggled to breathe.

I eased up a little. If she passed out, it would take time to splash water on her and wake her up. "What happened?"

"He left the bar and hesitated, like he heard something. Then he disappeared from camera range for about five minutes. After that, I got a clear view of him on the path between those big oaks. He was walking to the parking lot, maybe eight minutes behind Ms. Falcon. He was walking fast, like he was in a hurry to get somewhere, and he had his cell phone out and was dialing someone. Then this dark shadow came out of the bushes. The person was dressed all in black and ran up behind Graf. It looked like Graf was stabbed in the neck with a syringe of some kind. I couldn't be certain because the picture was grainy and not clear. But it looked like his attacker drugged him."

"And you've known this how long?" Judas jumping candlesticks, I had to kill her. It would be a civic duty. The woman needed to die.

She flipped her dark hair over her shoulder and struck a senior portrait pose. "Awhile. But I had to keep you focused on what I needed."

Cece karate-chopped my wrist before I could drag Olive back against the bars and beat her. I was forced to let Olive go. She slumped onto the cot. "Honestly, you don't have to get so irrational."

"What happened after he was injected?" Cece asked. Her tone told me she was as fed up with Olive as I was.

"He sort of crumpled to the ground. Then my camera went on the fritz. A very expensive camera, I might add." A little moue of disinterest settled around her mouth. "I don't know anything else. I was going to check on the camera when Coleman brought me here and locked me up." She spat the last sentence.

"Describe the attacker," I held no hope that Olive would give any reliable details, but I had to try.

"Average height and build. A little stocky. Moved with speed."

That ruled out Jeremiah, who was tall and slender. And the "moving with speed" ruled out Buford. He was out of shape and slow. But it could be any of their minions. Jeremiah had at least half a dozen men searching the fields for me. And there was no telling who was on their membership roster.

"Let's go." I motioned Cece from the cell.

"Hey! Hey! What about me?" Olive asked. "I haven't been charged with anything. You can't hold me here. This is a lawsuit waiting to be filed. I'll own every inch of this ratsuck little hellhole town."

"We aren't deputies," Cece said. "We have no authority to release you."

Olive lunged at the bars, but we were already moving back to the sheriff's office, where I'd left the tablet. We had work to do.

Cece took over. She was quicker and more proficient at button pressing. Jeremiah had compiled a number of files, and among them was a neatly typed list of members of the Heritage Heroes. Telephone numbers were helpfully included.

With her superior skills, Cece accessed the sheriff's office printer, and in a moment we both had a hot-off-the-press copy of the membership. I read the baker's dozen names twice, wondering if Graf languished in confinement—or worse, injured—in the hands of one of these men.

There were no women on the list, I noted. Jeremiah and Buford's club of haters allowed none of the "weaker sex." I would show them what brains and determination could do. I'd thwart them and save Graf.

I cross-checked the names with Cece, marking the handful of familiar ones with an X. Half the names we didn't recognize—a few were people I knew in passing. Folks who had recently moved into Sunflower County and I'd met in the grocery store or at some political function. In fact, I realized many of the men had injected themselves into the actions of Sunflower County's governing bodies. I could only assume they had moved to Sunflower County to join Jeremiah's Internet madness. Mayan calendar, the Rapture, sunspots, whatever it took to feed the fear. The people on the list had a desperate need to believe the world was coming to an end and they would be the chosen ones, the survivors. To me, it seemed like a form of mental illness, and I could never forget that out of those thought processes martyrs were born.

Using a county map, we plotted where each member lived. I urged Cece to ditch the sheriff's office and hit the road with me for a safari, hunting members of the militia group, but she refused. Tinkie was due any second, and Cece wouldn't consider confronting Jeremiah or his henchmen without a lawman, a search warrant, and a loaded weapon.

I thought the search warrant unnecessary, but there was no budging Cece. While we waited on Tinkie to arrive and Coleman to return, we perused the other files on the tablet. Cece kept up a barrage of constant chatter, an attempt to keep my mind off Graf and the ticking clock. I would thank her later, but at the moment I had visions of a ball gag.

When we got to the file on Tilda Richmond's history, Cece plopped into DeWayne's chair and I hovered over her shoulder. We skimmed the paragraphs. Much of it was what Oscar had already revealed. Tilda was a Richmond relative who ran away from home at the age of sixteen to avoid an arranged marriage. No news there.

She went to Washington, D.C., where she worked as a serving girl in a tavern near the Capitol for several years. She engaged in heated political debates with the customers, a fact that got her discharged, but not before she came to the attention of a newspaperman, William French.

Tilda's passion for freeing the slaves—couched as traitorous sentiments by the author of the article—but keeping the union intact appealed to French. He hired her to ghostwrite articles for his newspaper and introduced her to the political circles of D.C. She left behind the tavern and became a member of the fourth estate and the political elite.

In 1855, at the age of twenty, she met Montgomery Blair, a man destined to be Lincoln's postmaster general. In the next years, the Kentucky lawyer brought her into the circle of men who were Lincoln's political adversaries and who, in a brilliant political move, would later become his cabinet. It was a world where Tilda's sharp perception and understanding of the Southern mind-set was greatly appreciated.

Cece began to read aloud. "Tilda and Blair, an avowed abolitionist though his family owned slaves, became friends, an odd couple in the Washington political circles. It was in this friendship that Tilda drew up a plan for the federal government to buy the slaves from slaveholders and preserve the Union. It was a bold proposal, and it met with much resistance from all sides, though Lincoln strongly supported the idea.

"A friendship was forged between the President and Tilda, which we believe escalated beyond the boundaries of professional to personal. Tilda Richmond can reliably be called a traitor and a whore."

Cece looked up and frowned. "Could they do that? I mean, just buy the slaves and free them? Would it have worked?"

"I have no idea if it was a viable plan, but it sure would have saved a lot of anguish and lives." It had never occurred to me to consider such a thing. Could the war have been averted had the idea of a twenty-five-year-old woman been taken seriously? Would the Southern states have gone along with it? The Civil War remained a huge scar on the consciousness of the nation, and the South had never completely recovered from the shroud of defeated nation.

Cece returned to the tablet screen. "After the Southern states seceded from the Union, Blair arranged for Tilda to meet Secretary of War Stanton. A keen animosity developed between them. Stanton allowed that no woman had a role in government, but it was after Lincoln's assassination that Stanton turned vicious toward Tilda. He told her that soft sympathies for the Confederate states would be punished as treason. There is documentation he told Tilda she should have swung beside Mary Surratt."

"This is incredible. It's almost easier to believe Twist's version—that Tilda was involved in an assassination attempt on Lincoln."

"Women weren't even allowed to vote." Cece massaged her neck to relieve the tension. "This is amazing stuff. No wonder Twist and Webber are at each other's throats. This really could be a great book. A barn burner of a plot with bigger-than-life characters—a bestseller as Twist predicted. I wonder why they don't just collaborate?"

"That's like asking why two pit vipers tied in a sack can't get along."

Cece laughed. "They put the gloss on the shine of professional jealousy." She pushed the tablet my way. "You read. I'm hoarse."

I perched on the edge of the desk and found the place she'd stopped. "The proposal to buy the slaves was rejected as too expensive. No action was ever taken. Throughout the war, the traitorous Tilda traveled back and forth from Washington to the Southern states. At times, she carried messages between Lincoln and President Jefferson Davis. She used her status as the daughter of a respected Southern plantation owner and supporter of the Confederacy to move fluidly among Southern society and politicos. The damage she may have done to the Cause is unfathomable. Her death on Egypt Plantation put an end to her meddling in the affairs of men and the destruction of the nation she betrayed."

I had to stop reading before my blood pressure shot off the charts. The writer's tone was arrogant and condescending. I didn't doubt Jeremiah put fingers to keyboard to write this, but I was curious where he acquired his research. The whole thing was preposterous, but I didn't think he'd made it up. His imagination wasn't that good. He'd found this material somewhere.

And he'd tell me where before this case was over.

"Do you think my brother wrote this?" Cece asked.

"Yes. At least some of it."

"What happened to Jeremiah, Sarah Booth? He hates women. It's so clear. Do you think it's because I became a woman?"

I went to my friend and tipped her chin up. "Absolutely not. Jeremiah hates everyone. He's an equal opportunity hatemonger. What you did or do with your life shouldn't impact your brother's worldview. He's not only a misogynist, he's also a racist, a survivalist, and a kook. For whatever reason, he adopted hatred as his religion. Free will allowed him to chose, and he took the dark path. It's eating him alive, but he can't park any of this at your door."

"I should have tried to patch things up with him. Maybe I could have made a difference."

I remembered the abuse and hardness Jeremiah heaped on Cece. I'd thought he was misguidedly protecting his parents, but even after they were dead, he'd treated Cece like a pariah. "Stop taking on the blame for this. Jeremiah had every chance to be a decent, loving human being. He chose not to. You aren't responsible."

"How did Jeremiah come by this information?"

"I don't know. I'd like to ask him."

She nodded. "The vitriol. All Tilda wanted was a solution to a problem that ultimately tore the nation apart. And he calls her a traitor. It's unbelievably sad."

"He'll be hot when he finds out I stole his tablet." Boiling wouldn't begin to describe his fury.

She pointed to the apparatus I held. "Does it say what happened to Tilda? Did a Falcon relative kill her?"

It occurred to me Jeremiah had come across this information because it was part of the Falcon heritage. But Tilda was a Richmond by birth. She hadn't married a Falcon—or anyone as far as I could tell. But in the eyes of a Southern supporter, her death might be viewed as justified. Even to her friends and family, she would be a traitor. It was funny how hate could pervert every aspect of a person's soul. Tilda's work for a peaceful resolution to a way of life that even the practitioners admitted was wrong was defined as treachery and traitorous by men like Jeremiah, even today.

I scrolled down to the end of the file. "It doesn't say, Cece. That's the end."

"What do you think happened to her?" Cece was pensive.

"I don't know, but as soon as we find Graf, let's go to Magnolia Grove and scour the attic. Jeremiah found this information somewhere. Maybe there's more."

The sheriff's office door opened and Tinkie entered. "More what?" Her flushed face told me she was rattled.

"More information. Where's Oscar?" Cece asked.

"With Coleman and DeWayne." Her gaze slid around the room, and she turned a shoulder to me, avoiding eye contact.

"Did they find something?" My gut knew the answer, and I didn't want to hear it.

Tears pooled in her china blue eyes. "No. Nothing really—"

"*What?*" The iron taste of fear filled the back of my throat.

Tears spilled down Tinkie's cheeks. It was bad. I stumbled off the desk and started toward her but my knees jellied. Cece caught me.

"What? For heaven's sake, just tell me."

"They found blood in an upstairs bedroom at the old McCauley place." Tinkie clenched my hand. "There's no way to tell whose blood."

"It may not have been Graf's." I grasped at any straw that floated by.

"It may not be," Tinkie agreed. Her face said the exact opposite.

I knew then that Coleman and DeWayne believed Graf was injured. Seriously so.

"How much blood?"

"I didn't see it. Coleman called Oscar and asked him to drop me here and then meet them. So I could be with you."

"We need to tell Coleman what we learned from Olive." Cece spoke quietly and took action, pulling out her cell phone.

"Did Coleman say how much blood?" I had visions of Graf's blood sprayed over the walls and soaking the floors. Surely not. Surely it wasn't so bad.

"They're still searching for Graf. That's a positive. They must believe he's still alive." Tinkie realized what her words revealed and she put her hands on my cheeks and forced me to look into her eyes. "He's okay. If he'd been dead, they would have found him."

I couldn't stop the gasp that shuddered through me at the idea of Graf's body, the spirit gone from it.

"Get a grip, Sarah Booth." Cece was behind me. "This is no time to slump into a puddle of emotion. Graf is out there and he's waiting for you to find him. And you will. But you have to get yourself under control. *Now*."

The "now" did it. Graf's life hung in the balance. I couldn't flutter around, emotions rendering me totally ineffective. "Was Graf upstairs when I was in the house?"

"I don't know," Tinkie said. "The blood was older, I think. At least not fresh. It might not be Graf's. With that bunch of thugs, it could have been one of their relatives'. They'd sell their mothers down the river without blinking an eye."

"She's right," Cece threw in. They were desperate to keep me calm. "Did they happen to find any of the diagrams or the computer that Buford took from the camp? Sarah Booth didn't have time to do a thorough search."

"Nothing. The Heritage Heroes must have a headquarters somewhere else," Tinkie said.

Once Graf was found, I'd refocus on finding evidence against Jeremiah, but Graf was my first priority. "Would you drive me to The Gardens for Graf's Range Rover? Obviously my car is not drivable."

"Hank picked up the roadster, Sarah Booth. He towed it to his garage and said he'd work on it first thing tomorrow."

The car, though I loved it, was far down my list of

worries. "Thanks for checking on Pluto. Were the horses okay?"

"Everything at Dahlia House was fine. Coleman called a couple of volunteers and they're watching the place for you. Nobody seeking mischief will sneak down your driveway."

"Thank you. Thank you both."

Tinkie patted my back. "Coleman said he should have Jeremiah and his men running the roads looking for you rounded up and in custody within the hour. He said for us to wait here for him. He wants your input."

Coleman was worried about me. The need for my input was just an excuse to keep me cemented at the sheriff's office until he returned—a tactic doomed to failure. Coleman knew me too well to order me to stay, but he would certainly dangle a carrot if he thought it would be effective. Not this time.

"Ladies, let's talk to Gertrude. Based on Olive's information, Graf was taken before he made it to the parking lot. That means someone snatched him and then had to move his car. Gertrude may have seen something useful. While I'm there, I can pick up Graf's car."

"Don't you want to wait for Coleman?" Tinkie asked.

"We'll be back before he gets here."

Cece copied the list of Heritage Heroes members and gave one to Tinkie. "I'll fill you in on Tilda Richmond while we drive. Let's round up Gertrude and interview her. She's the nosiest woman I know. Maybe we'll get lucky."

By the time we arrived at the B and B, Cece had brought Tinkie up to speed on Tilda Richmond, Lincoln, and Jeremiah's role in the night's events.

Cece parked beneath the graceful limbs of a live oak and we walked toward the reservation desk and Gertrude's charming personality. Graf's car was parked somewhere on the grounds of the B and B. Coleman hadn't said if he'd left the key or what, but I had a spare and thank goodness I'd had the presence of mind to pull the ring from the ignition when I'd had my wreck.

The twinkle lights that circled the trunks and branches of the beautiful trees were still dark. Gertrude was tight as a tick, but the lights created a magical world around the B and B. Add to that the incredible flowers and lush plants that took on a fantastical appearance at night, and it was counterintuitive to save money by not repairing whatever wiring issue had caused the blackout.

As we walked along in the darkness, I searched for the camera Olive had installed and someone had crushed.

"Where's Dr. Webber?" I asked.

"I haven't heard anyone say," Tinkie admitted. "The focus has been on the Heritage Heroes. I don't think anyone has thought to pin down Webber."

"Gertrude can probably account for his whereabouts. She watches everyone." Cece wasn't paying a compliment.

"You ask, Sarah Booth, and we'll back you up." Tinkie caught my hand in hers and squeezed. "She loathes you. Have you ever asked why she has such an active dislike of you?"

"No, and I don't care." Because time was of the essence, I told Sweetie to sit at the door of the B and B. We'd waste too much time if Gertrude ranted about my hound in her business.

We found Gertrude in her usual perch behind the registration desk. I wondered if she ever slept. She was neither startled nor happy to see us.

"The bar is closed, Sarah Booth."

"Has the fire marshal inspected here lately?" Tinkie asked. "You know if there's a violation and you lose your insurance, the bank might have to call in your mortgage." Tinkie knew how to bludgeon a suspect without lifting a hand.

"What do you want?" Gertrude asked. In the dim light of the registration desk, her faced showed more wrinkles and there were smudges beneath her eyes. A guest had been murdered and my fiancé attacked and abducted on the premises of her B and B. Perhaps it was wearing on her.

"Were you aware that Dr. Twist installed cameras around the B and B?" I asked.

Gertrude blanched. "What do you mean?"

"In the bar, in the gardens, probably in the bathrooms. Hidden cameras are recording your guests. There's no telling how Olive plans to use the video. She's producing a self-aggrandizing movie about herself. A documentary of her work on the Lady in Red."

"Where are the cameras?" Gertrude was a lot more upset over this tidbit than I'd imagined.

I shrugged. "Ask Twist. When she's released from custody."

"She's in jail? For what?"

"Obnoxiousness." Cece stepped forward. "Do you recall Graf Milieu being here earlier today?" She checked her watch. "Or rather yesterday?"

"I know he's missing." Gertrude was peeved. "One of my guests found his car behind the tennis courts, hidden among the four o'clocks, so I reported it to the sheriff. A moron drove straight into the plants. It'll take them months to recover." She reached behind her and brought forth Graf's key ring. "I suppose you'll want these."

"Thanks." I grasped the keys.

"Did you see Graf leave?" Cece asked. "He was right behind me."

"I saw you both. You left and he followed a few moments later."

"Did you see anyone else?" I asked.

"It's a bed-and-breakfast, Sarah Booth. There are other guests. They aren't chained in their rooms. They walk through the gardens."

Cece shoved her face into Gertrude's. "She asked a civil question. Now, who took a walkabout in the gardens?"

"My, my, aren't we testy." Gertrude clucked her tongue. "At that particular time, I saw a man. Not a guest here. He'd skulked up to the front, and I'd been on my way to run him off the property. I can't have riffraff lurking around. The guests don't appreciate it. And that Twist!" She frowned. "If she can find something to complain about, she will. She wants to deduct fifty dollars off her bill every time a bird tweets or a door shuts and disturbs her."

I could almost sympathize about Olive, but I didn't have time. "Who was this man?"

"I haven't a clue. Medium height. A little chubby. He had a quick way of moving. That's why I noticed him. Very catlike."

My mouth went dry. "Think, Gertrude. This could be important."

"You think he stole the Lady in Red's corpse?"

It took a moment for her words to register. Tinkie recovered first. "Wait a minute. What are you saying? Someone stole a hundred-year-old corpse?"

"Well, slap a gold star on your forehead."

"How do you know this?" I asked.

"The coroner's office called to talk to Twist. I don't know where she took off to, but I took a message."

In the B and B there were no guest room answering machines. All messages were left at reception, which meant Gertrude. She wrote notes and put them in the little pigeonholes corresponding to the room number.

Sure enough, a swatch of paper stuck out from Olive's box.

"Did you tell Olive?" I asked.

"She hasn't been back. I don't have smoke signal capability here, Sarah Booth."

"She has a cell phone," I reminded her.

"Oh, posh. Those things don't work half the time. I never bother to call one. If she wants her messages, she can march her fancy self right here and pick them up like everybody else."

Gertrude was almost as tiresome as Twist, but so far she was our only witness. I had to press her. "If you saw this man again, would you recognize him?"

"The general build, yes. I didn't see a face or head. I went out to confront him, shortly after Mr. Milieu left, but the interloper was no longer on the property. I assumed he'd gone wherever vagrants go."

"You never fail to amaze me with your heart of gold," I said as I signaled Tinkie and Cece that it was time to leave.

17

When the three of us were out of Gertrude's hearing range, I pulled them into a huddle on the path. Sweetie sat patiently beside my hip, ready for action should it be necessary. "I can't wait for Coleman."

"You're aren't heading off half-cocked." Tinkie's jaw jutted forward. "I won't have it. You'll get yourself killed and then where will I be?"

I knew her well enough to realize she couched her sentiments as self-centric, but that was not the true reading of her heart. "I'm not going to get killed. I'm taking the Range Rover and I'm going to find Graf."

"The hell you are," Cece said. "And we're supposed to do what? Play checkers in the sheriff's office until you come back?"

"You have to find Webber. Someone has stolen that corpse. Twist is in jail. Obviously she doesn't have it. That leaves Webber. Who else would engineer the theft of some old bones?" They couldn't argue with my logic no matter how much they wanted to.

"He can have the corpse," Tinkie said, fists riding her hip bones. "I'm going with you to find Graf."

"Me, too." Cece wasn't about to be left out. "Right after I call Coleman and let him know the body has been stolen. Cadaver theft is just too sick. I mean, have they strapped the moldering bones to the hood of a pickup like hunters do? Ick." She punched up Coleman's cell, and in a moment had him filled in on the situation.

"We can cover more ground if we split up. The Lady in Red must be recovered. That's what you two need to pursue." My tone was firm. If I kept them focused on the stolen corpse, my plan stood a chance. My intentions required solitary action. No witnesses. Another issue was endangering my friends. Tinkie had already been on the receiving end of poison and attempts on her life. Cece, too, had been injured in my adventures. "I'll stay in touch. I promise."

"You won't cover any ground if you try to ditch us," Tinkie said. "I may be shorter than you, but piss me off and I can be a lot more devious. I will complicate your life like a stomach virus on a desert trek."

I couldn't allow Tinkie's vivid image to distract me. The minutes sped away like scattered stardust. I could stand there and argue, or I could take them along with me. Or I could trick them. Door number three. "Let's get the Range Rover."

I headed for the tennis courts, wondering why Gertrude hadn't moved the vehicle out of her precious four o'clocks and back to the parking lot. She had the key. There was no explaining the way Gertrude's mind worked.

What I was about to do would be hard for Tinkie and Cece to forgive, but I would worry about that later. I'd begun to operate in a place where right and wrong blurred. Saving Graf pushed everything else to the fringes. I'd often heard that a person was capable of anything under the right set of circumstances. Now I understood with my heart as well as my mind.

Walking through the dappled moonlight on the grounds of a paradise, I wanted to thank Cece and Tinkie for such devoted friendship. For such intelligence and heart. Maybe they'd let me when I got back.

The Range Rover was tucked deep in a jungle of flowers that smelled as sweet as any summer night from childhood. Four o'clocks sprouted from a tuber and grew wild. Their blooms opened at four o'clock each afternoon and released a heavy, sensual perfume that was gone by dawn's first light. The flowers, in variegated pinks and whites, yellows, and purples, covered the car.

"I'll back out of the plants so you can open the doors," I told them. "Keep Sweetie Pie with you."

As I got in, I locked the doors, reversed quickly, threw it into drive, and gunned it. In a matter of seconds I blasted down the path toward the highway. Tinkie and Cece, as well as Sweetie Pie, would have a hard time forgiving me for tricking them. Maybe there'd been a different choice, but I hadn't seen it.

I drove to Harold's house. I didn't expect approval, but of all my friends, Harold had the most complete understanding of me. Of who I was, and of what I might be capable of doing. My gender was not an issue when my anger and fear were aroused, and he would not treat me like a weak sister.

After a sleepy greeting, he stepped out of the entry to allow me to pass, but I stopped just inside. "I need a gun."

Harold's head tilted slightly. "What kind?"

"Something with a clip. I need several clips, too. Not a twenty-two." I meant to blow them up, not wing them. "I'm used to a Glock."

"Wait here."

When Harold returned, he had a Glock 17 and five additional clips. That gave me over a hundred rounds. Annie Oakley on steroids.

"Are you sure you know what you're doing?"

"They have Graf. Whatever it takes, I intend to find him and bring him safely home." The one thing I could not afford was to let my fear blossom out of control. I fought to remain tough, factual.

Harold handed me the gun. "Be careful. Can I come with you?"

"No. I'm headed to Buford's. If you don't hear from me, that's where I went. Cece and Tinkie will be looking for me. They'll call you."

"I won't lie to them. And you know I have to call Coleman. I'd stop you—"

"And I'd never forgive you. My choice, Harold."

"And my choice to send reinforcements."

I nodded. "Then delay them. I won't endanger my friends again." I felt a pinch on the back of my calf and looked down into the demented eyes of Roscoe. "If something should happen to Graf and me, I think Sweetie would love to spend time with you and Roscoe. Tinkie will take her. But Sweetie needs her dose of the dark side."

Harold caught my hand and kissed the pulse at my

wrist. "You'll be fine, Sarah Booth. Pity the fool who comes between you and your love."

"Take care of your daddy," I whispered to Roscoe and slipped out the door and into the night.

We were into the wee hours of the morning. Dawn wasn't far away, maybe three hours. If I meant to keep the element of surprise, it was now or never.

I headed east, toward Highway 55 and the center of the state. By logical deduction, I figured if the Heritage Heroes had Graf, then Buford was the go-to. He was absent from the cotton field shenanigans, so either he was busy with Graf or he was drunk.

He would, hopefully, be sound asleep. Buford knew the members of the Heritage Heroes and who did Jeremiah's bidding. Before I left his sty, I'd make him squeal like a piggy.

As I sped through the night, I turned the question I'd asked of Jeremiah on Buford. How had a man with a solid future ended up in this place? Buford had too great a fondness for the drink. He didn't have the mean streak Jeremiah had, or the desire to punish. His life was a caution for everyone—how easy it was to step from happiness into a world of dark emotions. Too bad Oscar hadn't convinced him to voluntarily enter a mental facility. Now he was going to deal with me.

Buford's white shell drive was surrounded by hardwoods that provided cover for a gracious, raised Creole cottage. Two elegant curved staircases led up to a beveled glass door and a veranda offering a shady rest on all four sides. Oscar was generous with the allowance he doled out to his cousin. Unlike Jeremiah, who had been given a lump sum inheritance to squander, Buford had been wisely kept on a financial leash.

I parked a dozen yards off the driveway and walked to the house, which was dark. I'd half expected guards or an alarm, but I'd underestimated Buford's arrogance. He felt safe, privileged, beyond the reach of those who opposed his madness. All the better for me, I thought.

Harold wouldn't be able to hold Tinkie and Cece off for long, so I had to get this done. I missed my hound and the redoubtable Pluto. But the kind of men who participated in this stupidity would think nothing of shooting a dog or cat. Probably not of shooting a woman, either, since they seemed to categorize living things into two categories—men and inferior beings. I couldn't risk the people and animals I loved.

But I would find Graf.

I made it up the stairs without creaking a board. The front window was locked. If the floor plan of the house was similar to others of that style, Buford's bedroom would be in the rear. I eased around to the back, trying windows as I went. If I had to break one, I would.

Which I did. Using the butt of the gun. Before I was certain whether the noise had awakened Buford or not, I ducked inside and made for the bedroom, Glock at the ready.

Buford was sprawled in a beautiful old sleigh bed, his mouth open, snoring. I smacked his feet with the gun barrel, and he awoke on a snort. "What? What's going on? Why are you here?" He fumbled at the bedclothes. "Sarah Booth Delaney?" Indignation began to inflate him. "You have no right to be here. Get out! Who do you think you are, breaking in like that?" He pulled the sheet up to his chin.

"Where's Graf?"

"That man you keep? How should I know?"

"Buford, there's no one here to help you or hear you scream. I brought bolt cutters. I'll start at the first joint of your toes. Each time I ask a question and you don't answer, I'll snip off another joint." I whapped him upside the head with my hand to show I meant business. "That's for tying up my friends."

It took a moment for him to regain his senses, but a new light of respect shone from his eyes. "I have no clue where Milieu is. Why would I know or care?"

"Let me tell you what I know. I know about the Heritage Heroes. I also know about the Evergreen Tree cell. I'm not certain what you're up to—yet—but I will find out. I suspect if you don't serve time for kidnapping, you'll end up in a mental facility where they'll keep you so drugged you won't be a danger to yourself or anyone else."

"I'm perfectly sane. What a ridiculous threat." He swung his legs to stand, but when I pointed the gun at his heart, he stilled. "In another few weeks, we'll have the state judicial system in our pocket. I've invested wisely, and we've got the money to support our candidates. Once the state supreme court is responsive to our agenda, you're going to see big changes. No more women running amok. No more illegals taking the jobs from our citizens. No more minorities getting a free ride."

State elections would be held the first week of November, but I'd hardly given them a passing thought. Buford was spouting another whole brand of craziness.

"Coleman will deal with this. My concern is Graf. Who is the most likely person to have him?"

"None of us. What use is he to us?"

"To keep me from investigating you."

Buford's laughter came deep from his gut. "You're kidding, right? Our goal was to run you and Cece off, not taunt you into more investigation. That Twist woman couldn't have come at a worse time to stir up controversy and get the media down here. I have no clue where your fiancé is and furthermore I don't care."

I didn't believe him. I put the gun to his head. "Where is Graf? Give me the wrong answer and someone will be cleaning your brains off the wall."

At last the reality of his situation sank in. He wasn't certain whether I would pull the trigger or not, but he'd sobered up enough not to risk it. "Wherever he is, we're not involved. I swear it."

"Not the right answer." I pressed the muzzle hard enough to make him whimper.

"Call Jeremiah. Ask him."

"You call. Put it on speakerphone, and if you say a word about me being here, I'll kill you and I won't blink an eye."

He fumbled with his cell phone and dialed. Jeremiah's gruff hello was tinny over the speaker. Buford had to clear his throat. "Jeremiah, do you have that actor fellow, Graf Milieu?"

"Have you lost your mind? What would I do with him?"

"Just tell me. Do you have him?"

"Are you okay, Buford?" Suspicion oozed in Jeremiah's voice.

I pushed the barrel a little deeper into the flesh at Buford's temple.

"No, I just woke up. Bad dream."

"Don't lie to me, Buford. What's going on?"

A glint of fire sparked in Buford's eyes. "That Delaney bitch is here. She thinks you're holding her boy toy hostage."

"Tell me where Graf is and I won't hurt Buford. Again." I smacked the gun on top of his head. Buford's cry of pain was gratifying. Another retribution for tying up my friends.

"Buford, don't let her bluff you. She won't kill you. We're on the way."

Before Buford could say anything else, I whipped the gun against his cheek. He went down like he'd been struck by lightning. I picked up the phone. "Buford's no longer conscious, Jeremiah. And I have news for you. The Lady in Red was stolen from the morgue in Jackson. Olive Twist is in jail, so she doesn't have her. This is going to have the national media down here by daybreak."

"Who took her? Who—"

"You answer my questions. If you don't have Graf, where is he?"

"I don't know, Sarah Booth. I'm not lying. We had no reason to take Graf."

In my gut I knew Jeremiah was telling the truth. He didn't have Graf or know what had happened to him. He and the Heroes weren't involved in Graf's disappearance.

If the hate group didn't have Graf, I had no clue where to find my fiancé or how to help him. The realization was as profound as a gut-kick from a mule. I'd wasted hours chasing the wrong lead. I'd assumed Jeremiah or Buford was responsible.

I'd gone off half-cocked, ready to blame the easy target.

I called Tinkie from Buford's phone.

"Buford?" she answered warily. "What the hell are you up to now?"

"It's me. And I need help."

The long silence told me how angry Tinkie was. And she had every right to be. At least she hadn't hung up on me.

I tried again. "Graf isn't being held by Jeremiah and his group. I don't know who has him and I don't know where to begin looking. I'm sorry, Tinkie. I was afraid I'd have to shoot Buford and I didn't want you to share the blame for what I did."

"You think if Buford was holding Graf hostage I wouldn't shoot him myself?" Her indignation couldn't be missed.

"Buford is Oscar's cousin. I hurt him. A little."

"Are you okay?" she asked.

"I'm fine. Do you know who stole the Lady in Red?" There had to be a connection between Graf's abduction and the body theft.

"Coleman talked with the lab. They have fingerprints from the break-in. The thing is they don't have Webber's to compare. Somehow he's avoided a criminal record."

But I knew where to obtain prints. "Tell Coleman to call campus police at Ole Miss. Webber has a leather sofa in his office. I'm sure his prints are all over it."

"You want me to *relay* that to Coleman?"

Tinkie was nobody's fool. She realized I didn't want to talk to Coleman. Furious wouldn't begin to describe his feelings toward me. "Please."

"Webber's in the wind. No one has seen him, either. I think he snatched the corpse—for what purpose I can't imagine. Maybe he has Graf, too."

"Thanks, Tinkie. And I'm sorry. Please tell Cece."

"Tell it to your dog. She's been frantic."

I hesitated. "I know. I'll pick her up."

She must have heard the hopelessness in my voice and she took pity on me. "We'll find Graf, Sarah Booth. We will. And he'll be fine."

Weariness clobbered me on the trip back to the courthouse. I was no closer to finding Graf than I had been when I left my friends in the dust. Adrenaline had carried me as far as it could. I was about to crash.

"Get the robot to drive the damn car."

Jitty had joined me, but I couldn't bear to look at her. Great private investigator that I was, I couldn't find my fiancé. Graf, the answer to Jitty's dream and heir-apparent dilemma, was simply gone. "I'm sorry."

"Sorry for what?" Her perky tone caught me by surprise.

I chanced a look at her and the SUV swerved onto the shoulder before I righted it. Jitty's red hair was parted in the center. Her minidress revealed full cleavage, slender thighs, and a tiny waist. Her face was all angles, from wide cheekbones to pointed chin. Jane Jetson rode shotgun with me. "Don't you know any cartoon characters who are fat or dowdy?"

"Of course I do. But who would want to be them? Pa-lease! Marge Simpson with blue hair, married to that moron Homer? By choice? What planet are you from?" She coyly cocked a shoulder. "I'm from Earth."

"Jane 'Jitty' Jetson. Where's L. Ron or Elroy or who-ever?"

"I'm not worried about my children, I'm worried 'bout your fiancé."

At least she'd cured my near energy collapse. I was wide awake, recharged, and thrumming with anxiety. "Why cartoons, Jitty? Will you just tell me that?"

"Sarah Booth, girl, that's not the important question." Her voice softened. "But I'll tell you. As a kindness to Miss Alice."

"My great-great-great-grandmother asked you to tell me something?" A million possibilities tumbled in my tired brain and I almost swerved off the road again. Why not ask Alice? She was alive during the Civil War. She *would have known*—or at least known of—Tilda Richmond. And all the other characters. She would have first-hand knowledge of the events surrounding Tilda's escape from unwanted matrimony, her years in Washington, D.C., the scandals of her affiliation with Abraham Lincoln, and her untimely death. Grandma Alice could lay out the past, and then I'd be able to figure out the future. "What did Alice say?"

"Alice says there's a future for you, Sarah Booth. No matter what happens, you come from people who don't quit. Who don't give up. She wants you to remember that."

Not what I wanted to hear. Icy fear tickled down my spine. "Why did she send that message? Has something bad happened to Graf?" Jitty could not play coy. She had to answer.

"I don't know, Sarah Booth. There are things even I can't see. But Alice wants you to hold on to the future. 'Hold tight, like you're ridin' a chargin' stallion in a wild wind.' Those are her words."

"Jitty, just this once, please, tell me if Graf is hurt. If he's—" I couldn't say it. "I'll never ask you anything from the Great Beyond again, but this time, *please*."

Jitty shook her bobbed red hair. "Oh, you'll ask, Sarah Booth. You'll beg. You've got plenty of drama in the future, and it isn't on a stage. You draw turmoil like a turd draws flies. If I could see the answers you want, I'd break all the rules to end this misery for you. All I can see are glimpses. And I know whatever happens now, you'll smile again."

Frustration fueled my hands and I jerked the SUV to a patch of dirt on the roadside and slammed on the brakes. If I could put my hands around her neck, I'd choke her. All I wanted was an answer. A simple yes or no. Was Graf alive? Was he injured?

In the milky light of the moon, Jitty was as cool as marble and just as calm. "Gather yourself, Sarah Booth."

"Tell me." I wasn't negotiating anymore. I wanted an answer.

"I can't. It's that simple. The fact I stay at Dahlia House to watch over you is a violation of the natural order. Alice and Libby and James Franklin, they're mighty strong-willed. But if I told you things, if I did that, I'd be called back."

"Where is Graf? Can you tell me where to look?"

"The way to the future is one step at a time. Now, get yourself together and get busy solvin' this case. The answers are there for you. Even the ones you won't like."

I would have sold my soul to the devil to know Graf was safe. The problem with such a bargain was I might not get the answer I wanted. I leaned down on the steering wheel and inhaled. I needed a cigarette, but I didn't have any and there was no time to stop and buy a pack. The nicotine craving was a reaction to stress. I pushed it away and pulled myself together. I had to. There wasn't a choice.

When I sat up, Jitty was gone.

Yet she'd left me with a clue to resolving the Lady in Red issue once and for all. But that was far down on my list. I didn't care what Olive or Webber wrote—or did. I wanted Graf home safe and sound.

When I pulled into the parking lot at the courthouse, Coleman's patrol car was there. And so was Tinkie's Cadillac and Cece's hybrid. And Harold's car.

Pausing for a moment beneath the statue of Johnny Reb that graced the courthouse entrance, I stared up into the bronze face. He was so young, and so tired. The men of both armies had walked into raging battles where thousands of their comrades died. They'd stepped forward, knowing they would likely die. And if not death, their reward would be crippling wounds and maimed bodies. Yet they'd soldiered on.

Where did such courage come from? Was it merely youthful foolhardiness?

I didn't have an answer.

Delay wouldn't give me false courage. I ran up the steps and down the hall, and pushed in the door of the sheriff's office. Heads swiveled in my direction. On the faces of my friends I read everything from pity to mutinous anger.

"I sent the ambulance to get Buford," Tinkie said, all business. "Oscar's meeting him in the ER. If Buford accuses you of anything, Oscar will shut him up. That's what friends do for each other."

The blood rushed into my cheeks. I had no defense. She was right. Friends looked out for each other, and though I'd been trying to protect her and Cece, she would never see it that way.

Coleman stepped into the awkward breach. "Webber's

vehicle was spotted in Jackson circling the morgue. The fingerprints on his office sofa matched prints at the morgue break-in. Good tip, Sarah Booth."

"I found out what the Heritage Heroes and the Evergreen Tree group are up to—they're trying to force the outcome of the state election. The supreme court justices. They want to control the judicial branch, but I don't know that they were doing anything illegal."

"That's a worry for tomorrow," Coleman said. "I'll put in a call to the secretary of state's election fraud unit and they can see what's what."

"There's been no sign of Graf." Coleman delivered the bad news, so I didn't have to ask. "And I cut Olive loose. She was in jail for her own protection, but she doesn't need safeguarding." Anger heated his words. "Olive received a series of death threats, which she reported to me. That's why I stayed so close to her. She wouldn't take them seriously, but I had to." Coleman's temper climbed. "It took me a while, but I tracked down the threats. Olive sent them to herself. This was all hype for her documentary and book. When this is done and Graf is safely home, I'll pursue action against Twist for wasting my time and the resources of this office."

"You were never involved with her?" Cece asked. "I wondered how you could be. Dah-link, that would be like a tumble with a role of barbed wire." She gave him a hug that ended in a pinch on the arm. "You could have told us, you know."

Coleman cleared his throat. "I've asked the highway patrol to set up roadblocks on the main routes to stop Webber. Of course there are dozens of cotton field roads he can use, and he's familiar with the farm-to-market road system. Why anyone would steal a corpse is beyond me, but if he has the Lady in Red, we'll recover the body."

Cece did a runway pivot as if rehearsing for the Black and Orange Ball. "Do you think he's holed up in some ratty motel with a corpse? Puts a completely different spin on *Psycho*, doesn't it?"

"I don't care about a corpse—I want to find Graf." Webber and Twist could go hang for all I cared.

"We should start at the B and B. I'll convince Gertrude to let me search the unused rooms. It's possible Graf is on the grounds." Tinkie lifted her shoulders and straightened her back. She had to be as tired as I was, but she found her second wind. "Gertrude will talk to me and she hates you, Sarah Booth. This is a job I can handle and I'll report back if I find a shred of evidence."

Tinkie was helping me, and it was more than I deserved. "Thank you, Tink."

"Take your dog home and check on your cat," Tinkie said with more kindness than I could have mustered.

"I need to buy a new cell phone first thing tomorrow." Oscar had retrieved mine, but it was in sad shape.

"Take mine." Harold handed it to me. "Your friends only want to protect you," he whispered.

"I have your gun. I didn't shoot it, but there's blood on it. I'll clean it and return it."

"Worry about such things tomorrow, Sarah Booth. Let's go. I'll follow you home to be sure you make it safely. For good measure, I'll check the house and grounds."

Even if I'd wanted to argue, I didn't have the grit. I could only be thankful that my friends cared enough to look out for me, even when I made them worry.

18

When I drew near Dahlia House, I was flagged down by the two guards Coleman had stationed there. They gave an all-clear report and said the horses were grazing peacefully in the back pasture. No one had bothered the house or the animals.

I eased to a halt at the front steps. Harold's car door slammed in tandem with mine. As we went up the steps, he took my elbow. "Roscoe's in the car. I could call him in and stay with you for a while. I'm too wired to sleep, and I don't really want to be alone." He was worried about me, but he was too smart to rub my nose in it.

"Bring him in to play with Sweetie. Maybe he can soften her heart." My dog had given me the cold shoulder on the ride home. Highly miffed at being left behind, she let me know it.

Pluto ran around the corner of the house to greet me, and Sweetie yodeled a mournful salutation at him. The cat walked past without even a whisker-twitch in my direction. I gathered Pluto in my arms. He was a rotund kitty, but it was all muscle, with a large helping of brains and courage. "You saved my life," I whispered as I kissed his head. Pluto didn't appreciate public displays of emotion, and he leaped from my arms, tail swishing, and led the parade across the porch.

The five of us, Pluto, Roscoe, Harold, Sweetie, and I, stopped in the foyer, gobsmacked. Dead silence echoed through the rooms. Dahlia House had felt this empty only once before—when I returned after my parents' funeral.

The smell of old furniture, wood polish, and the passage of time permeated the air. The hall clock, an antique grandfather model, ticked ominously. I hadn't wound it in weeks. Graf must have assumed the chore, but he never even mentioned it. He was like that, doing the small things that meant so much to me.

A sound of distress escaped me. Harold's fingers clamped my elbow—the steadying hand of a friend.

When he was here, Graf filled the house with a manly scent of spice and forest. His step on the polished wooden floors created a familiar creak and sigh—and I missed those sounds. I wanted Graf home, safe and unharmed.

I pushed forward to the kitchen and brewed a pot of coffee. It was nearly dawn. No point in trying to sleep now. Harold loaded the dishwasher, working with quiet efficiency. We both needed to stay busy.

"Sweetie? Roscoe?" I retrieved two special doggy bones from the freezer and put them in the microwave to thaw. It would take some doing to win my hound's forgiveness. She sat on the kitchen floor, facing away. When I called her name she wouldn't even acknowledge me.

Harold sat down beside her and snuggled her into his arms. "She wanted to keep you safe," he told her. "Don't be such a hard-ass."

"Be-yurlllll." Sweetie's response, though spoken in hound, was clear. I was in big trouble with her.

"I'll make it up to you," I promised as I stroked her long, silky ears. And when she began to thaw a little, I kissed the top of her head. Roscoe cackled—it sounded exactly like the Wicked Witch of the West. Harold didn't deny the dog was part imp. Maybe half. Roscoe sprang at Sweetie's face with demonic gusto. She growled and snapped at him—and the game was on. They tore out of the kitchen through the swinging door and I heard them thundering up the staircase.

"Thank you," I said. Sweetie could never deny a request from Harold.

Pluto was on a special low-cal kitty diet food, but I treated him to an expensive can of kitty cuisine, then poured two cups of coffee.

"Will you go with me to the attic?" I offered a cup to Harold.

"I'd prefer the Casbah," Harold said drily, "but the attic is a close second."

His reference to the 1938 classic movie *Algiers* called to mind a former client, the beautiful and mysterious Hedy Lamarr Blackledge, named for the exotic and mysterious actress who starred in the movie. "If I could close my eyes and wake up in Algiers, it might be tempting to run away."

"You're as beautiful as Hedy Lamarr, Sarah Booth. But you're as loyal as Sweetie Pie. You're never abandon a friend in need."

I retrieved two flashlights from a kitchen drawer and gave him one. When we reached the second-floor landing, he tilted his head to indicate the dogs were following us up the stairs. "And you're as determined to have your way as Roscoe. We'll find Graf, and everything will be set to right."

I blinked back the surge of emotion and trudged upward to the attic. I had a reason for wanting to explore the old chest in the far corner that had belonged to my great-great-great-grandmother Alice.

The attic access was behind a closed door that gave onto another flight of stairs. When Dahlia House was built, the attic had served as a ballroom. If I ever had money to spare, I'd renovate the high-ceilinged room and hold a fancy-dress ball. Maybe for my wedding reception. Maybe just this once I'd take the money Graf so generously offered to help with Dahlia House. Maybe I'd show him that I could share my history and my home. If he came through this okay, I'd change my ways.

Our footsteps echoed eerily in the cavernous room filled with furniture, clothes, and Delaney artifacts. When I found the pull string for the overhead light, I flooded the attic with illumination.

"This is a treasure trove," Harold said. "It isn't the Casbah, but it's something else."

I ignored the plastic-wrapped racks of dresses that dated back to the Roaring Twenties. Alice's clothing, which I would have loved to possess, hadn't survived the war.

Photographs had captured the antebellum splendor of her wardrobe, but none of the dresses remained.

"Help me open this steamer trunk." I set down my coffee and flashlight. Harold and I put our backs into the effort, and the lid of the trunk groaned wide. The musty odors of crumbling pages and old sachets made me think of Aunt Loulane. I could almost hear her—"The past is best left *in* the past." She had a homily for every occasion, which didn't mean she wasn't accurate.

"Are you seeking something in particular?" Harold asked. "Or is this just a side trip down History Lane?"

"I can't be certain, but I have this fuzzy memory of a journal or letters—records my great-great-great-grandmother kept during the Civil War."

Harold was quick on the uptake. "And you think this might link to the Lady in Red? Why did you just think of it?"

I couldn't tell him that Jitty, dressed as a cartoon character, had tweaked my memory. "When I was driving home from Buford's I was so tired. Exhausted. I was thinking back to the time when my parents were alive and life was so . . . safe. And then there were those years with Aunt Loulane. I was thinking about her and I remembered the chest."

"Loulane adored you, Sarah Booth. Did you know she was being courted by a lawyer from Lexington, Kentucky, but when James Franklin and Libby were killed, she declined his marriage proposal and took care of you instead?"

I pushed my straggly hair behind my ears and looked at him. He wasn't teasing me. He was dead serious. "That can't be. She could have moved me to Lexington with her. Surely she didn't give up a chance at marriage and her own family and happiness." Somehow, I knew this was true, though. The ghost of memory tickled me.

"And take you from Dahlia House? I don't think so." His smile was sad. "She never wanted you to know what she gave up. I've almost told you a time or two before, but I didn't want to burden you. Now, though, you should know."

Not a single time had Aunt Loulane ever mentioned the man she could have married. Not once. Not even when I went off to college. She stayed at Dahlia House, keeping it for me, until she died unexpectedly of a heart attack. "She sacrificed her happiness for me." Was there no end to the guilt I'd feel this day?

"No, Sarah Booth. She chose happiness *with* you over marriage. A choice you should understand. Dahlia House was her brother's heritage. She did it as much for James Franklin and Libby as for you."

"That doesn't make me feel a lick better."

"For someone to love you that much." He touched my cheek with the gentlest caress. "That should tell you how special you are. When we find Graf, if that man doesn't marry you, I'll take you for myself."

I put my hand over his. "You're many things in my life, Harold. I appreciate all of them."

Together we lifted the tray from the old trunk. Near the bottom, beneath the christening gown belonging to the child Alice lost to a fever during the war, was a stack of old letters.

I pictured my mother, on her knees leaning over the ancient trunk, bringing the bundle of letters up from their safe nest. For a moment, I was transfixed as I remembered the pale light from the dusty windows striking her wedding band as her fingers traced the letters.

"One day, you'll come here and read these. What's in them remains with the Delaney family, Sarah Booth. The secrets here aren't ours to tell."

I had been no older than four, but the image was too strong to be fantasy. I turned to my friend. His wry smile told me he'd anticipated what I was about to say. Harold knew me too well. "I have to do the rest of this alone."

He offered his hand to assist me to my feet. His kiss on my cheek was warm, creating the tiniest little pulse in my thumb. "Call me if you need me. Roscoe and I will show ourselves out."

His ability to accept me, without judgment or need to intervene, was rare for a friend and even rarer for a man. I watched him disappear down the stairs with the evil Roscoe at his heels. Had I not known better, I would've thought Roscoe had miraculously been domesticated. But I knew his capability for deception—he was merely waiting for an opportunity to break bad.

In the golden light of an overhead bulb, I sat on the dusty attic floor to read. Dawn was breaking outside the window, and there had been no word from Coleman on the search for my fiancé or the missing corpse of the Lady in Red. Unfolding the papers, I stepped into the past.

The letters were to Alice from her parents, from some childhood friends, and—the largest portion—from her husband as he crisscrossed the South as part of a cavalry regiment from Mississippi. The stiff old pages were filled with urgent declarations of love and the lingering sense that Fate would never allow their reunion.

I could guess at the letters Alice had written him— filled with lies about the bountiful crops and the availability of help on the plantation. She would never have added to his worries by writing of the dire circumstances of the women and children across the South. And he spared her the brutal savagery and waste of life in a war that pitted brother against brother.

I'd always been curious about Alice's and Jitty's early lives. I was learning more than I'd bargained for. The pain and loneliness and hopelessness, though disguised by the determination of both husband and wife to shade the other from the horrors, were clear to me from the vantage point of more than a hundred fifty years later. Everyone suffered, some just more than others.

Rifling through the documents, I came across one in a feminine hand. The return address was Washington, D.C. The postmark 1860.

"My dearest Alice," it began.

> *Since I fled Zinnia, my life has been more than challenging. The details would scandalize the pastor and the church ladies, so I will spare you. Just know I value and miss your friendship, offered with such a generous heart. As you no doubt know, our country is perched on a terrible precipice. I fear war between the Northern and Southern interests is unavoidable, but I intend to try to stop it.*
>
> *Should something happen to me, I wanted one person to know the truth. I fled the marriage to Percy Falcon for several reasons, but murder is the primary one and my son, Jedediah, is the second. Yes, I have a son. When he is a grown man and able to make his own decisions, he'll learn his family history, as sordid as it may be. Every man has a right to know his past and decide his future.*
>
> *My betrothed, Percy, murdered his mother in*

Georgia. She was an octoroon who belonged to the Falcon family and was the mistress of Fletcher Falcon. She gave birth to Percy, the only male Falcon heir. Percy, a blond, blue-eyed child, was adopted by his white father and raised as a natural son. But the truth will out; it always does. In a society where a Negro has no standing or freedom, Percy could not allow the truth to come forth, so he murdered the only person who could reveal the origins of his birth, his own mother.

I could not marry and conceive children with a murderer, yet Percy took that choice from me. He raped me in a guest room at Magnolia Grove while I was visiting. He said I would soon be his and he didn't have to wait. He is a brute and an evil man. My life with him would have been worse than that of a slave in chains. So I left, unaware that I carried his son.

I gave birth to Jedediah in Washington and have placed him with a good family. He has grown into a fine boy. I wish you could know him, Alice. He reminds me of your son, and some days when I am bereft and afraid, I pretend they are friends. Your son, the older and wiser, looking out for mine. If war is avoided, perhaps this fantasy can become a reality.

On different occasions, I've returned to New Orleans and other Southern cities as an emissary of the federal government. I hope to see you one day soon, if war can be avoided. I would love nothing more than a visit at Dahlia House with a glass of lemonade and the joy of your company.

Pray that war will not come, because I have no

doubt our beloved homeland will suffer terrible de-
feat and retribution. I have a plan to compensate
slave owners that may avert what can only be hor-
rific bloodshed. Keep me in your thoughts and heart.
　With great fondness,
　Tilda

So this was the high stakes Jeremiah had to keep secret.
His Falcon ancestor was a cold-blooded rapist and murderer. And there was black blood in the family. This was
what had driven him into the arms of the Heritage Heroes
and into a scheme to subvert a democratic election.

My first impulse was to shred the letter. As my fury
grew, I wanted to shove it down Jeremiah's throat. What
a bunch of ancient foolishness. What family didn't have
horse thieves or bank robbers or saloon girls somewhere
in their past? The Falcons had a brutal, ugly rapist and
murderer. And one branch of the family had "passed" as
white. So what? Who really cared? If DNA samples were
taken, would anyone be able to claim a "pure" heritage?
Nope. And what poppycock, anyway.

This was what had driven Jeremiah to kill Boswell
and attempt to kill Olive Twist? To hide these moldy secrets? Cece, too, shared this dark past, but she would
never take it as her burden. Jeremiah had nothing worthwhile to cling to in the present, so he put his emotions
on the past.

The man should be hanged for stupidity.

By the time I retied the letters with the crimson ribbon, my temper had cooled. The day outside had turned
from pink to lavender. I repacked the trunk and as I
stood, my hand brushed my side and I felt Graf's keys in
my pocket.

I froze.

Image fragments and bits of information swirled around my brain, a kaleidoscope of shrapnel pieces that snapped into one single question: why did Gertrude have Graf's keys? Coleman should have taken them from her. He or DeWayne should have kept them after searching the Range Rover.

But Gertrude had them. Graf had been taken on her property, his car hidden in a secluded part of her gardens.

Shortly after Graf disappeared, Tinkie and I left The Gardens' bar. I'd seen Gertrude hustling across the unlit grounds with sheets and towels. I'd figured a guest emergency. Now a more sinister possibility arose.

The night Olive's room was firebombed, Gertrude had appeared in the bar with shrubbery in her hair. I'd assumed it was from eavesdropping behind the bar's ficus trees. What if it had been because of a sprint through the flowerbeds after a failed attempt to kill Twist?

But why? What stake could Gertrude claim? She wasn't part of the high-society Daughters of the Supreme Confederacy. Why would she harm Boswell, or Twist? Or Graf? It didn't make sense, but at last I'd stumbled on what felt like the right path.

A terrible thought followed right on the heels of my revelation. Tinkie had gone to The Gardens to question Gertrude.

Fighting panic, I called Tink. She answered with a sleepy hello. She was home safe with Oscar. She'd found nothing to indicate Graf had been in any of the B and B guest rooms. I urged her to go back to sleep and promised I would do the same.

At the front door, I considered making Sweetie and

Pluto stay. The glare festering in Sweetie's eyes convinced me otherwise. They loaded into the backseat of the SUV and we were off just as the sun topped the sycamore trees that lined the driveway.

I parked on the road and hiked across the B and B grounds. Sweetie, Pluto, and I—the Mod Squad of Zinnia—trudged side by side. I'd brought along Graf's sock. If he was being held here, Sweetie would sniff him out.

I'd feared Gertrude might be working in the flower-beds in the cooler morning hours, but my worries were for nothing. The only living creatures in the gardens were the birds and squirrels, and a few butterflies that had endured the summer heat. It wasn't seven o'clock, but the mercury was already in the mid-eighties. The humidity added at least ten degrees. Summer would end, but not soon enough.

Sweetie darted off the trail and Pluto and I followed, dodging through a vividly colored bed of red salvias bordered with Sweet Williams. I was familiar with the inn proper, the gardens near the tennis courts, and those surrounding the pool, but there were areas I'd never explored, not to mention wilderness areas. My hand twitched to call Tinkie or Cece, who were far better versed on the layout of the facility. But I didn't. My intent was to scout the area. If Graf was here, I'd call for backup.

We cut across a beautiful bonsai garden and continued, Sweetie leading the way. Occasionally, she stopped to sniff the ground, circling in different directions. Then she'd be on the scent again.

We left the tennis courts behind, and I realized we were close to the spot the Range Rover had been found.

Sweetie sniffed the area where the car had been—and where I'd abandoned her—and gave me the stink eye and a low, mournful howl.

"A little forgiveness," I lectured.

Sweetie shook her ears at me and bolted northeast. She lunged into the four o'clocks and vanished. Pluto and I hesitated, then went after her. "Sweetie!" I called quietly. This was payback for leaving her. Now she was showing me how worry felt, and I had to agree—I didn't like it.

I couldn't call loudly—for fear of waking the sleeping dragon. Hot pursuit was my only option. Pluto and I sprinted after the dog. The cat, for a rather tubby specimen of the family *felidae*, zoomed like greased lightning.

My long night of no sleep became apparent as I struggled after my critters. I'd lost my sense of direction. We wove through beautiful oaks and a swampy area that reminded me of a river brake. Sweetie truly had struck a trail. She knew where Graf was—or at least where he'd been. And it was no place he should have gone.

I hurled myself through unkempt tangles far from the puritanical righteousness of Gertrude's regimented gardens. Dodging around a walnut tree, I stopped an inch short of ramming into Sweetie. She stood at attention. I followed her gaze to see Pluto batting at a grotesque brown, moldering mummy.

"Son of a—!" Sweetie hadn't found Graf, but she had found the Lady in Red. Or what was left of her. A ragged tatter of red velvet shrouded her rib cage.

I pulled my cell phone from my pocket. Coleman needed to be here. I'd punched in the first three digits when my feet were snatched out from under me. In one terrifying moment, I hung upside down. The phone flew from my grip and landed at least two feet beyond my dangling hands. Harold's pistol slipped out of my waistband and landed beside the phone.

Gradually, I stopped swinging back and forth and my stomach settled. I caught my breath and called to my dog. "Sweetie, get the phone." I'd stepped in a snare, and the rope circling my ankles would quickly become painful. "Sweetie—bring me the phone."

But Sweetie was intent on something else, a movement in the bushes surrounding the clearing. Cougar, bear, wolverine, giant python—what lurked in the bushes, eliciting a low, no-nonsense growl from Sweetie Pie? Hanging upside down and swaying, I was too dizzy and disoriented to discern the threat.

Just when I thought things couldn't get worse, I heard the familiar hum of blood-sucking insects. Mosquitoes the size of dragonflies swooped at me from all directions. This would be the most humiliating death of any PI ever. Drained by insects and eaten by coyotes.

"Sweetie, please, fetch the phone." Why hadn't I taught Sweetie to retrieve?

The long, low growl that came from the hound made my hair stand on end, but I couldn't see anything—until the bushes parted and Olive stepped into the small clearing.

"What in the world, Sarah Booth?" She circled me. "You're like a bug hung in a spider's web."

"Stop yakking and cut me down." I twisted so I could follow her movements.

"Why should I?"

"Because if you don't, when I get free, I'll hunt you down and hurt you."

"Oh, fiddle-dee-dee, as Scarlett would say. You do

talk a mighty ferocious game. Hard to back up a threat when you're hanging from a tree like Tim Burton's idea of a piñata. If I gave you a few good whacks, I'll bet roaches would fall out."

I would kill her, first chance I got. Something painful and slow. "You'd better let me down, Olive, I mean it."

"Sorry, no can do. I have a date with destiny, and Dr. Webber. If you're free, you'll try to stop us. We have big plans for the Lady in Red. Neither of us has tenure, and the halls of academia are suffocating us. No, it's the open road that calls to us, a siren song of adventure." Her hands fluttered in theatrical little gestures.

I burned with the desire to strangle her, but I had a bigger question. I couldn't have heard that correctly. "Richard Webber, your adversary? You're traveling with Richard Webber?"

"It seems the passionate fire of our first love was banked, not dead. We've rekindled the heat, and let me just say, he lights me up like a Roman candle! We're taking the Lady in Red and leaving town. We have it all planned out. We'll explore every state while traveling in the intimacy of a huge Winnebago. We'll exhibit the Lady in Red, just like they did outlaws in the Old West. You know, there was even a plot to steal Lincoln's body. We'll give lectures across the nation to communities who would never, otherwise, be exposed to rigorous academic research and professors of our quality. We'll draw crowds and charge admission fees. We'll coauthor a book about the Lady in Red and our incredible romance and sell it at our lectures. I'll add passion to Dick's dry research, and he'll add male gravitas to my voluptuous language. We'll hit the *New York Times* bestseller list together."

The woman was delusional. About a billion laws prohibited such spectacles. "You're nuttier than a can of Planters. There are health provisions against hauling a corpse around the country. Webber will serve prison time for stealing a dead person. If you involve yourself with him, you'll end up behind bars, too." Not that I cared. In fact, it was a great idea.

"Oh, Sarah Booth, I received the DNA results. The Lady in Red is a Richmond, no doubt about it. She had DNA matches to Buford. It cost an arm and a leg to do the testing, but it's well worth it. The things I learned!"

"How did she die?"

She squatted so we were face-to-face, though I was still upside down, which made her look even meaner. "You'll have to read my book to find out."

I didn't give two hoots about what caused Tilda's death, but I did care about Graf. "Where's my fiancé? If you've hurt him—"

"Why would I have Graf?" She crossed her arms. "Oh, I get it. You saw how Coleman Peters went after me, and now you think Graf Milieu has caught my scent. If I had more time I'd bring him to heel, but now I have Richard. He's the jealous type, you know. Can't stand it when another man shows his desire for me. I can't produce Graf. Haven't seen him in a couple of days. But just remember, I *could* have had him."

"Twist, untie the rope."

"What's in it for me?"

"The knowledge you did one decent thing in your life?"

She grabbed my hips for a big windup. "By the way, Sarah Booth, I never intended to pay Delaney Detective Agency. Never. Not one red cent. And there's nothing you can do about it."

When she let go, I spun in fast circles. The last thing I heard was her age-inappropriate giggle as she fled the scene.

The spin nauseated me, but I clung to the fact she'd be back. She had to get the bones of the Lady in Red—hopefully before all the blood rushed to my head and popped it like an overripe melon.

I was getting too old to take the abuse of a PI.

Before I could react, I slammed into the ground, head-first. Had I not been rotating a little, I might have broken my neck. As it was, I deflected my weight and flopped hard on my left hip. I was so damned glad to be flat on the ground, I didn't complain but scurried to gain my feet.

Picking up the rope that had held me, I saw where the fibers had frayed from rubbing against the tree limb. Olive's little cruelty had freed me. And I wasn't waiting around for another booby trap.

I picked up Harold's cell phone and gun. Thank goodness it worked. Now was time for the cavalry. I called Tinkie and filled her in. "Webber, Twist, and the corpse are here in the woods behind The Gardens. Call Coleman before the freaks take their traveling show on the road."

"Do you have a lead on Graf?" Tinkie asked. "Coleman searched all night. Jeremiah and Buford swear they don't know anything. The blood at the old McCauley house came from Arnold, not Graf. When Pluto attacked him, he bled like a stuck pig. There's no evidence Graf was ever there."

"Don't you find it a little suspicious that Gertrude had the keys to Graf's SUV? She didn't give them to Coleman. I'll bet they weren't in the ignition when Coleman searched the car. And Gertrude was the last one to see Graf."

Tinkie was silent for a long moment. "Coleman wouldn't have given her the keys. In fact, if the keys were in the vehicle, he would have driven it to Dahlia House once he checked it over."

"Exactly."

She came to the same conclusion I'd reached. "Graf is somewhere at The Gardens."

"I think so, too. Gertrude has to be involved. I don't know the specifics. But she has a stake in the outcome of the Lady in Red. Did she tell you anything useful?"

"She wasn't at the desk. I looked everywhere, but no one awake had seen her. I checked the empty rooms and found nothing."

"Is there somewhere else on the grounds she might hide a person?"

"What are you planning?" Tinkie would have me microchipped to track my movements if I wasn't careful.

"I'll sit on Gertrude. If she's involved with Graf's disappearance, the simplest thing to do is watch and wait. She'll have to take him food and water, right?"

"Yeah, right." Tinkie didn't sound positive that Gertrude would feed and water a hostage. "Wait for Coleman."

"Absolutely," I lied before I closed the phone.

I had no time to lose. "Sweetie, find Graf."

19

I couldn't be certain who'd set the man snare, but I was pretty sure it wasn't Olive or Richard Webber. Neither had the skills. A person with military or survival training had rigged it. Like . . . Arnold, or a Heritage Hero. But forewarned was forearmed, as Aunt Loulane would say. I wouldn't fall into another ambush.

The most encouraging thing was the trap's existence—an indication protection was needed from snoopers. A hostage would warrant such tactics.

It was disturbing to abandon the bones of a long-dead woman, but Coleman was en route. I made tracks and followed Sweetie's nose. She'd hit a trail. Graf was close. I could feel it. I just prayed he wasn't injured.

As I jogged through underbrush along the shady path,

I tried to connect Gertrude to Graf's disappearance and to Jimmy Boswell's death. No matter how I turned the facts, I couldn't make the dots connect. Gertrude simply didn't fit into any scenario I came up with.

Amid the thick underbrush and canopy of trees, I discerned a darker shadow. Sweetie, too, slowed, checking back to be sure I was paying attention. I drew abreast of her and she licked my hand. At last, I was forgiven. Pluto, panting a little from the extended exertion, brushed against my other side. Hidden by a screen of scrub brush, we crept close to an old building, probably a plantation foreman's home at some point in history.

Surrounded by woods, the place was well maintained. The clapboard was painted and the porch swept. Flowers surrounded it in a riot of blooms, and the yard was carefully mowed carpet grass. I wouldn't have been surprised to find the roof shingled in gingerbread. If I went inside would Graf be imprisoned in a cage, a hot oven waiting to toast him?

Time to do battle with the witch. If Graf was there, I meant to save him.

I started forward until I felt sharp claws hook my ankle. Right through the skin and into the bone. "King Herod waltzing with Freddy Krueger! What are you doing, Pluto?" I had to whisper, so the harsh words lost some of their impact.

I was about to shake loose when I heard a low rumble of wheels on gravel approaching the house. Cat, dog, and I hunkered down and hid. Peering through the leaves, I saw Gertrude arrive in a vintage golf cart. She balanced a food tray. From her pocket she withdrew a key and went inside.

Unless she was delivering room service to Olive and

Richard—and hell hadn't frozen over so that couldn't be possible—she had Graf in there.

Tearing free from Pluto, I scurried to a window and peered in. A nicely furnished living room held no human occupants. The next window showed a dining room, also empty. At last, I found a bedroom window. Tied to an iron bedstead was Graf.

Gertrude stood beside him, holding the food tray and talking. I could tell Graf was disoriented and weak by the way he struggled to sit up when she freed one hand for him to eat the sandwich she'd brought. It took all of my willpower, and a grip on Sweetie's collar, to keep from flying into the room. Good thing I stayed put. She lifted a gun off the tray and waved it around.

"We have to do something," I told my comrades. Great words, but short on action. I didn't know what to do.

Pluto had other ideas. He jumped onto the porch and hurled himself at the front door. There was nothing I could do to stop him. I watched Gertrude's shocked reaction as she dropped the tray and hurried to the front door, gun in hand.

By the time she opened the door, Pluto had streaked into the front shrubs. Gertrude scanned the front lawn. She was closing the door when Pluto darted through her legs and into the house. The sound of glass breaking followed.

Pluto was destroying her dishes.

"A cat! In my house! My lovely china!" Gertrude was furious. "I'll kill that black beast."

In her frenzy to extinguish Pluto's life, she left the door open. Sweetie and I took the opportunity. I zipped toward the bedroom where Graf was a prisoner, and Sweetie went to aid Pluto.

Graf saw me and tried to sit up, but I motioned him

to be still as I untied his other hand and his feet. His face was swollen and dark circles underscored his eyes. His left leg angled oddly under the covers.

"Don't move." I forced myself to stay calm.

He nodded. "Sarah Booth, I knew you'd find me. You're the best detective." A goofy grin heightened his pitiful physical condition.

I pulled the Glock Harold had loaned me from my waistband. If Gertrude got between me and helping Graf, I'd send her to her eternal fate.

I dialed the sheriff's office and DeWayne answered.

"Send an ambulance to The Gardens. Gertrude has a house down the road on the north side." Why had I never wondered where Gertrude lived? I'd assumed she had quarters in the B and B. "Graf is really hurt. *Hurry.*"

I closed the phone and my gaze fell on a photograph on her bedside table. It was Gertrude and Jimmy Boswell. I couldn't believe it. I picked it up for a closer look. He was younger, with shorter hair, but it was Boswell. The photo was maybe five years old. What was Gertrude doing with—I saw it then, the physical resemblance. Boswell was her cousin, nephew, child? Some relation.

"Put it down." Gertrude stood in the doorway, her gun aimed at my heart.

I returned the framed picture to the table. My own gun was at my leg, hidden from her view. If she was a decent shot, she'd hit me before I could raise the Glock. Distracted by the photo, I'd let her get the drop on me.

"Why did you kill Boswell? He's your blood." It was the first thing that popped out of my mouth. Judging by her thunder brow, it was the wrong thing to say.

"That selfish Twist *never* let him drink her expensive,

imported coffee. *She* should have drunk it. The poison was meant for her. Jimmy took her crap for months to infiltrate her research. He suffered abuse and denigration for the cause. Jimmy was a good boy."

Her wild eyes scanned the room. When she saw the cell phone in my other hand, she laughed. "You called the sheriff, didn't you?"

"And an ambulance for Graf. What did you do to his leg?"

"He tried to escape, so I shot him. The bone is shattered. I told him there'd be consequences. I couldn't get medical help for him because of you and your snooping."

Graf struggled upright. I pressed him back to the bed. Gertrude's nonchalance sent a jolt of fury through me. She'd traumatized his leg with a bullet and felt no remorse. Now she held a gun on both of us. If Graf moved too much, his wound might start bleeding again. Or Gertrude might shoot him in the other leg. "Is Boswell your son?"

She swung the gun barrel up, focusing on my head, but the tremble in her hands was a dead giveaway. Whoever Boswell was to her, she'd loved him. "Don't pretend you don't know. I've waited and waited for you to tell your fancy friends. I've put up with your knowing looks and superior attitude. You've made me suffer, so it was only providence when I was able to make you suffer in return."

"What are you talking about?"

"Your mother told you. She promised she'd never tell, but she didn't keep her word to me. You've lorded it over me ever since you came home."

"I have no idea what you're talking about." She was talking in circles, and none of it made any sense.

"Put the gun on the floor. Right now, Sarah Booth. I'm not blind and I'm not a no-count fool like you think. No one in this county has ever taken me seriously. You will now."

I had no choice but to do as she directed. I laid the Glock beside the photograph. "So poisoning Boswell was an accident?"

"Forget Jimmy. Don't you dare say his name."

"I never knew you'd married."

Anger whipped across her face and I thought for sure she'd plug me. "You aren't much of a detective, Sarah Booth Delaney. You never bothered to check into me. I was just a woman who planted flowers and ran a bed-and-breakfast. I wasn't worth your attention. I outsmarted you and the whole town. No one ever knew a true thing about me—except your mother. Not a single one of you cared what I dreamed about or who I loved."

"My mother?"

"Don't play innocent. She told you. You've made it clear you look down on me."

"Told me what?" She'd tackled my brain with a sideways swipe. "What are you talking about? My mother's been dead for twenty years. I was only twelve when she died. What should she have told me?"

"She swore she'd keep my secret, but I knew she'd tell. You've laughed behind my back for the last time."

Gertrude held a gun, but no one called my mother a liar. "My mother's word was gold."

"All these years, I've watched you sneering down your nose at me."

"I have no clue what you're talking about."

My denial incited her to hotter anger. "You knew I'd gotten in trouble and had to give my baby away. Libby Delaney promised me she'd take my sins to the grave with her, but she blabbed it to you."

"My mother never spoke a word of it."

"Your mother made the arrangements and paid the fees for me to leave town, have the baby, take some secretarial courses, and come back to Zinnia as if I'd been away at school. She promised never to tell. That I could come back home and pick up my life without anyone the wiser. She lied. She told you. I remember how close you two were. Thick as thieves."

"My mother kept her word." Pity warred with fury. "You didn't know her very well, Gertrude. She never told me your secret. The only person looking down on you is yourself. What happened to your child?"

"He was adopted by a family in Vicksburg."

"Jimmy Boswell was your son." Never in a million years would I have thought I'd feel sorry for Gertrude. She'd always been mean as a snake. But I saw a different view of her—a woman who got in trouble in a town where everyone knew her business. Fear of public ridicule had driven her to give up her son. Now she had to blame someone, and it was me and my dead mother.

"Well aren't you Miss Smarty Pants. It took you long enough to put it together. I gave up my son because I wouldn't have him grow up in a town that would never forget he was a bastard. I did the loving thing for Jimmy."

I did the quick calculations in my head, but came up without a name. "Who was Jimmy's father?" I glanced at the photo again, and I knew. How could I have missed it? There was the aristocratic nose; the serious, wide blue eyes; the tousled dark blond curls. "Jeremiah Falcon. He got you pregnant and refused to acknowledge the child."

"He did no such thing." She drew herself up. "I never told him. He had his hands full. He gave up everything that mattered to him—his love of drawing and painting, his dreams—so he could become what his parents demanded. You have no idea what it did to him. He had the soul of an artist, and they didn't recognize the value. He had to cut out the best part of him to please them. He was just a young man with a dream of creating masterpieces and they wouldn't let him have even that. Had he shown up with me, a mature woman from the wrong side of town, his sacrifices would have been for nothing."

"You seduced a teenager?" I'd seriously underestimated Gertrude.

Her laugh was bitter. "Things aren't so simple, Sarah Booth. I was older, but far less experienced. Jeremiah had seen more of the world in his short life than I had. He was young in age, but older than me in the ways of the world. We fell in love. As wrong as it might have been, I didn't take advantage of him. Your mother understood. Or at least she pretended to. She convinced me to give Jimmy up to a good home. She helped me start a new life. She promised I would forget about my baby, but I didn't. I couldn't."

"I'm sorry, Gertrude. I liked Boswell."

"And if you'd known he was my boy, what would you have thought?"

"The same."

"Liar!"

I wasn't lying, but I decided to lay it on even thicker.

Gertrude was completely unhinged. To save Graf, I would gladly play along with her. "Boswell was a gentle young man, and I wondered why he tolerated Twist's abuse. I understand now—he was on a mission. You should be proud of him. A fallen soldier."

Poor Jimmy Boswell had been born into insanity and he'd never had a chance. The son of Gertrude and Jeremiah, an unfortunate DNA donor team. He'd gotten all the way to Maine in a graduate program, but he'd never broken the tether to the craziness of his family and the past.

"Why are you being so nice?" she snapped.

I shrugged. She blocked the doorway, and she had a clear shot at me and Graf. I couldn't afford to piss her off. Or rush her. I just had to keep her talking until Coleman arrived.

"Water." Graf's voice was weak.

"There's water on his tray," Gertrude said. "Give it to him. I took no pleasure in hurting him. He shouldn't have tried to get away."

"Why did you kidnap Graf?" She might hate me, but kidnapping Graf was a surefire ticket to having half the county on a search-and-rescue mission. She wouldn't risk that kind of scrutiny just to hurt me.

"He overheard me arguing with Buford."

"You introduced Jimmy to Buford and Jeremiah so he could have some contact with his father, even if he never knew Jeremiah was his dad."

"Jeremiah respected Jimmy's intellect. They were like father and son in that way. I didn't want Jimmy to go to Maine but he won a scholarship to Camelton. He met Twist and read her publications. When he became aware of her interest in the Lady in Red, he told me and I told

Jeremiah. It was agreed he should offer to work for Twist."

The entire avalanche of disaster had been set in motion months before now. "And Twist happened to show up just when the Heritage Pride Heroes and their little political cell had put a plan in motion to subvert the judicial elections."

"Jeremiah thought of the plan. It's brilliant. No one pays attention to electing a judge. It was perfect. And Buford, with his investment background, was able to raise the funds."

"Sarah Booth, water, please." Graf sounded so feeble. Where was Coleman?

I opened the water bottle and handed it to Graf. His eyes were fevered, and the tiny movement of reaching for the water made him wince with pain. "I love you," I said.

"Fine lot of good your love will do him. Can he be a leading man with a crippled leg?" Gertrude asked.

That was it. Mocking Graf's injury was too much. "Who are you, freaking Annie Wilkes?" I'd intended to be nice but I couldn't take any more. She was like a Stephen King character.

"Shame on you, Sarah Booth. Didn't your mama ever tell you that your mouth would be the death of you? Now the real you comes out. You think you're better than me, superior."

"Screw you, you crazy bitch." She'd pushed me over the edge, but I wasn't alone in the house. Not by a long shot. While I'd been arguing with her, Sweetie had slipped up behind her, perfectly situated to trip the old bat. And Pluto waited, examining his claws.

I lunged at Gertrude, and Sweetie swung her rump to

hit the innkeeper just behind the knees. She sprawled backwards. The gun fired and hit the ceiling. I dove at her and in a matter of seconds, I was sitting on top of her with my knees pinning her arms and her gun in my hand. For good measure Pluto dug into her scalp with all four claws.

"Get that devil cat off me. He's tearing my head off." She ripped and snorted, but she couldn't budge us.

"Hold her, Sarah Booth. I'll get the rope." Graf grabbed his damaged leg and tried to move it. At his agonized cry I wanted to beat Gertrude damn near to death.

"It's okay, Graf. Listen." In the distance, sirens could be heard. "I have her. Just don't move." He was hurt so badly, but he was worried about me.

"Thank goodness." He fell back on the bed.

"Bring them here quick, Sweetie. If Timmy was ever in the well, it's now."

Sweetie ran down the lane, barking at the rescue vehicles and leading them to the cottage. It was only a few minutes, but it seemed like hours before Coleman swept into the room followed by DeWayne, Doc, Tinkie, Cece, and Oscar.

Coleman made short work of cuffing Gertrude and putting her in the back of a patrol car. Doc went straight to Graf. I knelt on the floor beside the bed and smoothed his dark hair from his forehead. He was burning up with fever. The wound was infected. His focus drifted in and out.

Doc drew the covers back and revealed the mess that had once been Graf's handsome leg. "No." It was one word that slipped from me.

After an injection for pain, Doc started an IV of antibiotics. The bullet wound was above the knee. The flesh was purple and swollen around the jagged entry.

"The good news is she missed the joint," Doc said, but I could tell by the tone of his voice that Graf's injury was severe.

The EMTs pushed me out of the room. Tinkie and Cece flanked me and Oscar stood behind, a hand on my shoulder. "Doc will patch him up," he said.

"Sure," Cece added. "Good as new."

"You'll be dancing on your honeymoon before you know it," Tinkie threw in.

The EMTs moved Graf onto a gurney and loaded him into the ambulance before I could ask a single question. "I want to ride with him," I said.

"Take Sweetie and Pluto home," Doc said. "Take a bath, have a drink. Relax a minute. He's going straight into surgery as soon as he gets to Jackson. I gave him enough painkiller, he won't be waking up for a while."

"Can they save his leg?" I asked.

"I've never lied to you, Sarah Booth. It's a nasty wound. The bone is a mess. He's gone a day without medical care. This is serious."

I was crying. "You could lie to me just this once and it would be fine."

"We'll take her home." Tinkie's arm cinched my waist, navigating me to the door. "Once she's showered, we'll drive down to Jackson."

"No." I broke free and ran to the ambulance. I couldn't leave Graf. I had to be with him.

Doc grabbed me and held on tight. "You'll need a vehicle, some clothes, his personal items. Gather them up."

He shook me lightly to make sure it sank in. "We aren't equipped for reconstructive surgery here in Zinnia. It's more than I can handle."

If Doc wasn't willing to work on Graf, he was in bad shape.

"I'm sending him to the smartest orthopedic group in the state. That's the best chance of saving his leg," Doc said. "Now, step back and let the ambulance go."

Before the whirling red lights disappeared in the trees, I turned to Coleman. "Where're Olive and Webber?"

"On their way to Memphis, but they'll be picked up. Don't worry, every road between here and the Tennessee line has an officer sitting on it. Thanks to you, we recovered the Lady in Red. She'll be returned to Lexington for interment in the Odd Fellows Cemetery. Olive and Webber will spend time in jail. Probably worse to them, they'll lose their academic credibility."

Fury was like a snake in my head. "And make a million dollars off their book. Graf will lose everything important to him."

"Not true." Coleman touched my cheek and whispered in my ear. "He'll still have you. There's nothing in the world more important." He tilted my chin up with a gentle finger. "They can perform miracles in medicine now. Be strong for him, Sarah Booth. Now I'm taking Gertrude to jail. And I've called in the election fraud unit. They'll investigate Jeremiah and Buford and that crowd. The feds may be brought in, depending on what the financial records show about election tampering."

Tinkie and Cece stepped up like bodyguards. "Time to leave."

"I want to talk to Gertrude. Alone." If I couldn't be with Graf, I could finish it with Gertrude.

They eased me toward Graf's Range Rover. "Not going to happen. Not today. Maybe later. Right now, Graf is all you need to think about. Gertrude isn't going anywhere."

"She poisoned her own son." I tried to make it fit into a world I could comprehend.

"She meant to kill Olive," Cece said. "That's enough to drive anyone nuts. But she's been crazy for years. Our mistake was assuming she was harmless."

Cece had no clue Boswell was her nephew. She, too, had suffered a loss through no fault of her own. I would tell her, when we had a moment to sit and have a drink.

"Cece, I'm sorry about Jeremiah."

Cece gave her one-shouldered shrug. "Legal fees will likely force the sale of the ancestral home, dah-link, but it's been gone a long time. It was never really mine. For a while, it was my cocoon, a place to be while I changed and metamorphosed. But it was never my home, not the place I was destined to live. Now I'm truly free of the web of the past."

"I love you, Cece." Tinkie blew her a kiss. "And you, too, Sarah Booth."

"All of this, and we were never paid a dime. Olive confessed she never intended to pay us," I said, because I couldn't bear to talk about Graf or the loss of Magnolia Grove or the death of a young man warped by foolish hatred.

I locked the bathroom door against Tinkie and Cece, not because I didn't appreciate their loving concern, but I was suffocating from fear and grief. I turned on the shower and stepped under the stinging spray with

my clothes on. As the water pounded me, I slowly un-
dressed.

"Sarah Booth, are you okay?" Tinkie tapped on the
door.

"I'm good. Please, I just want to stay here, in the water,
for a moment."

"I could hand you a towel."

"I don't intend to drown myself." I almost smiled.
Tinkie knew me too well. "I'll finish cleaning up and
then we'll drive to Jackson." It was pointless to believe I
could escape her a second time. Besides, I didn't want to.
Tinkie and Cece were my rocks. I couldn't face this without them.

I finished the shower, put on makeup, jeans, sandals,
and a cotton shirt in Graf's favorite color, green, to
match my eyes. I threw my belongings in a bag and
then packed his toiletries and clean clothes. He wouldn't
want to wear a hospital gown. He'd hate that, especially when he started rehab. He wouldn't want his
back door flapping. I found loose shorts, T-shirts, and a
robe.

Whatever awaited me in Jackson, I was as ready as I
could be. I picked up the suitcase and stopped. Jitty
blocked the doorway. I recognized her persona instantly—
the dark hair with reddish highlights, the strong eyebrows
and red lips, the business suit, down to the notepad and
pen she held. "I can't do this," I said, almost dropping
the suitcase. "I can't deal with you right now. Please, go
away."

"Don't forget the rest of the story," Jitty said. "Remember, you always get your man and your story. That's
your motto."

"Coleman has Gertrude behind bars. Graf may lose

his leg. There's no man to get, just a crazy old bitch who destroyed her son and shot my fiancé."

Jitty perched on the bed. "Love is a wicked blade, Sarah Booth."

"If Graf loses his leg, his career is over." I could confess my fears to no one else. "He will never forgive me. And he shouldn't."

"Graf's a strong man. Adversity will make him stronger."

I swung the suitcase at her head, but it went right through her as she faded away. "How dare you! How dare you say such a thing, as if he's developed a pimple. This is my fault, and he may suffer the rest of his life."

She materialized, still sitting on my bed. "You'd best get a grip on yourself. Put some bone in your spine. How much will it help if you go all to pieces and act like this is the end of the world?"

Her words stopped me cold. "He's going to lose the leg, isn't he? That's why you're here as Lois Lane. I'm Graf's Kryptonite. I weaken him and make him vulnerable, like Lois did Superman. I've brought this on him."

She stood up, anger simmering in her eyes. "It doesn't matter how this happened or why it happened. What matters is that it has happened and it's up to you to decide the best way to support Graf."

"He'll hate me."

In less than a blink, Jitty was in my face. "*Get over yourself*. Graf needs you to be strong. Show him what a Delaney can do when a loved one is hurt."

I didn't have a chance to answer. I heard Tinkie and Cece coming up the stairs, dogs and cat in the procession.

"Who are you talking to?" Cece edged past me into the bedroom and looked around.

"Myself." I hefted the suitcase. "I'm ready for the hospital."

My friends arranged for a comfortable chair in Graf's room. A good thing, too, since I'd spent twelve hours waiting for him to return from surgery and wake up.

At the first sign he was regaining consciousness, Cece and Tinkie went to the cafeteria on the pretext of getting coffee. They understood I needed to be alone when Graf awoke.

He tossed his head and moaned, and I was at his side, his hand clutched in mine. His leg was a massive swath of bandages, but they hadn't amputated. No one would give me odds whether his leg would heal properly, though. Modern medicine could do only so much.

"Where am I?" he asked.

"In the hospital in Jackson." I kissed his palm and held it to my chest. "You're safe."

"Gertrude shot me."

"I know." I put my hand on his forehead, relieved that he felt cooler. The infection was on the run.

"Why? Why did she do it?"

It would be difficult to explain, but I had to try. I told him about Boswell and Gertrude, about my mother's role in helping a woman trapped by a mistake. His breathing stabilized as I told him about Boswell and his connection to the Confederacy through generations long dead—and about his relationship to Cece, who still didn't know.

"You people are insane." Graf turned away from me.

You people. That's what Olive called us, because she was not of the South, not part of us. Now Graf felt the same way. And I couldn't blame him.

I squeezed his fingers and pressed a kiss to his cheek. "I love you. So many people here love you."

"Do you?" he asked. "Will you love me when I can't work?"

Anger would have been easier than the swell of sorrow. I mourned the loss of so many things all at once, it took a moment to speak. "The doctors say you have a chance to recover fully."

"What are the odds?" A pulse jumped in his beard-stubbled jaw.

"They won't say."

He shifted to face me. "Why did Gertrude do this to me? I was nothing to her. I overheard her arguing with Buford, but I couldn't make head or tails of what it was about. I started walking to the parking lot to pick up Cece. She attacked me with some kind of sedative. Why?"

"It's complicated. To protect Boswell and Jeremiah. And because Gertrude thought I looked down on her. She did it because she feels she's been cheated. Because she's mentally unbalanced."

He nodded.

"If I could take the injury, I would."

At last he squeezed my hand back. "I know, Sarah Booth. You'd trade places in an instant. But you can't."

He slumped back in the pillows, and in a moment he was lost in sleep again. I smoothed the hair from his forehead and watched his eyeballs shift beneath the lids. He deserved so much better than what I'd brought to him.

Squeaking rubber-soled shoes signaled the doctor was making rounds. When Dr. Kress, the orthopedic surgeon, stepped into the room, I discovered a man surprisingly young and fit. He motioned me outside.

"The surgery went smoothly," he said. "The nurse said Mr. Milieu is awake."

"He wants to know the odds he'll lead a normal life."

Dr. Kress tapped a pen against the chart. "It's fifty-fifty. We did everything we could. His attitude will play a huge role."

"Fifty-fifty." It wasn't the best, but it surely wasn't the worst. "Full recovery?"

The doctor nodded. "Keep him calm right now. It's a long road ahead."

And he was gone.

I closed the door and returned to Graf's side. Across the bed, Jitty waited, the sunlight from the window catching in the glitter of an incredible ball gown.

"Great. Cinderella." Now wasn't the time to rub my nose in a fairy tale. "Climb back in your pumpkin and beat it." I turned away.

"You need a dose of fairy godmother."

"And that's about as likely as a magic wand or ruby slippers to send me back to Kansas." A cool breeze touched my cheek and I sank down in the chair. Jitty was standing beside me. "Can't you just leave me alone?"

Graf mumbled in his sleep. I went to him. No amount of guilt or regret could undo what had happened.

"Cinderella's darkest hour was when she had her prince and was happy." Jitty stepped out of her glass slippers. "When she thought all was lost, her prince found her."

"Life isn't a fairy tale, Jitty. You of all people should know that. You lost your husband and everyone you ever loved."

"You don't know the half of it, Sarah Booth. My story didn't start at Dahlia House. I lost my whole family when

I was just a baby. But it didn't defeat me, and you ain't gonna let it tear you apart."

"I'm not you. I'm not as tough or strong or willing to endure."

"Maybe not today. Maybe not tomorrow. But you'll find your strength again."

She was so sure, she really pissed me off. "Leave me alone."

"I have a message for you."

"Tell my fairy godmother to buzz off."

"From your mother."

I swung to confront her and found her brown eyes filled with a golden light. "What message?" Hope suffered a painful resurrection. A second before, I'd been ready to wave the white flag and admit defeat.

A sad smile graced Jitty's beautiful face. The diamonds of her tiara glittered. "You'll never lack for love, Sarah Booth. No matter which path you choose, true love will find you."

The hard rock inside my chest began to melt. "There really is true love?"

"You ask such a question, after knowing Libby and James Franklin?" Her left eyebrow arched, and she lost every smidgen of princess élan. "Girl, you can't see past your own nose if you ask your mama that question."

"Tell her I love her." Before I finished the sentence, Jitty was gone.

The click of high heels told me my friends were back. Cece handed me a cup of coffee and Tinkie collapsed into a hard-backed chair in the corner and removed her red high heels. "Damn, these shoes are pinching me. I think my foot is growing bigger. Like a pregnant woman's. They fit perfectly when I bought them."

"The secret to a happy life is finding the right fit," Cece said. "In love and in shoes."

"Amen." I didn't have the answer I wanted, but I did have the man I loved and the friends who mattered most. And most important, I had my hope back. With hope, I could accomplish anything.

READ ON FOR AN EXCERPT FROM

Booty Bones

THE NEXT SARAH BOOTH DELANEY MYSTERY
FROM CAROLYN HAINES AND ST. MARTIN'S /
MINOTAUR PAPERBACKS:

1

The setting sun casts gold upon the white beach, and the azure curl of surf takes on a lavender cast as it rushes the shore and spreads a mantle of foam. The waves crest inches from my bare feet, a rhythmic tidal pull that comforts me, promising that life continues. The end of an October day is nothing less than stunning on the small barrier island named for French royalty: Dauphin Island, Alabama.

Graf Milieu, my fiancé, is in the beach cottage I've rented for a week. My hope is that Graf will find walking in the sand good therapy for his gun-shot leg and the island's beauty healing to his injured spirit. Graf's wounds go much deeper than a shattered bone, and they are my fault. He was abducted, shot, and held prisoner without medical care because my private investigative work spilled over into his life.

But that is the past and cannot be changed, no matter how hard I wish it. What I'm planning with this Gulf Coast getaway is to protect the future.

Sweetie Pie, my loyal hound, roots her nose into the back of my armpit, letting me know she sympathizes with my worry. My dog and Pluto, the black cat who lives with us at Dahlia House, my ancestral Mississippi Delta home, are here with me at the beach to aid in Graf's recuperation. I need all the help I can get.

The wind is chilly off the water, and my butt is damp from sitting in the sand. Pluto struggles toward me, his dainty little paws sinking with each step. With a kitty sigh, he plops into my lap. He has only contempt for the surf and for anyone who admires water—even the dazzling aqua waves of the Gulf of Mexico. Water is necessary for fish, and that's as far as Pluto is willing to go.

"Where's Graf?" I ask the critters, hoping he is not far behind them.

They both look back toward the beach cottage. Sweetie's long, delicate ears droop more than usual. The critters are worried about Graf, too. He's been in a terrible state since he was shot. The surgery to repair the bone was successful, but the recovery has been painful. The doctors saved his leg, but there is a chance he will always limp. Graf is an actor with a good chance of becoming a movie star. Physical disabilities don't fit into that equation. He's fighting hard against the anger, fear, and depression that are normal emotions accompanying such an injury.

And have I mentioned this is all my fault?

The wind whips off the water and sends a salty spray

into my face, and for a moment I remember this same beach some twenty-five years earlier, when I vacationed here with my parents. The beach cottages were much plainer, less luxurious, and no oil-drilling rigs dotted the horizon. The sand was pristine then and hadn't suffered the thousands of gallons of oil from BP's Deep Water Horizon well that blew and polluted the Gulf. My parents were alive, and I was safe, expecting only the best of a bright future. Life has certainly taken me down a peg or six.

Sweetie's cold nose against my armpit brings me back from those carefree childhood days. The sun has dropped below the horizon, and the skyline to the east is swiftly changing from peacock-blue to indigo. Time to gird my loins and do battle against Graf's worries. I shall bring joy back to his life. I shall do it with my bare intention and will.

I stand up suddenly, just in time to catch the image of a woman clad in widow's weeds on the other side of the sand dune. She is there one moment and gone the next. Sweetie sees her, too, as does Pluto, who puts on his Halloween arch. Like most felines, Pluto disdains unexpected company.

"Who was that?" I asked, even as I loped over the sand in pursuit of the strange figure.

When I rounded the dune, the light was fleeing the sky, but I could make out the feminine silhouette. Her antebellum dress grazed the sand and belled out behind her as the Gulf wind struck the skirt. A black veil floated like the banner of a dark empire. What the hell was going on?

Sweetie passed me and gave chase, but she wasn't baying like she would if she was on a scent. Pluto, too, for all of his heft and waddling belly, outdistanced me. The phantom floated across the deep sand while I floundered.

"You! Wait up!" I called. No one—not dog, cat, or woman—slowed his pace. I notched it up to a full-fledged run. "Hey! Stop, dammit!"

The stranger slowed and confronted me. Her gown and veil popped in the gusting air, and I was reminded of Deborah Kerr in the *The Innocents,* the film adaptation of "The Turn of the Screw." Brilliant and terrifying.

The figure seemed to wait for me, and I thought of death. I'd always expected the Grim Reaper to be male, but this black-clad raven of gloom persuaded me otherwise.

"What do you want?" I slowed to a stop in the deep sand two dozen yards from her. She was slender with perfect posture, but her features were obscured by the mourning attire.

She said nothing.

Sweetie and Pluto were frozen in place only a few feet in front of me. They made not a sound.

If this was death come to lurk around the shadows of my life, she would not find hospitality. "You've taken too much from me. Get away from here. You have no business with me or the people and animals I love. Be gone!"

"I've lost, too," she said. "More than anyone should."

In the softness of her voice and the plaintive tone, I realized this was no threat, but someone who knew suffering. "What are you?"

"A friend."

"A widow from the distant past?" Judging from the dress style, I'd estimate the mid-1800s. It took me a moment, but then I knew. "Jitty?"

She lifted the veil, and I saw sorrow etched in her mocha skin.

"Funeral crepe? That's the best you could do for a beach costume? No polka-dot bikini? No tawdry flip-flops and big hat? Miss Fashion Plate, where is your style?" I vacillated between relief and annoyance. "You scared the life out of me."

"I'm a haint. That's what haints do—we frighten people."

"But you're *my* haint, and upsetting me is not allowed. You live by the rules of the Great Beyond, but I live by Delaney rules, and I just wrote that one."

Her chuckle seemed to hold the fading sunlight for a moment longer.

"Why are you here, Jitty, dressed like a mourner from the eighteen hundreds?" My momentary humor was gone, and worry returned.

"Life is a cycle, Sarah Booth. You know this."

"I do. I don't like it, but I know it. I'm in the summer of life, and so is Graf. There's no cycle crap happening here that needs widow's weeds."

"Perhaps not." She made no promises. It was against the rules of the Great Beyond for her to tell me anything about the future. "But remember the wheel of life turns again and again."

"If you're warning me Graf is in some new danger, just spit it out."

"The French call orgasm 'the little death.'" Her smile was luminous. And still sad. "At the peak of joy is always the descent into death."

Too bad there was only sand around. Had there been rocks, I would have picked one up and thrown it at her. "Say it plain."

She shook her head. "So much history has happened on this island beach. The French settled here and named it Massacre Island because their first discovery was a mound created from human bones. It was a Native American burial site." She looked out toward the water, and the last lingering bits of peachy light played across her face. "Not a bad place to meet an end."

"And not a good place either. Who are you mourning here? Coker died in the war, not on a barrier island."

"Very true. My husband died on a blood-soaked battlefield with Alice's husband, your great-great-great-grandfather. But there's history here on Dauphin Island, Sarah Booth. Important history. I suspect you'll find out soon enough."

She flickered in and out, as was her wont when she was ready to take a powder.

"Jitty, will Graf be okay?"

But there was only the sound of the surf and the wind whipping my shirt like a tattered flag. Sweetie, Pluto, and I turned toward the three-story cottage. A light bloomed in an upstairs window, a smudge of cheer against the star-spangled night.

It was time to make dinner for Graf. I had a plan to enliven his spirits. A secret plan. And it would work, because I had no other alternative.

I took the stairs to the second floor. All of the beach cottages were built on pilings, a precaution against a tidal surge, but it also gave us a primo view of the Gulf. I found Graf on the balcony, leaning on the railing and staring out at the wind-whipped water.

I poured glasses of red wine and took them outside.

I handed him a glass and then snaked my arm around his waist. He'd lost weight, and he didn't need to.

"Thank you, Sarah Booth. You've been a perfect Florence Nightingale."

"Florence Nightingale died a single woman. Not going to be my fate, Graf Milieu. Just giving you a heads-up."

The long drive and then the lengthy walk on the beach had tired him. I traced the lines in his face with gentle fingertips as he spoke. "Once I'm healed, I promise, I'll make an honest woman of you." He drew me close and kissed me with lingering tenderness. "I'm getting stronger each day. Walking on the beach and climbing the stairs at the cottage—exactly what the doctor ordered. Thank you for convincing me to come here."

"I am your Gale Storm with full attention to social and recreational activities, and never forget it." I tiptoed and kissed his chin. "I've booked a tour of the old fort for tomorrow. This place has a fascinating history. Native Americans, French, Spanish, British, Confederacy, and United States. This area has been ruled by a number of different nations."

"You take the fort tour and I'll work out on the beach." Graf sipped his wine and gazed at the crashing surf. The wind ruffled his dark hair. He needed a haircut and a shave. He'd come so close to dying, and he'd fought so bravely to regain the use of his leg. Sometimes, though, depression snuck up on him. Doc Sawyer had warned me to be on the lookout and to keep him distracted.

"Aarrgh! Disobey me and ye'll walk the gangplank!" I used my finger to poke him in the ribs like a sword.

"Am I going to have to endure pirate parodies for the whole week?" he said teasingly.

"Maybe. I discovered the Gulf waters were swarming

with pirates and buccaneers. And the fort here, Fort Gaines, played a vital role in the War Between the States. Also in the two world wars."

"I never realized you were such a history buff, Sarah Booth. I always viewed you as a girl of the moment. All flash and dazzle and heat. Some very interesting heat."

My heart surged with hope. Since the gunshot, Graf had avoided intimacy. I'd seen him staring at the nasty wound on his leg and now the glaring scar. He was no longer physical perfection. I didn't care, but he did. I had to play this cool. "Wars don't interest me a lot. But pirates—now that's another story. I love pirate tales. Especially stories involving treasures."

"Shiver me timbers." Graf swept me backward, bending me over his arm as he held me and rasped his beard along my cheek and neck.

I tried to push him away, but he was too strong. "What does that even mean? You've been watching bad pirate movies. Next thing I know, you'll have an eye patch."

"And maybe a parrot." He drew me to my feet with ease. "Actually, I know a little about sailing. The phrase comes from the ship pounding up and down in rough seas or battle. The concussion would rattle the mast, which was made of wood."

"I may have to reconsider my engagement." I held out my left hand with the beautiful diamond. "I'm not sure I want to marry a know-it-all."

"No danger of that. But I can read. Maybe you should give it a try."

I punched his arm lightly. "Oh, I brought some books for the beach. I intend to enjoy the surf and an adventure while you complete your physical therapy. I can watch and make sure you're doing it right."

Before I'd packed to come to Dauphin Island, I'd met Doc Sawyer, my friend and family doctor, at Millie's Café for a cup of coffee and a chat. I needed his professional advice on dealing with Graf's emotional and physical wounds.

"Graf has to find his way, Sarah Booth. It isn't just the shattered bone and the pain. This injury has changed how he sees himself. It's shaken loose everything he ever believed about his life and his future."

"I have to help him."

Doc took my hand and gave it a hard squeeze. "Be there. Be strong. Supportive. Caring. But don't make the mistake of pandering to him or trying to make this easier. He'll resent you, and he'll hate himself because you pity him. Don't coddle him and for God's sake don't let him act like a tyrant."

I clung to those words as I inhaled the salty air and gripped the railing of the balcony. "I brought some cards. Care for a few hands of poker?"

"In a little while. I'm happy here, listening to the surf. To be honest, I'm tired. I never thought learning to walk could be so exhausting. How do babies do it?"

"They don't know any better," I said, kissing him. "I'll put the salad together. We can eat when you're ready. No rush." I picked up his empty glass and left him in the night and wind.

"Sarah Booth?"

I turned slowly, trying to disguise the hope I felt. Would he suggest an appetizer before dinner? "Yes?"

"I love the way you help me. You don't have to, though. I don't blame you for what happened."

"I blame me."

"Stop it." He spoke gently. "I'm healing, and you have to do the same. If you continue to blame yourself, this will always be between us. No one could have predicted what Gertrude would do. It wasn't your fault."

"Right now, let's focus on getting you back one hundred percent. After that, I'll work on my guilt issues."

"It's a deal." He blew me a kiss. "Just remember, I love you."

I took that tiny grain of joy and savored it as I went to the kitchen and threw together a curried shrimp salad, one of his favorites.

Sunday dawned with a mantle of lavender and gold. October was closing out, and the beach—normally filled with tourists and surf lovers—was empty in the chill morning. Graf had fallen asleep on the sofa, and I had left him there. It hurt me that he hadn't come to share my bed, but Cece had given me a primer on the subject.

Cece Dee Falcon, my friend, knew more about body image than most psychologists. She'd once been Cecil. Only her strong will and intense self-knowledge had given her the strength to fight family and often her community in a quest to become the person she was meant to be.

"Graf feels diminished," Cece had warned me. "Don't push intimacy. He has to see himself as sexually desirable before he engages. Let him come to you, Sarah Booth. And don't take it personally. This isn't about you. It's all about him."

So I tiptoed past him with Sweetie and Pluto following, and we went out on the sand so I could smoke a cigarette. I didn't do it often—had in fact fought and beaten the demon tobacco for years. Now I was cutting myself a little slack. Graf and I would both recover our strength and put this behind us, including the smokes.

A child's laughter caught Sweetie's attention, and she bounded over the sand dunes and disappeared. She was a gentle dog, but I didn't want her size to intimidate a kid. I stood up and followed with a disgruntled Pluto at my side. The cat was not a fan of early mornings either. The tang of salt in the air only made it worse for the water-disdaining feline.

I stopped on top of the dune. Down the beach, Sweetie Pie ran circles around a child with flowing brown curls that hung to her waist. She looked to be eight or nine. When Sweetie paused, the child spun cartwheels in the sand. She was too far away for a clear view, but her delight in the beach and water was obvious.

I'd been happy at her age. Endless laughter and adventure. The joy of sun and sand and movement. Shading my eyes with my hand, I searched for an adult. The surf could be dangerous, and the girl was far too young to be outside alone.

A slender woman with long blondish curls waved a scarf, and the child skipped to her and took her hands for a swing. Mother and daughter, I thought. They knelt side by side and lavished affection on Sweetie. One day Graf and I would have a child that beautiful. Two. A girl and a boy. Or two girls. Or two boys. It really didn't matter, as long as they were healthy.

Fear had kept me from starting my own family. I lost everyone I loved, and I didn't believe I could recover if something happened to my child. So I'd run away from the possibility. I'd held Graf off, postponing wedding dates and potential children. My miscarriage hadn't helped. Now, though, I was done with fear and running. Graf and I would build a family. I was strong enough now.

Not to mention the thing Jitty kept a countdown on—my biological clock was ticking away. This week, while my fiancé and I were on the beautiful beach, I would commit to Graf and a bicoastal life that included children, movies, horses, travel, and a deep and abiding love for my husband. And Jitty, of course.

The mother and daughter raced down the beach, and Sweetie returned to me, ears flopping and tail wagging with delight. Pluto, on the other hand, stared at me with golden-green eyes that seemed to say, "Look at that stupid hound. There is nothing more pathetic than a dog."

"Let's make some coffee," I suggested. "Graf and I have a guided tour of Fort Gaines at ten. Time to roust him up and get him ready for the day."

Fort Gaines was built for people much shorter than my height, and poor Graf had to stoop to pass under some of the arched entrances. The group for the Sunday morning tour was small, a handful of fall beachcombers taking advantage of the October weather. In the summer, I could imagine the fort would be crowded with tourists.

Our tour guide, Angela Trotter, was a slender young woman with navy blue eyes and a love of the old fort and its checkered history. Originally used as a port and defense point by the French explorer Iberville, the barrier island, which has shifted and changed shapes and locations as a result of hurricanes, played a role in the development of the Gulf Coast rim. Military strategists had used Dauphin Island to defend the vulnerable—and valuable—inner waterways. The island had also been a waypoint for pirates, and Angela Trotter brought the past to life.

"One of the most colorful pirates to sail these waters was Jean Lafitte. A French nobleman by birth, he attracted the best sailors, some of them French nobility who were more in the model of anarchists than Black Beard pirates."

Angela outlined Lafitte's colorful career—the island stronghold he built off the coast of Louisiana on an island in Barataria Bay, and how he declared the island a free state, where slaves kidnapped from the cotton, rice, and sugarcane fields were given the full privilege of citizenship.

"One such highborn lieutenant of Lafitte's was a pirate named Armand Couteau," Angela said. "It's rumored he hid a treasure worth millions on Dauphin Island. Many have hunted for the lost gold using all types of equipment, but nothing has ever been found. Most believe the hiding place is now underwater. Savage storms have shifted the island's contours too many times to count."

Unfortunately, I couldn't give the tour my full attention, because I was worried about Graf. He'd gone for a long walk up and down the beach before we came to the fort, and now his face was pinched with exhaustion and fatigue. He was trying too hard, another thing the doctors had warned me about.

When the guide moved us along the barricades that

gave a glorious view of the Gulf, Graf lagged behind. I dropped back to walk with him.

"Go with the group," he urged me. "My leg is hurting, and I'll take it slow for a little while. Make notes so you can tell me all the stories." His smile was more grimace.

"Let's head back to the cottage. I'm tired, too."

"Don't mollycoddle me." He ran his hand through his hair. "I'm sorry. I didn't mean to snap. I'm just spoiling it for you. Go listen to the tour. I'll catch up in a bit."

"I came to spend time with you," I said. "The tour isn't important. Look"—I pointed to the south—"This is the place where Union naval commander Admiral David Farragut tried to navigate the mine-salted Mobile Bay and declared, 'Damn the torpedoes, full speed ahead.'"

Movement across the fort's yard caught my eye. The blond woman from the beach disappeared into one of the old powder buildings. If she was on the tour, she'd dropped out to pursue her own interests. Maybe she was a local who already knew the history. I was about to ask Graf if he'd seen her when footsteps alerted me that someone approached.

The young tour guide joined us. "You guys okay?" she asked. "I haven't bored you into a coma, have I?"

"We're just enjoying the view," I answered. "My fiancé is a little tired."

"We'll wait for you in the hold." She didn't give us a chance to decline. She hurried away to catch up to the group.

"Ready to rejoin?" I asked.

"Let's see this to the end. Then I'm going to need a hot soak in that lovely bathtub and a long nap."

"You've got it." I turned to follow him and saw the

blond woman. She was half in shadow behind the powder house, and her attention was directed at Graf.

I wondered if she recognized him from one of his films, or if she was wondering what injury he'd sustained. With any luck, he'd heal perfectly before the Hollywood gossip machine found out he'd ever been hurt.